KT-074-906

## LOVE ON THE DOLE

Walter Greenwood was born in 1903 at Salford in Lancashire. He was educated first at Langworthy Road Council School, Salford, and then by himself. He began part-time work as a milkroundsman's boy when he was twelve then worked, again part-time, with a pawnbroker, before leaving school at the age of thirteen. He then worked as an office boy, a stable boy, a clerk, a packing-case maker, a sign-writer, a car-driver, a warehouseman, and a salesman, never earning more than thirty-five shillings a week, except while working for a few months in an automobile factory. He was on the 'dole' at least three times.

*Love on the Dole*, his first novel, was accepted for publication in 1932 and when it appeared in 1933 it was at once recognized as a classic. He has since published ten more novels, a volume of short stories and his autobiography, *There Was a Time*, which is now available in Penguins. He has also written plays, several of which have been filmed. Walter Greenwood, who lives on the Isle of Man, is now working on the dramatization of *There Was a Time*, to be presented at the Mermaid Theatre, and he is writing a new novel.

WALTER GREENWOOD

# LOVE ON THE DOLE

*The Time is ripe, and rotten ripe, for change;*
*Then let it come . . .*
JAMES RUSSELL LOWELL

PENGUIN BOOKS

Penguin Books Ltd, Harmondsworth, Middlesex, England
Penguin Books Australia Ltd, Ringwood, Victoria, Australia

—

First published by Jonathan Cape 1933
Published in Penguin Books 1969

—

Copyright © Walter Greenwood, 1933

—

Made and printed in Great Britain by
Cox & Wyman Ltd,
London, Reading and Fakenham
Set in Linotype Pilgrim

This book is sold subject to the condition
that it shall not, by way of trade or otherwise,
be lent, re-sold, hired out, or otherwise circulated
without the publisher's prior consent in any form of
binding or cover other than that in which it is
published and without a similar condition
including this condition being imposed
on the subsequent purchaser

# CONTENTS

'I would have liked to live this life, for a space, in any one of half a million restricted flats, with not quite enough space, not quite enough air, not quite enough dollars and a vast deal too much continual strain on the nerves. I would have liked to have come to close quarters with it and got its subtle and sinister toxin incurably into my system.' – *Those United States*. ARNOLD BENNETT.

'... and in 1917 I was only beginning to learn that life for the majority of the population, is an unlovely struggle against unfair odds, culminating in a cheap funeral.' – *Memoirs of an Infantry Officer*. SIEGFRIED SASSOON.

'Oh, it's time the whole thing was changed, absolutely. And the men will have to do it – you've got to smash money and this beastly possessive spirit. I get more revolutionary every minute, but for *life's* sake' – *The Letters* of D. H. LAWRENCE. Ed. ALDOUS HUXLEY.

'I feel that you are suffering because the years are passing irretrievably without one's "living". But patience and courage! We shall still live and experience great things. What we are witnessing first of all is a whole old world sinking, each day a piece, a new collapse, a fresh gigantic overthrow. . . .' – ROSA LUXEMBOURG. *Letter from prison to Frau Sophie Liebknecht*, 12 May 1918. Trans. by Evangeline Ryves. Vide *The Adelphi*, November 1932.

'The middle class has been reduced to a proletariat. I, too, can escape from starvation only if I find new sources of income. So I must once more struggle and worry. Once more I must thrust all spiritual and cultural interests into the background, and, like all the rest who find themselves in my position, hunt for shillings in order to keep body and soul together. More fighting – daily, repeated, exasperating, demoralizing, offensive and defensive fighting of man against man.' – '*Blockade!*' *The Diary of an Australian Middle Class Woman*. 1914–24. ANNIE EISENMENGER.

All the persons represented in this book are purely imaginary; moreover, while actual places and events are mentioned, certain modifications have, in some cases, been intentionally introduced with a view to preserving its fictional character.

# PART ONE

## CHAPTER I

# HANKY PARK

THEY call this part 'Hanky Park'.

It is that district opposite the parish church of Pendleton, one of the many industrial townships comprising the Two Cities. In the early nineteenth century Hanky Park was part of the grounds of a wealthy lady's mansion; at least, so say the old maps in the Salford Town Hall. The district takes its name from a sloping street, Hankinson Street, whose pavements, much worn and very narrow, have been polished by the traffic of boots and clogs of many generations. On either side of this are other streets, mazes, jungles of tiny houses cramped and huddled together, two rooms above and two below, in some cases only one room alow and aloft; public houses by the score where forgetfulness lurks in a mug; pawnshops by the dozen where you can raise the wind to buy forgetfulness; churches, chapels and unpretentious mission halls where God is praised; nude, black patches of land, 'crofts', as they are called, water-logged, sterile, bleak and chill.

The doorsteps and window-sills of the houses are worn hollow. Once a week, sometimes twice, the women clean them with brown or white rubbing stone; the same with portions of the pavement immediately outside their front doors. And they glare at any pedestrians who unavoidably muddy their handi-work in traversing the strip. Some women there are whose lives are dedicated to an everlasting battle with the invincible forces of soot and grime. They are flattered when you refer to them as 'house-proud'. But they are few. The others prefer to have a weekly tilt at the demon dirt and to leave the field to him for the next six days. Of a Friday evening when this portion of the housework is generally done, the pavements have a distant resemblance to a patchwork quilt. Women, girls and children are to be seen kneeling on all fours in the streets, buckets by their sides, cloth and stone daubing it over the flags, then washing it into one even patch of colour.

Families from south of the Trent who take up residence here are astonished at the fashion and say that from whence they came nothing like this is ever seen. The custom persists. The 'sand-bone men' who purvey the lumps of sandstone in exchange for household junk, rags and what-not, can be seen pushing their handcarts and heard calling their trade in rusty, hoarse, sing-song voices: 'San' bo - . Donkey brand brown sto – bo – one,' which, translated, means: 'I will exchange either brown or white rubbing stone for rags, bones or bottles.'

At one time, in the old days, when local men made their millions out of cotton and humanity, when their magnificent equipages trotted along Broad Street past Hanky Park from the local Eccles Old Road – or 'Millionaires' Mile' as it then was called – when large families lived in the Park's one room cellar dwellings and when the excess in population was kept in check by typhus and other fevers, it was the custom of the 'sand-bone men' to sprinkle sand on the newly scoured flag-paved floors of the houses in exchange for bones, which, I suppose, went to the tallow factories to be made into farthing dips. Most of the flag-paved floors are gone, now. The years have brought their changes. Water closets have superseded the earth and tin privies, though not so very long ago; the holes in the tiny back-yard walls from which the pestiferous tins were drawn when to be emptied of the ordure are still to be traced, the newer bricks contrasting in colour with those of the original wall. Fever is rarer; large families are no longer permitted to live in cellars; instead, by force of circumstance and in the simplicity of their natures, they pay much more than their grandparents did for the convenience of living in a single room over a cellar.

The identical houses of yesterday remain, still valuable in the estate market even though the cost of their building has been paid for over and over again by successive tenants. The houses remain: streets of them where the blue-grey smoke swirls down like companies of ghosts from a million squat chimneys: jungles of tiny houses cramped and huddled together, the cradles of generations of the future. Places where men and women are born, live, love and die and pay preposterous rents for the privilege of calling the grimy houses 'home'.

## CHAPTER 2

## GETTING UP

5.30 A.M.

A drizzle was falling.

The policeman on his beat paused awhile at the corner of North Street halting under a street lamp. Its staring beams lit the million globules of fine rain powdering his cape. A cat sitting on the doorstep of Mr Hulkington's, the grocer's shop, blinked sleepily.

'Tsh-tsh-tsh-tsh-tsh,' said the bobby and stooped to scratch the animal's head. It rose, crooked its back, cocked its tail, pushed its body against his hand and miowed.

The melancholy hoot of a ship's siren sounded from the Salford Docks.

A man wearing clogs and carrying a long pole tipped with a bunch of wires came clattering down Hankinson Street. His back was bent, beard stained and untrimmed, his rusty black bowler hat was tipped over his eyes. Blind Joe he was called, though he never gave wrong change out of a shilling nor had need to ask his way about. Whether or no he actually was blind none could say; he was Blind Joe Riley, that was all.

The bobby straightened himself as Joe approached: 'Mornin', Joe. Heigh, hei, ho. More rain, more rest,' said the copper.

'N' rest f' t' wicked, lad, 'cept them as is bobbies, an' they ne'er do nowt else. Ah don't know how some folks ...'

'Ah know, Joe. ... Ah know,' the bobby interrupted: 'Ah know all about it.'

'Well there's one thing Ah'd like t' know if tha knows all about it ... how thee and thy mates have cheek to hold hand out for wages just f' walkin' about streets. ... N' wonder folks call it a bobby's job.' He ejaculated, disgusted, clattered into North Street, stopped at No. 17, raised his pole and began to rattle the wires against the bedroom windows. A voice responded. Joe answered: 'Come on, now, Mrs 'Ardcastle. Hafe past five, Monday mornin' an' pourin' o' rain. . . .' He shouldered his pole to repeat the performance at other houses in the street. Then he turned the corner at the far end.

Silence. Not a cat stirring.

The solitary lamp half-way down the street emphasized the enshrouding gloom and silvered the gently falling drizzle.

Lights began to appear in the lower windows of the houses. The grocer's shop at the corner of the street blazed forth electrically, the wet pavement mirroring the brilliance. Unwashed Mr Hulkington, the gross, ungainly proprietor, shot back the bolts and stood on the step, wheezing, coughing and spitting on the roadway. He panted, shivered in the rawness of the morning, turned about and closed the door to stand behind the counter in readiness for the women who would come, soon, stealing like shadows, to buy foodstuffs on tick.

At No. 17, Mrs Hardcastle, an old woman of forty, came downstairs 'Ah-ah-ing' sleepily, hair in disarray. She groped on the tiny kitchen's mantelpiece for the matches, struck one and lit the gas. The glare hurt her eyes: she blinked and stifled a yawn, stretched and shrugged her shoulders. It was cold. She stooped, raked out the grate and stuffed it with a newspaper taken from a thick pile under the cushion of the rocker chair. Then she stood, indecisively, still sleep-dazed, as though at a loss what next to do: 'Oh, aye,' she said: 'Coal.' She picked up the shovel, trudged to the back door and paused by the stairs to shout: 'Harry, Sal. Come on, now; five an' twenty to six.' She unbolted the door. The cat ran in miowing noisily, tail in air: it leaned heavily against the table leg and walked round and round, still miowing. Other people in the neighbouring backyards were shovelling coal; the gratings of the shovels on the yards' flaggings rasped harshly in the still morning air.

In a few moments the fire was made. The shovel, balanced on the top bar with a sheet of paper spread in front, drew a great draught and sent flames roaring and leaping round the kettle. Smoke and flame roaring up the chimney, gushing out of the chimney-pot and into the sky; thousands of smoky fires;

millions of chimneys exhaling simultaneously; smoke drifting, converging, hanging, an immense pall over the Two Cities.

Mrs Hardcastle went to the foot of the stairs again to call the boy and girl. Still no response. She frowned, sighed, lit a taper at the gas and went upstairs to the back room. A candle, secured in its own grease stood on a chair-seat by the bed; over the chair-back was flung, anyhow, feminine clothes. The rusting iron bed-end was similarly adorned except that the clothes there belonged to a boy. Except an old chest of drawers and a curtain suspended in front of an alcove by the fireplace, doubtless a makeshift wardrobe, there was nothing else in the room.

'Come along, there. Come along,' cried Mrs Hardcastle, petulantly, as she lit the candle: 'Harry. Sal. ... D'y' hear?' She shook one of the forms.

A smothered grumbling. Sally withdrew her head from the thin coverings and yawned. Eighteen, a gorgeous creature whose native beauty her shabbiness could not hide. Eyes dark, lustrous, haunting; abundant black hair tumbling in waves; a full, ripe, pouting mouth and a low, round bosom. A face and form such as any society dame would have given three-quarters of her fortune to possess. Sally wore it carelessly as though youth's brief hour was eternal; as though there was no such thing as old age. She failed in her temper; but when roused, colour tinted her pallid cheeks such as the wind whipped up when it blew from the north or east.

'Tea brewed, ma?' she asked, rubbing her eyes.

'Long since,' her mother lied, adding, plaintively: 'Come on wi' y'. Get up. ... Havin' me trapesin' about like this. ... Why can't y' get up first call. ... When I was your age I was up wi' t' lark. ... Harry. *Harry.* Y'll be late for work. Oh, *willy'* get up. Sick an' tired I am wastin' breath.'

Sally prodded him with her elbow: 'Hey, dopey. ... D'y hear ...? Gerrup.'

He stirred, grumbled, struggled half-heartedly to a sitting position, and, still keeping his eyes closed, groped over the bed for his clothes: 'What day is it, ma?' he mumbled.

'Monday, lad, an' pourin' o' rain. They'll be wet through i'

Price's yard,' coaxingly: 'Come on, son. . . . Hurry, lad, or y'll ha' no time for y' breakfast.' She went downstairs.

Sally groaned: 'Rainin'. . . . Allus rainin'. . . . Ne'er does nowt else i' this hole.' She threw the bed clothes back, got out of bed and began to dress. Harry, fair hair all tousled, crawled on all fours to the edge of the bed and stepped on to the icy lino. He shivered, his skin pimpling with the cold: 'Stockings gone agen,' he mumbled, dithering and groping about the bed end: impatiently: 'Aw, Ah'm sick of it all.'

'Wrap 'em round y' neck of a night, then y'll know where t' find 'em,' snapped Sally. She pulled on her knickers and half-turned. 'Open y'r eyes: there they are on floor.' She stood in front of the candle slipping her clothes over her head, an enormous shadow of herself reflected on wall and ceiling.

Harry muttered something, dragged on his stockings and knickerbockers, stumbled past her and went below, his sullen expression mirroring the surly dissatisfaction he felt towards the day's prospect. Rebellion stirred in his heart. Bleak visions both of the school classroom and of Price and Jones's pawnshop where he worked as half-time clerk, rose to his mind. He would be writing tickets there from half past six this morning until school time; he would return after school and continue writing pawn-tickets until the place closed. Then it would be bed time again. He could smell the stale pungency of the place after it had been shut up over the week-end. His spirits retched. It was incredible, shameful, unbearable. No escape; *had* to go. And tedious lessons on top of it all. A lump rose to his throat as he pushed his hands under the cold water of the tap. The shock of the icy water roused him; the fair hairs on his thin arms stood upright. Then he remembered!

Why, how on earth had he overlooked – ! He'd done with schooling, had finished with it on Friday last! He now was free! His wondering spirits revived. Free! They contracted the instant he recalled Price and Jones's pawnshop and his mother's and father's desire that he should accept Mr Price's half-promise of full time employment there. Price and Jones's though! *that* above all things. Couldn't they understand that he'd had a surfeit of desks there? that the pawnshop was a worse prison than school? Imagine it, tied up there all day until eight o'clock of an evening and nine on Saturdays. He flamed with indignation. Three years now he'd been tied up there; three years before school hours and after; three years he'd sat in that dark corner of the pledge office writing out millions of pawn-tickets. Damned in a fair handwriting: 'See our Harry's handwriting. By gum, think o' that, now, for one of his years.' He had paid dearly for those flattering remarks. And now, if his parents were to have their way he was to be penalized even further; they wanted him to be a scrivener for the rest of his life. They *would* do. 'Well, Ah'm not doin' it,' he muttered, aloud.

'Eh?' answered his mother.

Harry did not hear her. He wouldn't obey them; couldn't; the thought was sickening; he would die. He began to cast about in efforts to devise a means of frustrating their plans. What could he do? Surely there was a way, a means. He wanted to . . .

Ah! Of course! But dare he? He paused, staring, unseeing into the gloom of the backyard transfixed by an idea. His heart swelled; a glow of eager anticipation suffused him; his eyes kindled. He would have to hurry, though. He'd to be at Price and Jones's by six-thirty; and his father would be home from the night shift at the pits presently. Better be gone before he returned; might ask awkward questions as to the reason of the early departure. Hurriedly he finished washing himself to sit down to the table. And by the time Sally came downstairs he was bolting his breakfast, mechanically, while staring with absorption at the tablecloth. Yes, it was a fine notion, indeed. What luck! Dare he hope that it would materialize?

Sally said, after she had washed herself: 'What's up wi' *you* this morning? Why are y' rushin' wi' y' breakfast; y've plenty o' time.'

She *would* say that. 'You mind y'r own business,' he muttered.

She smiled as she glanced at his rolled-up sleeves: 'Old Samson,' she said, with a provocative laugh: 'All muscle.'

He flushed hotly: this was her favourite trick, deriding his miserable muscles when she couldn't think of anything else to say; had been ever since once she had surprised him, stripped to the waist, standing in front of the small mirror over the slopstone endeavouring to emulate the posture of a notorious wrestler whose picture had lain propped against a jug on the table: it had been, for him, a most embarrassing moment. 'You leave my arms alone,' he snapped. He raised his brows accusingly: 'You watch yourself. Ah saw y' talkin' t' Ned Narkey, last night. What time did he let y' come in, eh? That's what Ah'd like t' know. If pa hears about –'

Her eyes blazed; the smile faded: 'You mind your own business,' contemptuously, and with a curl of the lip: 'Choir boy! Ha!'

'Now, children. Now children. Cant y' ever agree? Like cat an' dog, y' are. Ne'er seen a pair like y',' said Mrs Hardcastle, wearily: 'Get y' breakfasts an' let y' food stop y' mouths. Come on, Sal. Y'll be quartered' (fined a quarter hour's wage for impunctuality).

Harry mumbled something, resentful of Sal's allusion to his being a chorister. She seemed to delight in provoking him. Oh, this kind of thing took all the pleasure out of the idea. He rose from the table sulkily, put on his jacket, celluloid Eton collar and stud bow, picked up his cap and sauntered to the door.

'Where y' goin' now?' asked Sally.

'Aw. . . . Questions agen. . . . There'n back t' see how far it is . . .' With a gesture of impatience he stamped out of the house into the wet street.

Doors were opening and slamming. Men, women, boys and girls were turning out to work.

The lamplighter was on his rounds extinguishing street lamps. The rain was ceasing.

CHAPTER 3

# LOOKING FOR IT

DAYLIGHT waxed stronger.

Women wearing shawls so disposed as to conceal from sight and to shelter from the elements whatever it was they carried in their arms, passed him now and again. They looked, in profile, like fat cassocked monks with cowls drawn. He knew what it was they carried and whither they were bound. He paid no attention to them, proceeding, via by-streets, to fall in with a great procession of heavily booted men all wearing overalls and all marching in the same direction.

The drizzle had ceased by the time he reached the main thoroughfare.

Red and cream electric tramcars rattled by; alongside raced bicycles, municipal buses, privately owned charabancs crowded with men, the atmospheres within the vehicles opaque with tobacco smoke.

Tobacco smoke, blue and grey. It rose from the marching men like sweat vapour from distressed horses, hung in the still air or swirled, gracefully, in the draught of passers-by. Over all, the air resounded with the ringing rhythmic beat of hobnailed boots.

It fired Harry's imagination. A tremulous elation fluttered his heart; then a despondence stole across his spirits when he remembered that he was but a trespasser. He had no real right to be here with these men. A spiteful voice in his brain whispered that he was doomed to clerking, reminded him that, even now, he wore the uniform of offices, Eton collar, stud bow and those abominable knickerbockers. He felt ashamed of himself, slunk along by the walls trying to make himself inconspicuous. All these men and boys wore overalls; *they* weren't clerks, they were Men, engaged in men's work. Sullen obstinacy mingled with rebellious desperation stirred in his heart. 'They ain't getting me clerking,' he muttered.

He found himself listening to the beat of the men's feet again; an entrancing tune, inspiring, eloquent of the great engineering works where this army of men were employed. Reverently he murmured its name: 'Marlowe's.' Marlowe's, a household word throughout the universe of commerce; textiles, coal, engineering, shipping and home trade; a finger in the pie of them all.

And there, majestic, impressive, was the enormous engineering plant itself; there, in those vast works, the thousands of human pygmies moved in the close confines of their allotted sphere, each performing his particular task, an infinitesimal part of a pre-ordained whole, a necessary cog in the great organization.

He stared at it, unblinkingly. He had seen it before, often enough, but not in the light of the present as something in which he wished to be absorbed. Awe glowed in his intent eyes.

Three huge chimneys challenged the lowering sky; three banners of thick black smoke gushed forth from their parapets, swirling, billowing, expanding as they drifted, with 'unperturbed pace' to merge, imperceptibly into the dirty sky. A double row of six smaller chimneys thrust up their steel muzzles like cannon trained on air raiders. Tongues of flame shot up, fiery sprites, kicking their flaming skirts about for a second then diving again as instantly as they had appeared. An orange glare reflected dully on the wet slates of the foundry.

The colossal building itself sprawled sooty and grimy over a tremendous acreage enclosed within a high brick wall. Within was laid out in streets numbered in the American manner, 'First Street', and so on to 'Forty-First Street'.

Railway lines, like shiny snail tracks, trailed all over the place. Presently, men would come out of their small cabins to stand at junctions with red flags in their hands, waving on or holding up the light locomotives which pulled the railway traffic about the company's premises. At present, though, all within was quiet. The industrial city's streets lay as in a midnight silence. Deserted save for the solitary figure of a night watchman slowly traversing Tenth Street; a slow-moving speck hemmed in on both sides by the towering steel and glass façades of the riveting and machine shops. In a moment this silence would be shattered.

Shattered by the influx of the vast concourse of men congregated outside the walls. Before six o'clock the twelve thousand of them would pass through the gates. They crammed the wide thoroughfare, a black mass of restlessness; crammed, saving a strip of roadway kept clear for the frequently arriving, bell-clanging tramcars full of more overalled men. The air stank of oily clothes, reeked with it and tobacco smoke, and buzzed with conversation to do, mostly, with week-end sport.

How easily, negligently, these men wore their supreme importance; how infinitely, ineffably superior these gods of the machine and forge were to mere pushers of pens! Occasionally, as he pushed through the crush gazing at the faces of the men, he was filled with misgiving to remember his great temerity in presuming to aspire to their status. Could it be possible that those in authority would give Harry Hardcastle a job? No, no, it was too much to expect; those expectations, desires, which would give one great happiness rarely materialized. His courage ebbed; the thought of the likelihood of returning home disappointed, of going back to Price and Jones's, was maddening. He wouldn't do it; he'd run away first; he'd – Oh, they *must* take him on here; must, must, must.

Of course they'd take him on. They'd engaged the other boys, Tom Hare, Sam Hardie, Bill Simmons and Jack Lindsay. He pushed onwards towards the gates, an expression of desperate resolve and intense determination on his face. He kept a wary eye open for a chance meeting with the four boys with whom he associated of an evening at the street corner. He almost bumped into them but managed to withdraw and disappear into the crush; they were too preoccupied in consuming a cigarette which they were taking turns in puffing. He didn't want them to see him; they were too discouraging; chaffed him, with unmerciful derision, concerning his occupation at the pawnshop. Nor was there anything remained for Harry but to grin in a sickly, apologetic manner. Wasn't their contempt justifiable when their romantic work was compared with his own? Look what Marlowe's had done for them in three months' time! Three months ago they had been at school, marbles in their pocket. They and he now were poles removed. They talked, intimately and authoritatively in terms of magic; entrancing names such as 'machine shop', 'foundry', 'riveting shop' slipped from their tongues with spellbinding ease. They were men already; their speech and swagger made him outcast, filled him with gnawing envy. But think on it in a few moments, perhaps, he would be as they, an engineer in embryo!

Again he faltered. Where was application to be made? The place was so vast; he might wander through it all day without finding the person who had to do with engaging the apprentices. Indeed, he might not even be permitted entry. And he'd to be at Price and Jones's by six-thirty. He dared not prejudice his employment there until he was sure of occupation here. He heard the chains of the desk clanking behind him.

If only he could find someone who would introduce him to the right quarter. He would have to hurry; in a few moments this crowd would be gone.

He searched the faces of the men for one familiar.

There was Ned Narkey, a huge fellow with the physique of a Mongolian wrestler. But he wouldn't, couldn't ask Ned. There was something about the beefy hulking brute that repelled one; though Harry admired his strength; according to the boys Ned could lift a girder that four ordinary men couldn't move. But he wasn't a nice fellow; there was a foul side to his tongue, and there were tattoos on his arms of naked females which he could make perform the most suggestive postures by contracting his muscles. For this reason Harry glowered whenever he saw Sally speaking with him. Though he kept his dislike of Ned a secret; the boys would have laughed him out of countenance had they ever discovered it. Ned was popular with them; he'd had his picture in the paper when he won the medal during the war. And he'd a pocket full of money, what remained of the gratuity they had given him when he had been demobilized. No, no, he couldn't ask Ned; couldn't risk humiliation in front of all these men. Ned might be kindly disposed, then, again, he mightn't; and, as today was Monday and Ned probably not recovered from his week-end carousal, the latter mood would be likeliest.

Nearer the gates Harry glimpsed Larry Meath reading a newspaper and leaning against the wall. Larry Meath! Harry's heart leapt and his eyes glowed with eagerness. *He'd* understand; he was that kind. His quality of studiousness and reserve elevated him to a plane beyond that of ordinary folk; he seemed out of place in his lodgings in North Street. He wasn't for drinking, gambling, swearing or brawling. Though if you went to the library to look at the illustrated papers or to watch the old geysers playing dominoes, you sometimes saw Larry at one of the tables absorbed in some book or other that looked as dry as the desert. And argue! Hear him, when during election times, you and the rest of the boys went to the committee rooms to see whether there were any bills to distribute or any lamps to hold; hear him then! he could talk fifty to the dozen. Yes, he'd a reputation for cleverness: his face attracted you, too; lean, a gentle expression and a soft kindliness, a frank steadfastness in his eyes that invited confidence. People were always going to No. 21 with their troubles: 'Ah've had a summons for me rent, Larry. *Could* y' go for me? Ah'm feared t' death. Eeee, y' don't know what a relief it'd be if on'y y'd . . .' or if somebody had an official form to fill in they, demoralized by the questions set forth and distressed at the thought of having to take up pen and ink would come, nervous and stare eyed to ask his assistance, going home, beaming and relieved, with the completed paper clasped in their hands. Just the man to help Harry. Besides, he was sure to have some influence in the works since he was a cut above the ordinary engineer: he it was who assisted in maintaining the efficiency of the plant, saw to the overhaul of the gigantic crane that Ned Narkey drove; at least, so said the boys who spoke respectfully of Larry Meath's status.

He was about to approach Larry when he paused within arm's length and turned sidewise, alarmed, a sudden remembrance occurring to him that Larry's kindliness might take an unexpected turn. Yes! Remember when Jack Lindsay asked Larry to introduce him to Marlowe's? Larry warned him against it: told him that it was a waste of time serving an apprenticeship to engineering. Harry tried to edge away from Larry, but the crowd, growing denser about him prevented movement. He hoped, fervently, that Larry would not see him. He was putting his paper away now; out of the tail of his eye Harry could see Larry's gaze fixed on him. He ran a finger round his collar, fiddled, nervously, with his stud bow and pretended an absorbed interest in the activities of two gatekeepers come to stand on the inside of the great gates ready to fling them back at the appropriate time. He could feel Larry's gaze.

Larry, slowly stuffing his newspaper into his pocket regarded the boy sympathetically, thoughtfully. A thin, down-at-heel child dressed in a worse-for-wear knickerbocker suit, a celluloid Eton collar, yellowing, fiddling nervously with his stud bow.

Another recruit to this twelve thousand strong army of men

who, all, at one time had come, eagerly, to some such place as this on a similar errand. Larry too. All had been young Harrys then. They now were old, disenchanted Harrys; families dependent on their irregular and insufficient wages; no respite to the damnable eternal struggling. Discontented and wondering why they were discontented; each keeping his discontent in his own bosom as though it were a guilty secret; each putting on a mask of unconcern, accepting his neighbour's mask as his true expression, and, often, expressing inarticulate revolt in drunkenness, in making desperate, futile efforts to relieve their poverty in gambling hazards they could ill afford.

Sam Grundy, the gross street-corner bookmaker, Alderman Ezekiah Grumpole, the money-lender proprietor of the Good Samaritan Clothing Club. Price, the pawnbroker, each an institution that had grown up out of a people's discontent. Sam Grundy promised sudden wealth as a prize, deeper poverty as a penalty; the other two, Grumpole and Price, represented temporary relief at the expense of further entanglement. A trinity, the outward visible sign of an inward spiritual discontent; safety valves through which the excess of impending change could escape, vitiate and dissipate itself.

He regarded the boy thoughtfully; a thin, down-at-heel child fiddling nervously with his stud bow.

A man next Harry glanced at his watch and said to his mate: 'She'll blow any second, now.' Harry licked his lips and wiped his clammy palms on his breeches' backside. His face was flushed, brain in a whirl. What was he going to do? What ...

Suddenly, from the side of one of the tall chimneys appeared a plume of steam vapour instantly followed by the deep, loud, hoarse note of a siren. The warning signal telling the men that only five minutes separated them from the time to commence work. The great gates slid back. In concert the vast assembly seethed about the opening and spilled into the enormous rail-lined pattered streets and yards, spreading in all directions like an army of ants in panic.

Swept forward by the irresistible current, bewildered, apprehensive, it was only a matter of seconds before he found himself in the machine shop.

Rows of lathes, milling and drilling machines; overhead a maze of motionless countershafts, driving belts crossed and connected to the pulleys of the machinery below. Odour of oil everywhere; floor black with it. Yet there was no litter, no accumulation of dirt; the tidiness amazed Harry. Between the rows of machinery, white lines, painted on the concrete floor, had legends painted, also in white.

SAFETY FIRST.
KEEP BETWEEN THE WHITE LINES

Boards here and there suspended in conspicuous positions, said: 'Don't Run'. At various points men formed into queues from whence came the quick, repetitive 'ping-ping-ping' of bells. The men clocking on and swearing dreadfully if anybody fumbled a time-card which they had to take out of one rack, slip it into a slot in the time-recorder, depress a lever and restore the card to its appropriate place in another rack on the other side of the clock.

He stood there gazing about him, hypnotized by all he saw. His heart rose to think that, at this time tomorrow morning, he, too, might be punching a time-card!

'Hey, what the hell're *you* doin' here?' the rough voice of a tall man wearing a badge of authority in the lapel of his coat. The countershafts began to turn; men were divesting themselves of their coats and hanging them on long racks that would shoot up to the ceiling the moment six o'clock blew. Harry licked his lips, swallowed hard and stammered: 'Ah – Ah – ' Oh, what should he say? 'Ah – Ah – Oh, Ah've bin sent here for a job an' Ah don't know where the place is.' Would the man believe?

'You want time office,' replied the man: 'There t'is, o'er there. See Ted Munter. Come on, now, get out o' here.'

Ted Munter! Ted Munter who lived in the next street to North Street! Why, everybody knew him. What luck.

Ted, a semi-bald, pot-bellied individual with thick pebble steel-rimmed spectacles on his nose, said, surlily, as Harry knocked, timidly, on the open inquiry window of the time office: 'Wot the 'ell *d'you* want?'

'Please, Mr Munter,' replied Harry: 'Ah've bin sent here for a job.'

'Oo sent y'?' snapped Ted, peering at Harry.

Harry blinked. He drew a bow at a venture: 'Foreman, Mr Munter.'

'Ah know . . . which foreman?'

'Ah dunno his name. . . . He just tole me t' come here an' ask f' you. He was a tall man.'

Ted narrowed his eyes and contorted his mouth: 'Ah know oo it was,' said Ted, staring hard at Harry and making him feel extremely uncomfortable. Then, as Ted continued, Harry realized that Ted was not talking *to* him but *through* him to some foreman or other in the works with whom he, Ted, was at loggerheads: 'Ah know oo it was. 'Ee thinks ee's t' have *all* t' new lads as come here, the yellow-bellied rat. Yaah! Ah'll show him,' glaring at Harry. 'Y' go in machine shop, d'y' hear? *Ah'm* boss o' this office an *Ah* sends 'em where *Ah* think fit. . . . D'y' understand?'

'Oh, aye, Mr Munter,' Harry agreed, eagerly.

Ted grunted: 'Washer name?'

'Harry Hardcastle, sir.'

'Six o'clock t'morrer mornin'. . . . Machine shop, think on . . .' He cocked a glance at Harry's clothes: 'An see y' come in a pair overalls. This ain't a bloody school.'

Harry blushed: 'Yes, sir,' he mumbled, meekly.

'All right. Muck off. . . . Don't hang around here. Hey! Here, tek these here papers. Get y'r owld man t' fill 'em up. An' y' bloody clockin'-on number's,' glancing at a chart: '2510. Clock number fourteen. Clock on o' mornin' an' clock off o' night. *Don't* clock at dinner. Think on, now, don't you go'n make a muck of it like all t'others do, the dense lot o' bastards,' jerking his thumb: ' 'Oppit, now, 'oppit, 'oppit, 'oppit.' Confused with excitement, Harry made himself scarce. What luck! He really was engaged. And in so short a space of time! What would the boys have to say to this? He gazed at the papers in his hand. There was the magic word 'Indentures!' And they'd given him a number, 2510. There was the hallmark of his engagement. Better make a note of it. He wrote in on a corner of the indenture.

The man with the badge in his coat again intercepted him. Harry told him of his success: 'All right, clear off, now, until tomorrow,' the man said, not unkindly: 'Can't have y' hangin' about here.'

He went outside the gates thrilled, spirits soaring, paused and turned to survey the great place, enthralled as a child in a Christmas toy shop.

The roadway outside the works' wall was now bleak and deserted save for a few late comers, old and young who were running a race, the other competitors being the time clocks ticking imperturbably on the workshops' walls. A light railway engine clanked by; a couple of tramcars stood empty, their guards and drivers stealing an illicit smoke. Pavements and setts were littered with a million fag-ends of cigarettes, spent matches, tram tickets, screwed up balls of newspaper and disgusting plashes where sufferers from Manchester catarrh had spat. The yards were almost empty; a hurrying figure here and there.

A hissing plume of steam vapour from the side of one of the tall chimneys; the loud, deep hoarse note sustained much longer this time and accompanied by blasts and shrill pipings from the sirens and whistles of the factories and mills adjacent.

From the great works came a rumbling and a confused muffled banging; air throbbed. Two men with brass brooms came out of the Marlowe yard and commenced to sweep up the litter.

A new day's toil had begun.

CHAPTER 4

# PRICE AND JONES'S

PRICE AND JONES'S pawnshop stood at one point of a triangle; the other two points were occupied, respectively by a church and a palatial beerhouse, each large, commodious and convenient.

The pawnshop was entered by three doors, the front to the sales department, the side and back to the pledge offices. Three faded gilt balls on an angle iron stood out from the wall, the dents in the balls evidence of their having been used as targets by the youth of the neighbourhood.

For the convenience of policemen and the inconvenience of

burglars square peepholes had been cut in the window shutters and the back doors. A gas jet glimmered in the shop all night long and an arrangement had been made with the police whereby a pair of shop ladders should, when the shop was closed, be left directly in front of the safe. A peeping policeman noticing whether the ladders were in their customary place could tell whether all was well within or otherwise.

Mr Price's idea. Jones was fiction. Gaunt, cleanshaven, thin lipped, Mr Price's eyes were like those of a fish, glassy, staring: his high cheek-bones, sunken cheeks and sallow complexion, this last as a result of a self-imposed forty-year term of imprisonment in his shop, lent his countenance a death-mask-like appearance especially when, business being slack, he stood, motionless, in the shadowy alcove by the fireplace where fire never burned no matter how cold the day. Nothing could have been more full of life than his skeletonic fingers as they plunged into the heaped money of the cash drawer: as a symphony is to some ears so the jingle of coins were to Mr Price's. When staring at the rhino he was beatified. He was a high official at one of the local chapels; also, he was a magistrate. And to be sitting on the bench giving some cringing wretch a stern talking to was an occupation which inspired in him the greatest pleasure and appreciation of his public spirit.

Young Harry, standing shivering and sniffing on the damp pavement outside the shop, was reflecting, happily, on what had just occurred at home. At first his father had been reluctant in giving his permission. Happily, he had been too weary to give the matter adequate consideration. He had capitulated with: 'Aw, all right. Ah'm too tired t' be bothered. Go if y' want to. But think on, now. . . . Hark t' what Ah say. Once them there papers are signed y' bound f' seven years. Ah've no money t' buy y' out. Teks us all our time t' live here.' It had been as easy as that! And his mother was to come to Price's, soon, to buy a pair of overalls for him.

With such intoxicating thoughts in mind he stood, hands in pockets, shivering and sniffing by the padlocked gate guarding the porch of the door set there to keep urban courting couples out of the doorway.

Presently he saw Mr Price approaching dressed in the fashion of an explorer Antartctic bound. Mr Price's blue nose sniffed the raw morning air over the top of a long woollen scarf wrapped twice about his neck; his Homburg hat was pulled low on his head, its brim crooking his ears; his long heavy overcoat reached almost to his ankles but did not conceal the fact of his wearing stout leather leggings; his heavily soled boots made no noise as he crept along carrying umbrella in gloved hand, boots made no noise since he wore goloshes.

He grunted a muffled good morning through the scarf. Harry made answer. Mr Price regarded the boy: 'Hardcastle,' he said, magisterially: 'Hardcastle take the hands out of the pockets.' Harry blushed, blinked and withdrew the hands: 'Slovenliness,' Mr Price continued, gravely: 'Slovenliness, slovenliness. . . . Always to be deplored, especially in one so young. Where is the handkerchief? Blow the nose.'

Harry's desire was to retort, rudely; his indignation, though, robbed him of speech, and the glassy stare in Mr Price's eyes gave no encouragement. Still he could say something with impunity; this was to be his last day in the pawnbroker's employ. He said, with stammering impulsiveness: 'Ah'm leaving here today. . . . Start at Marlowe's in morning.' He quaked, inwardly, as he spoke in spite of the impatience he felt towards himself for so doing.

Mr Price said, as though Harry had not spoken: 'Hold the umbrella. Over me . . . over me . . .'

He felt Price had made a fool of him: he stared at the pawnbroker, resentfully, remembering the past three years in Price's employ: memories of the dreary mornings and the interminable evenings when his friends were free as birds whilst he was chained to the desk, crowded to his mind to resolve themselves into a frigid seizure of the spirits, a terrific recollection that made him helpless with incredulity to know that it had been a fact and not a nightmare. That it now belonged to the past was equally incredible. Tomorrow, Marlowe's! He took a deep breath: henceforward would be one long holiday.

Keys rattled. Mr Price, fetching out an enormous bunch, fitted one to the padlock and opened the gate. The front door was secured, extra to the ordinary lock, by a forged iron hasp and staple and another padlock. Keys rattled again; the door opened. The pungent odour of new sheets, blankets, quilts and what not floated out of the sales department; a revolting stench reminiscent of the unspeakable. Price entered, lit the gases and disappeared to put away his things. Harry removed the shutters, gleefully picturing himself replacing them tonight.

From the backyard came the confused buzz of conversation: through the iron barred windows Harry, if he had wished, could have seen a backyard full of women, their shawls so disposed as to conceal from the elements whatever it was they carried in their arms. They looked like fat, cassocked monks with cowls drawn. They had obtained access to the backyard by one of their number thrusting an arm through one of the peepholes and withdrawing the bolt. Harry cried: 'Shall I let 'em in, Mr Price?' and an exultant voice in his head added, with relish: 'Last time y'll say that, Harry.' He grinned.

Mr Price, wherever he was, made no answer.

Voices from outside, all in wheedling tones:

'Eh, 'Arry, lad, open door.'

' 'Arry, we're perished.'

'Come on, now, 'Arry, lad. We bin standin' here hours.'

He glanced at the barred windows to see what he had seen every morning these years past, a crush of unwashed women, hair tumbled, come to raise the wind so that they might have money to spend on food. Though, to him, custom had acquainted him with the notion that they merely had come to pawn things.

He glanced at them, blew into his blue fingers ostentatiously to indicate that he, too, was cold. Next moment, caught unawares, he received the fright of his life from Mr Price, who, creeping up to him, silently, stooped and whispered into his ear: 'You may let them in, Hardcastle.'

He climbed the counter, went to the back door, and, after shooting the three stout bolts, turned tail, a rowdy, pushing, shoving, squeezing crowd of women hot on his heels. By the time he was on the other side of the counter again the place was full. In the staring gas light, the women, throwing back their shawls from their dishevelled hair revealed faces which, though dissimilar in features, had a similarity of expression common, typical, of all the married women around and about; their badge of marriage, as it were. The vivacity of their virgin days was with their virgin days, gone; a married woman could be distinguished from a single by a glance at her facial expression. Marriage scored on their faces a kind of preoccupied, faded, lack-lustre air as though they were constantly being plagued by some problem. As they were. How to get a shilling, and, when obtained, how to make it do the work of two. Though it was not so much a problem as a whole-time occupation to which no salary was attached, not to mention the sideline of risking life to give children birth and being responsible for their upbringing afterwards.

Simple natures all, prey to romantic notions whose potent toxin was become part of the fabric of their brains.

As virgins they had cherished a solitary dream, the expectation of the climax of their wedding day. Wedding day, when, clad in the appropriate – afterwards utterly useless – finery, they appeared for a glorious moment the cynosure of a crowd of envious females.

For a moment only. It passed to add its little quantity to all their yesterdays.

The finery was discarded for less conspicuous apparel which devoured their identity; they became one of a multitude of insignificant women by a mere change of costume, and the only pleasure that remained was a vicarious living-over again of their magic moment in watching, from the back of a crowded church doorway, the scene enacted by later generations. And the satisfaction, if satisfaction there was, in knowing that the scornful tag 'left on the shelf', could never be attached to them.

Patronage of Price and Jones, and all that it signified and implied was an aspect of marriage unanticipated in their dreams.

Harry gazed at the women as a soon-to-be-released prisoner might stare at the stones of his prison cell, fixedly, slowly revolving memories of his long incarceration, half doubtful of freedom, rather afraid of it. They were the same familiar faces he had seen week after week for years, until they had become

as institutions; the same actresses in the same grim play. Week
after week, for years. New faces from time to time; young girls,
pregnant, wedding rings on their fingers, sometimes squalling
babies in their arms; they were rather shy at first; but they
became less and less shy, more and more married as weeks
went by.

Next Friday or Saturday (he wouldn't be here then!) they
would hand over their wages to Mr Price in return for whatever they had pawned today. And next Monday they would
pawn again whatever they had pawned today, paying Mr Price
interest on interest until they were so deep in the mire of debts
that not only did Mr Price own their and their family's clothes,
but, also, the family income as well. They could not have both
at the same time. If they had the family income in their purses
then Mr Price had the family raiment and bedding; if they had
the family raiment and bedding then Mr Price had the family
income. This morning Mr Price had the family income: the
women were come to redeem the moneys with the family
raiment so that they might pay off their tick account for food
which stood against their names in the books of Mr Hulkington,
the street corner provision merchant. So it would continue,
week after week, a tale, told by an idiot, never to be concluded,
until the characters had no further use for pawning or redeem-
ing anything else in this perplexing world.

Harry, staring at them all, said, to himself: 'Well, Ah'm glad
t' be leavin' all this,' repeating, with immense relief: 'Eeee,
glad t' be gooin'. Phoo, not half!'

Confused clamour resounded in the room; all conversing
simultaneously. Harry reached out the box of pins used by Mr
Price to secure the identification tickets to the pledges; long,
stout pins, instruments of death in Harry's hands, when, wanting better occupation, he impaled the starving stupefied vermin
crawling out of the pledged bundles of clothing.

By this time the counter resembled a cheap-jack's stall in the
market; boots, shoes, clogs, girls' cheap, gaudy dance frocks,
men's Sunday suits, mixed bundles of bedding, table linen and
underclothing done up in cotton print wrappers.

Mrs Dorbell, who had crushed in first, a beshawled ancient,

lugubrious woman, round shouldered, wizened, with a dewdrop at the end of her hooked, prominent nose, pushed a man's cheap serge suit to the spot where Mr Price stood when doing business. Then she stared, alarmed, into nothingness and clapped her bony hand to her placket as though something had bitten her leg. An expression of consternation appeared on her face, but only for a moment. She coughed, assumed an innocent air and drew the suit back to her side of the counter to stare, fixedly, at an imaginary stain on the lapel. Out of the tail of her eye she glanced this way and that, stealthily withdrew her hand from her placket and quickly slipped into one of the suit's pockets her old age pension book. She pushed the suit back to its former place, coughed, unconcernedly, turned to her nearest neighbour, a tall, restless-eyed old woman name Mrs Nattle, who had fetched, in a bassinette, nine suits, a dozen frocks, any number of boots and shoes, two wedding rings, three watches and chains, not to mention a couple of barelegged, barefoot children whose mottled legs shivered with the cold whilst their scraggy arms ached with the bundles they carried – Mrs Dorbell, after the manoeuvre with the pension book, turned to Mrs Nattle and said, off hand: 'It's a wery cold mornin' this mornin', Mrs Nakkle,' a mournful look then a slow inclination of the head towards the blank wall behind opposite which, across the street stood the public-house: 'Ah wish *they* wus open,' Mrs Dorbell said; 'Could jus' do wi' a nip, Ah could. Ne'er slep' a wink las' night, Ah didn't. *Daily Express* is right. 'Taint bin same since war. Before *that* started things *was* reas'nable. A body could get a drink wi'out hinterference wi' this 'ere early closin' an late openin'. But Ah ne'er did hold wi' Lloyd George nor wi' any o' t' rest of 'em neither. Vote for none on 'em, say I. All same once they get i' Parli'ment. It's poor as 'elps poor *aaaall* world over.'

Mrs Nattle permitted her to finish, staring at her, meanwhile, with suspicion, her lips tightly pursed. Then she leaned towards her and whispered, out of the side of her mouth and very much after the manner of an amateur ventriloquist: '*I* seed performance,' she said, mysteriously, adding, explanatorily: '*I* seed y' slip pension book into pocket,' she put back her head, raised her brows and stared at Mrs Dorbell accusingly.

Mrs Dorbell opened her mouth and stared back. But Mrs Nattle turned to the two children who had accompanied her. She smiled at them and said: 'Here, gie me the bungles. . . . Y' can go, now. See me when Ah come back an' Ah'll gie y' penny each.' She relieved them of the bundles and they disappeared, as did the smile from Mrs Nattle's lips. She addressed herself to Mrs Dorbell once again who was staring at her, stolidly. Making no immediate reference to what she had seen Mrs Nattle remarked: 'Them there's two wery obligin' childer o' Mrs Cranford's, Mrs Dorbell. Me round's gettin' that there big these times that Ah'll not be able t' manage it, soon.' She looked up to the dirty ceiling waiting for Mrs Dorbell to reintroduce the subject of the pension book.

'It don't,' said Mrs Dorbell, with a significant stare: 'It don't do t' tell everybody *all* y' know. Still tongue in a wise head. Wise as a sarpint, an' 'armless as a dove, as it says i' Bible, though I haven't bin t' church for 'ears an' 'ears. If it's too far for parson to come t' see me, it's too far f' me t' go t' see him.' She sniffed: the dewdrop disappeared, but slowly grew again.

Mrs Nattle nodded and announced, loudly: 'Least said soonest mended, Mrs Dorbell,' leaning towards her and whispering into her ear: 'Though Ah ne'er knew he tuk in pension books, bein' agen law as is printed on book back an' him bein' a churchgoer an' a magistrate,' putting her head back and continuing so that everyone could hear: 'Though Ah'm surprised at nowt wot nobody does, be what they may . . .' whispering: 'Course, Ah knew it were done a lot during war wi' ring papers' (official documents issued to soldiers' wives during the Great War enabling them to draw their allowances at the post offices). 'Ah tuk many an' many an' *many* a one.'

Mrs Dorbell was suddenly bent double by a spasm of coughing; her head went below the counter level as she spat upon the floor. 'Chest bad agen,' she said, panting, when she recovered: she added, confidentially: 'If you was to go to front shop when nobody wus about – *front* shop, mind, business bein' of a privit' natur' – go there an' hexplain things to him, y'know, that you've got a round o' customers an' pawn on commission for 'em as is too high an' mighty t' come themselves – Well,' a wink and a deep breath, 'Well, *he* knows that if he teks their pension books i' pawn they can't draw their pensions till book is redeemed,' a nod and a wise look: 'Y'*can* stay in house when y' can't afford t' get y' clo'es out o' pawn,' emphatically: 'But y' can't afford t' miss y' ten bob pension for sake of half a crown,' muttering: 'Which is wot he lends on pension books.' Pause. Still keeping her gaze fixed on Mrs Nattle she jerked her head towards the other side of the counter and raised her brows: 'An' '*e* knows it, Mrs Nakkle, '*e* knows it. Be 'e church goer, magistrate or King Dick hissel', 'e *knows* it. An' he'll oblige a lady wot asks him privit' an' proper when nobody's about.'

Mrs Nattle winked: 'Ah'll,' she said, referring to those whose pledges she negotiated on commission: 'Ah'll see my customers, Mrs Dorbell, an' thank y' for the 'int and hinformation.' Mrs Dorbell looked at her as a head waiter might look at a departing millionaire who had left a threepenny piece as gratuity. Mrs Nattle sensed her disappointment, pondered a moment then added, impulsively: 'Well, go on, then. Call round arter Ah've finished me business. There's a drop left i' bokkle.'

Mrs Dorbell licked her lips and . . .

Conversation hushed. Mr Price appeared carrying day book, ledger, perforated sheets of pawn-tickets, bag of silver, packets of copper and bundles of treasury notes. Reverent gazes watched the fascinating rite of long, bony fingers caressing the ready and stowing it into the proper compartments in the till of the cash drawer.

A moment later the drawer was shut: Mr Price gazed at the suit Mrs Dorbell had fetched: 'Same agen,' she said: 'An' *it*,' nudging Mrs Nattle with her knee: '*It's* in the pocket, as oosual. Ahem!'

Without a word Mr Price conveyed the suit to the front shop where was the safe. The door was heard to open and close. Mrs Nattle looked at Mrs Dorbell and nodded, wisely. Price returned: 'Four an' six on the suit, Mrs Dorbell. Fraying at the turn-ups,' he said briskly.

'Oh, go on wi' y' blarney,' protested Mrs Dorbell, pouting: 'Y'know Ah've t' get it out o' week'end.'

'Four and six,' replied Mr Price, unmoved: 'Hung or folded?'

(An extra charge was made if a suit or frock was put on a coat hanger instead of being done up, anyhow, in a bundle, which would, of course, fill it as full of creases as a concertina.)

' 'Ang it,' muttered Mrs Dorbell, sulkily. To Mrs Nattle: 'That lodger o' mine's eyes like 'awks' for creases in his Sunday suit. It may as well be here, say I, as hangin' up at home doin' no good t' nobody. But he don't believe i' pawnshops nor don't believe in obligin' his landlady. Dammim.'

'Blue suit, four and six,' cried Mr Price, loudly: 'Hung.' Harry made out the tickets, one for Mrs Dorbell as a receipt and one to pin to the suit, afterwards entering the item in the day book. Referring to the old age pension book Mr Price cried: 'And "goods", half a crown. Same name.' Mrs Nattle gently pushed her arm against Mrs Dorbell's, who coughed.

Harry passed the tickets to Mr Price then blew into his purple fingers. He tore a fragment from his blotting-paper to wrap round the upper steel portion of his pen; it had been as though the steel was ice. Then he tucked his hands under his waistcoat armholes, hunched his shoulders and dithered staring, unseeing at the blank wall in front, the cold creeping under his scalp and giving him a sensation as though his hair was standing bolt upright. A voice in his brain said: 'Seven o'clock, eight, nine, ten, eleven, twelve. Five hours and then dinner time.' Five hours, though! Back again at one o'clock, then another seven-hour penance in this dim, perishing alcove until he put up the shop shutters at eight o'clock, or, more likely, half past, since there was always a last-minute rush.

A lump rose to his throat; he wanted to cry. He shuddered at the thought of having to take up pen, to remove his frozen hands from the warmth under his armpits. He felt his stomach cleave with hunger as a vision of a steaming cup of tea floated, with maddening vividness, through his brain. Suddenly, a light of alarm appeared in his eyes; he removed his hands from their snug nest and thrust them into his coat pockets. Yes! In his eager excitement of the morning he had forgotten his lunch. It was the last straw. He gulped. Five hours. He turned his face to the wall, sniffed and commenced to weep. If only it were eight o'clock tonight and he could go home. Even the thought of

Marlowe's in the morning brought no comfort; he wanted to go home. If only he had not finished his schooling. His tears ceased as he paused, wondering, amazed at the full revelation of the awful fate he had missed by getting work at Marlowe's. If he had not succeeded there, this present would have been a daily experience. This dark foreboding corner would have been his daily prison indefinitely. At Marlowe's was warmth, variety, new experiences, companionship of boys his own age, and, above all, free evenings and Saturday afternoons. He marvelled anew; clung to the soon-to-be realized dream, trying not to hear the voice of Mr Price concluding the morning's first transaction which heralded the approach of a second. Ah, yes! His mother would be here soon to buy the overalls for him: he could ask her to fetch him some bread and butter. He licked his lips in anticipation, ran his cuff along his wet nose and sniffed. He felt his spirits returning.

'Half a crown and four an' six is seven shillings,' Mr Price was bawling: 'Threepence for hanging the suit and twopence for tickets leaves six and sixpence. *Thank* you, ma'am.'

'Six an' seven, it leaves, if *Ah'm* not mistaken,' corrected Mrs Nattle, eyeing the pawnbroker with a steely, suspicious glance. Mrs Dorbell gazed at her friend in gratitude.

'My mistake,' replied Mr Price, gruffly. 'Six an' seven, ma'am. Next please,' he banged the money down while Mrs Dorbell's hovering claw gathered it together. Meanwhile a wave of restlessness animated the customers. All pushed and squeezed, loudly proclaiming that they were next to be served. And Mrs Nattle, being the loudest voiced, the most domineering character and the most plausible liar present, prevailed, silencing, ultimately, a tiny woman by the name of Mrs Jike, a transplanted sprig of London Pride from Whitechapel, who, extra to other accomplishments, was gifted oracularly, being able to read the future in teacups and playing cards. Mrs Jike wore a man's cap and a late Victorian bodice and skirt; she was an inexpert performer upon the concertina, a student of the Court and Personal column of her penny daily and dated the world's decay from the time of the passing of Victoria the Good. She complained, to Mrs Nattle: 'Shime on y'. . . . Y' know my bloke wownt gow to work till he gets money for his dinner beer. Yaah, measly old 'ooman, y'.... Gow to Petney.'

Mrs Nattle ignored her, turning to Mrs Dorbell and asking her to wait, afterwards facing Mr Price in readiness for the bargaining. All present sighed, patiently, shifted the weights of their bodies to their rested legs and wondered how long it would take for Mrs Nattle's barricade of pledges to be transferred to the other side of the counter.

Negotiations commenced. Finally Harry handed to Mr Price four full sheets of pawn-tickets not one detached from its perforations.

Muttered conversation on the part of the spectators regarding Mrs Nattle while Mr Price totalled up the sums due to her. She was 'a marvel', an 'amazin' old 'ooman'. 'How she remembers what she wants on all them there, I – don't – know.' 'Second natur'; her's bin doin' it for 'ears an' 'ears.'

Mrs Nattle heard all; stood there, aloof, clothed in professional pride. In a moment she had departed, hands full of money and pawn-tickets, Mrs Dorbell, shuffling and sniffling, tailing on behind.

Business was resumed. A constant stream of women coming with pledges and departing with money. All kinds, lively and garrulous, morose and silent, young and old; coughing, spittings, wheezings, complaints; births, marriages, deaths and causes; illnesses, remedies, matrimonial differences; court news (police and royalty); cost of living, state of employment, scandal and all the gossip that trips from the tongue when women meet.

But not a sign of Mrs Hardcastle.

She had promised to put in an appearance before eight o'clock. It now wanted minutes of noon. For hours past Harry had started, eagerly, each time some customer had entered by the sales department; each time he had been disappointed. Sulky expressions had abided on his face most of the morning. He had been filled with self-pity. Didn't his mother know that he was weak with hunger? Hadn't she seen, remembered that he had not taken a lunch? Besides, what of the overalls she had promised to buy? Was she going to disappoint him in this, too?

Things were always happening this way: you looked forward to something, and, sure enough, you'd be disappointed. Sullen anger gnawed his heart.

Then, when he least expected her, he heard his name whispered from the front shop. He slipped from his stool, went to the sales department, raised his brows and said, petulantly: 'Where y' bin, ma. I bin waitin' all mornin'. I've had no lunch neither.'

She gazed at him apologetically: 'I bin busy lad. It's washin' day,' she murmured.

He frowned, depressed. He noticed her hands and arms were wrinkled and uncommonly clean from long immersion in water. The tiny kitchen would be full of steam, table wet and soapy; clothes would be bubbling in the copper; the peggy tub would be in the way; everywhere would be damp; no chance of snatching a moment's warmth from the fire; clothes, draping the maiden would screen its heat from the room. Worst of all there would be a makeshift dinner, cold and unpalatable. Washing day! Ooo, wait until he fetched wages home from Marlowe's; then, perhaps, his mother would be able to afford the services of a laundry.

He noticed that his mother was licking her lips and glancing, nervously, over his head. He turned. Mr Price was standing behind him slowly rubbing his hands.

'Ah want t' get lad pair overalls, Mr Price. So Ah've – ' She lifted her coarse sacking apron to the counter and out of it withdrew Hardcastle's spare suit. As Price picked it up to examine it, she added: 'Ah'll have t' get it out o' week-end.'

He hummed and ha'd, and said: 'Six shillings, ma'am,' then directed Harry to make out the ticket.

The boy returned with it: money was exchanged. Meanwhile Harry went over to the rack where the boiler suits and overalls were stored, reaching out a suitable pair. A ticket pinned thereon said '5s. 6d.' and, in code: 'US/–' which, to Harry's experienced eye, meant that each overall cost Mr Price two shillings and sevenpence, or, thirty-one shillings a dozen less 5 per cent, cash in seven days.

The key to the code was written on a postcard pinned up for reference in a dark corner by the safe. On every article for sale, the cost price was written in code over the retail so that Mr Price could tell, if circumstances demanded it, by how much he could reduce the marked price without missing a sale and without selling below cost.

Itself, the code was a piece of advice all Mr Price's customers were unsuccessfully, but perpetually, striving to obey.

| S | H | U | N | P | O | V | E | R | T | Y | X |
|---|---|---|---|---|---|---|---|---|---|---|---|
| 1 | 2 | 3 | 4 | 5 | 6 | 7 | 8 | 9 | 10 | 11 | 12 |

Privately Mr Price took good care to shun it: professionally was a different matter; lacking it in others there would not have been a Mr Price. Anyway, so as none could tell how much profit he was making out of them he used the simple code of which he was author. If he wished to indicate that such and such a thing had cost him nine shillings and sixpence, he first looked at the letter above the number nine 'R', then at the letter above the number six 'O', placed a stroke between them 'R/O' and there it was, plain as a pikestaff, nine and sixpence cost. Under it, also as plain as a pikestaff, the retail price: '19/11.'

Business.

Unconcerned with Price's cryptic markings Harry was absorbed in holding the overalls in front of him. Yes, they had the long, narrow, intriguing pocket down the leg side for the reception of the two-foot steel rule. And, look, the trousers leg reached to his ankle. No more would he be ashamed of his spindle shanks. Farewell, embarassment!

Mrs Hardcastle blinked at Price: 'How much are they?' she asked. He hummed and ha'd anew, took the garment from Harry, looked at the ticket and inspected the stuff and seams with the assidutiy of an ape vermin hunting. Harry and his mother stared at him. For her part she had always looked upon him with awe; it amounted to downright reverence since he had been made magistrate.

'They are the best,' said Mr Price, warningly, staring at her and slowly rubbing his hands: 'They are the best, ma'am. . . . Five and sixpence they're marked, ma'am. . . . But – er – h'm – ah!' squinting at the ceiling and pulling his lower lip: 'Suppose we say five and fou — five and threepence. A little dis-count.' He laid stress on the 'dis' instead of the 'little'.

She laid the money on the counter. And Mr Price picked it up. Harry reached for a sheet of brown paper. Mr Price, hearing the rustle, said, quietly, without looking at the boy: 'I'd roll them and put them under the arm, Hardcastle. No use wasting paper.'

Mrs Hardcastle's heart beat faster for the boy. She said, hur-riedly: 'Ah'm sorry lad's leavin' y', Mr Price. 'Taint our wish as he should go engineerin'. .... Ah'd rather he was kep' wi' you.'

Harry blushed. His mother was apologetic! She spoke as though indebted to Price! 'But Ah don't want t' stay, ma,' he complained, indignantly, red in the face. She embarrassed him. Why hadn't she held her tongue.

'Hush, lad, hush,' she murmured, her lips parched. She was glad Mr Price was looking elsewhere. Harry shouldn't have said that; Mr Price might be offended.

Price, looking at his fingernails, murmured: 'After careful consideration, I find I would have had to get another boy in any case, ma'am. There isn't enough work here for a full-time clerk. Things're bad.'

'Then isn't — Don't y' want me this afternoon?' Harry asked eagerly.

'Well,' answered Price, shrugging: 'You may as well finish the day out now that you are here . . .'

Mrs Hardcastle murmured something and went out, fumbling awkwardly with the latch. Harry, disappointed, found himself watching Mr Price who had opened a drawer in the counter, had reached out Indian ink, brush, piece of Bristol board and now was writing, in bold letters:

Boy Wanted
Must Be Good Handwriter
Part Time     Good Wages

'Aye,' said Harry, to himself: '*He* calls half a crown a week good wages.' He was annoyed, resented a successor in a way. The thought that, when he had left, business would proceed as before made him feel rather negligible, unimportant. Still —

Who cared? He became happily conscious of the overalls under his arm. ... Lathes, milling machines, engineering, 25*10* and evenings, and Saturday afternoons free! FREE!

Suddenly the air was filled with the concerted blasts of factory, mill and workshop sirens. The noon respite. His eyes kindled. Listen to Marlowe's! With rising spirits he said: 'Dinner-time, Mr Price,' slid over the counter and went outside.

CHAPTER 5

## GIRLS MAKE HIM SICK

CLATTER of clogs and shoes; chatter of many loud voices; bursts of laughter. Hundreds of girl operatives and women from the adjacent cotton mills marching home to dinner arm in arm, two, three, four and five abreast. They filled the narrow pavements and spread into the roadway.

A generation ago all would have been wearing clogs, shawls, tight bodices, ample skirts and home-knitted, black wool stockings. A few still held to the picturesque clogs and shawls of yesterday, but the majority represented modernity: cheap artificial silk stockings, cheap short-skirted frocks, cheap coats, cheap shoes, crimped hair, powder and rouge; five and a half days weekly in a spinning mill or weaving shed, a threepenny seat in the picture theatre twice a week, a ninepenny or shilling dance of a Saturday night, a Sunday afternoon parade on the erstwhile aristocratic Eccles Old Road which incloses the public park, then work again, until they married when picture theatres became luxuries and Saturday dances, Sunday parades and cheap finery ceased altogether.

Harry, gaze fixed on the pavement, was become acutely self-conscious of the incongruity of his schoolboy clothes and believed that every girl he passed must be similarly impressed. He felt a fool to be wearing such now that he was a Marlowe employee. Why hadn't he had the foresight to slip on the overalls before he came out of the shop? He then could have walked proud and unashamed in the centre of the roadway. Still, he was always doing things like that; always upside down. And another thought was bothering him.

'Hallo, Harry.' A girl's voice; belonging to her whom the bothering thought concerned. He looked up. Helen Hawkins beamed on him with her winning smile. Her shapeless coat was open revealing a short print frock faded from many washings: she was hatless and the cotton fluff adhered to her hair like a veil of blown snow.

She beamed on him: he did not like it. There was a concentrated, undivided fixity in her gaze, an expectant questioning: he felt uncomfortable. Her smile was eloquent, unique, existed for none but him. And because of what he was thinking it filled him with a creeping self-reproach, or with that conflicting emotion named being at 'sixes and sevens' with oneself.

Things were changed, now. Time had been, lately, when, in his moods of black despair concerning the servitude at Price and Jones's, he had been grateful of Helen's sympathetic ear attentive to his troubles. He felt that her acceptance of his confidences had placed him under a puzzling kind of obligation to her; a vague, tacit understanding that irked but could not be hinted at or expressed, that gave her the privilege to take a proprietary interest in his affairs. He felt uneasy. He sensed a restraining influence, a lack of freedom to associate himself with the boys. And that was impossible now that he had to work with them. Though Helen knew nothing of this, yet. It would come to her as something of a shock when he told her.

He remembered a fortnight ago, in the heat of a sudden impulse to appear impressive, having told her that, on leaving school, he was to seek work in a 'proper' office. Why had he said it? He never had the remotest idea of so doing. The memory of the incident returned to him vividly; he recalled his puffed-up self, proud as a pigeon, revelling in her admiration. Perhaps she would have forgotten it by this time. Oh, but what did it matter whether or no: he could change his mind if he so wished. Why should he be scared of her? This was the kind of thing that made friendship with a girl so undesirable; they were so troublesomely inquisitive.

43

He forced a smile: 'Oh, hallo, Helen,' he said, adding, unnecessarily, as they walked along: 'Goin' home for y' dinner?'
She sensed a constraint in his demeanour instantly. She looked
at him, questioningly, wondering, her smile fading, the light
dying in her eyes. After a pause, she said: 'I didn't see y' over
week-end, Harry. Where were y'? Y' weren't in choir, either.'

He shrugged: 'Aw, Ah stopped in house, readin'. Didn' want
t'go out.' He could not confess that shame of his schoolboy
clothes was the real cause. It occurred to him that it would be
weeks, possibly, before his mother would be able to afford him
a pair of long trousers for Sunday wear. That meant sitting
at home over the week-ends. It would be humiliating, after
wearing overalls during the week to appear in knickerbockers
of a Sunday. Until now, this prospect had not occurred to him.
Glum discontent stirred in his heart. Why had some such occurrence as this always to rise to spoil one's new-found pleasure?
Tomorrow's prospect was robbed of half its savour.

'You left school Friday, didn't you, Harry?'

It was coming: he could sense her thoughts. He gripped the
overalls tighter: 'Aye,' he said, moodily.

'And the job ...?' a timid eagerness appeared in her expression.

She hadn't forgotten! He forced a laugh: 'Oh, Ah've got a
job. Start at Dicky Marlowe's in morning. Machine shop ...
2510's me number. Here's me overalls.'

She raised her brows, incredulously: 'Engineering? I thought
you ...'

'Oh, Ah know. Ah know. Office,' a grimace and a deprecatory
gesture: 'Naow. ... Had enough o' Price an' Jones's t' last
me a lifetime.'

They turned into North Street; halted by the open door of
No. 7 where Helen lived together with the remaining dozen
comprising the family. A number of very young and very dirty
children played in the gutter. Women passed, occasionally,
carrying basins of fried fish and chipped potatoes leaving a
pungent odour of the mixed dish in their wakes; lines of washing decorated the street billowing in the fitful breeze.

She stared at the pavement. This occurrence was the handiwork of Bill Simmons and his clique. Jealousy of their influence on him pinched her. He was a cut above their kind. Besides, what a bathos, after all her fond expectations, to imagine Harry dressed in overalls instead of as she had always pictured him, clean, tidy, going to an office where gentlemen worked. Nor was it that such an aspiration was impossible; being a chorister at the parish church was guarantee that he could have had such a job; all the boys in the choir went to offices. In overalls, though, working with street-corner louts.

And she had been led to believe. ... Her dream crumbled. Oh, why had he given her his confidences? Why had he permitted her to glory in that she, of all the street girls, nay, of all the girls of the neighbourhood, had been the one to whom he had unburdened himself. Didn't he know that his friendship had drawn the teeth of that ogre, rendered it innocuous – that ogre, the squalor and discomfort of her home? The yearning sadness of a farewell stole plaintively across her heart as she recalled those sweet sessions when she stood with him in the shadowy upper reaches of the street listening to his murmured tale of woe. She felt that happiness being furtively withdrawn, stolen by sly hands which she could not resist. No longer would he feed the deep longing in her heart; no more could she escape, through him, those bleak lonelinesses which sometimes stole upon her; she murmured: 'Vicar can get y' job, if y'd ask.'

'Yaah,' he replied, impatiently: 'Ah know.... Tart's job. But not for me,' staring up into the sky and adding, fervently: 'I want proper man's work,' with a shrug: 'Besides, I've left choir. Voice is broke.'

'It isn't,' she cried, accusingly, suddenly animated; 'You know it isn't.'

'Oh, yes it is. It's broke, Ah tell y'. *Ah* know,' obstinately, and with finality: 'An' Ah'm goin' to Marlowe's.'

Appealingly: 'But look at fellows y'll mix with, Harry.... Swearers like Ned Narkey, and ... and ...' hotly and with impatience: 'Oh, it's Bill Simmons and his crowd as've put y' up to this ...' her eyes sparkled.

He stared at her: 'What's it to you?' he asked, incredulously: 'Ah can please meself, can't Ah? *Ah* knows what Ah'm doin'.'

The impudence; the manner of her assumption! Oh, aye, *she'd* have him go to office work! And the way she referred, disparagingly, to Bill Simmons and the rest. His nostrils dilated; he glared at her: 'Mind y'r own business,' he said, indignantly.

She stared at him; her spirits froze. Could this really be the Harry Hardcastle around whom she had woven an ideal? 'Oh, Harry,' she murmured, appealingly: 'Let's not fall out.'

He brimmed with self-confidence: 'What d'y' mean, *us* fall out? Ha! Ah like that.'

'Oh, Harry, I never meant . . .'

A loud voice came from the open door at Helen's back, her mother's: 'Hey, there. How much longer are y' gonna stand there argefyin'? Dinner's goin' cold here.'

Harry muttered, impatiently: 'Aw, Ah'm goin' home for me dinner. . . . Girls mek me sick. S'long.' He stamped away, moodily.

She watched him with sinking heart until he disappeared through the door of No. 17, then she turned, eyes shining, and went into the child-infested rowdiness of her home.

CHAPTER 6

OVERALLS

His initiation was disappointing.

Visions of being conducted to a bolted and barred room where, in hushed whispers, he would receive careful instruction concluded by a solemn adjuration to keep the knowledge a sworn secret, proved to be entirely without foundation. There was no painstaking instruction, no enlightenment of the 'mysteries' of the trade as had been promised in the extravagant language of the indentures. That was pure bunkum, evidently. What a fool he would have made of himself had he apprised the boys of his silly expectations.

Instead of being set to work on a lathe he found his duties consisted in running errands for the elder apprentices and the men.

There was only one whom he knew would be sympathetic;

instinctively he unburdened himself to Larry Meath; though Larry's was cold comfort.

'You're part of a graft, Harry,' he said: 'All Marlowe's want is cheap labour; and the apprentice racket is one of their ways of getting it. Nobody'll teach you anything simply because there's so little to be learnt. You'll pick up all you require by asking questions and watching others work. You see, all this machinery's being more simplified year after year until all it wants is experienced machine feeders and watchers. Some of the new plant doesn't even need that. Look in the brass-finishing shop when you're that way. Ask the foreman to show you that screw-making machine. That can work twenty-four hours a day without anybody going near it. Your apprenticeship's a swindle, Harry. The men they turn out think they're engineers same as they do at all the other places, but they're only machine minders. Don't you remember the women during the war?'

'What women?' Harry asked, troubled by what Larry had said.

'The women who took the places of the engineers who'd all served their time. The women picked up straightaway what Marlowe's and the others say it takes seven years' apprenticeship to learn,' a wry smile: 'Still, if you want to be what everybody calls an "engineer", you've no choice but to serve your seven years. Oh, and you were lucky to be taken on as an apprentice. I hear that they're considering refusing to bind themselves in contracting to provide seven years' employment. There is a rumour about that there aren't to be any more apprentices. You see, Harry, if they don't bind themselves, as they have to do in the indentures, they can clear the shop of all surplus labour when times are bad. And things are shaping that way, now,' a grin: 'You've no need to worry, though. You've seven years' employment, certain.'

Hum!

It chilled Harry, momentarily.

Only momentarily. With all its disadvantages it was infinitely a more enjoyable occupation than Price and Jones's.

Variety here! Any of the men requiring such and such a tool

gave him a brass check with their number stamped on it; he took it to the stores and exchanged it for the desired tool. Towards noon, in company with other new apprentices, he brewed tea for those men it was his duty to attend. Afterwards he ran to Sam Grundy's back entry with their threepenny and sixpenny bets. At week-end, he learned with pleasurable surprise, the men would give him coppers for the services, extra if the bets he had taken proved profitable. Yes, despite what Larry Meath had said, this method of earning a living was far more desirable than Price and Jones's or any other office.

As for Bill Simmons and the others, they were liars. From their talk at various times he had concluded they were in charge of machines. Nothing of the kind; errand boys, 'shop boys' they were, nothing more. Rather discouraging to learn that, generally, over a year elapsed before you were permitted to use even a drilling machine. Drilling machine, though. A child could be entrusted with it: all that was necessary was the depression of a lever; a device prevented the drill from boring too deep; it was foolproof. Nevertheless, he was not permitted practice on the machine. As yet he was errand boy, and a zealous one into the bargain.

But that period soon passed when, sent on errands to the stores, he hurried there and back resisting the temptation to have his attention engaged by the numberless absorbingly interesting engineering operations to be seen on all sides. From the other apprentices he learnt the circuitous routes to the stores, routes which led through the various departments.

The foundry! What a place.

Steel platforms from which you saw great muscular men dwarfed to insignificance by the vastness of everything: men the size of Ned Narkey who had charge of the gigantic crane. Fascinated he saw the cumbrous thing, driven by Ned, unseen, move slowly along its metals: leisurely, its great arm deposited an enormous ladle by the furnace. A pause; a hoarse shout; a startling glimpse of fire then a rushing, spitting river of flames that was molten metal running out of the furnace's channel into the ladle until it brimmed. The river of fire was dammed, ceased as by magic. The crane's limp cable tautened; slowly the ladle swung, revolved, white-hot, a vivid, staring glare that stabbed the eyes; slowly it swung, twenty tons of molten metal to the moulds.

Men, red in front, black behind and trailing long shadows after them; men with leathern aprons, bare, sinewy arms and coloured goggles shading their eyes, ran about in obedience to shouted instructions: chains creaked on strain, unseen mechanism 'clank-clanked', then, as with calculated deliberation, the glowing cauldron tipped forward as though held, jug-wise, by an invisible giant's hand. Harry held his breath as the metal brimmed the lip to fall, splashing off a teeming fountain of heavy, quick-dying sparks like a catherine wheel, before the metal ran to earth forcing off hissing plumes of burning rainbow-coloured gases through the mould vents.

A magnificent, inspiring sight; made you feel proud of being identified with the great Marlowe organization.

The forge, too, where, amongst others, old Pa Scodger worked. Mr Scodger was a blacksmith. A blacksmith, though! Ha! A diminutive, harassed fellow with a bald head and a huge moustache. He worked in the tiny smithy adjoining the forge, and, out of working hours, sometimes afforded amusement to the boys of North Street by the differences that occurred between him and his termagant wife. As though he hadn't enough dinning in his ears where he worked.

The forge! Impossible to stand still here. Rows and rows of drop hammers, small and large; ten ton to over a hundred. Great blocks of steel lifted by eccentric pulleys shaped like an egg, motivated by electricity and compressed air; blocks of steel crashing upon the white-hot forgings with a shattering BUMP. Earth shook, trembled beneath your feet. If you stood within yards of the largest hammers you actually were lifted off your feet. A most peculiar sensation; a tickling of the stomach, a giddiness. Outside the works' walls even, three hundred yards away, the reverberations of the enormous things could still be felt.

As for the riveting shop. Bedlam.

The din here was insufferable. On the walls were the furnaces, each a little smaller than a kitchen oven, one every four yards or so; a fire-clay-lined box without a front. They were fed by two pipes, one gas, the other compressed air: the air roared, centrifugally, driving the gas in fierce orange-coloured spirals, making white-hot the rivets lying within. The operatives were adept as jugglers. A pair of long-handled pincers shot into the furnace; out came a white-hot rivet, plump into the rivet hole; then a steel bar was rammed on to the rivet head to hold it secure whilst the riveter, with a revolver-like pneumatic riveter, jammed it home, pressed the trigger, and: 'tat-tat-tat-tat-tat'. Such a row. As though a million boys were running stakes along iron railings, simultaneously. Every man stone deaf after a six months' spell of work here. Phew! But they *were* men.

And such as would take advantage of a greenhorn's inexperience and credulity in playing him tricks. Such as when Billy Higgs, one of the senior apprentices whose behests it was Harry's duty to obey, sent him to the stores for the 'long stand'. Harry went, unsuspectingly, made his request, wondering on the shape and use of the instrument. The storekeeper answered, solemnly: 'Long stand? Oh, aye, just stand there,' and went on with his work. Minutes elapsed: Harry watched the traffic of boys coming with brass checks and going with tools. Jack Lindsay, a thickset boy with a ready grin and a fondness of striking pugilistic attitudes for no reason at all, came up whistling: ' 'Allo, 'Arry,' he said, 'What y' standin' there for?' Harry told him. Jack shook his head and said, sympathetically: 'They mek y' wait for that summat awful.' He went off chuckling. Soon Harry began to blush and to wonder why all the apprentices who now came up looked at him as though he was some odd animal: they grinned or laughed, nudged each other and winked. Bill Simmons, blue-eyed, over-grown, with an unruly mop of hair and a chronic habit of prefixing almost every noun he used with the idiomatic term for copulation, laughed and said to his companion, Sam Hardie, an undersized, bow-legged, low browed boy with long, strong, ape-like arms: 'Did y' ever, Sam. They ain't gev him the – stand yet!'

With a sickly grin Harry asked him the meaning of the joke. Sam, grinning, advised him to ask the storekeeper. Blushing, Harry turned to the busy man who had forgotten all about him: 'Hey,' he protested, mildly indignant: 'Hey, what about that there long stand?'

The man looked up: 'What! Ain't you gone *yet*?' he asked, raising his brows.

'I come here for long stand an' you told me . . .'

'Well, y' bin standin' there hafe an hour. . . . Ain't that long enough?'

Truth dawned; red in the face Harry licked his lips, turned on his heel and slunk away. 'You might ha' told me,' he said, reproachfully, to Bill Simmons and the others. Bill sniggered: 'Wait till *you* see some gawp doin' the same. See whether you tell him.'

A more humiliating experience awaited him. His desire had been, on walking home, to have oil and dirt smeared on his face as evidence of the nature of his work. Vanity demanded it: it was imperative. And for two nights now, on arrival home, the first thing he had done was to glance into the mirror there to see a most disappointing reflection. Instead of a really oily face such as most of the boys and nearly all the men managed to acquire his skin was pale. He resolved on artificial methods. Unfortunately, whilst daubing grease on his face during the noonday respite behind what he had thought to be the privacy of a milling machine, Tom Hare, a steel-spectacled sly-eyed, foul-mouthed, untidy boy with stoop shoulders, bulging forehead and decayed teeth, surprised him.

Jeering he summoned the other apprentices.

Harry's hate of Tom, lively at all times – he was a disgusting fellow who thought nothing of exposing himself in front of the boys, was obsessed with matters sexual, laid grasping hands on girls, and, sniggering, told tales of the filthy behaviour of his parents in whose bedroom he slept, there being a very large family and the usual inadequate accommodation – Harry's hatred of him increased.

The boys congregated in front of him, chortling. Someone asked what should be done with him, asked in such a way that suggested there being only one answer.

Harry retreated, slowly, panting, eyes staring. He guessed what was to follow: 'Leave me be . . .' he cried, casting wild

glances about for a weapon. There was nothing to hand. Tom
Hare shouted: 'Tek his trousis down,' and giggled.

'You leave me be. ...' His voice rose shrill: he pointed a
quivering, threatening finger at Tom: 'I'll blind you, Tom Hare.'

They all laughed and closed in on him. Sam Hardie's ape-like
arms encompassed him. In a moment he was on his back,
struggling impotently, and bawling hysterically. His cries were
drowned in the roar of laughter that rose when rough hands
tore at his trousers and exposed his nakedness. He screamed,
struggled frantically. Somebody ran up with a pot of red paint,
a brush and grease; anonymous hands daubed it on him where-
ever exposed.

Then, laughing, they released him. Harry, sobbing, covered
his oily painted nakedness, drew on his overalls and retired to
the lavatories to wipe away as much of the mess as he could. He
felt that never again could he look any of the apprentices in
the face. What would they think of his girlish screaming? of his
patched undershirt and ragged shirt lap? Then there was the
knickerbockers! They now would know that he wore the
abominable things underneath his overall. He shrank, inwardly.
What an altogether humiliating episode.

He snivelled, blew his nose on a corner of the oil and paint
daubed newspaper he was using. He still was catching his breath
in sobs. This to happen when he wished to identify himself with
the boys! His impulse was to steal away, run off and never return. He felt abysmally lonely and miserable. He remembered
Helen: instantly he yearned for her soothing company. But even
she he had alienated: 'Aw, girls mek me sick!' What a fool he
had made of himself in his vain impatience.

'Eh, 'Arry. ... A' y' there?' a shouted interrogation. Jack
Lindsay.

'Aye,' Harry muttered, sniffing.

'Aach, what're y' shrikeing for, man. Come on. Come out'v
it.' He kicked the privy door: 'Open door and let's in.' Reluctantly, Harry slipped the catch. Jack entered, grinning, lit the
fag end of a cigarette and offered Harry a puff. Grateful, Harry
accepted; he translated the gesture as symbolic of comradeship.

'Ah wasn't shrikein' because Ah was feared,' he mumbled in

an attempt to excuse his tears and screams: 'It 'urt.'

Jack made a grimace, leant against the wood partition, crossed his legs and said: 'They'll leave y' alone, now. Y'll be one 'v us. Y've all got t' g' through it when y' first come. . . . Hey! Save us a draw: that's th' on'y tab end Ah've got.'

Harry's spirits revived: 'Y'll be one of us!' The phrase warmed him. Suddenly, his apprenticeship assumed an aspect of maturity. He felt profoundly grateful to Jack. He passed the cigarette-end back to him: 'Ah'll gie y' packet o' week-end, Jack.'

The deep note of the siren. Countershafts began to revolve. Beneath his feet he felt the reverberations of the drop hammers: his ears caught the distant muffled 'tat-tat-tat-tat-tat' of the pneumatic riveters.

'Aw,' said Jack, deprecatingly: 'Ah don't want y' cigs. . . . Come on, let's get out o' here.' He led the way, Harry, with an uncertain access of self-confidence and with a sheepish grin on his face following.

<br>

CHAPTER 7

## SATURDAY

TEN bob a week: ten bob every Saturday! 'Seven and a tanner more'n Price paid me!' A stimulating experience.

Ah, and Saturday. Saturday, free! The day had a peculiar atmosphere; an air all its own. It pervaded everywhere, communicated itself to everybody.

The birth of noon blazoned forth by fanfares, as it were, blaring dissonances on all the mill and factory sirens: an exuberant tumult of sound that shouted: 'Work's done until Monday! Hurrah!' At Price and Jones's he would have had a nine-hour stretch ahead of him. Phew! And Blimey!

Noon.

The great exodus from Marlowe's began. Twelve thousand boys and men surging through the gates, a black, agitated river of humanity breaking into a hundred tiny streamlets and

scurrying off in all directions. Lines of empty stationary tramcars and fleets of charabancs; corporation buses, push and
motor bikes: mad rushes, pushings, shovings, cursing, jangling
of tram bell, honkings of motor horns: 'Gerrout of it, y' dreamy-
eyed sod, y' ...' changings of gears, rattlings of tramcar wheels,
clouds of pungent exhaust: 'What a bloody stink ...' ragged
boys calling the midday sporting newspaper: 'One o'clock. ...
One o'clock edition,' football and racing talk. Everybody all
smiles on account of wages in pockets and because they
wouldn't see any more machinery until Monday morning.

There'd be a flutter on the two-thirty, football match this
afternoon, the public house tonight and a long morning in bed
tomorrow with the missis. No sirens; no alarm clocks; no Blind
Joe to rouse one with his eight-foot pole tipped with a bunch of
wires. Luxury! All smiles and good nature.

Harry, among the twelve thousand, dirty faced and jingling
his money, swaggered home, walking with the rest of the
street-corner boys. This Saturday feeling was intoxicating. He
was happy, contented, oh, and the future! A delightful closed
book full of promise whose very mystery enhanced its charm.
It justified, fully, his choice of occupation. There was something indefinable about Marlowe's, something great and glorious, something imminent, but, as yet, just out of reach.
Optimism told him to rest content, assured him that joys un-
dreamt of were in store. And who can question optimism? It
seduces. Anticipation filled him with unwonted buoyancy, with
sensations of reckless abandon.

Affluence entered his life. This day, Saturday, became one to
live for. When at Price and Jones's earning a half-crown a week
his personal share of the money amounted to a solitary penny.
His mother now gave him a shilling. Added to this were the
coppers he received of the men for services rendered, brewing
their tea, taking their bets to Sam Grundy's back entry and
fetching home the winnings.

The winnings!

Who ever could forget yesterday? Yesterday, the occasion of
Billy Higgs' winning five pounds odd as a consequence of a shilling wager, a 'double'. Yesterday Harry had fetched Billy the

winnings. This morning Billy had given him a half-crown!

Phew! As he handed the money over to Billy, Harry had gazed upon him awed, watching him, with forced nonchalance, stuff the money into his pockets under the cynosure of envious eyes. What a moment for Billy: how everybody crowded round to offer congratulations, pushing Harry aside as though *he* had not taken the bet, as though *he* hadn't drawn the winnings, as though part of the transaction's glory wasn't *his.* Even Billy admitted it: 'You've fetched me luck, son,' he had said. Harry swelled with pride and importance, and, for a moment, visualized himself as a kind of infallible luck charm with queues and queues of men ranged in front of him begging, imploring him to take their bets thereby to exert his magical influence upon them. Of course, it was silly.

Ah, wait until he was as old as Billy Higgs; wait until *he* was twenty years of age and winning over five pounds for a shilling. Though he wasn't complaining now. The half-crown which Billy had given him was in his pockets, plus the other half-crown he had earned for brewing tea and what not. Then there was the shilling he would receive of his mother. Six shillings! More than twice as much as Price gave him for a week's work. There was not sufficient air to breathe.

Hanky Park shed its dreariness; its grimy stuffy houses took on cheerful aspects; the acrid, pervasive stench of the rubber proofing works became imperceptible. Over all was an air of well-being for the day was Saturday. Pay day.

No scratching and scraping today; kitchen table littered with groceries; sugar in buff bags; fresh brown crusted loaves; butter and bacon in greaseproof paper; an amorphous, white-papered parcel, bloodstained, the Sunday joint; tin of salmon for tomorrow's tea; string bag full of vegetables; bunch of rhubarb with the appropriate custard powder alongside. Ma rushing about, now to the slopstone, now to the cupboard stowing things away, now to the frying-pan on the fire where the dinner was frizzling, now impatiently lifting the cat out of the way with her toe as it, the cat, clawed the table leg, miaowing, licking its lips and sniffing the Sunday joint, hungrily: '*Get* out o' my way, cat. Ain't y' ne'er had enough?'

After handing his wages over and receiving his spending money, he, while waiting dinner, sauntered, unwashed, to Mr Hulkington's, the grocer's corner shop where swarms of noisy children were spending Saturday halfpennies. He purchased two penn'worth of Woodbines, then stood with the rest of the boys on the kerb, hands in pockets jingling his money.

This was life! Nothing else was to be desired than to stand here smoking, spitting manfully, chatting wisely on racing and forking out threepence for a communal wager: 'Ah tell y', lads, the — thing's a dead cert, a dead — cert,' said Bill Simmons, adding, confidentially: 'Ar owld man (father) heard it from another bloke whose sister-in-law's one o' Sam Grundy's whores. *He* wouldn't tell *her* that i' he hadn't heard summat good, him bein' a bookie. Anyway, Ah'm havin' thippence on it. Wha' d'y say?'

They handed their threepences over, Bill departed and returned a moment later from Grundy's back entry all smiles: 'It's on,' he said. But, like most 'dead certs', the information rarely proved profitable. Still, it gave one something of a thrill; inflated one with the anticipation of success, caused one to expand and to respond to the entertaining bustle of Hanky Park of a Saturday noon.

Harry surveyed it with complacence.

Crowds of shabby mill girls clattering home, arms linked, four and five abreast. There would be a metamorphosis wrought in their appearances after tea; arrayed in their cheap, gaudy finery in readiness for dancing, nobody would recognize them as the same girls. Tom Hare, naturally, had to observe, aloud, on their anatomies: he was a disgusting fellow.

He turned from him to watch the women scurrying from Price and Jones's loaded with redeemed pledges. Mrs Nattle, pushing with great dignity, a perambulator piled with bundles, three of Mrs Cranford's children at her heels carrying the superflux. Mrs Dorbell, withered and threadbare, shuffling out of her stricken home talking to herself as she walked. Drawing alongside Harry she stopped, suddenly, and, interrupting her own conversation, exclaimed: 'Eee! Ah've come out bout (without) me baskit!' she about faced, shuffled into the house to reappear with an old basket on the crook of her arm. She trudged away talking to the pavement.

Two handcarts, with attendants, stood in the middle of the street, the one selling cooked ribs, the other fish, and around the last swarmed nearly every cat in the neighbourhood, stalking, fawning round the fishmonger and his conveyance, tails in air or sitting on their backsides waiting the trimmings which he flung to them whenever he made a sale.

A second-hand clothes dealer crying his trade, stopping by Blind Joe Riley who was standing puffing his pipe on his doorstep: 'Any ole clo'es, mate?'

'Aye, lad, all on 'em,' replied Joe, and went on puffing.

Clothing-club collectors and insurance men, afoot or riding into the street on bicycles, knocking briskly upon the open doors, poking their heads within and shouting the name of the company or firm whom they represented.

'Prudential, Mrs Jike.'

'Good Samaritan, Mrs Bull.' (The Good Samaritan was a clothing club owned by Mr Alderman Ezekiah Grumpole, a fat and greasy citizen who, also, was a money-lender.) The collectors withdrew their heads from the doorways, flourished pen or pencil in a businesslike manner, then beamed upon the tribes of dirty children standing or lying about the pavements, all of whom would have breathed more freely had they blown their noses. Afterwards, the hopeful collectors whistled or hummed tunes and surveyed the grey skies with such unconcern as suggested that the collection of money was the last thing in their minds.

'Call next week, lad,' from stout Mrs Bull, the local, uncertified midwife and layer out of the dead. She sat at her kitchen table, jug and glass at hand: 'Call next week, lad. Ah broke teetotal last night,' with assurance: 'Ah'll have it for y' when y' call agen. Mrs Cranford's expectin' o' Tuesday, an' owld Jack Tuttle won't last week out. Eigh, igh, ho, hum! Poooor owld Jack,' a guzzle at the glass.

'But y' missed payin' last week, y' know, Mrs Bull,' plaintively, from the collector, scowling at the snotty-nosed children standing on the kerb endeavouring to ring the bell on his bicycle.

'Aaach. .... Get away wi' y',' loudly, so that Mrs Cake, Mrs Bull's mortal enemy standing on her doorstep across the street waiting the collector, heard every word. Mrs Cake curled her lip, shrugged her shoulders and displayed her payment book conspicuously as she heard Mrs Bull exclaim: 'Tell owld Grumpole t' put me i' court,' louder, as she glimpsed, through the window, Mrs Cake's contemptuous expression: 'An' y' can tell her wi' lum – ba – go across street wot thinks she's a lady that we ain't *all* married to 'usbands wots lets wife wear the trousers.'

'Aye, it's all right, Mrs Bull,' sulkily, from the collector: 'But y' get me in trouble keep missin' like this.'

'Aach, trouble, eh? Tha'll thrive on it when tha gets as owld as me.'

The collector turned, grumbling, pushed his bike across the street, removed the scowl from his face to smile, unctuously, upon Mrs Cake, who, lips pursed, eyes a-glitter, handed over her book and money: 'Some folks,' she cried, loudly, staring at Mrs Bull's open front door: 'Some folks as could be named ain't got principle of a louse,' to the street, generally, as she received her book of the collector who prepared to ride away: 'Fair play, *that's* my motto. Owe nowt t' nobody an' stare everybody in face!'

'Willage blacksmith!' jeeringly from Mrs Bull who laughed, hugely, into her glass. Mrs Cake slammed the door and retired to the kitchen where to express herself irritably on her husband and children.

At the street corner Jack Lindsay chuckled and pointed to one of the houses. The boys turned to see tiny Mrs Jike, accordion under her arm, disappear into the home of Mr and Mrs Alfred Scodger. Grins broke on their faces. 'Now for it,' said Jack.

Presently, from the Scodger abode, came the concerted cacophony of accordion and trombone. As an accordionist Mrs Jike was as ungifted a performer as Mrs Scodger was upon the trombone, nevertheless, between them, they managed to provide musical accompaniment to the hymn singing at the spiritualists' mission situated over the coal yard at the far end of the street.

The noise of the music attracted the children: congregating round the door and under the window, some, more curious than the rest, muscled themselves on to the sill to peer through and to feed their gazes on the strange spectacle of the two musicians, tiny Mrs Jike stretching and pressing her instrument, buxom Mrs Scodger, puffing, pushing and pulling on the brass, between them managing to arouse the suspicion in a chance auditor that the tune they were playing was 'Whiter than the Snow', a hymn of which the mission was inordinately fond. Though not Mr Alfred Scodger, the unmuscular blacksmith.

Disturbed from his after-dinner nap, the peeping children saw him appear in the threshold of the door dividing the two rooms: his face, enormously moustached, wore an expression of indignant protestation: his sparse hair bristled wryly as one just risen from bed or sofa; he held his rusty billycock in his hand, his coat was on his arm and his boots were unlaced, the tongues protruding like those of rude boys making faces at the teacher behind his back: ' 'Ere!' he cried, elevating his brows and holding out the hand carrying the billycock.

The music ceased: Mrs Scodger lowered her chin and frowned at the blacksmith over her spectacles. She jerked her thumb, rudely, towards the room at the back and replied, peremptorily: 'Kitchen,' adding, imperiously: 'An' tek them there Sunday clo'es off. You ain't goin' out o' this house till I'm ready to' go wi' y'.' Mrs Jike watched, patiently, resting her instrument in her lap, fingers still engaged to the stops.

' 'Ere!' repeated Mr Scodger, more indignant than before.

'You heard me . . .'

He stared at her, indecisively, but, as he saw her knee commence to bob up and down beating time, and as she nodded to Mrs Jike and then raised her instrument to her lips, he, with a sudden blaze of revolt, stamped to the front door, opened it, turned upon his wife who had lowered her instrument and now was gaping at him incredulously, turned upon her and exclaimed angrily: 'Sick an' tired of it, Ah am. . . . If you think Ah'm gonna spend me Sat'day afternoon listenin' t' that there –' stabbing the air with his forefinger in the direction of the trombone – 'that there *thing*, you're – you're. Oh, Yaah.' He stamped out, slamming the door, taking good care to hurry off down the street. Mrs Scodger, when she found herself able to believe her ears, hurried to the door and fulfilled the expectations of the boys at the street corner by shouting out, loudly, and, at the same time, shaking the trombone as she would have a club: 'ALFRED SCODGER!'But Alfred, though he heard, did not heed.

Instantly, Bill Simmons, Sam Hardie, Tom Hare and Harry, at the instigation of Jack Lindsay who beat time with his hands, exclaiming: 'All together boys,' commenced to sing, in harmony, a vulgar parody of the mission's favourite hymn.

Universal laughter; grinning neighbours, accustomed to the boys' irreverence, came to stand on their doorsteps. And Tom Hare, who was an expert, made a very loud and extremely rude noise with his mouth which caused still more mirth. It embarrassed Mrs Scodger, who, red in the face, retired, muttering, whilst Alfred, trembling with emotion, passed through the open doors of the Duke of Gloucester public-house, where, leaning against the bar, Harry saw Ned Narkey, mug raised to his mouth. Phoo! The way he could guzzle beer! At half-past two he would go reeling down the street to his digs, sleep off his drunkenness in readiness for evening. Harry thought him a fool; wondered how long Ned's army money would last at this rate. Everybody knew how he was spending it on women (he'd the nerve to invite Sal go dancing with him! Harry had heard it from Helen who had heard it of Sal herself. The impudence of Narkey, classing Sal with those women with whom he associated! It filled him with unease to think of her even speaking to him). Narkey. Harry regretted Ned's muscularity; nobody could gainsay his striking appearance: either in his workaday apparel or his flashy week-end clothes his figure rendered him conspicuous. He'd be all right if he wasn't so overbearing, so downright, so ostentatiously vain. He thought every girl in the place had only to see him, to fall in love with him. Although Harry did not know it his lip was curling as he stared at Ned's broad back, so engrossed was he in telling himself how much he disliked Narkey.

He dismissed the thought from his mind, stretched, yawned, and, seeing Larry Meath passing on the other side, rucksack on his back, cried, warmly: 'Aye, aye, Larry,' and grinned.

'Hallo, Harry. Still like the job?'

'Not half,' Harry answered; 'It's great.'

Larry smiled, nodded and turned the corner.

Bill Simmons, throwing away the end of his cigarette, spat and said, as he stared after Larry: 'He's a queer bloke, if y' like. I seen him up Clifton way when I was out ferritin' wi' Jerry Higgs, y' know, along cut bank. Aye, an' there he was, large as life, lyin' on his belly in grass watchin' birds through them there glasses o' his,' curling his lip: 'Fancy a – feller seein' owt in watchin' bloody birds. He's barmy, if y' ask me.'

Tom Hare laughed: 'Jus' depends on what kind o' birds he's watchin'. Them as wear skirts is more i' my line. . . . An' there's some hot 'uns down cut bank. Maggie Elves. Ha! She'll let y' do owt for a tanner.'

Harry scowled: 'Aw . . . tarts agen. Blimey, don't *you* e'er think about nowt else?'

Tom winked, clapped his hands together, grinned and showed his decayed teeth: 'Ay, Harry, lad. Y' want t' go out wi' Maggie f'r a night, it'd do y' good. . . On'y a tanner, then y' could call y'self a man.' He winked again at the others, sniggered and added: 'He knows nowt about tarts, does he?'

Harry blushed: he hated to give the other boys the impression of his being a prude; at the same time he shrank from the thought of being in a class with Tom Hare. He protested, with warmth: 'Aw, you wouldn't talk like that if y' ma heard y'. An Ah' don't believe y' anyway, about this Maggie Elves. She must be a bright spark an' hard up t' have owt t' do wi' a guy like you.'

'Me?' replied Tom, not at all put out: 'Me? Ha! Any tart'll let y' do what y' want if y've enough money. Aye, *any*!'

'Oh, no, they won't,' Harry retorted, thinking on Sal and Helen: 'Ha, the kind as'd luk at *you*, might. They ain't partic, anyway,' impatiently: 'Oh, but you make me sick,' raising his brows and concluding, in tones of warning: 'You let y' ma hear y' talkin' like that. She'll gie y' Maggie Elves an' cut bank.'

Tom made a grimace: 'Me ma, eh. They're all same, her an th'old man. . . . So're all of 'em as is married. That's what they get married for. . . . Your ma an' pa . . .'

'Shut it, Hare,' snapped Harry, white, a threatening stare in his eyes: 'You leave me ma and pa out of it . . .'

'Yaaah,' Tom mumbled: 'You're just daft, that's all.' He glanced, furtively, at the others who were staring at their toes in silence. Their demeanours abashed him. He sensed he had overstepped the mark, and, accustomed as he was to have their attention only at the expense of relating the behaviour of his parents, in whose bedroom, owing to pressure on the accommodation, he slept, he laughed forcedly and said: 'Aw, y' get t' think nowt at all about it when y' get used to it. .... Why, on'y last night they came home drunk, and he . . .'

He was interrupted by Helen Hawkins who was passing, carrying a basin of the inevitable chipped potatoes. Tom Hare lowered his voice as Helen, a timid smile on her lips, paused in front of Harry. The others moved farther away to listen to Tom's story. Now and again they chuckled.

He smiled, forcedly. The sight of her after his words with Tom Hare filled him with a discomfort. He was glad, though, that she had preferred to forget his impatience when he had told her that he was sick of girls. He felt he wanted to make amends for his rudeness. Yet, somehow, all that Tom Hare had said seemed related to the basin of chipped potatoes in Helen's hand, related in a vague way, yet related. The food typified her home: the Hawkins family seemed to live on nothing else. Ach, her mother was too lazy to cook proper meals: she and her husband were too fond of going out boozing in the company of Tom Hare's parents and letting the house go hang.

Suddenly, it dawned on Harry that Helen's environment was precisely that of Tom Hare's! A fearful thought flashed through his brain. Was it conceivable that Helen might have to listen to or even witness the drunken sexual behaviour of her parents? It was revolting, shameful.

It gave place to others. Did Helen sleep in the same room as her parents or was her bed in the back bedroom? Did her grown brothers sleep in the same bed as she? 'Like me and Sal?' a voice in his brain added the question.

The question bewildered him: 'Me and Sal? I'd ne'er thought of it like that, afore.' But his sleeping with Sally was not the same as Helen's sleeping with *her* brothers. Sally was his *sister*. Of course, they were Helen's brothers. But in her case it didn't seem right at all. It puzzled and plagued him. Then a deep hatred of all the families and the houses of Hanky Park swelled his heart. Aw, but who cared? Thinking things like this only spoiled Saturday. Forget all about it! There'd be the picture theatre tonight and there was money in his pocket, more money than ever he had possessed before. Why, if he'd been at Price and Jones's he wouldn't have finished until nine o'clock tonight when everybody else was enjoying themselves. Away with these perturbing thoughts; today was Saturday!

Helen, gazing at him, said, quietly: 'What's come over you lately, Harry?'

He forced a grin, knocked his cap to the back of his head: 'What d'y' mean?' he asked, gazing at her. On a sudden he found himself marvelling at the charm of her girlish femininity: the thought that she *was* a girl and not a boy was wholly pleasing. He saw her instantly, in a new light; perceived qualities in her that were never before apparent to him; softness, freshness, an indefinable, elusive characteristic that seemed to fill, completely, some equally indefinable hiatus in his nature. Withal, a cautious voice bade him beware; friendship, exclusive friendship with her had its penalties. And, at the moment he did not wish to be penalized. Oh, he did not know what he wanted: she disturbed him: he didn't want to be disturbed; wanted to preserve, indefinitely, this happy-go-lucky, carefree Saturday air, these sensations of reckless abandon as were inspired by today's affluence and the prospect of the evening's search for diversion in the company of the boisterous boys. No, look what happened when he contemplated Helen: it left him miserable; made him think on such unpleasant things as her sleeping with her grown brothers; made him target to jealousy's stinging barbs such as when thoughts of, say, Tom Hare's laying his vile hands upon her, occurred to him. Absurd, impossible thoughts, yet such as filled him with exquisite pain. No, better remain fancy free; to love Helen was to embrace sadness. Oh, he did not know what he wanted. Staring at her, he knocked his cap to the back of his head and asked: 'What d'y' mean?'

She hesitated a moment, gazing at the pavement: 'What have I done?' she murmured: 'I mean . . .' she hesitated again, then looked up and said, haltingly; 'I mean . . . I thought you and me were . . .'

He thrust his thumbs into the straps of his overall bib, smiled and asked: 'Thought we was what?'

'We. . . . You know what I mean, Harry.'

He noticed that she was blushing; he saw the pulse beating in her throat. He felt intensely flattered. He lit a Woodbine.

With restrained eagerness she said: 'We could be . . . *you* know, Harry. Ah've allus liked you best of everybody. You hurt me when y' didn't go in office, but that don't matter. Ah'd like to have seen y' in office, that's all; you were cut out for it an' could ha' . . .' impatiently; 'Oh, well, you're different from that lot there.'

'Oh, they're all right, Helen,' he said, smiling in the direction of the group of chuckling, whispering boys. He looked at her, paused awhile and knitted his brows: 'It's like this, y' see,' anxious not to give too much offence and lowering his voice so that the boys could not overhear: 'Ah like you, too. Really, no kidding. But . . .' the eager light died in her eyes: 'But, well,' a shrug; 'Ah don't want t' go out reg'lar wi' anybody, yet. . . . Ah. Oh; Ah dunno, Helen, Ah just don't want.' A pause, then, impulsively: 'Ah want t' have some fun.' Instantly he saw her disappointment, and, in a desire to offer some sort of consolation, added, ingratiatingly: 'Come t' t' Flecky Parlour (a local theatre) t'night? Y' know, wi' the gang,' expansively: 'Ah've got plenty o' money.'

She stared down the street. One of her brothers, a bow-legged rickety child just able to walk, came out of the house clad only in his shirt. He toddled to the kerb, and sucking his dirty fingers, made water down the sough then returned to the house.

She sighed, dispirited. She did not know what to make of anything, and everything. Harry's attitude of easy complacence (was it genuine?), his refusal to accept her offer of exclusive friendship, to forsake the company of those street-corner boys charged her with a heavy listlessness.

Harry did not understand.

Hanky Park and its squalor could be made invisible if only he would permit her to devote herself to him in the little things.

Such happiness as this would. . . . Oh, but it was too impossible a happiness. If only he and she were grown older. She felt herself to be matured already; but Harry still was a boy, and he was out of reach. His refusal drew back the veil of sweet fancy with which she had shrouded the staring horror of her home.

No, that dirty, misshapen, half-naked child who had stood on the kerb a moment ago was not a character out of an absurd nightmare. His name was Tim Hawkins, one of a swarm, which lived, somehow, in the littered, mouldering kitchen which defied all efforts to keep clean. He and all that was associated with him; the unmentionable things, her parents' shamelessness which she herself dared not believe; these shut the door to idle dreaming and left her companioned only by her sole self.

Mother? Father? Brothers and sisters? Home? What meaning was there in them? A strange sensation stole over her, a perplexed incredulity. That dirty hovel, home? Where else? In all the wide world, of all the sweet dreams and fond imaginings of such homes as were writ of or projected at the pictures, of them all, hers was that in North Street. None else. The rest were words in a book, shadows flickering on a screen. Dreams. If she went elsewhere and asked for admittance the people would say: 'You don't live here. We don't know who you are.' Something within her contracted, recoiled; she shivered with loneliness. Oh, Harry, Harry Hardcastle. She could only look away from him, conscious of a hungering desire for his confidence and company.

Dully, insistently, crushing came the realization that there was no escape, save in dreams. All was a tangle; reality was too hideous to look upon: it could not be shrouded or titivated for long by the reading of cheap novelettes or the spectacle of films of spacious lives. They were only opiates and left a keener edge on hunger, made more loathsome reality's sores.

When you went to the public baths and stood, after a day's work, in a queue waiting your turn until the attendant beckoned you to a cubicle where was a bath half-filled with dirty water left by the girl or woman just quitted the place – you couldn't, by any stretch of imagination, even when the attendant had drained off the water and washed the muck away, see it as anything other than what it was, Hanky Park, the small corner of the wide, wide world where you lived.

Escape there was, or, at least, relief, in friendship. In Harry, in none other, could she have confided, unburdened herself. She wanted him to herself; someone to whom she could talk, to whom she could confess the superflux of feeling; someone with whom she could dream her dreams.

But he did not understand.

He had given her opportunity to be with him tonight, though. She mustn't, couldn't, daren't neglect the chance. Better share his company with others than be denied it altogether.

She saw her mother come to the door, a pot-bellied, middle-aged woman, teeth missing, hair in disarray about her face, her gait that of premature decrepitude. 'Hey,' she growled, and her stomach convulsed with the exclamation: 'Hey, come on wi' that there dinner, will y'. How long're y' gonna stand there gassin?''

Helen forced a smile and said, to Harry: 'All right, Harry. Ah'll come. Ah'll be waitin' here for y'.'

'Righto, kiddo.' She was blushing. Unaccountably, he felt a deep sympathy towards her. In an impulsive burst of generosity, he added: 'Ah'll treat y'.' He watched her depart.

They'd have a great time, with the boys, at the pictures, tonight. He'd buy her a tanner's worth of chocolate. There'd be the picture queue – always fun there – the fourpenny seats; perhaps a penn'orth of chipped potatoes each, wrapped in a piece of newspaper; wouldn't be Saturday night lacking these. Then the noisy hilarity inside the Flecky Parlour. Tom Hare provoking the attendants by making that vulgar noise with his mouth which set the audience in convulsions of laughter. Oh, and the happy genial rowdiness of everybody infected by the Saturday night atmosphere.

Great not to be working until nine o'clock tonight; great to have money and to spare. His eyes sparkled, he raised himself on his toes and beamed. In the light of the happy present the allure of the future seemed without end. Soon they would put him in charge of a machine, and then . . .!

He breathed, deeply, stared into nothingness, transfixed.

# PART TWO

## CHAPTER I

# REVELATION

THESE new experiences, compatible work, money to spend, Saturday nights' entertainment, brought with them a calm serenity which gradually assumed an air of permanency as though it had come to stay for evermore. Memories of Price and Jones's receded, were forgotten.

The human nature in him, though, found errand running become stale and uninteresting: he fretted for promotion, never allowed an opportunity pass without pestering Joe Ridge, the foreman, who, often as not, answered, snappily: 'Aw, f' God sake gie o'ever mitherin' me, son. Y'll be shoved on a bloody machine when it's y' turn. Tek things easy while y've chance. When y' workin' agen a stop-watch y'll be bloody sick o' sight o' machines. Blimey, some o' you kids don't know when y're cushy. Hop it, now, Ah'm busy.'

Sorry, though! Sorry to be entrusted with a lathe; a machine. Machines! MACHINES! Lovely, beautiful word!

He would stand staring unblinkingly at the elder apprentices at work on the machines. Imagine it, they all were under twenty-one years of age! Sudden doubts clutched his heart. Had he their intelligence? Would he, ever, be as proficient as they? Suppose, when opportunity came his way, he proved to be a miserable failure! But he wouldn't fail . . .

'Hey, Hardcastle, go t' t' stores for this. Come on, man. Luk alive. Don't stand dreamin' there . . .'

Errand boy. Roll on, time. Come the day when some other boy would take his place. He became an assiduous student of the others' working; flattered them, cunningly, that they might be induced to impart scraps of knowledge; was ever ready to watch a man's work who wished to absent himself from the machine for a short spell. Then, when wanting a few months of his sixteenth birthday, promotion came.

Strange movements were afoot: change taking place everywhere. A great deal of the old machinery was taken away and replaced by new: beautiful, marvellous, wonderful contraptions that filled the eye with pride to look upon. Hundreds of the old faces were missing one Monday morning. A batch of new boys came into the machine shops, and, strange to relate, none of the indentured apprentices. Nobody knew why; nobody cared. Rumour said that trade was bad. But how could it be with all this new machinery, this general upset, reshuffling and re-organization. All this was more suggestive of busy times. Anyway, they couldn't sack him; he was bound apprentice for seven years, only two of which had elapsed.

Promotion! After waiting for it so long its coming found him quite unprepared. Still, one could soon use oneself to it. And the day the batch of new boys came into the machine shops all wearing brand new overalls, all self-conscious and awed by all they saw, he found no difficulty in demeaning himself with mature superiority.

He was glad that many familiar faces of the time-served apprentices were missing; in their presence he could not very well pretend to omniscience. Besides, he never had been able to look on the older apprentices *as* apprentices; they had belonged to a different generation; some of them even had grown moustaches; they had been more akin to men than to boys. Anyway, they now were gone; their places occupied by much younger fellows to whom you could speak on terms of familiarity.

'Now,' said Joe Ridge the foreman: 'Now, p'raps y'll stop y' mitherin'. There's machine y've allus bin shoutin' for. See as y' don't make a muck of it. An' if y' want t' know owt, ask.'

Harry stared from the foreman to the capstan lathe, a smile growing on his face: 'Oh, ta, Joe,' he said, beaming: 'Oh, Ah'm glad, really.'

'Aye, Ah know all about it,' replied Joe deprecatingly: 'Jus' watch y' work's done proper, an' don't start messin' about. If owt guz wrong stop machine an' report it straight away. Allus y've t' do is t' watch; there's nowt i' this job. An' if y' behave y'self y'll p'raps be shoved on one o' t' new lathes as'll be ready next week, so tek care o' y'self.'

True enough, this task was child's play. But he was in charge of a lathe at last even though it was of the simplified capstan variety. He regarded it with pride of possession, ran his hand along it caressingly, touched its mechanism and stared, raptly as the tool shaved off fine ribbons of steel, which, spring-like, curled on themselves and snapped off. Fascinating. Thrilling, too, to know that promotion might be repeated again next week. In that case would be treble promotion since, in the ordinary course of events, he should first have had a spell on a drilling machine. He felt vastly pleased with himself, more especially when he remembered that Tom Hare, who had served three months longer than he, had been put to a drilling machine.

Tom resented it, apparently. At noon, he said, sulkily: 'Tain't fair, you bein' shoved on that there lathe in front o' me. Ah'm gonna see somebody about it. . . . Ah've bin here longer'n you,' aggressively: 'Why have they done it? That's what Ah'd like t' know.'

'*Ah* dunno,' Harry answered, secretly feeling that natural superiority must be the cause: 'Ah dunno. Don't ask me. Ah'm on'y doin' what Ah'm told.' Then, before he knew what had happened, he had added: 'Y' shouldn't lark about so much, an' y' should stop comin' late of a mornin'.'

Tom opened his eyes, incredulously: 'Y' what?' he cried indignantly: 'Who the — d'y' think *you* are?'

Harry frowned: 'Don't you swear at me or Ah'll swipe y'.'

'*You* will?' jeeringly, and showing his decayed teeth in a forced grin: 'Ha! Luk who's talkin'.'

'Aye, Ah will!' raising his brows and glaring.

'Ah'd like to see y' do it.'

'Dare me to – ' clenching his fists. The other boys, hearing the altercation gathered round and commenced to egg the boys on to fight with cat-calls.

Tom, who never had any intention of fighting, cast about for a means whereby he could extricate himself from his difficult position. 'Dare me to,' Harry had said, and now stood, fists clenched, lips set, desperately hoping that Tom would not dare him.

Tom curled his lip: 'Yaaah,' he sneered, 'It was either Larry Meath or Ned Narkey as got y' put in front o' me. . . . On'y a-cause they're dead nuts on your Sal!'

Harry blushed: 'Liar! They ne'er have nowt t' do wi' our Sal.'

'Liar y' sel'! She's bin jazzin' wi' Ned an' Ah've seen her talkin' t' t'other feller.' He pushed his prominent nose towards Harry and glared at him through his steel-rimmed glasses, adding, defiantly: 'Call me a liar now,' then, with contempt: 'Narkey's pet!'

The jibe was monstrous. Before Harry knew what had happened he had punched out, wildly hitting Tom upon the nose. Tom roared, clapped his hand to his face and screamed: 'Oh, me eyes, me eyes, me glasses. . . . Oh, me eyes!'

The spectators chorused approval, urging Harry to sail in to finish off Tom on the grounds that Tom's roars were mere pretence with which to hide his cowardice. Even had he wished Harry could not have continued. He was trembling with agitation and nervousness. Besides the very idea of striking Tom again was absurd: he was crouched, cowering against a lathe holding his hands to his face, still shouting.

Jack Lindsay went up to him, gripped a handful of his limp, oily hair and pulled his head back revealing a bloody nose: 'Yaaah,' he cried contemptuously: 'Shut y' row, y' ain't hurt. . . . You make me sick, y' big squawker.' He gave him a push which sent him on his knees: with a shrug he said, to the others: 'Carm on, leave him to have his squawk out.'

They moved away, Harry following. But he scarce had gone a half-dozen paces when curiosity made him pause to gaze back at Tom who now had risen to his feet standing, lonely and forsaken. His face was averted; he was sniffing and wiping his incarnadined nose. A sudden access of pity and compassion compelled Harry to return. He felt in his pocket and withdrew a cigarette: 'He' y' are, Tom,' he said, impulsively: 'Ah didn't mean t' 'urt y'. . . . An Ah didn't want t' fight.'

Without looking at him Tom took the cigarette, sniffed awhile, then shot a sheepish glance at Harry and mumbled: 'Ah didn't mean owt agen your Sal. . . . Though she *has* bein jazzin' wi' Ned Narkey an' Ah *did* see her talkin' t' Larry Meath,' with warmth, and in self-justification: 'You'd ha' felt same if somebody had bin put in front o' you,' recklessly: 'But Ah don't care. Let 'em stick their — lathes!'

'Ne'er heed, Tom,' replied Harry, feeling very magnanimous: 'You ne'er heed. There was a mistake, Ah bet, that's all . . .'

The siren interrupted. They returned to their work. In a moment all was forgotten.

2

What a change to hand over brass checks to raw apprentices! Brass checks with '2510' stamped upon them. To say to the boys, in impressive tones of voice: 'Hey, you, tek this t' t' stores an' see y' quick about it,' watch them scurry off, as zealously as he had done when first engaged. Pleasant, too, to answer, condescendingly, their timid questions regarding the machinery's mechanism, to pretend to a thoroughly comprehensive knowledge of all the engineering processes, and generally, to act as though *your* work was of the supremest importance.

He inspired, deeply, vastly pleased with himself.

Suddenly, the pleased expression faded: he stood, transfixed, as a shocking thought raised tumult in his brain: his skin crept; involuntarily his hand went to his mouth; he gaped, unseeing, at the lathe's remorseless revolutions.

'Blimey!' he muttered, scared.

He had been superseded by younger boys! This was the price that had to be paid for promotion. Its consequences were crushing.

No longer would he run errands for the men; the new boys would do that, and, at week-end, they would receive those coppers which had made all the difference to his life. Incredulously, he asked himself to imagine the fact that, for the future, he would only have the shilling spending money his mother gave to him. Two packets of Woodbines, admission to the pictures of a Saturday, two penn'orth of sweets, a threepenny bet, and, lo! he would be penniless until the following Saturday. It was monstrous. Nor would there be any relief until four years had elapsed, until he had concluded his apprenticeship and found another place where he would receive the full rate of pay. 'Blimey!' he muttered, and repeated: 'Blimey, Ah ne'er thought o' this.'

His world was upset; everything appeared in a new, unfamiliar and chilling perspective. Terrifying intimations tiptoed through the numb silences of his mind; insistent voices whispered the harsh truth that he was no longer a boy. This new batch of shop boys had pushed him, willy-nilly, along the path of Age, a road he had no inclination to follow. And they had given no warning; the transition had not been gradual but precipitate.

He looked back a couple of years. Why, the 'men' as he had called them, Billy Higgs, for example who had given him the half-crown when he, Billy, had made that very profitable bet – these 'men' hadn't been men at all; they were grown up apprentices, nothing more. Theirs had been precisely the same circumstances as his own: they had earned no more money than he. Yet how did they manage to buy a new suit once a year, to give pennies to the boys and to afford sixpenny and shilling wagers? They went to football matches, too, and occasionally, treated 'tarts' to the pictures. It perplexed and bewildered him. He was now in their class: as things now were he could not afford to do any such thing. What he could do, the only thing that remained, was to arrange with his mother to have a greater share of his earnings than had been customary and to depend upon her for new suits and the rest of his clothes and other requirements.

Of course, there was nothing else for it, those older apprentices whom, in his ignorance, he had considered men, must have made precisely similar arrangements. They weren't men at all, never had been. Even those with moustaches, who were twenty-one years of age, were, from the point of view of money, only overgrown boys, dependent on the support and generosity of their parents. Yet they were doing men's work. It was outrageous. Something ought to be done about it.

A sense of heavy responsibility crushed him. He now was in the class of senior apprentice: he was sixteen, the eldest among them was only four years and a few months his senior. Year by year would see him taking a step upward as the eldest were gradually displaced until he, too, reached the top rung five years from now when to be numbered among the time-served men.

For a moment the inexorable quality of Time's flight appeared to him in an alarmingly vivid glimpse. Until now a year had seemed an interminable age, something that stretched away into the hazy infinity of the future and could not be comprehended. In a flash he saw twelve months each treading on the other's heel in a never-ending suffocating circle, monotonous, constrained, like prisoners exercising mechanically in the confines of the prison yard.

He'd been at Marlowe's nearly two years now. And they were gone! Irretrievably. He felt perplexed, puzzled, cheated.

Sixteen years old, seventeen, eighteen, nineteen, twenty, twenty-one. Five years hence he would be a man. 'A man.' It was inconceivable. Yet Billy Higgs was a man and always had looked it. Think on it! When he first had commenced here Billy was only nineteen, just three years older than he, Harry, was at this moment. Why, in three years' time . . . !

A vivid recollection of the war years occurred to him. He saw himself standing on the kerb clutching his mother's skirts and thrilling to the martial music as he watched the latest batch of Lancashire soldiers marching to their death in the Dardanelles. He had thought how fine and big and strong the nineteen-year-old soldiers had looked and had been strangely perplexed by hearing his mother say, to Mrs Bull who stood with her:

'Ay, ain't it shameful. Childer they are and nowt else. Sin and a shame, Mrs Bull. Sin and a shame.'

'Them as start wars, Mrs 'Ardcastle,' Mrs Bull had replied, emphatically: 'Them as start wars should be made t' go'n fight 'um. An' if *Ah'd* owt t' do wi' it, fight 'um they would. They'd tek no lad o' mine. Luk at them lot there, boys an' nowt else.'

The recollection amazed Harry. Why, those soldiers had only been three years older than he. They were men at nineteen, then. Had he been their contemporary he, too, would have been a soldier; a corpse, probably, in some foreign land. He shivered.

Try as he would he could not bring himself to think himself a man. Did he lack some masculine quality which others possessed? Lacking it or no he would be forced into it.

There were some little boys at school at this moment, who, two years from now would be engaged by Marlowe's. He licked his lips. These newcomers would see him as he had seen Billy Higgs, a man. He blinked and licked his lips again; wanted to go search out these boys to tell them that he wasn't a man at all, had no intention of being a man: 'Ah ain't no man,' he told them, in his mind: 'Ah ain't no man. . . . D'y' understand? Ah'll on'y be eighteen when you start here. D'y' see? On'y four years older'n you. Aye, an' y'll be gettin' more'n me to spend an' Ah'll nearly be out o' me time,' to himself: 'Blimey, kids o' fourteen gettin' more'n me to spend when Ah'm eighteen. Blimey, Ah'll on'y be earnin' sixteen bob a week then and pay me own insurance.'

Glimmerings of truth began to dawn. A million mysteries slowly unfolded their secrets; what had been tinged with glamour crumbled to stark and fearful reality.

He saw groups of young men lounging at street corners; young men serving their time or not serving their time: the sight was so commonplace that nobody ever noticed it. Why were they lounging there? Why didn't they go to the picture theatre or some place of amusement? Why didn't they smarten themselves by wearing their Sunday suit of an evening? He knew why they never went in search of amusement, because they were as he, lacking the necessary money. And the remembrance of rows and rows of Sunday suits at Price and Jones's told their own tale. The suits belonged to Price: every week-end he hired them out to those who had bought them. And even those who didn't pawn them daren't wear them every evening. The clothes had to be made to last a twelvemonth, the procurement of which explained the presence of the Good Samaritan Clothing Club collectors in Hanky Park every Saturday noon. Two shillings a week for fifty-two weeks equals one new suit, etc.

But there was a point on which he still was puzzled. Take Billy Higgs, a typical example. Never, to Harry's knowledge, had Billy been inconvenienced by his penury: contrary, Harry had vivid recollections of Billy's throwing money about prodigally; he saw him oozing complacence and beaming good-naturedly on everybody.

'How many times?' he asked himself.

'Aye,' he murmured, 'How many times?' Once, and once only, when Billy had made that profitable bet.

Slowly the explanation crystallized. Billy's extraordinary good fortune on that solitary occasion had made him a cynosure;

attention had been focused on him, nothing more. It was so unusual for anyone to have a temporary sufficiency of money that when such good fortune did fall an individual's way, all the other penurious wretches saw a nimbus of glory glowing round the fortunate one's head. It was a seven days' wonder. You remembered them and their luck as you remembered the fire at Harmsworth's mill. In the ordinary course of events you never looked at Harmsworth's mill: it was a mill, part of the landscape and nothing more. But when it was blazing people rushed from all parts, and, ever afterwards, the memory of the conflagration stuck. When the fire was extinguished and the damage repaired, things resumed normalcy, nobody raised their eyes to the sooty buildings. The same with Billy Higgs. Nobody looked at him now; the nimbus had faded with the spending of his money. He was now unemployed. Only last night Harry had seen him lounging at the street corner with the rest of the dole birds feeling in his pocket for a fag-end that wasn't there.

All in the same boat: all hard up; there was a sorry kind of consolation in being one of a crowd.

But he resented the intrusion of the new boys: they had stolen money out of his pocket with their coming. He felt resentful of everybody who was prosperous. Resentful of Sam Grundy, the bookie, of Alderman Grumpole the fat money-lender proprietor of the Good Samaritan Clothing Club, and of Price, J.P., the cadaverous pawnbroker.

Then fears and panic clutched him: he became afraid. Was this what was meant by growing older? And money. A shilling a week was impossible. Cigarettes, pictures and threepence for a bet and – broke until next pay day. Gosh! He *must* find a winner; must be extremely painstaking with his threepenny wagers. His heart contracted to remember that only once in two years had he won, and then only two shillings.

Ah, but he had been careless, then; hadn't spent time studying form. Then there were the competitions in the newspapers: '£500 for First Four in the Derby'. 'Spot the Ball and win £1,000'. But the prospect of winning here was remote. And, ten to one, if he did succeed in placing the Derby horses correctly, his prize would be like that of the man's in the next street who had performed, successfully, the difficult prognostication and had received, instead of £500, a letter and a package from the Competition Editor, saying: '... therefore, owing to the huge number of successful competitors, list of which may be had on application plus cost of postage, it has been found impracticable to divide the money prize. Enclosed, however, is a magnificent photogravure plate of H.R.H. the Prince of Wales.'

'Aw, blimey,' he muttered: 'Ah'm fed up, Ah am.'

Where was that feeling of confidence of the future? of the imminence of joys to be?

Where was Helen? He wanted her, urgently; wanted to confess his fears to her attentive and sympathetic ear. He'd take her to Dawney's Hill tonight where they could talk, confidentially, without fear of interruption. Take her, if she would go.... Suppose she declined. Imagine if she transferred her affections elsewhere!

Oh, Helen, Helen. Only she could assuage this fear of the future that loomed, large and foreboding like a great, dark cloud on the horizon.

### CHAPTER 2

## HE IS HAPPY

DAWNEY'S HILL (how it came by that name I cannot say) lies about a half-mile to the west from Hanky Park. It is a huge deposit of sand, a high eminence with a grass-capped brow. In genial weather and when the darkness falls, urban lovers sit out their evenings here kissing and fondling, wisely snatching happiness whilst it is there.

If the heavens have ears they must have listened to millions of promises and plans from the lips of young factory hands scheming as to their futures..

The hill's popularity as a rendezvous may be accounted for in that there is free access, no pay-boxes, turnstiles or warnings to keep off the grass. At sunset Venus presides. And the dirty grass has provided the nuptial couch for many and many a moment's ineffable bliss, prelude, sometimes, to premature and hasty marriages. No doubt it will continue so to do for just as long a period as the Two Cities Municipal Authorities take to sell Dawney's Hill, a cart-load at a time, to any and all speculative builders who find themselves in need of sand.

From its brow, if you sit with your back to the setting sun, the huge, stricken area of the Two Cities sprawls away east, north and south. Like a beleaguered city from which plundering incendiaries have recently withdrawn, a vast curtain of smoke rises as from smouldering ruins. And the tall chimneys standing in clusters like giant ninepins, spouting forth black billowing streamers, write their capricious signatures on the smudgy skies. The same today as in the not-long-ago when old people told tales of cows being called home from where below were once lush meadows; days when the soaring larks beat wings against unspotted skies, and, of a night, gawmless calves, the daft loons, stood gaping at the moon, and, aloft, the stealthy midnight owl sharply eyed the moonlit green below.

By east, north and south sprawls the cities' area.

The sensible lovers never face it; they look towards the northwest where the prospect is pleasanter. There still are fields, and, where the river twines and turns about a mile distant as the crow flies, its steep northern bank gives hospitality to congregations of trees. Town trees and town fields.

Helen sighed contentedly and gazed at Harry lying supine in the grass by her side.

His attitude towards her this last day or so had changed completely. He seemed to desire her company, her exclusive company; yet she was cautious, distrustful of her optimism. She did not wish to build on the premature hope of its permanency.

There were encouraging signs, though. He was growing older perceptibly; no longer did he seem to hanker for the company of the other boys. Indeed there was a change in the demeanours of them all; they all were more or less subdued. Its cause was not far to seek. Of a Saturday evening nowadays only a ghost of their erstwhile boisterousness remained; no more did they fling money about carelessly. A new generation had taken their places by Hulkington's, the grocer's shop; the same in the Saturday picture theatre queues. The younger boys evinced the same habits, the same prodigality; different boys, that was all.

'It's rotten, Helen. Kids like that gettin' more to spend than me. Older y' grow, more work y' do an' less money y' get t' spend. 'Tain't fair.'

As she sat here with him by her side she recalled his words, turned them over thoughtfully. They pleased her: yet they made her feel very sorry for him. She gazed at him, he was lying staring into the sky, a hand carelessly plucking at a tuft of grass. The more she looked at him the more urgent and warm her love of him seemed to grow, until, at last she could not resist an impulse to confess her feelings. On a sudden she leaned towards him and murmured, with suppressed ardour: 'Oh, Harry, Ah do love y' . . . Ah do, really.'

He looked at her, pleased, surprised: 'D' y', Helen?' he murmured, with a tiny smile.

She glanced this way and that, then, lowering her head, kissed him, hastily, sitting up again immediately afterwards to assure herself that they had not been seen. She saw that the other couples were too preoccupied with their own love affairs to be concerned with those of others.

She gazed at Harry again, a faint tinge of colour in her cheeks.

'Do it agen, Helen,' he murmured, his hand closing on hers.

'Nooo,' she replied, feeling it to be her womanly duty to deny him: 'Nooo. Somebody'll see us.'

'Oh, go on,' he urged: 'Let 'em. I don't care.'

'No. . . No,' she said, with finality, as she glanced about her again. Hastily, she pressed her lips to his whilst he placed his disengaged hand about her neck in a protracted embrace. So that when he released her she was flushed, her hair and hat awry. 'You should ha' let me go, Harry,' she protested, straightening her hat and trying to restrain her smiles. His answer was to close his eyes and sigh, contentedly.

As he lay there, a curious sense of luxurious indolence, of brain-laziness stole over him. With Helen by his side he felt safe and secure from what he did not know. Safe and secure; tranquil, lulled into a state of harmonious quiescence, of peace and quiet breathing.

He took a deep, sighing breath. He opened his eyes, reluctantly. Helen, leaning on an elbow was bending over him. They smiled at each other.

'Are y' happy, Harry?' she asked.

He sighed anew: 'Eee, Ah am,' he murmured: 'Just then, when Ah closed my eyes, Ah'd such a lovely feelin' about me an' you.'

'What was it?'

He stared at the sky; tried to find words with which to express himself: 'Ah dunno,' he murmured: 'It was all nice, that's all. It made me feel sleepy-like.'

She did not answer; stroked his hair whilst her gaze roved over his shabbiness. She discovered that she was profoundly grateful for his present circumstances: tremors of fear disturbed her as she thought on what might have been the consequences had he taken up office work. Suppose, in the place of that soiled mercerized cotton scarf he had worn collar and tie; a nice suit instead of oily overalls; neat shoes instead of hobnailed boots. She never would have dared expose her own shabbiness alongside him, even if he had been agreeable. Perhaps he would have found a different circle of acquaintances; might never have given her a glance. Oh, what rubbish. Might have been was only might have been; precious reality was hers.

She said: 'Would y' rather be here wi' me than wi' streetcorner lads, Harry?' She gazed at him with steadfast anxiety.

He did not answer, straightaway, stared, unblinkingly into the sky. Her question recalled days that were gone; days when he could anticipate, regularly, the three shillings a week spending money instead of the miserable shilling as at present. What the devil could a fellow do with a shilling? he needed more money now than ever; he wanted to demonstrate his affection for Helen in buying her things: wanted to buy clothes so that he might appear smartly dressed. But – he frowned; some restless part of him writhed, impotently.

His hesitation chilled her; his frown was frightening. Could it be that he still was in doubt regarding his need of her companionship?

'Would y'?' she repeated, searching his face apprehensively.

He sat up, made a deprecating pass with his hand and replied: 'No fear. Ah ain't goin' wi' them no more . . .' He did not hear her sigh. She laid her head on his shoulder and closed her eyes as he drew up his knees, clasped them and rested his chin atop, staring at the scene below.

At the foot of the sandfaced hill, at the other side of the unpaved road, is a large railway siding; there are main line tracks atop a high embankment, and engine sheds and more rail lines on the embankment's farther side. Express passenger trains, bound for Liverpool and the north-west coast resorts roar by periodically. Shunting takes place perpetually: goods engines puff about the network of lines with seeming leisurely aimlessness: detached wagons in motion deceive the eye as to their destination, rumbling between the stationary rows of wagons when one fully expects them to collide, then, colliding, with a crashing of buffers when one expects them to proceed.

Although the noise was considerable Harry was not attentive. He murmured: 'It troubles me, though, havin' nowt t' spend on y', Helen. There's many a time Ah'd like t' . . .'

She pressed his arm and nestled closer: 'Ah don't want nowt, Harry. Ah only want you.'

Daylight was declining: darkness crept stealthily from nowhere and spread its dim veil over the townscape. A train that rattled along the far embankment whistled shrilly, its uncurtained windows gleaming brightly and emphasizing the gloom.

The bestarred universe of the Two Cities twinkled as lamplighters went about their work. There was no moon.

'All the same,' murmured Harry. 'Ah wish Ah had more money so's we could have a bit more fun.' He noticed the passing train. The incredible appreciation that he never had been aboard one in his life, dawned on him, startlingly. He swallowed, hard, paused awhile as a daring thought tempted his mind; then he blurted out: 'Ah want t' be able t' tek you an' me away for holiday, Helen . . .'

She interrupted: 'Oh, Harry,' in awed tones: 'But where could *we* get money for holiday?'

Her tones of voice nettled him: 'Aw, Ah'll get it,' he muttered: 'You see if Ah don't. . . .' A voice reminded him that a shilling a week saved was only two pounds twelve in a year's time. He concluded, lamely: 'Ah'm havin' a threepenny treble (a wager upon three horses in which the winnings from the first horse, if any, are re-invested in a compound manner upon the second-named and then upon the third-named animals). Ah'm havin' a threepenny treble every week wi' Sam Grundy. An' Ah'm havin' a go at competitions in newspaper,' confidently: 'Oh, you see, Ah'll pull it off one o' these days.'

'Oh, Ah don't care if y' never have nowt, Harry,' she murmured: 'S'long as we're happy, that's all that matters.'

Her arm stole about his waist. They sighed, simultaneously.

CHAPTER 3

'RASPBERRY, GOOSEBERRY . . .'

SALLY, an expression of preoccupation on her face, came out of the house and sauntered down North Street. Although she was dressed in her dance frock, her dawdling gait and her bemused expression suggested that such a way of spending the evening failed to please.

She had dallied over dressing; had, indeed, once made up her mind not to go, but the thought of there being nothing else to do but to sit mooning about the house, had forced her, in desperation, to her original, half-hearted intention. Her vague desire was to be enabled to have a room to which she could retire where to feel secure from trespass; some place where she could think in quietude; where there would be no family interruption. She did not know what she wanted to think about except that there was a feeling of irksome restlessness gnawing within her. She felt that she wanted something urgently, but what it was she wanted she did not know.

She did know that there was no privacy in the house: knew that if she stayed in the bedroom her mother, sure enough, would shout upstairs: 'Sal, what're y' doin' up there all this time?' The same if she, as sometimes she did, used the tiny privy in the backyard as a retiring room: 'What're y' doin' there,' would remind her that seclusion, as she desired it, was not to be had at home.

Oh, and this dancing in the arms of such as Ned Narkey. She was disgusted with it, had had enough and more than enough. It was worse than no substitute for what it was she lacked. If only she knew what she wanted. If only she could rid herself of these dreadful feelings of aimlessness, of this perplexing sensation of being lost, out of place.

She sighed, heavily, wearily, as she halted by the Duke of Gloucester public-house.

A group of children were playing a game close by; their piping voices merged into that of a street-corner orator who was addressing a handful of people on the other side of the street. She was too engrossed in her thoughts to heed either. She stood on the edge of the kerb, staring into the roadway as one absorbed in the orator's argument.

Ned Narkey, dressed in a smart suit, came out of the public-house wiping his lips on the back of his hand. He caught sight of Sally standing there and frowned. 'Hey,' he said, sourly: 'What d'y' mean keepin' me waitin'?'

She looked up: 'Eh?' she said. He repeated his utterance, adding: 'Why did'n y' come in pub an' tell me you was here?' darting a glance at the orator across the street: 'Ah suppose y' was more interested i' that muck *he's* spoutin', eh?'

'Who're y' talkin' to, Narkey?' she snapped, her eyes kindling: 'Who d'y' think you are?'

'You kept me waitin' . . .'

'Aye, an' a fine place y' was waitin' in, too . . .'

'Here,' he replied, warmly: 'Who d'*you* think y're talkin' to?' raising his brows: 'Blimey, y' might be Queen of Sheba,' warningly; 'but Ah've had enough o' your frisky ways. Ah can get tarts ten a penny, aye, an' them's don't keep a feller waitin', neither. D'y' understand? Ah'm gettin' sick o' tailin' you around like a shadder an' all for nowt.'

She narrowed her eyes: 'You're a dirty dog, y'know, Narkey. An' y'ain't the only one as is sick. Ah'm sick of you and the rest o' the crowd y' muck around wi'. Allus *you* want out o' girls is one thing only. But y' don't get it out o' me, d'y' understand. Best thing you can do is to go wi' them as is ten a penny.'

He swallowed his mortification and forced a smile: 'Aw, come on, Sal,' he cried: 'Ah was on'y kiddin'. You know me.'

'No,' she said: 'Ah'm not goin' dancin'.'

'Why?' he snapped, frowning: 'Y've got ready t' come.'

'Ah'm not goin'. Ah've changed me mind.'

His lips tightened across his teeth. His impulse was to strike her; she was maddeningly provocative; she was overwhelmingly desirable. Oh, to embrace her, crush her, hurt her. Why was it that out of all the girls and women of his acquaintance, she, who was so unattainable should be so desirable? Perhaps that was the reason. But that she should treat *him* with indifference! He swelled with anger: 'Aaach,' he snarled: 'Aw right, then, if y' don't want t' go. Y'ain't th'only tart around here,' sneeringly: 'P'raps y'd rather listen t' him and his blather.' He stamped off, fuming, promising himself that this high-handed attitude towards her would teach her a lesson and that she would come back to him of her own accord to ask his pardon.

She shrugged her shoulders and stood there, unmoved: 'P'raps y'd rather listen t' him and his blather.' She was puzzled as to Narkey's meaning. Then she became conscious of the orator opposite. Twice Narkey had referred to him. It was Larry Meath. Evidently Narkey was jealous of him. Jealous of Larry Meath, though! Imagine having her name coupled with Larry's, even though only in the imagination of a jealous mind!

Well, why not? She found that she was vastly pleased, immensely flattered by Narkey's jealousy. Her spirits, for some reason, soared like a rocket; a sudden, animated expression stole across her features. She smiled, breathed deeply, felt delightfully perturbed and nervous. She called herself a fool; yet she did not walk away, stood there, gazing at Larry, fixedly; found herself indulging in a cross-examination of herself regarding him. Why should she feel so towards him now and at no time before? She remembered having regarded him, previously, with something akin to awe. Not that she had never spoken to him: contrary often-times he had paused to pass a pleasant word with her. Imagine it, they *had* spoken to each other, previously. She tried to recall the words that had passed between them on those occasions. She could only remember herself as someone shy and tongue-tied. Larry's presence, somehow, seemed to demand your best behaviour. You became so very conscious of the loose way of your speech when you heard him speaking. She suddenly discovered a thousand faults in herself, and, for a moment felt dispirited at their enormity.

The moment passed: she listened to what he was saying.

'... And to find the cost of this present system you have only to look at our own lives and the lives of our parents and their parents. Labour never ending, constant struggles to pay the rent and to buy sufficient food and clothing; no time for anything that is bright and beautiful. We never see such things. All we see are these grey depressing streets; mile after mile of them; never ending. ... And the houses in which we are compelled to live are as though they have been designed by fiends in hell for our especial punishment. When work is regular we are just able to live from week to week: there is no surplus. But for ever, there hangs over us that dread threat of unemployment. Unemployment that can and does reduce most honest working folk to pauperdom, that saddles them with a debt that takes years to repay. Even at its best I say that this is not life. And it is not the lot of one or two individual families. Look around you here in Hanky Park; not a part but the whole of it is so affected. This existence is what is fobbed off on to us as Life. And Hanky Park is not the whole of England. In every industrial city of the land you will find such places as this, where such people as us who do the work of the world are forced to spend their days. *That* is the price we will continue to pay until you people awaken to the fact that Society has the means, the skill, and the knowledge to afford us the opportunity to become Men and Women in the fullest sense of those terms.' He stepped down; another man took his place.

He crossed the road. In her direction. Her cheeks flamed, her pulse quickened; she felt excited, elated, yet, at the same time, wished to withdraw so that he might not see her. She stood her ground, eyeing him, fascinated.

He glanced at her as he passed. He stopped, smiled, as one who is pleasantly surprised. 'Hallo, Sally,' he said, warmly, adding, with mock incredulity: 'Don't tell me I've made a convert.'

She laughed, murmured something incoherently, then averting her gaze, said: 'I was listening. But I don't know nowt – er – anything about politics.' She raised her eyes to his. The street lamp's beams caught her upturned face, and enhanced, in the pale contrast of her skin the glowing darkness of her eyes.

She blushed; thought she perceived an appreciative attentiveness in his gaze. Or was it imagination on her part? He had not yet answered; they still were looking at each other. She was embarrassed but could not avert her gaze.

'I was listening. But I don't know anything about politics,' she had said. He suddenly roused himself. She thrilled to notice an unwonted awkwardness in his demeanour. He said: 'Why not join us at the Labour Club?' a light laugh: 'It isn't all politics there, Sally. . . . Though you can't altogether escape them. . . . There's the Sunday rambles into Derbyshire; they should interest you; and they're a jolly crowd of young folks who go . . .'

'I'd like it,' she said. 'You go, don't you?' hesitantly: 'I don't know anybody there. I . . . I . . .' she smiled at him.

'Oh, yes, I'd take you. They're a sociable lot of people, you know. If you'd care to come up – let me see. . . . I'm engaged speaking at two or three street meetings tonight. If you're free tomorrow evening we could go to the club and I'd introduce you.'

'All right,' she said.

A pause. They eyed each other, smiling. 'Tomorrow evening, then,' he said, raised his hat, wished her goodnight and departed. There was a mysterious, nameless, perturbing significance about the episode that astounded him. But it invoked the most pleasurable sensations. As he strode along he found himself impatiently anticipating tomorrow evening whilst the vivid recollection of her upturned face and haunting eyes lingered in his mind. He marvelled that such emotions as now were his should have been engendered by one whom he had seen and spoken to time and time again. He whistled a gay tune.

Sally stood there on the kerb enchanted. He had raised his

hat to her. Charming? Who amongst the other men would have dreamed of such a gesture? Who . . .

Her mother, passing by, interrupted her thoughts. Mrs Hardcastle said: 'Ah'm just goin' t' Mrs Jike's, Sal. We're havin' a spritualis's meetin' in her kitchen. Ah've left Harry in th' 'ouse. He ses that if Ah saw y' to tell y' as he wants y'. . . .' She crossed the street to Mrs Jike's home.

Sally turned and sauntered homewards.

As she passed the group of children playing in the roadway their sing-song voices struck her ear. She smiled as she heard:

'Raspberry, gooseberry, apple jam tart.
Tell me the name of your sweetheart . . .'

2

When she entered the house she found Harry standing by the slopstone staring into the small mirror suspended there. Around his neck was a collar far too large for him, one of a number given to him by Larry Meath who had discarded them. He had accepted them with beaming gratitude; they were such as he always had dreamed of possessing, for, outside working hours, Larry was always neat about the neck. Even though the collars required altering, a glance at their effect upon him through the glass was sufficient to waken in his heart an abysmal discontentment with his shabbiness. Lacking a new suit would make the wearing of these incongruous. A new suit; a *proper* new suit; one made to special measurement, shaped at the waist, not a reach-me-down that fitted like a sack.

As Sally came into the kitchen he was imagining himself wearing the desired garment. It was made of blue serge; it embraced him, creaseless, precise.

She frowned as she looked at him. She wanted to be alone to think. She said, rousing him: 'What're y' gawping – I mean staring at y'self, for? You're worse than a girl.'

He started, removed the collar, turned, gazed at her and said: 'Would y' like t' mek these to fit me, Sal?' He held out the collar, adding, persuasively: 'Go on, Sal, y're a good sewer.'

She frowned: 'Aaach, what d'y' think I am? And don't say "mek", it's "make". Oh, I've no time to muck about – I mean, mend collars for nobody. I'm goin' to a dance,' impatiently: 'Get Helen Hawkins t' do them for y'.'

His hand fell to his side; his collar, wagging between his fingers, attracted the cat's attention; it clawed up at it, playfully.

He stared at Sally's averted face. Lately she had been more than usually inclined to snappy moodiness; on the least provocation her temper flared. He wondered what ailed her; she was spending much time dancing. She ought to be having a good time, he thought. He sighed, murmured, 'Ah wanted you t' do 'em, Sal. Ah didn't want Helen t' know as Larry Meath gev 'um me.'

She looked up, quickly: 'Who?' she asked.

He stared at her, astonished: 'Larry Meath gev 'um me,' he said, in surprised tones: 'Ah ain't pinched 'um.'

'Oh,' she said. She turned away, confused, picked up the cushion of the rocker chair and straightened it unnecessarily: 'You can leave 'um. ... Leave them there,' she said, without looking at him, 'I'll do them.'

'Thought you was goin' to a dance?'

'I'm not partic'.'

'All right. Thanks for doin' 'em, Sal.'

She did not touch the collars; they lay on the edge of the table. Dawdling around the house he perceived a certain restlessness in her: every time he made a move she glanced at him, quickly, expectantly. Finally, she exclaimed, with a trace of exasperation: '*Aren't* y' goin' out tonight?'

He muttered something, picked up his cap and sauntered to the front door not caring to offend her. Her attitude was puzzling: he lingered by the front door, curious. He heard her reaching for the work-basket; there came the metallic rattle of scissors then the creak of the rocker chair as she sat down. He heard her humming.

'She's daft, must be,' he said to himself, and moved off.

## CHAPTER 4

# FINE FEATHERS

THE question of a new suit became an obsession. He dreamed on it; wore it so often in fancy that, on waking of a Sunday morning, he was fully convinced that it hung behind the bedroom's curtained-off alcove which served as wardrobe.

It wasn't there. What met his eyes when he opened them was grim reality decorating the bed end, those wretched reach-me-downs bought second-hand from an auction at the Flat Iron Market. Sulkily he would rise.

Of a Sunday the streets did not see him nor would he give Helen truthful reason why. He lay abed until noon, sat in the house the remainder of the day fretting and brooding, sometimes sneaking out for a half-hour after darkness had fallen.

When alone with his mother and father he pestered them unceasingly: 'When am Ah goin' t' have that there new suit?' he mumbled with an expression of sulky petulance.

His mother sighed: 'Ay, lad, what can Ah do? Y' know Sal's on short time, an' y' pa's ne'er sure of a full week's work.'

'Ah know, ma. But Ah've ne'er had a proper suit yet. An' me nearly eighteen. Ah'm ashamed t' go out of a Sunday,' warmly: 'Luk at Bill Lindsay an' th' others. They can have 'em. Why can't I?'

Mrs Hardcastle glanced at her husband nervously, then said to Harry, apologetically: 'They get 'um from Good Samaritan, Harry. . . . Y'know y' father don't like weekly payments.' She glanced at her husband again. Harry, too, looked at him.

Hardcastle removed his pipe from his mouth, spat into the fire and addressed his newspaper: 'Y'll have t' mek do wi' what y've got, lad. It's tekkin' us all our time t' live. Y'll get one when things buck up.'

Tears of vexation swam in Harry's eyes. The awful indefinitiveness of: 'When things buck up.' He felt sickeningly impotent. He was tired of it, tired of everything. 'Prosperity in sight. Trade turning the corner.' He had thrilled at that when first he had become interested in newspapers about a year ago; the headline had seemed so full of promise of impending universal joy. The same line appeared every three months or so. But the prosperity was an unconscionable time a-coming.

'It's lies,' he said to himself.

'Trade turning the corner?' *He* was employed busily enough; so were the rest of the young men and boys at Marlowe's. Then to what part of the community was the headline addressed? There was Billy Higgs and his generation mouching the streets, threadbare and unemployed. There was Hardcastle irregularly employed at the pits: Helen and Sally were finding it unusual to have a full week's wages of a Friday. And he, Harry, although fully employed, was only earning a boy's. . . . A glimpse of truth frightened him: scared, he appreciated that he was fully employed only on terms. Nearly all the hands who were working full time at Marlowe's were youths such as he: youths, young men – nay, had the present been war time the authorities would have termed him a man and would have hauled him off to the trenches. Youths, young men, men, performing men's work but only being paid boys' wages. Seventeen shillings a week they gave him now. Why, before long he'd be out of his time, a fully qualified engineer. Then, if trade didn't improve he would join Billy Higgs at the street corner.

Trade improve? Well, suppose it did improve, aside from the fact that he couldn't see how trade could improve more since he and the rest were fully employed. Just suppose, though, that it improved in some mysterious fashion. Would Marlowe's re-engage Billy Higgs and the rest of the displaced time-served men? Or would more machinery be installed, everybody find themselves promoted and the gap at the bottom filled by hordes of raw boys just left school?

His spirits withered. Remember the installation of that new automatic machinery previous to the wholesale dismissal of Billy Higgs's generation? At that time it had held no significance for him except that it had meant promotion; it was merely newer and more up-to-date machinery whose functions were marvellous, whose capacity was manifold and infinite. The screw-cutting lathe that needed only the assistance of a hand to switch on the current; that could work, ceaselessly, remorselessly, twenty-four hours a day, seven days a week without pause for meals; a Thing that fed itself, functioned with mathematical precision, 'could do anything except talk', as someone had put it.

The novelty of such machinery was gone now; they were commonplace, established; their predecessors were antediluvian. They made of inexperienced boys highly skilled men. And the latest boys knew of nothing else; were as to the manner born.

Every year new generations of schoolboys were appearing, each generation pushing him and his a little nearer to that incredible abyss of manhood and the dole.

Why, the supply of boys was inexhaustible; there were millions of them at school; Marlowe's could keep going for ever. What was to become of him and his when their time was served? Where would openings occur if every firm was playing Marlowe's game? *If!* A horrible suspicion clutched him. Suppose that this present was an already established new order, that once a fellow came out of his time he remained unemployed for ever!

But what had all this to do with the question of a new suit? Oh, it made you dizzy, weary, having to think on all these things. His mind switched back to the question of the suit. 'Y'll have to make do wi' what y've got. Wait till things buck up,' his father's answer.

Harry's lip quivered: at that rate he'd remain shabby for ever: 'Why can't Ah have one through t' Good Samaritan like th' others?' he mumbled.

'Ah'm shovin' no millstone o' weekly payments round me neck,' replied his father, bluntly: 'What we can't pay for cash down we'll do bout (without).'

'But th' others do it,' Harry grumbled: 'An' here Ah am workin' full time an' ain't got nowt t' go out in o' week-ends.'

'Aaach! Ah've worked all me bloody life, lad, and what Ah've Ah got? All me bloody clo'es i' pawn t' get food t' eat,' warningly: 'Don't you set me off, now. Don't you set me off.'

Nettled, Harry, in a burst of uncontrollable temper, blurted out: 'Well, Ah'm sick of it all Ah can tell y'. Nowt t' spend an' nowt t' wear an' me workin' full time.'

Hardcastle jumped to his feet, blazing and flung his newspaper aside: 'God A'mighty,' he cried, 'This *is* a bloody life, this is. Ah come home t' rest an' what do Ah get? If it ain't you it's her (Sally). Blimey, man, d'y' think blasted money grows on trees. . . . Aaach, let me get out o' here.' He snatched up his seedy cap and coat and stamped out. Nobody understood a fellow's feelings. Here he was, a man, married to a woman, father to a couple of grown children, working hard and had always worked hard, yet couldn't afford to dress his children respectably. Blimey, didn't either of them ever think how he must feel about it?

Mrs Hardcastle, awed, fingering her apron, nervously, stared at Harry and murmured; 'Now see what y've done.'

Harry flung himself upon the couch and wept unrestrainedly out of sheer impotence.

Such episodes became common. He even invoked God's assistance: '*Please* God let th' old man get me that there suit. Ah ain't ne'er had a proper un an' Ah'm sorry Ah stopped goin' t' church an' choir.' Uninvited, a choir, in his brain, complete with organ accompaniment, began to make a nuisance of itself by singing that interminable composition, the sevenfold Amen.

He did not, however, place his cause wholly in the hands of the Deity. He persisted on his own behalf plaguing his father on every suitable occasion. After all, what disgrace was there in availing oneself of the facilities offered by Alderman Grumpole's Good Samaritan Clothing Club? Everybody hereabouts were its patrons, otherwise nobody would have new clothes. The Good Samaritan was a firmly established institution. It angered him to think that only his father's obstinate prejudice against credit dealings stood between him and his desires. Blimey, all this to-do arising out of a legitimate desire to be dressed properly. It made him boil.

His querulous complaints began to wear his father's nerves. The boy seemed absolutely impervious to reason. Weren't they in debt enough without contracting more for such inessential things as new suits? Such a suit as the lad desired would cost three pounds easily. That meant three shillings interest to be found before Grumpole would issue an order to the outfitter; then would follow twenty weeks' instalments of three shillings. Three shillings a week, though!

This kind of thing, not being able to provide adequately for one's family made a man feel an irresponsible fool, humbled him, haunted him to the point of driving him to frantic, foolhardy expedients. Money, money, money. The temptation to go drown worry and misery in drink was, betimes, almost irresistible. Walking abroad he would find himself brooding, muttering to himself 'Worked every hour God sent, every day o' me life. An' what have Ah t' see for it? Every bloody day, every bloody hour an' worse off'n when Ah was fust wed.'

Harry was unaware that his father's absences from home were contrived. Every time he caught the boy's gaze it said, mutely: 'When am I to have the suit, father?' He couldn't bear to look. Better to keep out of the lad's way as much as possible. His cause was just; the poor little devil wasn't fit to be seen; he was the only one in the house working full time; and he gave up every penny of his wages. Oh – ! Hardcastle felt an urgent desire to be able to take out his brains and plunge them in cold water.

To Harry, his father's stern visage was a perfect mask: had he known he would have been astounded that his father should be afraid of meeting him.

He persisted until one Sunday evening, Hardcastle, in desperation, exclaimed: 'Oh, missis, for God's sake get him that blasted suit. Blimey, sick of it all, Ah am.'

Victorious, Harry's hungry joy amounted to hysteria. In his excitement the haggard, relaxed expression on his father's face meant nothing to him.

## CHAPTER 5

# CONSULTING THE ORACLE

HARDCASTLE closed the front door. Sally and her mother were left alone in the house.

'Have y' 'ad enough t' eat, lass?' Mrs Hardcastle asked, preparing to clear the table.

Sally murmured an affirmative, linked a leg over the arm of the rocker chair and stared into the fire. She could feel her mother's gaze upon her: knew that she, her mother, was burning with curiosity to have an account of what had transpired on the ramble yesterday. Eagerly, Sally waited her mother's introductory query; listened, impatiently, to the series of nervous coughs with which her mother usually primed herself on such occasions. Oh, why did she hesitate? Couldn't she see that Sally was bursting to confide in her?

Mrs Hardcastle's heart was fluttering. Out of this promising affair of Sally's with Larry Meath, she, Mrs Hardcastle, was stealing a vicarious enjoyment. Already, in her heart, she had built up a wonderful romance out of the situation. It was delectable food to that starved side of her nature whose existence she would not admit even to herself.

But how to introduce the subject? If she asked a direct question Sally might resent it. Children could be very uncommunicative to their parents: there was an even possibility of Sally's answering: 'Mind your own business.' They never thought how their callousness hurt. It wasn't that she wished to interfere: she only wanted to steal a little of Sally's pleasure second-hand. Would Sally understand?

She coughed, nervously, made a great noise with the plates in the enamel wash bowl on the slopstone then ventured, timidly: 'It was late when you come in last night, Sal.' She did not look at her daughter.

'Um,' Sally replied.

Pause.

Sally tapped the pegged rug impatiently.

Mrs Hardcastle sighed, picked up the pot towel and said: 'Ay, he's a nice young man is that Mr Meath. Ah do like him, Ah do.'

Beaming, eyes shining, Sally strained round in her chair: 'D'y' really, ma?' she exclaimed, eagerly.

'Ah do. Ah reckon he's a gentleman,' she answered, emphatically, 'an' a credit t' t' neighbourhood an' ne'er heed what folks say about Labour men.'

Sally, still smiling, relaxed in the chair and stared into space: 'Ay, ma,' she murmured, happily: 'We had a grand time. Over mountains as high as y' never saw. An' he knows names of all the birds,' turning round once again: 'An' he paid me fare! Oh, Ah was in a stew when Ah heard th' others say fare was two shillings an' me wi' only tenpence in me purse,' she blushed at the recollection: 'Ah ne'er knew it'd be so much. But Ah think he knew how Ah was fixed, cos when Ah started t' blush an' stammer – y' know how he smiles, ma? – well, he smiled like that an' said he'd got tickets for both of us an' that it was all right. Though he said it different,' with restrained anxiety: 'He wouldn't ha' done that if he hadn't . . . didn't . . .'

Mrs Hardcastle nodded: 'It was tuk' for granted when Ah was a lass that when a lad paid for y' t' places he meant summat serious.'

Pause.

Sally stared into the fire: 'There was a girl in party that made herself free wi' him. She was tryin' t' rile me, Ah know. But he tuk no notice of her much, an' he kept wi' me all while,' sighing, heavily: 'Oh, Ah love way he talks. An' he's so – so – nice. Ah ne'er enjoyed meself so much in all me life,' brightly: 'An' he asked me would Ah go next time!' fervently: 'Ooo, Ah do hope Ah get some overtime in at mill. Ah want t' get a rig out like rest o' the girls. Ah felt proper out of it against them and their heavy boots an' jerseys and short trousers.'

Mrs Hardcastle looked at Sally with dubiety: 'D' y' think y' father'd like y' t' be dressed like that, Sal?' she murmured.

Sally frowned: 'Aw, who cares what he thinks? Ah'll buy 'um an Ah'll wear 'um. Let him mind his own business.' She folded her arms and glared at the fire. Then her expression relaxed as she pictured herself dressed in the manner desired. Every item would become her; the sweater would reveal the glorious femininity of her figure in such a way as would attract admiring glances. She would wear a vivid coloured bandeau to set off the blackness of her hair. Surely, Larry would be proud of her. She thrilled to see herself swinging along by his side.

Then, remembering the kind of people comprising yesterday's company, she found that she was not so sure of herself. She felt herself to be greatly inferior to them all. It was as though they belonged to a different species. Somehow she identified them as people who could afford pianos and who could play them; people who lived in houses where there were baths. Their conversation, too, was incomprehensible. When the talk turned on music they referred to something called the 'Halley' where something happened by the names of 'Baytoven' and 'Bark' and other strange names. They spoke politics, arguing hotly about somebody named Marks. Yes, they were of a class apart, to whom the mention of a pawnshop, she supposed, would be incomprehensible. Suppose they saw her home; her bedroom! She blushed, ashamed.

Yet, why need she be ashamed? She pouted. Suppose they saw Larry's home? His was no different from her own; it was in the same street, anyway. And, from the respect his opinions had been paid by those who had listened, she had concluded that, of them all, *he* was the superior.

Besides, since he was in no hurry to disavow her on account of her home life, why need she worry about what others might think about it? She almost became indignant with herself for entertaining such thoughts.

Her mother said, with fervour: 'Ay, lass. Ah'd be glad if y' could sekkle down wi' a young man like him. There's so many o' the wrong sort knockin' about these days.'

'Chance is a fine thing,' Sally murmured.

Her mother looked at her with sudden interest: 'Ah say, Sal,' she said: 'Let's go across t' Mrs Jike's. She's a rare 'un for tellin' y' fortune.'

Sally shrugged: 'Oh, that kind o' thing's daft,' she replied, in tones that lacked conviction. She felt a sudden fear, a quick distrust, an apprehensive foreboding. This present happiness, she thought, was too fragile a thing to be trifled with. Yet curiosity grew, tempted her, became irresistible.

'It ain't daft at all,' said her mother: 'Ma Jike tells fortunes true. Come on, let's go across to her house.' She straightened her apron and went to the front door. Sally hesitated for the millionth part of a second, then she followed.

2

As Mrs Hardcastle raised her hand to knock upon Mrs Jike's front door Sally arrested the movement; there was a suggestion of relief in her voice as she said: 'There's no light in house, ma. She must be out. Aw, come on, let's go back home.'

Mrs Hardcastle shook her off then raised a finger to her lips: 'Husht! Her's in.' There came sounds of Mrs Jike's voice speaking within. 'Her's holding a circle t'night, lass,' explained Mrs Hardcastle, 'that's why light's out. If we knock we'll scare spirits away then Ma Jike'll be riled.'

Sitting round a light bamboo table in the pitch dark kitchen were tiny Mrs Jike, withered Mrs Dorbell and stout Mrs Bull. The tips of their fingers rested upon the table top, feet, save Mrs Jike's, were firmly planted on the floor, Mrs Jike's feet rested upon a stool, this elevating her knees to within an inch of the table's underpart. A necessity if communication was to be had with the spirits who conversed through questions and in negatives and affirmatives only. A double knock signified a negative, a treble, an affirmative. Mrs Jike, being the medium through which questions were answered, permitted her knees to supply the necessary motive power.

Addressing the shades, she said: 'Is the spirets present here tonight? Answer three for "yes" and two for "no".' She saw nothing contradictory in the capacity of the 'spirets' to be able to say, in effect, by a double knock: 'Yes, we are not present tonight.'

However, her knee bobbed three times, and three times the table legs bumped upon the floor.

Outside, Mrs Hardcastle said: 'Ay, Ah wisht we'd ha' come sooner. We could ha' joined in circle.'

'Has anybody,' asked Mrs Jike, in businesslike tones: 'Has anybody got anything to ask the spirets about?' She pronounced the word 'spirits' in her peculiar way out of a belief that the pronunciation constituted good manners, which, of course, was essential when presuming to address the departed. One never knew to whom one might be speaking.

'Ya,' said Mrs Dorbell, 'Mrs Nakkle's got a ticket in Irish Sweep an' her wants me t' go shares. Ask spirits if Ah do will ticket draw horse.'

Having read in the newspaper that the odds to anyone's ticket drawing a horse were millions to one against, Mrs Jike concluded that there could only be one answer. The table bumped twice.

'Right. An' thank y',' said Mrs Dorbell: 'Her can keep her owld ticket. Ah want none of it.'

'Hush, Mrs Dorbell, hush,' chided Mrs Jike: 'Spirets don't like too much talking. Any more questions?'

'Ask if Jack Tuttle's there,' suggested Mrs Bull.

Knowing that Mrs Bull had laid out Jack Tuttle only a fortnight ago, and consequently, since he was dead and buried there could be no contradiction as to his whereabouts, Mrs Jike caused the table to bump three times.

'Oh,' said Mrs Bull: 'Y' there, Jack, lad, a' y'?' In the darkness, her companions could not see the roguish twinkle in her eyes: 'Well, hark t' me. When Ah laid thee out, lad, Ah found half-crown i' th' pocket an' Ah wus hard up so Ah tuk it. Ah knew tha wouldna need it where tha's gone, an' Ah'm on'y tellin' y' this so's y'd not think Ah'd pinched it. How d'y' find things where tha art, Jack? Is it owt like that tha thowt it'd be?'

Three bumps.

'Eh, lad,' continued Mrs Bull, hardly able to suppress her smiles as she gazed at Mrs Jike in the gloom: 'Eh, lad, God forgie me for sayin' it, but it tuk thee a long time t' go. For 'ears an' 'ears Ah was expectin' y' goin' every day.'

'Ask questions, Mrs Bull,' interrupted Mrs Jike: 'The spirets don't like y' to be too familiar.'

Mrs Dorbell, whose interest in the seance had flagged now that she had learned what she wished to know, saw Mrs Hardcastle and Sally through the window. She said: 'There's somebody at door, Mrs Jike.'

'Now – !' said Mrs Jike, with simulated annoyance: 'Now y've done it. They've gorn.' She rose and went to the door. 'Oh, it's you, is it, Mrs Hardcastle. An' Sally, too! Well, I never. Come in. Half a mo'. I'll mike a light in back room. There's a fire there and it's more comfortable.'

Sally and her mother entered. Mrs Hardcastle closed the door and said: 'We heard y' havin' circle, so we waited till y' was done.' She added, as the gas popped in the other room, revealing faces: 'How are y', Mrs Bull? How d'y' do, Mrs Dorbell?'

Mrs Dorbell complained of her cough. Mrs Bull, winking at Sally, said: 'Ah just come t' ease me conscience, Mrs 'Ardcastle,' to Sally: 'What's brought you here, lass? Come t' 'ave y' fortune told?'

'Cards or tea leaves?' piped Mrs Jike from the other room. There followed the hollow sound of a marble rolling around the kettle as Mrs Jike lifted the receptacle to see whether or no there was water in it. 'Kekkle's empty,' she said: 'Ik'll have t' be cards. Will y' all come in here, now?'

Sally said, in answer to Mrs Bull: 'Ah don't know why Ah've come, Mrs Bull, cos Ah don't believe in it.'

'Who does?' Mrs Bull chuckled: 'It's a bit o' fun an' it costs nowt.'

'Anyway,' said Mrs Dorbell, blowing her moist nose lusciously, on her filthy apron: 'Anyway, Ah'd ha' bought share o' ticket if spirits had said it was gonna draw horse, fun or no fun. Eee! Fancy me winnin' thirty thousan' quid! Ah'd buy meself a fur coat an' . . .'

'Aye,' Mrs Bull grunted, quite unable to visualize the possibility: 'Aye, an' Ah'd be layin' y' out in a month, drunk t' death, fur coat an' all.'

'Ah'd risk it, too,' sniffed Mrs Dorbell: 'Ah'd have a good once, anyway!'

They all went into the back room where, sitting on the table,

Mrs Jike was shuffling a pack of greasy cards: 'Cut 'um,' she said, to Sally: 'Three times, dearie.'

And, whilst Sally obeyed, Mrs Jike remembered that Ned Narkey had little chance of winning Sally's affections; that there was more likelihood of Larry Meath's success in this direction, and, finally, she did not overlook the fact that rumour had it that Sam Grundy had his eye on Sally. In a word she concluded that Sally was a most fruitful and interesting subject on which to practise her clairvoyance.

Half-heartedly, Sally turned up the ten of spades, the king of diamonds and the knave of hearts. Her mother watched with eager interest, Mrs Dorbell gazed stolidly, Mrs Bull rubbed her nose.

'Strike me pink!' cried Mrs Jike: 'Look at that!' She picked up the king of diamonds: 'Money! Lots of money!'

'In t' bank,' chuckled Mrs Bull.

Mrs Jike ignored her, looking at the card beneath which was the deuce of diamonds: 'And in a two,' she added. To Mrs Hardcastle: 'Might be two weeks or two months, or two years. But there's money, and plenty of it.'

Mrs Hardcastle sighed: 'Ah *do* hope it comes true,' she said, fervently.

'Y'd be daft if y' didn't,' Mrs Bull grunted.

Mrs Jike was shaking her head. She had picked up the ten of spades and was reminded by it of Ned Narkey. She put her mouth to one side and said, to Sally: 'I down't like this here. D'y' know a tall, dark man?'

Sally frowned. The silliness of all this rigmarole was becoming unbearable. She shook her head: 'Think hard, lass,' her mother urged: 'Think hard,' she gazed at her daughter, anxiously.

'Whether y'know one or y' down't,' said Mrs Jike: 'Cards siy there *is* one. He ain't y' colourin'. So be on y' guard. He means dinejer.'

'Tall or short, fair or dark, they're all same if they ain't got no money,' said Mrs Bull, chuckling, irreverently.

'Will y' hush, Mrs Bull, will y' hush,' protested Mrs Jike plaintively.

She picked up the last cut, the knave of hearts: 'Ah,' she said, with relish: '*Here* he is!'

Sally found herself gazing at her mother. Her expression of concentrated undivided attention was sickening. She remembered a time when this kind of thing would have affected her as it now was affecting her mother. She shrank from the thought of what she imagined Larry would think were he to learn of her having been a party to such triviality. She hated herself, flushed hotly. Eyes sparkling, she surprised her mother and Mrs Jike by flaring out with 'Aw, Ah'm sorry Ah came. This is all daft, this is, an' Ah'm going.'

'Well!' gasped Mrs Jike, as Sally left: 'Well!' she gasped, the cards falling from her hand: 'Well! Now – did – y' – ever!'

'Eh, Ah'm sorry for what she's done, Mrs Jike,' mumbled Mrs Hardcastle, apologetically: 'She's a strange, wayward lass, is Sal. An' just when y' was gonna tell her summat about *him*, too!'

Mrs Jike looked hurt and disappointed, a fact noticed by Mrs Dorbell who said, 'Ne'er heed, Mrs Jike, y' can tell us mine.'

Mrs Bull rose to go; she paused by the door gathering her shawl about her, and glancing at Mrs Dorbell's bent-backed, withered, shawl-shrouded frame, said: 'Ah can tell it, lass, an' Ah'm no fortune teller. Tha'll keep on drawin' thy owld age pension and then tha'll dee. Ah'll lay thee out an' parish'll bury y'.' She waddled away, chuckling.

Mrs Jike reshuffled the cards.

CHAPTER 6

LOW FINANCE

MRS NATTLE, pushing a dilapidated bassinette down North Street stopped by the door of No. 35. The soiled card suspended in the window by a piece of dirty string said:

AGENT FOR THE

GOOD SAMARITAN CLOTHING CLUB

Beneath appeared in Mrs Nattle's laborious handwriting:

*Pawning on Comission.     Naybores Obliged.*
*Yours truly Mrs Nattle.*

The triple underscoring had a cryptic significance. It referred to one of Mrs Nattle's illicit and profitable activities. Though this was conducted on very orthodox lines; to be precise, none other than those of the Bank of England's or of any other large money-lending concerns. Having no licence to lend money the triple underscoring of the significant word was a covert advertisement of the opportunities Mrs Nattle offered.

Conducted on very orthodox lines. Interest was charged, security – note of hand, or, preferably, a more material asset – demanded. The markets, or stocks that she watched, and from which she formed her conclusions as to whether or no her prospective patron was safe for a loan – or overdraft – was the labour market. If a woman was reputable and her husband working and of the kind who meets his obligations faithfully, that patron's stock, as it were was gilt edged and a short term loan (seven days) would be forthcoming. Otherwise the application would be referred to Alderman Grumpole who, if he took it up, would pay Mrs Nattle a 'commission' for the introduction of the business. Nobody would have been more surprised than Mrs Nattle to have been told that her business methods were closely related to those of the Bank of England. In this regard, though, she was in the company of that host of credulous Philistines who, though far from being deficient of their full share of capacity, permit themselves to be awed and humbled by the imperious patronizing demeanours of the expert. Philistines whose ordinary common sense leads them, unconsciously, into the successful undertaking of such tasks which, under a different name and in a more luxurious and refined environment, the experts would have everybody believe are capable of performance by themselves only.

She opened her door and walked into the stinking hovel leaving the door wide open so that the house's pestilential odours swept, an inexhaustible river, into the street.

She grunted and emptied the contents of her placket on to the table, pushing up the newspaper tablecloth and the accumulation of soiled crockery so that a foot square or so was left clear. Then she spent a few moments arranging numerous pawn-tickets in rows, placing upon each the appropriate amount of money. When she had finished, the table's corner had a resemblance to a game of draughts.

With another grunt Mrs Nattle seated herself to wait.

Presently, sluthering footsteps sounded, footsteps of someone who was wearing shoes or slippers far too large for their feet: accompanying came the sounds of someone's speaking to themselves. The footsteps halted by the door and a voice asked: 'A' y' in, missis?'

'Is that you, Nancy?'

Nancy shuffled in. It was Mrs Dorbell, shawl wrapped tightly about her skinny person, dewdrop at the end of her beak-like nose: 'Ah,' she grunted, staring at Mrs Nattle with rheumy gaze: 'Ah, y' there. Ah must ha' missed y'.'

'Sit down, lass. Mek thisel' at home.'

Mrs Dorbell complied, sighing. 'Ne'er,' she began: 'Ne'er got a wink o' sleep agen las' night. Cough, cough, cough, cough till Ah could hardly breathe.' Mrs Dorbell's way of telling her friend that her cough had kept her awake for about a quarter hour: 'Ah'd give owt for a nip, Ah would,' a long sigh: 'Ay, Mrs Nakkle, glad Ah am as y've tuk my advice. Ah knew as y' wouldn't be out o' pocket wi' it.' She glanced at Mrs Nattle who was regarding her with mute interrogation. She nodded and concluded: 'The oosual.'

Without answering, Mrs Nattle rose, placed a chair near the cupboard, opened the door, stood on the chair seat and strained after something on the top shelf. There followed the 'chink-chink' of glass against glass; her hand reappeared gripping the neck of a whisky bottle. Her other hand sought the cupboard for a number of small glasses. She stepped down with a jog and a grunt. Mrs Dorbell, eyeing the bottle with alarm, urged her to be careful.

Mrs Nattle could not answer since she had withdrawn the bottle's cork with her teeth where she held it so that it looked as though she was smoking the butt end of a cigar; then she lifted a small glass in a line with her eye and poured out a minute quantity of spirits with the care of a pharmacist dispensing a poison prescription. She replaced the cork and glanced at Mrs Dorbell who was licking her lips furtively: 'Drop o' hot water?' she asked. Mrs Dorbell shook her head and produced her purse from beneath her shawl: 'Thrippence,' said Mrs Nattle, and the transaction was complete.

'Habout that there sweep ticket,' said Mrs Nattle, picking the threepence up: ' 'Ave y' decided?'

Mrs Dorbell raised the glass to her nose and took a long sniff. She did not put it to her lips. Queen Victoria, in a chipped picture frame with a broken glass, looked down upon Mrs Dorbell as she answered: 'Ah've decided Ah ain't botherin' . . . Ah can't afford it.' Mrs Nattle grunted and a pause ensued.

The growing silence was dismissed by the sounds of more than one pair of approaching feet; voices conversed; the footsteps halted outside the open door. Instantly, Mrs Nattle whipped the bottle off the table and concealed it beneath her dirty apron. Mrs Dorbell placed the hand holding the glass beneath her shawl. Both women assumed expressions of bleak innocence.

The visitors entered. Mrs Nattle, identifying them all, sighed, replaced the bottle and said, apropos its concealment: 'Pays y' t' be careful, these days.'

Mrs Bull eyed the bottle and voiced a monosyllabic exclamation: 'Huh! paused and added: 'Three penn'orth. *Some*body's bin doin' 'emselves well. Bokkle was nearly full yesterday.' She eyed Mrs Nattle suspiciously.

Mrs Nattle, however, was attending to those 'naybores' whom she had 'obligded' on 'comission', shy, retiring types of womanhood for the most part. To have asked them to do their own pawning would have been asking the impossible; their consciences never would have forgiven them had once they passed through Mr Price's shop door. Happily, the enormity of the crime was lessened when indulged vicariously; Mrs Nattle's services were a blessing. They accepted pawn-ticket and money gratefully from Mrs Nattle who first deducted the few coppers 'comission', then they disappeared, each to her own way which, doubtless, led to some local hovel within whose walls were daily played the same scenes by the same cast with brain-dulling monotony.

The transactions were completed, everybody satisfied. Mrs

Nattle announced, with a gleam of pride in her eyes: 'Promp' sekklements, that's me. 'An'some is 's 'an'some does, say I, an've allus said it an' allus will,' to Mrs Bull: 'Now, Mrs Bull, threepenn'orth, y'said?'

'Aye, 'n luk sharp about it. Froat's nearly cut,' with a sour expression: '*Some* folks know how t' make money, by gum they do! Agent for owld Grumpole's clubs, pawnin' f' naybores, obligin', wi' three lines under it, an' sellin' nips. Ah'll bet y've a tidy pile hid away somewhere i' this house, Sair Ann!' Mrs Dorbell shifted in her seat: she had always thought exactly the same and nursed a secret hope concerning the hidden pile that, should ever Mrs Nattle drop down dead in the house, she, Mrs Dorbell, would be lucky enough to make the discovery. She had everything planned in readiness for such an eventuality. Though, to repeat, this was a secret.

Sair Ann, first measuring out the nip with customary care, replaced the cork and said, in answer to Mrs Bull: 'When a 'ooman's left a widder her's got t' do *summat* t' live. Thrippence, please.'

More footsteps outside: disappearance of bottle and glasses.

'It's ownly me,' said a voice, and Mrs Jike, the tiny lady from London, wearing an old cap of her husband's, a shawl loose about her shoulders, entered the house: 'Ay,' she said: 'I've ownly jest got thet blowke o' mine off to work.' She set threepence upon the table, sat down next Mrs Dorbell on the couch, tipped the cap over her eyes and scratched the back of her head: 'He jest wown't gow to work wivout his dinner beer money. Cont'ary, cont'ary through an' through, like all the rest o' the men,' brightly, as she set her cap straight, composed her hands on her bosom and gave herself a tiny hug. 'Well, gels, how are y'all this morning?' reaching out her snuff-box: ' 'Ere, have a pinch o' Birdseye, gels.'

Mrs Dorbell raised her mournful eyes and skeletonic yellow hand, took a pinch and sniffed it in with the dewdrop. Mrs Nattle passed Mrs Jike a nip, picked up the threepence and helped herself to the snuff as did Mrs Bull, who, lowering the glass from her mouth said: 'Yaa – Ah don't know what's comin' o'er folk these days. Ah remember time when ne'er a

day hardly passed without there was a confinement or a layin'
out to be done,' bitterly: 'Young 'uns ain't havin' childer as they
should. An' them as die're bein' laid out by them as they belong
to which weren't considered respectable in th'owld days. When
Ah was a gel a 'ooman wasn't a 'ooman till she'd bin i' childbed
ten times not countin' miscarriages. Aaach! How d' they expect a body t' mek a livin' when childer goin' t' school know
more about things than we did arter we'd bin married 'ears?'
Nobody had an explanation to offer.

Mrs Dorbell fetched a deep sigh: 'Things,' she said, dismally,
'Things ain't bin same since genklefolk left th'owld Road,' her
reference was to the bosky Eccles Old Road, the westerly con-
tinuation of Broad Street which runs at the top of Hanky Park.
Until the coming of the electric trams in the early years of
the century, the Old Road was the place of residence of many
millionaires whose source of wealth was cotton plus seven
generations of operatives to each of masters. In those days the
road was termed 'millionaires' mile'. The mansions still remain.
'I' *them* days,' Mrs Dorbell continued, 'I' *them* days a body
could allus depend on summat new t' pawn,' reminiscently:
'Ay, aye, Ah remember when Ah was a likkle gel how my owld
ma – God rest her soul i' peace – ' she crossed herself with the
hand that held the glass: 'My owld ma used t' fetch us all in
out o' street when charity ladies came round i' their kerridges
hinquirin' for them as wus hard up: "Come on, now," she used
t' say: "Off'n wi' them pinnies an' y' clogs an' stockin's." Then
she'd send us out into street an' ladies'd tek us names for a new
rig out. Ay, many a bright shillin' they've fetched at pawnshop. Many an' many a bright shillin'. Y' don't see nowt like
that nowadays. If y've got nowt y' get nowt an' nobody cares.
Ah, aye, oh 'twas a sad day for likes of us when kerridge folk
left th' Owld Road. If my owld ma was alive t' see things t'day
she'd turn o'er in her grave, indeed she would.'

Mrs Jike, who had been shaking her head all the while,
sighed: 'The world's ne'er been the sime since the old Queen
died.' She eyed her Majesty on the wall with reverence: 'Look
at Lenden! I see in me piper this morning as they're havin'
boxin' matches in the 'Elbert 'All!' scandalized: 'The 'Elbert*

'*All*!' holding up a hand then narrowing her eyes: 'Eh, *she'd* give 'em snuff if she were alive. She would thet. But they wouldn't ha' dared t' done it. Naow ... I mind the time when she was alive – Phoo! Talk about gentry! Strike me pink! Y' couldn't get wivin miles and *miles* o' the 'Elbert 'All for kerridges 'n pairs. *Real* gentry they were, too; none o' y' jumped-up uns; wore fortunes on their backs,' a sigh and a shake of the head: 'Look at 'Elbert 'All now – Boxin' matches ...' words failed her.

Mrs Nattle uncorked the bottle and poured out for herself an outsize nip. She wished all present a good health, sipped, took a deep breath preparatory to saying something when furtive footsteps at the door caused a general concealment of evidence: 'Who's there?' cried Mrs Nattle, staring with mixed apprehension and suspicion at the door.

Mrs Hardcastle poked her head round the door, smiled at Mrs Nattle ingratiatingly, then, as she noticed the other old women, her smile faded, she licked her lips and made as though to withdraw, saying: 'Ah, didn't know y' 'ad comp'ny, Mrs Nakkle.'

'Oh, come in, lass, come in,' responded Mrs Nattle, warmly. Evidence reappeared; all breathed more freely.

'It'll do agen when y' ain't busy,' said Mrs Hardcastle: 'Ah'm in no 'urry.' Mrs Nattle repudiated the idea of being busy. She pressed Mrs Hardcastle to state her requirements.

'Well,' said Mrs Hardcastle, hesitantly, shooting nervous glances at everybody: 'It's ... Ah – Y'see, Mrs Nakkle, our Harry wants a new suit.'

'Oh,' said Mrs Nattle: 'Y' mean y' want a club check?' Mrs Hardcastle beamed, relieved. 'That's easy sekkled. How much did y' want it for, Mrs Hardcastle?'

'Well,' she said indecisively: 'He did say he wanted it made t' measure.'

'He'll get one for three pahnds, Mrs Hardcastle,' said Mrs Jike, 'Which is wot I pide for my ole man's.'

Mrs Hardcastle agreed to the sum. Laboriously, Mrs Nattle filled up a form of application requiring much information, of Hardcastle's occupation, length of tenancy at 17 North Street, name and address of his employers, how long he had worked there and in what capacity. 'Get y' 'usbant t' sign here, missis, then Ah'll see as owld Grumpole gets it an' he'll send th' inspector t' see y' rent an' insurance books so's he can tell whether y're a good payer. Then y'll get check. . . . There'll be three bob interest t'pay afore y' get it then there'll be three bob a week for twenty weeks. Y'understand?' Mrs Hardcastle nodded and took the form of application.

Mrs Bull, glancing at the ceiling, said, off hand: 'Y'can put me down, too, for a check for five pounds, Sair Ann.'

Had Mrs Bull been looking at Sair Ann a glance at her expression would have been enough: 'Ah'll do nowt o' t' kind,' she said: 'Wot about last one y' had?' to the others: 'Went an' sold it for fifty bob cash down an' made owld Grumpole sing for his money cause he knows it ain't no use puttin' *her* in court, bein' as she can tell beak a good tale and ain't got change for a penny,' gazing at Mrs Bull: 'Five pounds, indeed. Huh! Such as you as get street a bad name. Grumpole's talking about puttin' it on blacklist.'

'Oh,' said Mrs Hardcastle, eagerly: 'Me 'usbant'll be a good payer all right. He don't believe i' checks an' weekly payments. He ain't comfortable owin' debts. . . . But what can y' do?'

Mrs Bull grunted: 'That 'usbant o' thine's got a lot t' learn, Mrs 'Ardcastle, a lot – to – learn. They can't get blood out of a stone, an' while Ah can get tick (credit) somewhere, well, here's one wot doesn't intend t' go owt short. Y'dead a long while, an Ah've had a bellyful o'sorrer if Ah ne'er have no more.' She drained her glass at a gulp, passed it back to Mrs Nattle and said: 'Gie's another threepenn'orth, Sair Ann . . .'

Mrs Hardcastle, knowing of nothing else to say, excused herself. A few days later Harry obtained his new suit.

# THE SMILE OF FORTUNE

IT was staggering, paralysing, incredible, unique.

As the news flew round people came out of their homes stare eyed, followed the crowd to the back entry where, if the congregation and their animated conversation were any indication, a murder, surely, had been committed.

The back entry was shaped in a triangle and was the place where Sam Grundy, the street corner bookmaker, received the threepenny, sixpenny and shilling bets of the neighbouring population. It wanted five minutes to six o'clock. Sam, or, as should be said, his hireling, commenced paying out winnings at six precisely. Except on special occasions Sam kept to the background, the business like others that are profitable, being illicit. Business was conducted over a backyard door, the clerk in charge standing on a chair seat on the other side of the bolted door.

The atmosphere was electric: people still flowed into the back entry through the three openings, where, at each, an unemployed man, unable to find other occupation offered himself ostensibly as paid sentinel to keep a look-out for Two Cities policemen, all of whom knew that at any day and at the appropriate time, law-breakers could have been arrested by the score. For some reason or other their beats took them elsewhere than the back entry's vicinity during Sam's business hours. Though, occasionally, plain clothes men did come upon the scene to take away the sentinels whose fines were paid by Sam. Though Sam looked upon this expenditure as a kind of rent due to the law for permitting his transgressions.

Passers by, their curiosity aroused by the general commotion, swelled the numbers, interrogating their nearest neighbour with a whispered, urgent: 'What's up? What's happened?' and darting quick glances at the house backs as though expecting to see flames consuming one of them. Here and there were closely packed groups peering over the shoulders of people engaged in making calculations on the margins of their newspapers. Now and again when the calculations were concluded, hats were pushed to the backs of heads followed by whistles expressive of incredulity.

'. . . Aye, an' he's had a thripp'ny treble every week for last three years. This is fust time it's come up. . . . Twenty-two quid for thrippence. What d'y' think o' that? He ain't twenty 'ear old, yet, either!'

Incredulously: 'Twenty-two quid for thrippence? – Yaaah. Some hopes.'

'True as God's above. Thrippence win on a twenty t' one chance, that's five an' three; all on Jackdaw, that won three o'clock at twenty t' one, that made it o'er five quid, an' he played it all on Tea Rose in three-thirty an *that* come up at three t' one. What d'y' think o' that?'

'An' will Sam Grundy pay him?'

'Ah, now y're askin' summat. That's what we're all here to see. If he does then he gets all my bets in future, you bet he will. Aye, there's lad o'er yonder. . . . Him as won, Ah mean.'

Harry, cap pushed up from his brow, white mercerized cotton scarf disarranged about his neck, stood right up to the back door a set smile of nervousness on his lips. The evening newspaper which he held in his hand was opened at the page giving the day's racing returns.

A stupor lay on his brain; now and again his skin crept and he shivered when his gaze fell upon the calculations he had made on his newspaper. Whenever anybody spoke to him he laughed, hysterically, scarcely hearing a word they said. His mind was plagued by an oft-recurring vision of himself coming out of Marlowe's half an hour previously, Jack Lindsay had bought a paper to see which horses had won; Harry, glancing over his shoulder as they walked along had eyed the results in such a manner as he had done ever since he first had indulged in the weekly bet, that was, in a furtive hope of the speculation proving profitable.

His first horse had won, he noticed. That wasn't anything new. 'Got one winner home, Jack,' he murmured. His eyes roved the three o'clock race: 'Jackdaw. . . .' He stared, licked his lips: 'Two up,. Jack,' he put an arm about Jack's shoulder: 'Have a luk at three-thirty. .... Ah played all on Tea Rose. It'll be on back page; stop press,' he grinned: 'It'll ha' let me down, you bet.'

Jack obliged: 'It's won,' he said, casually, not having paid any attention to Harry's remarks: bluffing was not unknown among them.

Harry stopped: 'Y' what?' he whispered, gripping Jack's shoulder. Bill Lindsay and Tom Hare, following a pace at the rear, also stopped.

''Ere,' complained Jack, shaking his shoulder free: 'What y' doin'. . . . Leggo.'

Harry snatched the paper from him; his face was white. He looked from the paper to Jack and said, weakly: 'Ah've gorra treble home. ... Two twenty t' one chances all on a three t'one ... !' They expressed their disbelief unequivocally. Harry's trembling hand produced a copy of the bet. They read it and stared at him, awed.

They were blocking the pavement; crowds of other young men and apprentices were passing; they cursed them and told them to get out of the way. Bill Simmons, with a dazed air, said to a passing group: ''Arry 'Ardcastle's got a treble home.' The others stopped, curious. The group swelled in numbers. A crowd was soon attracted. Somebody asked for a pencil: a voice cried, breathlessly: 'Twenty-two quid. ... Bloody hell!' The first part of the phrase passed from lip to lip accompanied by glances of sheer amazement. Harry, mystified, gaped at Jack Lindsay; Jack grinned: 'Good owld Harry,' he said generously: 'Ah hope Sam Grundy pays up. .... Sky's limit wi' him, so he ses . . .'

Congratulations from all sides; everybody wanted to shake Harry's hand. He commenced to laugh, hysterically; still doubted his luck. And the little shop boy who ran Harry's errands and who brewed tea for him, pushed forward to stand by Harry's side, grinning and preening himself in the warmth of the reflected glory he was snatching from Harry. Something to remember for ever.

A few moments later saw Harry, Bill, Jack and Tom running

homewards pell mell. Harry went directly to Grundy's deserted back entry where he stood, leaning and panting against the appropriate door.

Jack, Bill and Tom flew into North Street to apprise, first the Hardcastles then the rest of the neighbours. News spread; teas were left go cold; all roads led to the back entry.

Cap pushed up from his brow, white mercerized cotton scarf disarrayed about his neck, Harry stood right up to the back door, a set smile of nervousness on his dry lips. The crowd about him spoke to him often; he laughed, scarce hearing a word they said.

Footsteps sounded in the backyard. Sam didn't live here; he had a fine residence in a middle-class suburb; he rented the back portion of the house. Conversation in the entry subsided as by magic: in the silence that ensued carts could be heard rumbling over the setts of the main street two hundred yards away.

The back door opened; an unprecedented occurrence. A small, upturned box was to be seen ready as for the reception of an orator. A buzz of murmured conversation arose from the crowd accompanied by much neck straining as a small fat man, broad set, with beady eyes, an apoplectic complexion, came out of the house, crossed the tiny backyard and stood upon the upturned box, thumbs in waistcoat armholes. Preposterous-sized diamonds ornamented his thick fingers and a cable-like gold guard, further enhanced by a collection of gold pendants, spade guineas and Masonic emblems, hung heavily across his prominent stomach. He chewed a match stalk; his billycock rested on the back of his head; he wore spats. Self-confidence and gross prosperity oozed from him. The notorious Sam Grundy himself.

He gazed, paternally, upon the trembling Harry: 'So y' thought y'd brek bank, eh, lad?' Roars of obsequious laughter from all sides. Sam was popular.

Standing immediately behind Harry was Ned Narkey, upper lip elevated in a half-smiling leer, and Ted Munter, the Marlowe time clerk. Ted put his hand to his mouth, glanced at Sam through his thick pebble spectacles, then strained to Ned's ear:

'Luk at him, Ned, lad,' he said, apropos Sam: 'Ah knew him when he'd no breeches arse to his pants. Me an' him ran a crown an' anchor board i' th' army. Pots o' money we made. He saved his, but me, like a bloody fool as've allus bin, blewed it in on women and wine. . . . Eeee, if on'y Ah'd me time t' go o'er agen.'

'Bloody women an' wine, eh?' muttered Narkey. 'Yaaah!' He lifted his lip, turned his head stiffly, and spat. The spittle missed a bystander by the fraction of an inch. He glared at Ned who scowled back contemptuously then turned his great bulk away to regard Sam Grundy who, now, hands thrust deep into pockets was jingling his loose money noisily.

'You know, young fellow me lad,' cried Sam, loudly: 'You know, some bookies have a limit. Y' know that, don't y', eh?' continuing, before Harry had time to answer: 'There's fellers as call 'emselves bookies as'd on'y pay y' a fiver on your bet an' no more,' taking off his billycock and gazing about at the assembled crowd as though in acknowledgement of applause: '*That* ain't honest Sam Grundy.'

'Good owld Sam . . .' from many lips.

'Honest Sam's gotta motter – "Sky's the limit". – This here young feller me lad,' indicating Harry with a sweep of the hand: 'This here young feller me lad had a thrippenny treble,' turning round cautiously and resting a hand on the coping of the backyard wall: 'Charlie,' he cried, 'fetch a chair.' The man, Charlie, a tall, thin, consumptive-looking individual, hurried to obey: 'Stand up alongside o' me, son,' said Sam. Harry complied. 'Now, you had a bet wi' me, lad, didn't y'?' Harry nodded, blushing deeply under the concerted gazes of the crowd. 'How much were it, lad?' Sam shouted.

'Thrippence,' mumbled Harry, palpitantly.

'Speak up, lad, there's nowt t' be ashamed on. There ain't nobody here as wouldn't gie' ten pun t' be in your shoes,' to everybody: 'Eh?' Tumult. Sam held up his hand: 'Now, lad, speak up: How much were the bet? Turn t' t' crowd, son, turn t' t' crowd.'

Harry, gazing over the housetops, bawled: 'Thrippence.'

'An' how much d'y' reckon t' draw for y' thrippence?'

Harry went very red, gazed at Sam guiltily and whispered: 'Twenty-two quid.'

'Now, Harry,' said Sam, with good-natured reproach: 'Y' can speak louder'n that. The ladies and gents at back can't hear y'. Up, now, out wi' it.'

Harry mastered his shyness with a supreme effort and shouted: 'Twenny-two quid.' A universal sigh; a buzz of murmuring.

Sam lit a cigar, leisurely: 'Twenny-two quid for thrippence. How many bookies'd pay out that much?' No answer; a respectful silence. 'Well, y' all know Honest Sam's motter ...' half turning: 'Charlie. ...' Charlie appeared with a handful of notes which he passed to Honest Sam.

'What's Honest Sam's motter, Harry?' Sam asked. Harry, at the sight of the money, turned to the crowd and bawled, hysterically: 'Sky's limit.'

'Hold out y' cap, Harry, lad.'

A wave of restlessness on the part of the crowd; it surged forward simultaneously; necks strained, eyes bulged, as, one by one, Sam dropped twenty-two one-pound notes into Harry's cap. Everybody counted them fascinatedly as they fell. At the last Sam turned to the crowd, held out his billycock at arm's length and cried: '*That's* Honest Sam for y'. Wot can't speak can't lie.' He paused, saved further breath out of regard of the noisy expressions of admiration rising on all sides. Carefully, he stepped from the box and tapped the smiling bewildered Harry on the shoulder as he, Harry, was about to push his way through the crowd hugging his cap to his bosom jealously: 'Hey, Harry lad,' said Sam, a genial expression on his face: 'Ain't that your sister, young Sal?' Ned Narkey, overhearing the question, narrowed his eyes; his lips became thin lines; the tips of his strong yellow teeth could be seen; he clenched his fist and glared at Sam, resentfully.

'Ain't that your sister, young Sal?' Sam's question.

'Oh, aye,' Harry answered, wondering what Sally could have to do with this.

Sam nodded and smiled, thrust his hands into his pockets and rattled his money: 'Don't you forget to treat her, then. D'y'

hear, young fellow me lad. ... Tell her as Ah've said she's t'
have a couple o' quid out o' y' winnin's for some new clo'es.
An' think on, Ah'll ask her if y' have done when Ah see her.'
He patted Harry upon the shoulder: 'Better go through th' 'ouse,'
turning: 'Charlie, show Harry t' t' front door.' Harry followed.

Sam turned also and was about to pass through the back door
when Ned Narkey tapped him on the shoulder: 'Hey, you,' he
said, thickly: 'What's y' game wi' Sal Hardcastle, eh?'

Sam stared, astonished, not a little nervous of Ned's threatening demeanour: 'What d' y' mean, Ned?' he answered, with a
weak attempt at bluster.

'Don't "Ned" me. ... You know what Ah mean,' snapped
Ned, his enormous chest inflating: 'You've got women all o'er
place. ... Ah know. ... Kate Gayley was mine when Ah'd a
pocket full o' dough. ... Shuts bloody door i' me face sin' you
tuk her out in y' car. Told me she'd cut me out cos she was
feared o' neighbours talkin' an' gettin' her widder's pension
stopped. ... Ah ain't daft, though. But you can keep the bitch.'

'Aw,' murmured Sam, pacifically, shooting furtive glances
this way and that: 'Aw ...' he laid a friendly hand on Ned's
arm: 'Now, Ned, lad. Now, Ned ...'

Ned shook it off, impatiently: 'Yaa! Cut that out; y' can't soft
soap me!' His angry tones and the impatient gesture attracted
the attention of a number of the immediate bystanders. Their
conversations concerning Harry ceased instantly and were forgotten. They stared at Sam and Ned and came closer, all ears.
Ted Munter blinked, and such was his envy of his erstwhile
army comrade's post-war success in the bookmaking line that
he fondly hoped this totally unexpected occurrence would cul-
minate in Ned's giving Sam a thoroughly humiliating public
thrashing. Sam Grundy! Paah! Sam who always treated him,
Ted, as though he were invisible, as though they were strangers,
as though the gambling partnership of their army days had
never existed. Go on, Ned, lad, bash him; wipe the floor with
him; tumble his maddening, gross, intolerable prosperity into
the gutter; prosperity, that, but for the fool I was, I would now
be sharing. With such thoughts in mind Ted, suddenly perceiving in the situation a chance of ingratiating himself into Sam's

favours, gave his belt a hitch and said, with effusive amiability: 'Aw.... *Carm* on, Ned. Carm on into t' yard.... Y' don't want everybody listenin' t' y' business.' He took Ned by the arm and gently urged him into the yard. Sam, staring with fear, followed. Ted, assuming control of the situation, closed and bolted the back door and cried, dictatorially: 'Charlie.... Begin payin' out. Quick about it man, quick about it. Toot sweet!'

Charlie, a leather bag full of money slung about his person, jumped on to the chair seat to attend to the claimants for winnings who pushed about the back door. Ted, breathing freely, assumed a genial expression, thrust his thumbs into his broad leather belt and stared at Sam paternally, a high hope in his mind that, as a reward for his masterly control of a difficult situation, Sam, surely, would satisfy the ambition of a lifetime in giving him a working interest in the bookmaking business.

Sam, having recovered some of his lost composure, held out an appealing hand toward Ned: 'Now luk here, Ned,' he began: 'You've got me all wrong,' raising his greasy brows: 'Ah was on'y kiddin' the lad about his sister,' a forced laugh: 'Why, man, Ah don't know the lass. An' Ah'm old enough t' be her father!'

'Aye,' replied Ned, unimpressed: 'Y're owld enough t' be Annie Smith's grandfather. But that didn't keep her from goin' t' that there whorin' house o' yourn i' Wales, did it, eh? Aye, an' all t'other judies y' keep,' raising his great clenched fist to within a half inch of Sam's purple nose, adding, warningly: 'Think on, now, Grundy. Keep y' paws off'n Sal Hardcastle. If anybody has her it's gonna be me. D'y' hear?'

'Course, Ned, course. You have her ... *Ah* don't want nowt t' do wi' her.' He continued, strenuously repudiating any evil intention towards Sal, meanwhile, boiling inwardly at the necessity of having to hold the candle to the bullying of such a penniless lout as Narkey. Still, Ned had to be pacified; his reputation for brawling had been earned by deeds and not by words, and a blow from one of those immense fists of his, irrespective of the unwelcome and humiliating publicity – for Ned was boastful in his cups – would be extremely painful. Imagine this situation, though, he, the great Sam Grundy, having his desires thwarted; he, whose potent purse and patient persistence had never failed, yet, in consummating his illicit sexual desires; it was goading to think that in Sal Hardcastle, the latest, best and most disturbing of all his desires, a precedent might be created in Ned Narkey's interference.

'Think on,' said Ned, concluding: 'Hands off Sal Hardcastle. . . . If she's gonna be anybody's she gonna be mine. An' ah feels sorry for anybody wot tries any games on wi' her.' He turned his back on Ted and Sam, and, bracing his magnificent shoulders, stamped into the house and through the front door.

Ted, thumbs in waistcoat armholes, eyed Sam with an expectant and expansive smile: 'Well, Sam, lad,' he said, ingratiatingly:'Ah . . .'

'You, y' bloody fool,' Sam interrupted, thickly: 'What did y' want t' bring that big – in this here yard for?'

Ted, astonished, held out an appealing hand and opened his mouth. Sam scowled: 'Yaaa! Get out o' me sight. . . .' He turned on his heel and left Ted standing there, mouth gaping, blinking, like a fool.

CHAPTER 8

## MAGIC CASEMENTS

REMOVED from it as he now was he reviewed it with intense pleasure. The commotion in North Street yesterday, this, for the second time in the month! Which had been the most pleasurable? The occasion of Sam Grundy's paying him the money or that of yesterday, the preparations for departure to this glorious place?

He saw himself coming down the street at noon yesterday, smiling, self-consciously, laughingly ignoring the forest of upstretched hands accompanied by childish piping appeals for pennies. No, he told himself, he had not done wrong in not distributing largesse amongst the children. He had given a sufficient portion of the proceeds of his good fortune gratuitously. Less than half of it remained after he had given a proportionate share to his parents, Sally, and Helen whom he had insisted should spend her share on new clothes.

Then, of course, there was Jack Lindsay and the rest; they all expected treating. Neither could the shop boy who ran the errands be overlooked, and in the boy's wide-eyed amazement on receiving a half-crown, Harry saw himself years ago, responding, similarly, to Billy Higgs's generosity.

The remainder of the money burned to be spent; its possession filled him with a sense of the carefree; bewildered him. What could he do with it? Nay, what *couldn't* he do with it?

His father settled the question for him. And his father's suggestion recalled the daring thought he had rashly uttered to Helen as they had sat watching the trains from Dawney's Hill long ago.

'Harry, lad,' said his father, quietly: 'Y're on'y young once an Ah've ne'er had enough money t' tek y' away. So if Ah was you, Ah'd tek that lass o' thine away on a holiday. Me an' y' ma 'd on'y one in us lives; but it were worth it an' neither on us 'll forget it.' He glanced at his wife who was standing by the table staring unseeing and smiling at the recollection: a strange, rare smile that smoothed away, quite, that expression of worried preoccupation which habitually dominated her features. She looked even young. ' 'Twas worth it, eh, lass?' Hardcastle's stern, honest countenance relaxed; he, too, was smiling.

'Oh, go on wi' y',' she murmured, blushing shyly.

Sally laughed; her gorgeous eyes twinkled: 'Oh, pa, why don't y' kiss her. She's blushing!'

An atmosphere of warmth, affection and light-heartedness suffused the room.

'Aye,' continued Hardcastle, a reminiscent light in his eyes: 'Aye, Sal, lass, me an' y' ma had a gradely time, then. 'Twas th' on'y time we e'er had away but Ah'll ne'er forget it,' a sigh, then, to Harry: 'Y'll spend y' money on summat or other, lad, so y' may as well spend it on summat y'll remember.'

Five days was decided upon: Marlowe's would not permit him longer leave of absence.

Where to go was the problem until Larry Meath suggested a place where he once had spent a few days. He also obliged by writing the letter to the woman at the boarding-house. And he excited Harry by describing the place; harbour, rugged coast line, glorious country walks, such intimations as provoked Harry to a tingle of impatience.

When, in his eagerness of relating Larry's descriptions to Sally, he saw no significance in her sighs, her pensiveness, nor, for a moment, could he translate anything other than curiosity in her question: 'Did anybody go with him when he went?'

He shook his head: 'Ah dunno. Why?'

She shrugged her shoulders but did not answer, turned, rested a foot on the fender and stared into the fire. He regarded her with sympathetic gaze. He couldn't understand her affair – was there an affair? – with Larry. There was nothing definite about it, at least, from what he could gather. Sally was so reticent. Yet there could be no doubting her inclinations: he had never before known her to be so affected: her eagerness, sometimes, with which she interrogated him concerning Larry was almost painful to see; certainly he felt uncomfortable on such occasions. Of course, everybody knew that Larry Meath never bothered with girls; he was always too preoccupied with incomprehensible affairs up at the Labour Club. It was hard on Sally, though, if she thought so much about him. Still, what business was this of his. He now was away on holiday; it was foolish to mar these precious days, by revolving such depressing thoughts. Away on holiday! Free as a bird! Alone with Helen! Helen!

To her all was of the quality of a sweet dream: too sweet; caused one to move about in a trance-like state of incredulity half the time. How different, ineffably different from the crude, vulgar warnings of the married women at the mill who had offended her ears by references to the opportunities she and Harry would have for sexual indulgences. The prospect had been almost spoilt by their unpleasant suggestions. How different, though, reality.

Comparing the boarding-house with her home was not possible: there was nothing at all in common between them.

Here, the bedroom's furnishings, cold bare lino, tiny chest of drawers, small, flecked cheval mirror, iron bed, chair and the washstand with its large water beaker and chipped bowl, represented something quite foreign to her experience. It had two priceless, intangible qualities; it was clean; there was privacy. To have a room in which she could be secure from trespass once she closed the door! The luxury of a bed to herself! She did not know what to make of it. She lay awake for long periods revelling in the delightful novelty of such an environment: she even grudged her sleep, after a fashion. Though, to close one's eyes and to listen, lulled, by the murmuring of the sea, was irresistible.

Sunday, and the endless prospect of a whole week in front of them: repeatedly, Harry murmured: 'Ah say, Helen. Just fancy, all next week an' no work t' go to.' They stared at each other, smiling, marvelling.

This unusual mode of life was full of witchery; for the first two or three days they were unappreciative of their surroundings: wearing the wide-eyed expressions of a couple of children lost in fairyland they wandered, arm in arm, the lanes and the cliff paths, sat on the springy turf and stared into the haze over the wrinkled shimmering sea, inarticulate, enthralled.

'Ain't it champion, Helen?' he murmured, on a sigh.

'It's like what y' see on pictures,' she murmured, in reply: she, too, sighed, lay back on the turf and said happily: 'It makes me feel as though I want to do nowt but sleep.'

All was different here: sunshine and even the rain. Once they were caught in a lane by a shower, and, when it had ceased, they were fascinated by its quick evaporation: patches of damp dappled the road's surface; over all a fresh serenity breathed and lingered; the rain cloud, silvered at its edges rolled away; gulls sailed in the vivid blue, calling plaintively.

The natives were objects of reverence, their white-walled cottages of awe. To *live* here was something incredible; it was unimaginable that people should live ordinary lives in a place where others came to holiday. Holiday! 'Green days in forests and blue days at sea.' In a small rowing-boat following the rugged coast line to the south and on an evening when the sea was as motionless as a child asleep, the sky a fading blue from end to end. Air was still; day dying peacefully. Sometimes the sea would gurgle musically in an unseen rocky cleft; occasionally the creaking of the rowlocks and the plop of the oar blades insinuated themselves to the ears of Harry and Helen; then the sounds would recede and a delicious indolence drug the brain; the gaze dawdled idly on such things as the swirl left by the oars or the sparkling drops dripping from the blades.

Helen trailed a hand in the water; it was cold, slightly numbing; the chilly element saddened her; she stared, pensively, unseeing.

'What 're y' thinkin' about, Helen?' Harry, smiling, was gazing at her.

She listened to the creaking of the rowlocks and the dip of the oars, translated from the sounds a melancholy significance. Staring at her submerged fingers she answered, tonelessly: 'Just think, Harry, we've got t' go back t' Hanky Park ... leave all this behind. *Got* to.'

He shipped the oars, slowly, allowed the boat to drift. Sounds of sea birds' querulous cries echoed up the cliff faces; deep down on the sea bed and through the lucid water he could perceive, vaguely, purple patches, and, where the sea floor rose could discern the long weeds waving in the currents. Where the waves rose on the rocks they did not break; with oily silence they submerged their mark, receded and left a glistening line. A glimmer of the significance of the word 'beautiful' began to dawn on him, and, even though it yet bewildered him, what was meant by its opposite 'unbeautiful' struck him vividly. Hanky Park was unbeautiful. Hanky Park and all that it stood for to which they *had* to return. North Street, smoke, bricks and mortar, seas of slates, Price and Jones, Sam Grundy, Mrs Nattle and her companions, swarms of dirty children. A goading, incredible, awful fact for which there was no explanation. Except that money would solve the problem; with this they could prolong their stay here as long as the money lasted; lacking it they had to surrender themselves to Hanky Park once again. 'Surrender,' that was the word; they only were here on sufferance, even though the thought of having to leave made him homesick to stay. They were Hanky Park's prisoners on ticket of leave. Why Hanky Park, though? He tried to reason it out. When you had no money you had to go to whichever place you could earn it. And in all the wide, wide world Hanky Park was the only spot they knew of where they could find someone to buy their labour. Wages controlled their lives; wages were their masters, they its slaves. Staggering!

Still, that being so – if they could find someone here to employ them. But his heart shrank at the thought. This had occurred to him earlier, the occasion after he and Helen had discovered a whitewashed cottage to be let at a half-crown a week. He had inquired, cautiously, tentatively regarding employment here of an old fisherman. The old man had disillusioned him instantly; had told him that the winter saw most of the folk hereabout unemployed. Unemployed, here, though! Did its stinking carcass foul the air everywhere? Was there no place where it did not lie in wait for your coming? Despite it all revolt stirred in his heart when he had to acknowledge his impotency.

'It's a bit thick, Helen,' he mumbled: ' – a bit thick when y' can't do what y' want. Yaaa, who wants t' go back t' Hanky Park?' He unshipped oars, headed the boat round and pulled with an energy expressive of his feelings. Helen was silent.

Over the hills the pale moon was sailing, growing more brilliant as the western horizon lost colour. The lighthouse on the breakwater's extremity was flashing when Harry restored the boat to its proprietor.

A high eminence, little frequented, the home of sheep, deep bracken and blazing yellow gorse, overlooked the white-walled town. They followed the track to a point half-way up, branched off to a hollow they had discovered hard by a clump of conifers and seated themselves. They sat silent for a while each brooding.

'It's all right for you, Harry,' Helen murmured.

'What d'y' mean, Helen?'

She shook her head and stared into her lap: 'Oh, Ah dunno,' a sigh of weariness: 'What's good o' talkin' about it ...'

'Talkin' about what, though?' He persisted, and, slowly, wrung a confession from her. The story was not unfamiliar: he had heard a similar from Tom Hare regarding the sexual behaviour of drunken parents. But, whereas Tom's story disgusted him, Helen's shocked him. He hated her parents savagely. He – He – Oh, what could a fellow do?

'Ah want t' get away from 'em, Harry. . . . An' Ah would ha' done long ago if Ah could ha' found a place where they'd take me in for what Ah'm earnin'. But strangers won't do it when they know y' work at Marlowe's mill, them allus bein' on short time . . .' a pause, then, with sudden passion: 'Oh, Ah hate sex. Ah *hate* it.' She laid a hand on his arm: 'It's them, Harry, Ah mean. It's *them* . . . Ah could be sick when Ah think about it. An' livin' here wi' you for a week with all this here,' a pass in the direction of sea and town, 'An' a clean bed an' a room – an' knowin' that *they* won't come home drunk an' go in next room. Oh – ' Her head drooped, her hands went to her face.

He put his arms about her and held her close to him. He did not speak for a while. Presently, he said: 'Ne'er heed, Helen . . .' ardently: 'Ah love y', Helen. Ah *do* love y' . . .'

Without thinking as to its practicability he suddenly burst forth, eagerly: 'Aye, 'Elen, an' as soon as Ah'm out o' me time we'll be married. Really. . . . No kid. An' Ah'll be out of it in a few months now.' Then a rebuke rose to his mind by way of an afterthought; a disturbing picture of automatic and other devilishly self-sufficient machinery. Things that made the serving of his apprenticeship a waste of time. Here he was promising marriage with such a competitor to fight. It was all very well for those fellows who invented them; their inventions put them on velvet. But they didn't pause to consider how many poor devils had to go under on their account. Blimey, look at Billy Higgs and his generation, still mooning around; skilled engineers supposed to be.

Then an access of confidence: 'Maybe,' he told himself: 'Maybe Ah'll land a job when Ah come out o' me time. There's *sure* to be jobs *somewhere*.' He breathed with greater freedom. He said, impatiently: 'Aw, let's forget about home, Helen. We ain't there now, thank God. Let's mek most of it while we can: there's on'y another day.' She relaxed in his arms. He felt her arms stealing about him: she said: 'Y'll allus love me, wont y', Harry? Things don't seem so bad when Ah've got you.'

'You know me,' he replied, stoutly: 'When we get back home

we start saving up straightaway for – well, you know what.'
Pause: 'Funny, ain't it, Helen ... Ah mean it's funny we ain't
ne'er thought o' getting married afore. You know. ... Fancy,
though, us livin' in different houses when there's nowt t' stop us
from gettin' a home of our own!'

It came in the way of a revelation this appreciation of their
liberty to marry. It was as though, previously, no such thing as
marriage existed, or, at least, if it did exist it was not for such
as they. On a sudden, as it were, they felt they had cast the
shell of boy and girlhood and had emerged, adults. A most inspiring sensation suffused them both; in an instant everything
seemed possible. They now were responsible for themselves,
the arbiters of their own destinies. Going home now to the prospect of marriage minimized the pang of parting from this
lovely place.

He assured her, with confidence and ardour, that his promises
would soon come to pass: 'Once let me get back to work. ...
Let me get out o' me time an' on full money. Ah'll show y' ..
Ah'll find a job ... Ah'll – Oh, you wait an' see.'

She lay back in the bracken, sighing. He brushed her sun-
burnt cheek with his lips. She murmured his name, her lips
sought his, and, abandoning themselves, they surrendered to
ecstatic oblivion.

The waxing moon climbed higher in the heavens: brilliant
beams bathed land and sea. Where shadows lurked the blackness was intense, impenetrable; elsewhere was eerily white. No
wind, no sound save the distant cool swish of the sea: rabbits
kicked their heels, sheep grazed, bats flitted and owls were on
the wing. The road the lovers were to traverse home wound, a
silver ribbon by the empty white-walled cottage, through sable
coppices and between high thorn hedges heavy with honey-
suckle and blossom.

PART THREE

CHAPTER I

## PLANS

THE return to the Two Cities was not so dismal an event as they had thought: nevertheless, despite their plans of marriage they bade farewell to the holiday with many pangs. Still, it was inevitable, Harry concluded, and, the sooner he settled down again to humdrum existence the quicker the time would pass which now separated him from the termination of his apprenticeship. All that would then remain would be the finding of an employer willing to pay him the full rate of wage due to a time-served engineer. Already he had accomplished this in fancy. He assured himself that he would not fail. His optimism communicated itself to Helen; their confidence grew and engendered a delightfully new sense of intimacy and devotion.

They considered the necessity of having to settle down again to the squalor of Hanky Park as a period merely of probation; a kind of temporary stage which had to be endured whilst the money necessary to marriage was saved. Their fancies and the seductive pictures it painted of a home of their own obscured reality and made bearable what, otherwise, would have been intolerable.

With ten shillings in his pockets, the residue of what remained of his winnings plus a shilling each which they had managed to save, he and Helen, arm in arm, went window gazing in the furniture shops. The most expensive establishments drew them as a magnet; luxuriously upholstered lounge furniture held them spellbound. Their imaginations were fired by the show-cards' sketches depicting suggested arrangements of the furniture in spacious, oak-panelled rooms whose open French windows looked on to a sunny garden with a dovecote on a pole in the centre of the lawn: such a place as never existed within miles of the Two Cities and whose upkeep would require at least an income of two thousand pounds a year.

An economical form of entertainment and much more

satisfyng than the picture theatre. Satisfying whilst one could keep up the pretence of being able to purchase the things displayed. But, when the illusion faded and the solemn stillness fell between them, they could only practise deception on each other in glum silences or in forced cheerfulness: 'Aw, ne'er heed, Helen. Just let me get that there job on full money an' we'll soon have things like that.' With the utterance of the words his heart contracted: what a shallow, ill-considered promise. He knew that on full rate of pay he would never be able to afford decent furnishings. Of the things he would have liked fine dreams only were his portion.

They would drift, by degrees to the cheaper shops. Ugly furniture; imitation this and imitation that; skimped jerry-built stuff that hurt the eyes, that boasted its inferiority shamelessly, brazenly and filled the brain with a bleak dullness. No showcards here save: 'Join Our Club. Weekly Payments Taken.'

Homewards with moody, resentful discontent in their hearts.

'Seems as though we've ne'er to get nowt we really want,' Harry grumbled. He scowled. Then, remembering his solitary stroke of good fortune, and, with dreams of a successful repetition, added, hopefully: 'Still, we *will* get what we want if Ah win newspaper competition. An' somebody's *got* t' win.'

Alone, he sometimes dared to look the problem straight in the face. Here he was, within hailing distance of completing his apprenticeship. For nearly seven years he had been working for a boy's wage, and, these last four years he had been performing a skilled tradesman's work, though it had made no difference to his wages. So far was quite clear: his income had been such as had precluded the possibility of saving, nay, but for the communal pooling of wages at home he would have been in debt. The future was the bugbear; *that* gave him pause. All his plans of marriage were on the other side of a very large 'if'. *If* he was successful in securing a situation on full pay.

Each time he saw Billy Higgs and his generation, ragged and down at heel lounging the street corners, each time he stared at them he stared at reality. But it was only an incomplete appreciation: every attempt to realize it fully was vitiated by a hope that he would evade their fate.

The ominous menace looming on the horizon of the future only served to set a keener edge upon his ambitions; the more impossible he recognized his circumstances from the viewpoint of marriage the more maddeningly desirable it became.

He could not restrain his pent-up feelings betimes; sought reassurance of everybody who would lend a sympathetic ear, though he referred to marriage guardedly, in a general sense.

Joe Simmons, Bill Simmons's elder brother, who was married and a labourer at Marlowe's, scowled when Harry, one evening on the way home, introduced the subject: 'Marriage. Yaaaa,' he growled: 'Blimey, you tek notice of a mug wot got married. Luk at me now. Nowt t' wear an' ne'er a blasted penny t' call me own,' indignantly: 'An' me *workin'*, too!' bitterly: 'Ah wus one o' the clever devils, Ah wus. . . . Oh aye, Ah knew all about it when Ah was single, Ah did. We was gonna be different from rest, we wus. But, bli-me! Eeee! Ah wisht as 'ad me time t' go o'er agen. By Christ, Ah do an' all.'

A week's holiday at the seaside, fifteen pounds and the girl of his pre-nuptial fancy – now his wife – had been the basis of Joe's venture into matrimony. There, by the sea, everything had been ideal: they had spent the fifteen pounds, or, in other words, had lived for a glorious week at the rate of £750 a year and had found such happiness as had inclined Joe to the belief that marriage would be one long repetition of the holiday. He overlooked the fact of the difference between the £750 and the £104 which last was the amount he earned after a full year's hard labour at Marlowe's.

Even now Joe still dreamed on the now remote happiness that had been his and his wife's on their only holiday. And though he felt, keenly, the need of money he never acknowledged it as the cause of his present discontent. He did not appreciate the fact that money's value was determined. He endowed it with a quality of elasticity when it was in his wife's hands and accused her of incompetence when she failed in producing the miracle of all their wants. He scowled when she gave him his half-crown spending money out of his wages every Saturday noon, said, surlily, that he didn't know what she did with the money he earned.

And when their language and temper became heated nobody would have thought them the same couple, who, years ago, strolled the Blackpool promenade arm in arm, perfectly happy.

Nor were others more encouraging; all warned him against it on grounds of financial stringency – all except one. The diminutive Mr Alfred Scodger whose termagant wife performed upon the trombone. Alfred said: 'Bein' wed's like a feller wi' a bald head: there ain't no partin'.' He removed his oily trilby so that Harry might see his shiny pate: 'Yaah, you be careful, Harry. Y' can allus get a new lass but y' can't get a new wife once y' married. Remember wot owld Alf Scodger says wot's bin through it all an' knows. Be careful, lad, be careful, an' be wary o' them as is musical inclined.'

Anon the vision glowed seductively; he day-dreamed on it, talked of it so to Helen that sometimes it was difficult to believe it actually hadn't occurred. And, long before his apprenticeship was complete it had ceased to be a vague ambition and had become a necessity shot with fearful apprehensions lest something unmentionable should arise to thwart its consummation. He came to put out of mind such daft, impossible notions of a decent home; they were futile wastes of time. Came to treasure and to be glad of the likelier possibility of obtaining such a house as any in Hanky Park. Oh, the deep yearning to imagine any one of them as his and Helen's; the poignant sweetness of picturing himself shutting the front door and feeling secure against all trespass! He came to regard all front doors with a deep respect.

His own home, what little he saw of it these days, was intolerable. He and Helen spent most of their time walking the canal bank or sitting on Dawney's Hill planning and scheming until darkness fell, then, under the stars, lovemaking.

At home was discord. This mysterious business of housekeeping was insoluble. His father's work was become chronically spasmodic; the new industrial revolution had stolen, insidiously, upon every enterprise, it seemed, and now was an accomplished fact. Though the three days' working week that it had established was still looked upon by all whom it affected as 'bad trade'; a phase that would pass when 'things bucked up'. Meanwhile there was no sign of this, and Hardcastle's wages were halved with the inevitable consequences on his temper.

There was something amiss with Sally, too. Gloomy, moody, she sat about the house as though nursing a perpetual grudge against everybody; at the least provocation she would flash out tempestuously.

Harry was relieved to be away from it: 'Ach, you make me sick, you do,' he snarled at her: 'Allus on the growl like a bear wi' a sore head. Why don't y' get married an' get out of it?'

She raised her gorgeous eyes to his at the taunt: he saw in them a look of intense pain. She did not speak. He blushed, picked up his cap and slunk outside, leaving her alone in the house.

CHAPTER 2

## TANGLE

NED NARKEY, standing cross-legged on the doorstep of his lodgings, thumb of one hand in belt, the other hand resting on the door frame and supporting his great bulk, lifted his lip in a scowling snarl as Larry Meath passed by on the other side. As he passed Ned spat contemptuously on to the pavement and voiced a harsh, growling exclamation, glaring at Larry and still wearing the scowl until he turned the corner.

Harry, sitting on the doorstep of his home, witness to the incident, wondered idly on its cause. Some days later he made a startling discovery by an accidental act of eavesdropping.

It was noon, he was standing by an open window viewing the smoky prospect and resting in the time that remained before the siren blew at one o'clock. To his left a wood partition enclosed the lavatories, a cramped place where were a half dozen chipped washbowls. Conversation on the other side was quite audible from where he stood. There were peepholes, too, cut in the wood, the work of idle apprentices who wished to watch for the approach of foremen and any other persons invested with authority.

The gush of water from a couple of taps first attracted his

attention, then, amid the splashings of hands being washed he heard the surly voice of Ned Narkey say: 'That there crane o' mine wants fixin' agen'; a short pause: 'Y'd berrer gerrit seen to. ... Y' made a right muck of it last time,' contemptuously: 'Mechanics. Aaach! Aaach! Ah've seen berrer wi' skirts on.'

Curious, Harry stooped to one of the holes in the partition. Ned was speaking to Larry Meath. Wonderingly, Harry remembered the incident of a few nights ago when Ned had spat as Larry passed by. In what way had Larry given Ned offence. He listened, puzzled.

Without looking at Ned Larry answered: 'If there's anything wrong with the crane you know where to lodge the complaint. It will be passed on to me.' He continued washing his hands.

Ned took a couple of heavy steps forward: 'Don't you come the bloody sergeant-major stuff on me, Meath,' he snapped: 'You ain't kidding a tart when y' talk t' me.'

No answer.

'You know what Ah mean,' continued Ned: 'Ah know y' game. ... It don't kid me.'

'What are you talking about?'

'Come orf it. Come orf it. You know who Ah mean. Y've bin stuffin' her up wi' all that there high-falutin talk o' yourn an' she swallows all y' say.'

Larry gazed at him and said, patiently: 'Who are you referring to, Ned?'

Ned curled his lip. 'Referrin' ... referrin',' in rising tones: 'Ach. The bloody edge you put on makes me sick,' indignantly: 'Who the 'ell d'y' think y' are?' threateningly: 'Anyway, you leave her alone. It's Sal Hardcastle Ah'm speakin' about.'

Harry's heart leapt; his skin crept. Larry, as he saw, was folding his towel; he was frowning as he regarded Ned whose enormous muscularity seemed magnified in comparison with Larry's slightness of build. Ned's expression was frightening; his chest rose and fell; his upper lip blue, like his jaw with stubble, was stretched tightly across his teeth; his unsleeved arms, muscles taut, fists clenched, hung, crooked, by his side.

Larry said, quietly: 'Don't you think you're making a bit of a fool of yourself, Ned?'

'Don't – you – talk – to – me.'

Larry turned to go but Ned's hand fell on his shoulder and whipped him round again: white, Larry faced him: 'You listen to me,' Ned snapped: 'What're y' goin' t' do about it?' he thrust his face forward, his huge chest rose and fell agitatedly. Larry made no answer immediately, regarded Ned interrogatively: 'Y' makin' no move t' marry her, a'y'?' Ned demanded.

'How can that concern you?' Larry answered, spiritedly.

'Me? Don't concern me?' Ned spluttered: '*Me*, as's ast her t' marry me ...' passionately: 'Turnin' me down for a white-livered conchie like you ...' angrily: 'Ah fought for such bastards as you. Sergeant-major Narkey, that's me. Aye, an Ah wus o'er there while yellow-bellied rats like you wus sleepin' wi' owld sweats' wives an' landin' soft jobs for y'selves,' pointing a threatening finger at him: 'Think on, now, Ah'm warnin' y'. If y' don't want that there dial o' yourn smashed in, keep away from Sal Hardcastle. Unnerstand, Ah mean it.'

Larry straightened his collar, disarranged by Ned's rough usage. He recognized the uselessness of argument in the face of Ned's jealousy. Besides, there was nothing he could have said. Yet, despite his usual equanimity he resented Ned's autocratic usage of his physical superiority and could not refrain from the retort: 'If I were you I'd consult Sal before you make any more arrangements for her,' gazing at him, steadfastly: 'As for your threats,' a shrug, 'you'd have time to regret them in jail.'

'Aaach,' Ned snarled; he clenched his teeth, glared and made a sudden movement as though to strike Larry. But he restrained himself: hatred burned in his eyes as he muttered, thickly: 'You an' y' bloody talk. You've got it comin' t' y', s'elp me. Y'll open that trap o' yourn once too often ...' the rest of his utterance was lost in the din of the siren. Harry saw Larry turn and walk out leaving Ned standing there his face contorted with impotent anger.

The memory of the incident plagued Harry, filled him with a restless perturbation all the afternoon.

He vowed not to tell Sally of the occurrence but he could not keep it to himself. Soon after tea, when they were alone in the house, he mentioned it casually. Her immediate response was something of a revelation. Her anxiety and the appeal in her eyes disconcerted him; never, previously, had he considered her capable of deep feelings, say, as existed between Helen and he. It came as something of a shock to find that she, too, had problems to face. 'Go on, Harry. What did Larry say. ..? Try to remember.'

She drew it from him, phrase by phrase.

'You don't like Ned, d'y', Sal?' he asked afterwards and saw the angry colour mount her cheeks.

'*Him*,' she answered: 'He's a dirty pig. Him an' Sam Grundy's a pair.'

'Sam Grundy? Why?' murmured Harry, staring. Surely ...! There returned to mind a memory of the evening Sam Grundy had paid him the winnings: until now he had never dreamed that there might have been an ulterior motive in his inquiries concerning Sally and in the adjuration: 'Tell her as Ah've said that she's t' have a couple o' quid out o' y' winnings for new clo'es.' A suspicion dawned. Hateful beast. It was common knowledge that Sam had kept women up and down the place; everybody knew of his house in Wales where, so people said, his mistress of the moment resided. It was perplexing to know that one could act so with such amazing impunity. Money, it seemed, could do anything. But to think of Sally's having anything to do with such ...! 'You ain't ...' began Harry, falteringly: 'You ain't ...? *He* ain't ...?' His cheeks burned.

'Ach, he's allus on to me, the fat pig,' in imitation of Sam Grundy: 'Y've no need t' work, Sally. Y'd have all y' want,' curling her lip: 'Puh! Ah'd want summat t' do t' let a thing like him or Narkey muck about wi' me.'

Imagine it! Men regarding her with desire! She, Sally, his sister! She, who, previously, he never had suspected her being a woman as, say, Helen. And such men: it was shameful: he experienced a bitter hatred towards both of them; such a sensation of disgust as though they had made an improper suggestion to him. He clutched the remembrance of Larry Meath, gratefully. He had confidence in him; his unaffected superiority inspired it.

He said, gazing at her: 'And won't Larry ...?' and left his

question unfinished. How mature she looked. Why, she was a woman: he had not noticed it before.

She was staring into the fire, head drooping slightly, one foot resting on the steel fender. She shook her head slowly, mechanically as she revolved memories which reopened the wounds of her discontent; memories of conversations with Larry, of confidences exchanged, of ideas expressed on his part – sometimes incomprehensible, otherwise depressing – ideas on and against marriage which rebuked her high hopes. She could have reconciled herself more easily to her disappointment had she known him to harbour no affection for her; it would have been inevitable, then. But he did not, could not deceive her; intuitively she felt him to be wilfully suppressing, evading his love of her, that he was as unhappy about it as she, and she responded, thrilling, to the remembrances of those times when it refused to be suppressed, times when it looked out of his kindly eyes eloquently and ravished her with an agonizing, hopeful happiness. At the thought she tingled with dissatisfaction and impatience; her heart expanded in an overwhelming desire to be in his company. She turned from the fender, picked up her hat and coat and made towards the door without a word to Harry. She knew where Larry would be.

'Where y' goin', Sal?' Harry asked, anxious in the face of this sudden activity. She must not have heard him; she went out without answering. He stared at the door, perturbed. What an uncomfortable state of affairs. Ned's threats to Larry: Sally's revelation of Sam Grundy's proposals. What a hopeless tangle; made his head swim to think about it. Oh, it didn't concern him, anyway; he'd his own worries. They came crowding back to him at the thought: he groaned, inwardly, reached for his cap and went in search of Helen.

2

Larry was not at the Labour Club where Sally guessed he would be.

'He'll ha' gone down cut bank, shouldn't wonder,' said one of the men at the club: 'He'd them there field-glasses wi' him an' that's where he gen'ly gus. Thee be careful a-goin' down theer, lass. 'Tain't fit place f'r lass t' be alone.'

That people might suspect her of 'running after' Larry, as the saying goes in the Two Cities, did not occur to her: even though it had she would not have been deterred. She never made a pretence of her infatuation, could not have dissembled it; rather was she proud of it and was naïvely, disarmingly frank with Larry concerning it.

In a sense she was relieved that Larry was not at the club; confidential talk was not possible there. And she knew the spot Larry generally affected on the canal side. It was about two miles west of Pendleton.

Anybody seeing a snapshot of some select corner might imagine it as being representative of the heart of the country. Beauty was there, doubtless, but not to the eyes of slum dwellers who walked there. They take with them what exists two miles away to the east. Still, beauty is there in the tall, limp-leaved beeches and hairy elms, the long grass and sedge and the water meadow sweeping down to the serpentine river a quarter-mile distant. Beauty, pockmarked by glimpses of gaunt, pit headstocks rising between trees and scarecrow electric pylons sprawling across the meadows' bosoms.

Often the eye is offended by the ribald handiwork of obscene boys and youths who, with lumps of chalk make crude suggestive drawings on the canal bridges' masonry, write disgusting doggerels and phrases and inscribe the names of girls beneath. Sometimes the songs of the lark and blackbird are overwhelmed by raucous screams of counterfeit shocked laughter from groups of mill and factory girls parading the banks who have been surprised by louts from the slums lying in the grass peeping at lovers, and, on occasions such as when they are encouraged by the presence of groups of girls, exposing themselves then bursting into raucous, hysterical laughter. Less egregious pastimes are indulged: colliers use the banks as training tracks for their whippets; gamblers hold 'schools' for the pitching and tossing of coins: in season the bat slogs the ball in adjoining meadows: racing pigeons are loosed; ferrets put down holes to start up squeaking rats and bolting-eyed rabbits which are chased to a bloody death by pitiless greyhounds. Here and there patient sportsmen puff pipes as they contemplate their floats bobbing on the still water, hook diminutive roach and gudgeon, carry their catches home alive in tins of water, put the fish in glass bowls when they arrive home then throw them into the midden two or three days later when they are dead.

Altogether, a pleasant place, marred by the activities of unpleasant people whose qualities, perhaps, are sad reflections of sadder environments.

As she walked the canal bank she brooded on Narkey's threats to Larry, flushed, resentfully. Then her spirits leapt as a wild hope warmed her. Perhaps these threats of Narkey's would set Larry on his mettle, as it were! Instantly she rebuked herself. Such would not be Larry. Not he whom she had followed round from street corner to street corner, blessed in the privilege of giving out – what were to her – dry-as-dust pamphlets, watching him as he mounted the seat of a borrowed chair wherefrom to proclaim his political faith to an audience of street-corner mouchers, who, for the most part, stood awhile then drifted to the pubs or where not. Nearly always she thought on him thus; it pleased her, charmed her so to do: as such she saw him 'attired in brightness as a man inspired', a character full of such qualities as those of an ideal. The very thought of having his caresses was stifling, ecstatic. There would be no giving on her part, only taking: she would be the receiver, he the giver. What had she to give? Who was she? Sal Hardcastle, an insignificant weaver at Marlowe's cotton mills. She shrank from the acknowledgement of her abysmal negligibility: by comparison Larry seemed more remote than ever.

The moment passed; she remembered occasions when the gentle expression on his face and the soft light in his eyes had told her all that she wished to know; occasions when he had made a confidante of her; although some of his confessions had been, in a sense, akin to warnings. How dreadfully disenchanting his repudiation of marriage when he spoke of it in general as concerning people in their circumstances. Yet, she told herself, he must have contemplated it in regard to himself else why should he bother talking to her about it? She was on shifting sands, here; was full of doubts of her surmisings, failed, entirely, to agree with his strange notions, but would not permit her courage to be shaken in her hope that, ultimately, all this perplexing tangle would be straightened. His notions were so perverse. Yet, she told herself, setting her chin, if he didn't want marriage then neither did she: it was Larry Meath she desired and not so much marriage. But even that, so it seemed, was not suitable to him: 'No, no, Sal, you misunderstand me. It isn't this marriage business that matters: marriage is only for hogs anyway. It's this damned poverty. My wages. What are they? Forty-five shillings a week. How on earth could we live decently on that? It isn't enough to keep us decently clothed and fed: it means a life of doing without the things that make life worth while. And – ' a gesture of helplessness: 'It can't be explained, Sal. If you don't see it as I then you just don't see it, that's all.'

What a supremely bewildering person he was. It was marriage, then it wasn't marriage but poverty. Imagine that, too! His wage was forty-five shillings a week *regularly*. And here he was crying poverty! Why, who in North Street could depend on forty-five shillings *every* week? Nobody. There never was a week but what the family income fluctuated. Yet these people ventured into matrimony.

'Doing without the things that make life worth while.' What did he mean by that? And by all his other incomprehensible talk which he uttered when addressing the crowds at street corners. Words and phrases of which she was jealous since they meant so much to him; jealous of them because they meant something to him whose secret was hid from her; jealous of them because she wished to be the inspiration in him of such animation as they occasioned. She could only have blind faith in his beliefs. She resented them, yet, at the same time, acknowledged them as the medium by which, in her eyes, he was elevated above other men. She wished him an ordinary type whilst preserving his extraordinary qualities. She . . .

'But what *do* you want, Larry?' the remembrance of her questioning him interrupted her thoughts. He had answered:

'What do I want eh? Ha! What I'm not likely to get,' an impatient gesture indicative of the street and neighbourhood in general: 'Aw, having to live amongst all this. Blimey, day after day and no change at all. Work and bed and work again. . . . Oh,' an expression of intense disgust: 'It's enough to drive a man mad.'

Mad! Enough to drive a woman mad too. She found herself in a bog of conflicting emotions. Out of the chaos rose the question: 'What could be denied a home that had a constant income of forty-five shillings a week?' She could not think of anything. Then what was it that Larry referred to: 'doing without the things that make life worth while?' There'd be enough for food, rent and clothes, surely. What else was there? He must be wrong. She could not be sure. He was so different from others. If only she could understand.

Still, to meet him this evening meant more confidences. It occurred to her that she should consider herself fortunate; he *might* have chosen some more intellectual girl in whom to confide. She smiled, reassured: an impelling force surged in her heart: she quickened her pace; her lustrous eyes took on an added glow as she gazed expectantly into the distance.

She did not find him. Three-quarters of an hour later saw her retracing her steps, dawdling along, her listless fingers holding a sprig of hawthorn blossom. She had visited all Larry's customary haunts: the meadows where he had shown her larks' nests in the deep grass, the nettle beds by the river side colonized by the Red Admirals, and the sand deposits there, pitted with holes into and out of which sand martins darted like shadows. Disconsolate and further depressed by the melancholy cries of the wheeling lapwings, she returned, and, passing a flowering thorn, idly plucked a sprig of blossom.

It was deeply disappointing, especially so when she dwelt on the delectable image of the pleasure that had been denied her; that, doubtless, he *had* traversed this path this evening and that she had missed him perhaps by only a few moments, was an irritating thought. As she left the canal bank and set her face towards Hanky Park she remembered that if she waited at the street corner she would, likely enough, meet him returning.

Until then she knew that this present irksome feeling of bleak loneliness would remain with her. Imagine it! At one time, not very long ago, she had found pleasure in dances and the picture theatres. What had come over her? Those diversions gave only a transitory pleasure: she saw herself returning home when pictures or dance were done, returning to the dreariness of No. 17 North Street. It wasn't that kind of life she wanted: she wanted something real and permanent, not the mere whiling away of time watching flickering shadows on a screen or the trumpery gaiety of a dance-room. She wanted Larry and a home of her own. . . . Dreariness of No. 17 North Street. A stupendous suspicion pounced upon her. The dreariness of her home represented marriage, to her father and mother both of whom, before their marriage must surely have been as she now was, desirous of homes of their own. They now had obtained it and, to her, it represented something that filled her with overwhelming dreariness. Could it be possible that Larry in his condemnation of marriage, was really suggesting that her mother's and father's married life with all its scratchings and scrapings was only removed from a newly married couple's experiences by the matter of a few years? Her mother and father had never been away from North Street on even a day's holiday since their honeymoon: Hardcastle himself was a smouldering volcano ready to erupt the moment she or Harry suggested expenditure on clothes: 'D'y' think bloody money grows on trees?' He was worried eternally over money. And Larry had said: 'It isn't this marriage business that matters. . . . It's this damned poverty . . . doing without the things that make life worth while. . . .' Was *this* understanding. She crushed all her thoughts. 'I want Larry . . . I want Larry,' she defied herself.

Night was falling. She was on Broad Street now passing the parish church. Her train of thought was interrupted by the sound of a hoarse voice speaking her name. She turned her head. Sam Grundy's fat, apoplectic visage smirked at her from the illuminated rear windows of his car. It kept pace with her walking; doubtless the chauffeur was obeying Sam's instructions. He put his face out of the window: 'Hey, Sal,' he cried, winking: 'Wharra bout a little ride, eh?' he nodded and winked

again: 'Ah'll get y' back, early. .... Go on. .... What'j'say, eh?'
Another grin and a wink.

She scowled at him, voiced a contemptuous exclamation,
walked behind the car and crossed the road without even another glance. Surlily she turned into Hanky Park. The fool to
think that his most tempting offers could ever be of interest to
her. She put him from her mind.

The public-houses were closing. Slatternly women, dirty
shawls over their heads and shoulders, hair in wisps about their
faces, stood in groups congregated on the pavements in the
shafts of light thrown from the open doors of the public-house.
Now and then they laughed, raucously, heedless of the tugs at
their skirts from their wailing, weary children.

In front of Sally was gloomy Mrs Dorbell, tiny Mrs Jike, fat
Mrs Bull and the resourceful Mrs Nattle who 'obligded' her
'naybores'. Mrs Dorbell was saying, as the party turned into
North Street: '. . . an' Ah say agen it's a fair sin an' a shame that
they should be closed at ten o'clock,' she referred to the public-
houses. Mrs Nattle answered, in reference to the bottle she kept
at home: 'An Ah say there's nowt t' stop workin' folk from
havin' a nip i' their own homes sociable like. Them as mek
laws g' nowt short, Ah'll bet . . .' Mrs Dorbell tripped, tipsily,
and clutched Mrs Bull's arm which caused Mrs Bull to suggest
that Mrs Dorbell had had enough for one evening. Mrs Dorbell
thought otherwise since she continued walking with them to
Mrs Nattle's home.

Sally was disgusted. It did not occur to her that they had
been as she now was, young, once upon a time. She saw them
as she saw them, four ragged old women, creatures divorced
from the species, institutions, as part and parcel of the place as
the houses themselves.

As she passed the clog shop next the Duke of Gloucester
public-house a hand stole out from the doorway's dark recess and
touched her arm. She started and turned. It was Kate Malloy,
one of the girls who worked in the same shed at Marlowe's.

'Oh,' cried Sally: 'Ah wondered who it was. What a turn you
gave me,' curiously: 'Whatever are y' doin' there, Kate?' She
stared at her, searchingly.

A thin, pale-faced girl, Kate's facial expression reminded one of a hunted animal; always there was a light of furtive nervousness in her eyes. She rarely spoke to anybody at the mill save Sally for whom she nursed a dog-like devotion, which, sometimes, became something of a nuisance. Though, since she had no parents and lived in lodgings, which, Sally thought, may have been the cause of her nervousness and reticence, Sally never could find it in her heart to rebuff her.

Kate whispered: 'Is he there?' She inclined her head towards the crowd just loosed from the Duke of Gloucester.

'Who?'

Kate reproached her with a glance: 'Ned, o' course.'

Sally sniffed: 'Ah dunno. Why, what d'y want him for?'

'Oh, Sally,' again, reproachfully: 'An' all Ah've told y' about how he ses he likes me.'

'Yaa,' replied Sally. 'What d'y' listen t' his gab for? He tells same to anybody as'll listen. Ah've told y' before. Leave him alone. All he wants y' for is what he can get out o' y',' imperiously: 'Come on, now. Get off home wi' y'.'

'Oh, no, no, Sal,' alarmed: 'Oh, no. He told me to wait here.'

Sally sneered: 'H'm. Fine 'un he is, makin' a girl wait till he's finished his boozin'. Yaa, ain't y' got no sense? What'll he be like if ever y' was daft enough t' wed him, which y' won't ... he ain't that kind.'

'Oh, Sal. He promised.'

Impatiently: 'You – make – me – sick, Kate. Hangin' around after a feller. Y'd catch me doin' it. ... Not for best man alive. How long have y' bin waiting there?'

'Not long. ... On'y since half eight. ... Ah guess they kep' him talkin' an' he forgot. ... We was goin' t' go t' t' pictures.'

'Y' daft,' replied Sally, with emphasis. 'What y' can see in a bloke like Narkey, Ah – don't – know.'

'Eh, Sal, but Ah love him ... really, Ah do. ... He's bin good t' me ...'

'Aye, an he'd be good t' me if he could get what he wanted. Don't be a ninny. Get off home t' bed while y' safe. Ah'd have no boozer muckin' around wi' me.'

'But Ah can't go, Sal. Ah promised Ah'd wait. – An' Ah don't want him to – Oh, Ah want t' see him. *You'd* be the same about a feller if y' thought owt about him like Ah do.'

'Aw,' said Sally, impatiently: 'You make me sick, Kate. Ah'm goin'; see y' tomorrow.'

She had not taken more than a half dozen strides when, passing the Duke of Gloucester public-house she suddenly found herself confronted by Ned Narkey who, having seen her, detached himself from the group outside the doors, and, with unsteady gait, intercepted her. A drunken smirk parted his lips; he planted himself in front of her, thrust his thumbs into his belt and stood there, grinning, swaying slightly: 'Hallo, Sal,' he said, warmly.

'Get out o' my way,' she snapped, and made as though to pass him. Instantly his expression changed: he scowled and caught her by the hand holding the sprig of blossom: 'Here,' he growled: 'Half a mo',' a thorn pricked his finger; he glanced at her hand: 'Ha!' he sneered: 'Bin in t' country, have y'?' thickly: 'Ah suppose y've bin wi' that . . .'

She snatched her hand away: 'You tek your dirty hands off me, Narkey.'

His lips tightened across his teeth: 'Dirty hands, eh. They wusn't dirty when Ah'd got plenty o' jack an' Ah wus payin' for y' t' go dancin', wus they, eh?'

'I ne'er asked y' t' pay. Ah'd ha' paid my whack an' you know it.'

'Luk here, Sal Hardcastle,' he muttered: 'No tart can make a runt out o' Ned Narkey. Ah've offered t' marry y' fair and square an' Ah mean it. . . . But if Ah don't have y' Ah'll mek sure that *that* yellow-bellied rat up street don't either. . . . Not if Ah have t' swing for him,' his voice was low with passion, his small, deep-set eyes glittered.

She curled her lip: 'You touch him, that's all, Narkey. Just touch him once, if y' dare. Our Harry told me what y' said t'day. . . . He heard y' . . .'

Ned flushed, glad in a sense that Sally had been informed of his passage of words with Larry. In Sally's being unaccompanied at present he was convinced that his threats had intimidated Larry. Doubtless she had been walking with him this evening, else how had she come by the blossom? He grinned, hitched up his belt: 'He's yellow,' he sneered: 'You've bin out wi' him tonight. . . . An' Ah suppose he left y' at top of Hanky Park an' sneaked down back way so's Ah wouldn't see him. . . . Yaa,' with a return to his threatening demeanour: 'He knows what's good for him . . .'

'An' if you know what's good for you you'll leave him be, Narkey. Ah'm standin' no more from you. Next time Ah'll call a copper,' raising her brows warningly: 'Ah've told y'. . . .' Blazing, she pushed by him to stand by Mr Hulkington's the grocer's shop window.

Fuming, in defiance of Narkey's threats, she prepared to wait for Larry.

CHAPTER 3

'TAKE A PAIR OF SPARKLING EYES . . .'

INSISTENTLY a part of him, a most imperious part, insistently it clamoured for Sally. At one time its influence had been controllable; he could reason it out of countenance. But it had grown in strength; its potency had developed until, now, it would brook no argument; it *demanded* and stopped its ears to the lips of his brain. Like a cuckoo fledgling in the nest it crowded out of mind all thoughts than itself.

Bemused, he had walked past his favourite haunts, and it was only when twilight stole abroad that he paused, turned about and set his face homewards. 'Oh,' he kept saying, wearily, until the tedious repetition took meaning from his words: 'Oh,' appealingly, as though to some invisible, unbending arbiter: 'Oh, if only there were a loophole, just a frail, unlikely possibility of getting out of Hanky Park . . . God, if only there was. . . . I wouldn't hesitate. . . . I'd marry her tomorrow.'

Then the tormenting bitter knowledge of his helplessness receded. His worried facial expression relaxed, a load slipped from his heart as an alluring picture of Sal appeared to his mind's eye.

Haunting eyes, dark, lustrous, full of mute appeal; pallid

146

cheeks emphasized by the abundance of her raven hair. Oh, the shining brightness, the eternal summer of her presence. Inspiring, radiant Sal! At the very thought of her he could feel a genial warmth suffusing him.

'I'd marry her tomorrow. ...' A malicious voice in his brain quoted his thoughts, adding, with a sardonic laugh: 'Where's the money to come from? Where's the money, man? And what of all your high-falutin notions and great expectations? You, with your forty-five bob a week. Yah, and buying your furniture on the five year instalment plan. *You'd* marry! Ha, ha, ha!'

His brain contracted. He awoke to the fact that he was entering Hanky Park.

Thoughts! Ach, daft dreams. Harsh reality was about him. Wails of children coming from suffocating bedrooms; beshawled old women shuffling off into gloomy areas; alley cats, gaunt as famine slinking down mephitic back entries; a couple lovemaking in the clog shop doorway; he could hear the girl's voice timidly protestant, the man's hoarsely insistent: sounds of a domestic quarrel somewhere near; shrill accusations from the wife, loud denunciations from the husband; a scuffle and a crash of crockery in the street; screams followed by the sound of many hurrying feet of people rushing to witness the brawl.

To be away from it all; to have the heart's desire. Someone to love, someone to caress when the brain was weary; to feel the soft, soothing, unresisting presence close to your own; to dissolve into exquisite oblivion for a precious moment and to be submerged in tranquil seas of deep forgetfulness. He heard his name called softly as he turned into North Street.

Sally was standing by Hulkington's shop window. Involuntarily his heart leapt, a beaming smile grew on his face. He crossed the street and seated himself on the shop front's wide wood sill.

Pale, heart fluttering, she sat next him. She sighed.

The few general remarks that passed between them were uttered self-consciously, as though each seemed conscious of the inward perturbation on the part of the other. Out of the tail of her eye she saw him grip the edge of the sill; her own hand, that holding the blossom, was scarcely an inch away; she experienced a tightening of the throat.

Conversation flagged. Then she remembered Harry's story of Ned's threats to Larry. She murmured, hesitantly: 'You. . . . Our Harry was telling me what Narkey said to you today, Larry. He heard it all.'

Larry stared into the roadway: 'Oh,' he said.

'But you aren't afraid. . . . I mean. . . . You'll take no notice of him, will you?' she could not conceal her concern; she regarded him, anxiously.

He smiled: 'Of course not. He was out of patience with himself.'

She curled her lip: 'He's a bad 'un.'

'Let's not talk about him,' he said.

Pause.

Her hand closed on his; he felt her shoulder touching him; something leapt within him, urgently responsive. The impulse to lean towards her was irresistible. He heard her murmuring, hesitantly: 'Y' won't be vexed wi' me if I tell you, will y', Larry?'

He looked at her, wondering; her lustrous eyes, regarding him steadfastly, held him: 'Vexed?' he whispered, lost to all but the contemplation of her loveliness.

'I followed you down canal bank tonight . . .'

A new expression grew on his face; he was filled with an extraordinary elation, a throbbing harmony; her eyes held him.

Colour tinged her cheeks; her lips parted slightly, she felt there was no air to breathe. Almost imperceptibly she inclined towards him, impelled by overwhelming emotions.

He could feel the quick sharp gusts of her breathing; her lips were almost touching his: his head drooped involuntarily, effortlessly and a wild, dizzying ebullience swept through him. His arm stole about her in a close embrace.

Then they regarded each other, fascinated, amazed, inarticulate. She whispered his name ardently, kissed him again and would have again, but for a couple of men, who, pausing at the street corner, stood conversing. She glared at them.

'Let's go round the back, Larry,' she murmured.

His spirits contracted on the instant; the magic trickled away. A back entry for a love bower! A three-foot wide passage, house backs and backyard walls crowding either side; stagnating puddles in the broken flagging; the sounds of the traffic of people's visiting the stinking privies, and, hark, over the roof-tops, the sound of a cracked voice singing shrilly. Mrs Dorbell's, the old hag, who, when drunk, always chose the privy seat on which to sing the same song:

'We'll laugh and sing an' we'll drive away care;
Ah've enough for meself an' a likkle bit t' spare.
If a nice yeng man should ride my way
Oooow, Ah'll make him as welcome as the flowers in May!'

He could imagine the expression of glassy-eyed vacuity on Mrs Dorbell's face. His arm, round Sal's waist, relaxed. He could feel the dulling sense of utter hopelessness creeping over him.

The voices of the two men at the street corner were audible; they were discussing horse racing.

Voices raised in altercation came from the Hawkins's home. Helen and Harry made a sudden appearance and stood upon the doorstep in silence listening to the raucous oaths of her parents. Ned Narkey, with Kate Malloy following in his shadow, strode round the corner and made towards his lodgings without seeing Sally or Larry. Papers were blowing about the street making grating noises as they slid along the pavement.

As she felt the pressure of his arm relax Sally regarded him with curiosity: 'Why, Larry,' she murmured, apprehensively: 'What's the matter? What's come over y'?'

He awoke to himself. He said, tonelessly, without looking at her: 'Oh, I shouldn't have kissed you, Sal . . .' impatiently: 'Oh, but what's the use . . .'

She stared, interrupted: 'But . . .' she protested: 'It was . . .' with intense concern: 'Oh, didn't y' mean it, Larry? . . . Didn't y' mean it?' pained, she searched his face.

He didn't answer straightaway, sat there staring at the pavement as again the miserable realization of his poverty crushed his heart. How frigidly inexorable it was.

'If only there were a loophole; a frail, unlikely possibility of evading the consequences of poverty.' Ach! how many times had he repeated that this evening? And how many times had he repeated: Forty-five bob a week: ten shillings rent, twenty-five shillings food, five shillings coal, gas and insurance; five bob left for clothes, recreation, little luxuries such as smokes and holidays. You gave a week of your life, every week, so that you might have a hovel for shelter, an insufficiency of food and five bob left over for to clothe yourself and the missis in shoddy. 'Aye, and what of the other things?' he asked himself. Books, music, brief holidays by seas that made the heart ache with their beauty, whose very memory sickened one with nostalgia of the soul. His brain refused further contemplation.

Helen was saying to Harry, in listless tones as both stared at the pavement, while, behind them, the brawl continued in the Hawkins's kitchen: 'Won't y' go home, Harry. . . . Ah hate y' t' be about when they're carryin' on like this,' shooting an apologetic glance at him: ' 'Tain't my fault, y'know.'

He put his arm about her reassuringly: 'Ne'er you mind, Helen,' he said, stoutly: 'You'll be out o' this here as soon as Ah get out o' me time an' find a job. Don't you worry, now. We'll be all right,' as an afterthought: 'An' Ah'm not goin' home till they've gone t' bed,' with suppressed passion: 'Gor blimey, it doa-narf mek me wild t' think y've got t' go in there t' sleep.' She did not answer; put her head on his shoulder and closed her eyes.

Kate Malloy, staring up into Ned's face as he stood, back to the door of his lodgings, thumbs thrust into his belt, Kate said, timidly: 'Aw, Ned, don't send me home yet. Ah didn't mean what Ah said. Ah'll wait till *you're* ready t' wed me.'

He smiled wryly: 'Thank y',' he said, sarcastically: 'Aaach! Some o' you judies mek me sick. Christ, if Ah'd married every bloody tart wot came t' me wi' your tale, Ah'd have a harem b' now,' staring at her: 'Y'll be all right. What the 'ell a'y' worryin' about?' hitching his belt and spitting: 'Y' ought t' be glad Ah luked at y'.'

'Oh, Ah am, Ned . . . Ah, am, really.'

'Well, go on. Y'd better hoppit, now, Ah'm tired. Meet me outside o' Duke o' Gloucester tomorrer night.' He turned about and lounged into his lodgings, closing the door on Kate. She stared at it awhile, then sighed heavily, and trudged off to her own lodgings, staring unblinkingly at the ground.

Larry turned to Sally; her eyes were full upon him. He saw the pale oval of her face, the graceful curve of her throat losing itself in the cheap material of her blouse; a glimpse of white teeth between slightly parted lips. The dew of youth was upon her, exuding fragrance. His eyes shone; he wanted to catch her in his arms; wanted to smother her with passionate kisses; wanted to feel her arms clinging about him. He made the shadow of a movement, then restrained himself.

'No, no,' cried an alarmed voice in his brain: another voice answered, recklessly: 'Damn the money and damn the consequences.'

He made a great effort to control the confusion of his thoughts: he said, in naked tones: 'Let's not deceive one another any longer, Sal. We both want the same thing. But you know my ideas,' bitterly: 'Forty-five bob a week. What a wage to build a future on. And look at Marlowe's: we none of us know when we're going to finish. What can I offer you? What can I . . .'

Impatiently she brushed aside his words: 'D'y' love me?' she asked, bluntly.

He stared at her: 'Why d'y' ask that, Sal, when you know.'

'D'y' love me?' she insisted.

'Yes . . .'

She rose, stood in front of him, regarding him with an earnest expression: 'Then let's get married.' He made as though to answer: she interrupted, eagerly, excitedly: 'Ah'll go out t' work so's we can have more money. Ah'll . . . Ah'll . . . Oh, Larry, Ah'd do owt for y' . . .'

He gazed at her, eyes kindling with deep affection: 'I know you would, Sal. But . . .' desperately: 'Aw, blimey, what the devil can we do,' an impatient wave of the hand towards the hovels of North Street: 'It's this. We can't get away from it . . .'

passionately: 'We'd go on and on but it'd get us. ... It gets everybody. Aw ...'

'But y' can't have *everything*,' she objected, wide-eyed.

'We not only can't, but *don't*,' he answered, warmly; then wearily: 'Oh, what's the use of talking, Sal. ... It's. ... It's wanting decent things and knowing they'll never be yours that hurts. Aw, but what am I talking about.'

She stared at him, mystified. She said, with a touch of impatience: 'It aint where y' live, it's who y' live with,' warmly: 'Besides, we'll soon be old and best part of our life gone. An' dreamin' about things y' can't have don't get y' anywhere ...' persuasively: 'Does it, Larry? Does it, now?'

He remained silent for a while, her words sinking deeply. He shook his head and sighed: 'Sometimes I think it does, Sal. But you don't know the misery of dreams. ... Be glad they don't plague you ...'

'Me ...?' she cried, wide-eyed: 'Me ...? Don't know dreams?' a bitterness tinged her tones of voice: 'You don't know. You don't know what Ah dream about you an' me. For ages, Larry.' She seated herself next him on the sill, said, appealingly: 'There's nowt for me to live for without you,' with unexpected passion: 'God, y' don't know what Ah'd do for you. ... Get house an' Ah'll come an' live wi' you. Who wants t' get married? Who cares what folk say?'

He was transfixed. Her earlier remarks still stuck in his throat. '... dreaming about things don't get y' anywhere.' 'We'll be old soon and best part of our life gone.' We'll be old soon. ... *Soon!* But not yet! A sensation of sudden gladness warmed him. He still was young; so was Sally; gorgeously young! On this dunghill of Hanky Park a rose was blowing for him. It, like all else, would shed its bloom. Not yet, though! Its intoxicating fragrance filled his nostrils. Grasp it, grasp, before it is too late. The thought of its passing was sickening. She was offering something priceless; balm, solace, affection: 'It ain't where y' live, it's who y' live with.' Voices whispered seductively; alluring visions of a clean kitchen radiant with the presence of Sally, rose to his mind. Ineffable home-comings!

He looked at her, his heart melting towards her. He surprised

her, saying: 'I'd have to start saving, Sal. ... I've no money
laid by. But if you'd wait ...'

Her face lit up with incredulous joy, became transfigured,
beatified. Breathlessly she whispered his name.


CHAPTER 4

## MUSICAL CHAIRS

AN erstwhile reformatory school for erring boys, an ugly,
barrack-like building, serves as one of the Two Cities' labour
exchanges. Hemmed in on three sides by slums, tenements
and doss houses, the remaining side stares at the gas works and
a cattle-loading mound, into, and out of which, bleating sheep,
cows and bulls, their eyes rolling, their parched tongues lolling,
are driven by loutish men and cowed dogs. And the slum children, seeing in the inoffensive creatures a means to exercise their
own animal instincts, come out of their dens armed with whips
and sticks and stones to belabour the animals as they pass,
meanwhile indulging in the most hideous inhuman screams,
shouts and howls such as occasions horror in the mind of a
sympathetic observer and, doubtless, terrified bewilderment on
the parts of the doomed beasts as they, smarting under whip,
stick and stone, run blindly along the dinning unfamiliar streets
finally to find themselves packed, suffocatingly, in wretched
cattle trucks.

A high wall, enclosing an asphalt yard, ran round the building. On it was scrawled in chalk, and in letters a foot high: 'Unemployed Mass Meeting Today 3 o'clock.' The handiwork of
Communists five or six weeks ago.

Harry Hardcastle, white mercerized cotton scarf wrapped
loosely about his neck, a tuft of fair hair protruding from beneath the neb of his oily cap, patches on the knees and backside of his overalls, stood in a long queue of shabby men, hands
in pockets, staring fixedly and unseeing at the ground. At street
corners, leaning against house walls or squatting on the kerb-
stones, were more men, clothes stinking of age, waiting until

the queue opposite went into the building when they would take their places in forming another. And all through the day, every quarter-hour, would see another crowd of fresh faces coming to sign the unemployed register at their appointed times.

The day was Monday. The Saturday previous, Harry's apprenticeship, together with those of Tom Hare, Bill Simmons, Jack Lindsay, Sam Hardie and the rest of their contemporaries, had come to an end. They now were fully qualified engineers. They also were qualified to draw the dole.

Harry had not yet told Helen. Perhaps there wouldn't be any need. As he stood there his thoughts were often infused by glows of high optimism as he marvelled on the immense possibilities of the situation. Imagine it! If, now that he had served his time, he found another situation, his wage would be that of a skilled man! Forty-five shillings a week! Wealth unspendable! It was incredible.

Already, in fancy, he had found himself a job; had bought himself and Helen endless necessities and, with excitement and exhilaration, was making elaborate plans for their wedding.

His confidence would ebb, precipitately; chill terrors froze his heart. Suppose. ... Billy Higgs had been unemployed these three years now. You wouldn't know the man; such a change; a threadbare, shuffling, stoop-shouldered furtive old man, that, not long ago, had known laughter. Suppose ...

Then, again, Helen had to be told. ... Still, after he had 'signed on' he could, nay, *would* go the rounds of Trafford Park and visit the other engineering shops. Why, it only needed a 'Yes' from a foreman and everything would be as it never had been before. He would use all his powers of persuasion and ingratiation. He would. ... Oh, hurry there, hurry, hurry, hurry.

Someone struck him a flat hand blow on the back. He turned, startled. Jack Lindsay, grinning: 'Wharro, Harry,' he cried, falling into the queue by Harry's side: 'Ain't this a bit of a lark, eh, lad?'

'What?'

'Why, y' silly sod, lyin' abed listenin' t' t' bloody buzzers when rest o' t' folk 're sloggin' at it.' He grinned anew. Harry grunted. Jack continued: 'Ain't it funny the way streets are . . . y'know . . . all quiet-like an' nobody about': a laugh: 'Ah felt as though Ah was playin' wag.'

A pause.

Harry said, impulsively: 'Ah'm gunna g' round lukkin' for work when Ah've signed on. A' you?'

Jack made a wry face: 'Ah'm gunna have a week or two's grass fust. Cuss work an' cuss them as made it. It's bin nowt but work e'er sin' Ah was owld enough t' peddle newspapers. They give us seventeen an' a' tanner dole an' that's more'n we got at Marlowe's after they'd stopped us our insurance money and we'd paid shop lads for runnin' us errands,' as an afterthought surlily: 'Besides, there ain't no bloody work. Y'on'y waste shoe leather lukkin' for it. Another crowd o' schoolkids tuk on at Marlowe's this mornin'. Ar Albert wus one on 'em an . . .'

There was a sudden shuffling of feet; a movement on the part of the queue. It surged into the asphalt yard and broke into two rivers, one comprising men already on the books, the other, new claimants for benefit. These last ran pell mell across the yard to a room on the ground floor marked: 'New Claims'. Instantly, the men at the street corners crossed the road to assemble in a new and quickly growing queue; newcomers sauntered to the street corners, some seating themselves on the kerb-stones to wait.

The room in which Harry and Jack, with the rest of the crush, found themselves, was oblong shaped, the upper parts of its bare brick walls painted a dull green, the lower, chocolate. An L-shaped counter ran the length of two sides behind which clerks sat at tables or searched filing cabinets for documents. Here and there, at regular intervals, more clerks sat to the counter attending to the new claimants. A dozen or so rows of chairs faced the counter's shortest arm, and were quickly occupied the instant the men rushed in. Those coming later lounged against the wall.

When one of those seated was called to the counter, his immediate neighbour took his seat, the remainder, with much shuffling of feet and grating of chairs, all moved up a place so that none of the chairs ever were vacant, the queue waiting for them often stretching into the yard. The proceeding had come to be known as 'Musical chairs', prefixed, always, by unprintable epithets.

Harry and Jack found places on the third row from the front.

He looked about him, scanned the notices plastering the walls. Government subsidized schemes for emigration illustrated by a couple of pictures, the one of a down at heel unemployed man standing staring up at a miniature facsimile of the picture, the other of the same man, now dressed like a cowboy, smiling broadly, looking very prosperous, holding a hand out, invitingly, while waving the other towards the distant prospect of a nice homestead, and beyond, of wide, rolling cornlands where hundreds of the erstwhile unemployed man's employees garnered his wheat. 'Canada for me!' he was saying. Pasted next to it was a pink bill, a warning to the unemployed, telling how a local man who had drawn benefit for his employed wife whom he had represented not to be working, had been sentenced to 'THREE MONTHS' HARD LABOUR'.

His gaze wandered; was attracted by a constant procession of men visiting one part of the counter marked: 'Situations Vacant'. Engineers in overalls, joiners and painters and clerks in seedy suits; stevedores, navvies and labourers in corduroys. They came singly and in couples, stood in front of the taciturn clerk, offered their unemployment cards, received answer by way of a shake of the head, turned on their heels and went out again without speaking.

They were soon attended to, Harry thought. Different from having to sit here where the waiting was interminable. He sighed and shifted restlessly, as he eyed the clerks behind the counter working with leisurely indifference. He wanted to be off in search of work; felt petulant that this business should delay him.

From the rooms above came the ceaseless rumbling of the feet of the unemployed who, segregating into a dozen or so serpentine queues, two, three, and four deep, moved forward, slowly, over the sawdusted floor towards the long counter divided into compartments and numbered, where the registers were signed.

'This *is* a bloody, blindin' lousy hole, anyway,' said Jack Lindsay: 'Luk at that,' he jerked his thumb towards a conspicuous notice forbidding smoking: 'Watch me seat, Harry,' he said: 'Ah'm off for a puff in t' yard.'

A quarter-hour passed: every five minutes or so the end seat on the front row would be vacated: all would move up a place, noisily. Jack returned: 'Hey,' he said: 'Jesus! Ain't y' moved? Blimey, if Ah'd ha' known Ah'd ha' fetched me dinner.' Harry forced a smile: 'Ah'm goin' for a smoke, Jack. Not be long.'

He went into the asphalt yard, lit a cigarette and stood staring at the constant traffic of unemployed men. Staring, depressed, the cigarette smouldering unheeded between his fingers.

He found himself fretting and fuming, petulantly indignant that he should be numbered as one of them. Just when he and Helen were making plans for the future: 'Oooo, Ah *do* hope Ah can get a job afore tonight,' he muttered to himself, fervently.

He found that he had lost the desire to smoke, extinguished the cigarette and returned to the room, writhing inwardly with impatience and asking himself, angrily, how the devil could a fellow get a job when all these men were out of collar. Still, he reassured himself, when he calmed down, still, perhaps it was true what the papers and people said about these fellows. Perhaps these fellows never looked for work, didn't want it. Yet –. He glanced, surlily, at the 'Situations Vacant' counter. There was a steady trickle of men there. He stared at the floor, brooding.

Presently he was called to the counter to answer many questions which were documented by the clerk. When this was concluded and Harry had received a yellow card with instructions to sign the register twice weekly, he with a timid, ingratiating grin, asked the clerk: 'Any chance of a job?' Without looking up the clerk inclined his head towards the far end of the counter: 'Apply at the vacancies,' he said. The man at the vacancies shook his head but did not speak.

Harry went outside. You couldn't very well expect them to find work for you: you'd got to find it yourself. 'Ah wus daft for askin', anyway. Ah should ha' known.'

Queues still were forming. Women, with unwashed faces and matted hair stood on their doorsteps, arms folded, leaning against the doors idly watching their filthy, half-naked children playing in the gutters. Some of the women held loud conversation with their neighbours across the street.

Jack had asked Harry to await his coming. Harry forgot him the moment he stepped into the street: only one thought was in mind: would he succeed in his quest for work? 'Gor, blimey, Ah hope Ah do. Aw, God, let me gerra job, will y'?' So much depended on it, nay, *everything* depended on it. Phew! suppose he was unsuccessful. He wouldn't have the nerve to tell Helen. Something akin to panic clutched his heart: he quickened his pace as though a job waited on speediness.

Trafford Park is a modern miracle. Thirty years ago it was the country seat of a family whose line goes back to the ancient British kings and whose name the area retains. Thirty years ago its woodlands were chopped down to clear the way for commerce and to provide soles for Lancashire clogs; thirty years ago the park-roving deer were rounded up and removed; thirty years ago the lawns, lately gay with marquees, awnings and fashionably dressed ladies and gentlemen, were obliterated. The Hall still stands though it now houses only dust and memories and echoes. And the twin lions surmounting either side the wide flight of steps now survey, instead of lawns alive with guests, a double railway track only six yards away, and, where the drives once wound their serpentine paths through the woods, the fungus of modern industry, huge engineering shops, flour mills, timber yards, oil refineries, automobile works, repositories for bonded merchandise, choke and foul the prospect. The river that flows at the foot of the adjoining paddocks is changed also: it now gives hospitality to ocean-going shipping from the seven seas, shipping whose sirens echo mournfully in the night: a river no longer in name even, but the Manchester Ship Canal.

A Five Year Plan thirty years ahead of the Russian. Yesterday the country seat of an aristocrat, today the rowdy seat of commerce. Revolution! and not a drop of blood spilt or a shot fired!

At this hour there were few pedestrians abroad though there was much traffic; heavy and light lorries, motor- and horse-drawn; railway engines pulling long lines of wagons in the tracks by the roadside. Great cranes lifting and lowering. A heartening sight; surely, in such a place, he could find a job.

How familiar, companionable, the rumbling of the machinery in the first place he called on; his heart leapt in response to the din. Eyes shining, a tiny smile on his lips, he put his question to the man at the time office: 'No we don't want nobody.' Harry thanked him and withdrew, hurrying towards the next. Of course, he reassured himself, of course, one couldn't expect success at the first time of asking. He was *certain* to find a berth with persistence. Why, he'd be running home before noon, running to meet Helen full of the good news. Even at the next place, and the next, hope failed to die.

Then gloomy forebodings insinuated themselves, forebodings that soon transformed themselves into scaring haunting dread. Billy Higgs and his generation – three years, now. That such a fate might be his . . .

Gosh! And Helen had to be told yet.

He stared up at the huge buildings furtively, licked his lips and ran a finger round his scarf: 'Aw, God, just let me get a job. Ah don't care if it's on'y half pay,' he found comfort in this conversation: kept it up: 'An' if y' can't find me a job Ah wish y'd mek Helen see it like as though it won't be for long. Ah mean, that if Ah don't get a job t' day let me get one soon. . . . Blimey, suppose she gets fed up wi' me if Ah'm out o' collar long. Suppose she gets another bloke wot's workin'. . . . Gor blimey, Ah ne'er thought o' that.'

Some of the works anticipated such callers as he; there were notices at the entrances: 'NO HANDS WANTED.'

He ignored them. You never knew but what somebody had just been sacked.

'Please, sir, d' y' want any hands?' A holding of the breath, an anxious stare.

'Do we hell as like. Go on, sod off. Can't y' read? Blimey, we're sackin' 'em 'usselves. An' don't bang the door when y' go out, either, or Ah'll be after y' an' kick y'r backside.'

There were no more places to visit.

He trudged homewards, staring, a strangulating sensation in his throat, a feeling in his heart as though he had committed some awful crime in which he was sure to be found out.

A solitary figure in the midst of busy commerce; a solitary figure wearing a surprised expression, hands thrust into pockets, white mercerized cotton scarf loose about his neck, the down of youth on his pale cheeks. He tried to explain it all to himself, to reason it out. There was no response to thought, only a mystified silence.

As he approached Hanky Park he heard the discordances of the noonday sirens. The sound was prostrating. Those sounds were no concern of his now; they weren't addressed to him telling him that it was time for him to refrain from work for an hour.

'Ah'm not workin'. . . . Ah'm out o' work.' Someone else had his place at Marlowe's and no other firm required him. He was OUT.

He felt icily alone.

A tinge of shame coloured his cheeks; he licked his lips and slunk along by the walls. Then a burst of resentment swelled his heart. Didn't the people responsible know what this refusal to give him work meant to him? Didn't they know he now was a man? Didn't they know he wanted a home of his own? Didn't they know he'd served his time? Didn't they know he was a qualified engineer? Was he any concern of anybody's? Oh, what use was there in asking the air such questions? What sense in . . .

'Hallo, Harry.'

It was Helen.

'Oh, hallo, Helen,' he forced a smile. She regarded him, perceiving instantly that there was something amiss: 'Why, what's matter, Harry?' she asked, all concern.

'Ah'm out o' collar,' he muttered, looking from her. She knew, now.

'Well,' she answered, brightly: 'Y' knew y'd have t' finish at Marlowe's when y' came out o' y' time, didn't y'? It'll be better for us both when y' find a job, now.' She was amazed at his gloom. Here was their opportunity.

Her attitude was surprising. He said, dolefully: 'Aye, but Ah've just bin round Trafford Park. They don't want nobody.' He stared at her with misgiving.

'Well, y' don't expect t' walk into a job straightaway. Pooh, y' ain't bin out o' work half a day,' confidently: 'Y'll find one soon.'

Her optimism was infectious: 'D'y' think so?' he said, smiling eagerly.

'Of course. You see.'

His eyes kindled, he smiled, intensely relieved: 'My,' he murmured, fervently: 'Won't it be grand for us both when Ah do?'

CHAPTER 5

# THE PLOT THICKENS

THE rain hissed and bounced on the pavements choking soughs and forming large pools in the roadways; air was full of the sounds of gushing water; downspouts a-rush, cascades from the eaves where gutterings were perished.

Mrs Nattle, sitting by the table in her stinking kitchen stared through the streaming windows wondering when her patrons would appear.

The table top said that the day was Monday. It was set out with many rows of pawn-tickets, many more than usual, each partly covered by a small heap of silver and copper. Also there were a half dozen tumblers handy, and, unbeknown to anybody except Mrs Nattle, a three-quarter-full bottle of whisky stood on the floor between her feet entirely obscured by her trailing skirts. She said, to the cat curled on the arm of the dilapidated horsehair couch: 'It's rain wot's keepin' 'um away,' adding, as an afterthought: 'Dammit.'

Shuffling footsteps without; sounds of someone's holding a conversation with themselves: Mrs Nattle pricked her ears: a voice asked, as the footsteps ceased outside the front door: 'A' y' in, missis?'

'Is that you, Nancy?'

Mrs Dorbell came in, drenched.

'Tek y' shawl off. Spread it in front o' fire,' said Mrs Nattle.

Mrs Dorbell complied: 'Wot weather,' she said: 'Ne'er stopped for a week.' She turned, eyed the glasses, sniffed, glanced at Mrs Dorbell and said: 'The oosual,' and, while Mrs Nattle reached for the bottle hid beneath her skirts Mrs Dorbell, pressing down her thin hair with her thin yellow hands sat down on the couch and said, mournfully, that she had not had a wink of sleep all the night owing to her 'cough, cough, cough . . .'

Further complainings were not possible since she was interrupted by the appearances of portly Mrs Bull and tiny Mrs Jike who both entered uninvited and unannounced and who divested themselves of their dripping shawls simultaneously. Mrs Jike also removed her husband's cap from her head and hung it to dry on the rusty knob of the oven door. She sat next Mrs Dorbell, gave herself a tiny hug and said, brightly: 'Well, gels, how a' y' all this mornin'?'

'As oosual. Bad,' said Mrs Dorbell.

'Ah'd be all right on'y for a twinge o' rheumatic,' said Mrs Bull, 'but Ah don't worry none. There's a rare lot on 'em i' Weaste (cemetery) as'd be glad of a twinge or two.'

'Ay, aye,' said Mrs Jike: 'The Lord loves a cheerful soul,' feeling in her placket for her snuff-box: 'Here, have a pinch o' Birdseye,' to Mrs Nattle as the snuff-box went round: 'Three penn'orth, Mrs Nakkle,' she grinned ingratiatingly and made a wrinkle-nosed grimace.

Mrs Bull eyed the many rows of pawn-tickets and put out her lower lip: she said: 'All this here unemployment's doin' *some*-body some good, Sair Ann.'

Sair Ann glanced at her, sharply, pausing in her occupation of dispensing drinks: 'What ails y' now?' she asked.

Mrs Bull grunted, her copious belly shook and her pendulous bosom wobbled: 'Luk at table. Full o' pawn-tickets. Why, y' ne'er had quarter as many customers a year ago.'

'Things is bad, that's why,' murmured Mrs Dorbell, gloomily, holding glass in one hand and pinch of snuff in the other; she added, with relish, after she had consumed the snuff: 'But thank God, unemployment or no, they can't touch me owld age pension. Wot a blessin', wot a blessin'.'

Mrs Jike laughed: 'That ne'er gowse on short time,' seriously: 'Eh, but did y' ever see sich a crowd as is at Price and Jones's nowadays? My – my – my! Full to the doors an' a queue all way round beck entry and half-way up street like it might be the Elbert 'All.'

Mrs Dorbell added her refrain: 'Things is bad.'

'Well,' said Mrs Nattle, corking the bottle with a flourish after pouring out a generous drink for herself: 'Well,' she said, replacing the bottle beneath her skirts then glancing at Mrs Bull, significantly: 'Well, there's nowt like worry for poppin' folk off. An' that'll be no ill wind for thee, chargin' like y' do for layin' folk out. Wot Ah've seen o' some folk round about here – worritin' their guts out like damn fools – What *Ah've* seen of 'em there'll be plenty o' work for you, soon enough.'

'Yaaach. They . . .'

A knock, sounding upon the door, caused glasses to disappear as by magic. 'Who's there?' cried Mrs Nattle, suspiciously: 'Come in. Don't stand in pours o' rain.'

It was Mrs Hardcastle. She was smiling with apologetic nervousness and, her own shoes being useless save for the house, she wore Hardcastle's clogs: 'Ah've on'y come for . . .' she said: glancing from one to the other, timidly: 'Ah'd t' pawn me weddin' ring. Though *he* don't know this is a brass 'un Ah'm wearin'. He'd murder me if he found Ah'd bin t' pawnshop wi' it. So Mrs Nakkle tuk it for me – An', Ah've come . . .' she smiled, expectantly, at Mrs Nattle.

'There 'tis, lass,' replied Mrs Nattle, picking up one of the pawn-tickets and the money thereon: 'There 'tis. Y' wanted hafe a crown on ring. But Ah on'y asked for two an' five. Y'see, if Ah'd ha' got y' hafe a crown y'd have had three'a'pence interes' t' find. But being as it's under hafe a crown owld Price can't charge more'n a penny. So, two an' five, wi' a penny for pawn-ticket an' tuppence for me trouble, leaves two and two. There y'are, lass. Two an' tuppence.' She gave her the money, adding: 'Now, what about y' Good Samaritan?'

'Well, y' see,' murmured Mrs Hardcastle: '*He's* finished at pit till further notice. An' our Harry ain't found a job yet. . . . It's gettin' on for nine months sin' he's bin out an' no signs yet. Ah don't know what Ah'd do if it weren't for our Sal's bit . . .'

'Aw,' said Mrs Bull, with impatience: 'Damn owld Grumpole an' his Good Samaritan. Thee put thy money in y' belly, Mrs Hardcastle and mek him wait.'

'Tek no notice of her,' snapped Mrs Nattle: 'Y' wouldn't like y' husband t' get a summons, would y', now?'

'Oh, no,' replied Mrs Hardcastle, alarmed: 'Here, y'd better tek a shillin'. Ah can't spare any more. There ain't a bite o' food in house for their teas. An' y' know what a temper our Sal's got. Eee, though, she's a changed lass e'er since she's bin goin' out wi' that Larry Meath,' she looked at Mrs Bull and smiled: 'Did y' know they're gettin' wed in a fortnight?' to them all: 'Though they want it kep' a secret.'

'Now I *am* pleased,' said Mrs Jike, turning to Mrs Dorbell: 'A weddin' in street. Did you ever?'

'Ay,' answered Mrs Dorbell, shaking her head: 'These weddin's today ain't like when Ah wus a gel. There wus free beer an' jiggin' in street i' them days.'

'Well,' said Mrs Bull to Mrs Hardcastle: 'Larry's a gradely lad an' that lass o' thine's lucky t' ha' gotten him. He ain't o' the strongest, though, an' he'd do better if he luked to his health more. Ah don't like that there cough of his. An' all that politicianin' he's bin doin' lakely in this kind o' weather should ne'er have bin done,' emphatically: 'Luk what's happened wi' all his talk. National Gover'ment, an' Labour nowhere. 'Tain't no use talkin' socialism to folk. 'Twon't come in our time though Ah allus votes Labour an' allus will.'

'Ah votes for none on 'em,' said Mrs Dorbell: 'Me ma an' her ma was blue (Conservative) or they wus red (Liberal), just depended on which o' t' two gev most coal an' blankets. But there ain't none o' that now as kerridge folk've left Eccles Owld Road.'

'Yaa, y' owld scut,' snapped Mrs Bull, contemptuously: 'Yew and y' kerridge folk. Tuh! Y'd sell y' soul for a load o' coal, some o' y'. Y' – make – me – sick. Eddicated an' well-read fellers like Larry Meath talkin' till they're blue in face and you ...' disgustedly: 'Aw, what's use o' me talkin'?'

'Ah ne'er bothers me head about wot don't concern me,' replied Mrs Dorbell unruffled: 'Ah understands nowt about poli-

tics, an' nowt Ah want t' understand. But Ah do understand a
load o' coal.'

Mrs Nattle made a face and raised her glass to it: 'They're all
same once they get i' parleyment. All on 'em, red, white or blue.'

'Well,' said Mrs Bull, draining her glass: 'Wot Larry Meath
said long enough ago's all comin' true. Everybody's comin' out
o' work. Not house in street but what somebody's finished or
feard o' finishin' any day. Aye, even Larry Meath, too. He told
me he's feard for it any week-end. Him wi' a safe job, too. And
how're t'others gonna go on? It's gonna be hard on young-
sters; specially them gels as is in family way like poor Kate
Malloy. She ses him as did it – though she won't say his name –
can't afford t' marry her. What d' y' make o' that?' to Mrs Hardcastle: 'Aye, an' if Larry does come out it'll put paid t' weddin'.'
Mrs Hardcastle shook her head as did Mrs Bull who concluded:
'Ay, Ah don't know what's gonna come of us all. Ah ne'er remember nowt like it in all my born days and Ah've seen some
hard times.'

Mrs Jike tittered: 'We'll all end up in workhouse. Somebody'll
have to keep us,' with a bright smile: 'It down't do to look on
dark side,' offering her empty glass to Mrs Nattle: 'Another
sip, Sair Anne. While y've got it, enjoy it, say I. If it down't gow
one wiy it'll gow another.'

2

Sally, nostrils dilating, stared at Kate Malloy who stood in front
of her, quavering; she demanded, on a note of incredulity: 'An'
he said he ain't to blame?'

Kate, fearful of the consequences of Sal's impetuosity, laid a
restraining hand on her arm and replied, anxiously: 'He don't
mean it, though, Sal. Drunk he was when he said it. He loves
me. . . . He told me he did.'

She shook Kate's arm away impatiently: 'Oh, what a *fool*
you are,' she declared, vehemently: 'Fancy bein' such a mug to
let a thing like that muck about wi' you. Ya! Just like him it is.
Him all o'er,' staring at Kate, pityingly: 'An' y' still want t'
marry him?'

Kate fingered the link of Woolworth beads round her neck, licked her lips and regarded Sal with a hungry light in her eyes. She did not speak. Sally shrugged and added, resolutely: 'Well there's no two ways about it. If he won't marry y' he's got t' give y' summat towards its keep. Where is he?'

'Duke o' Gloucester,' Kate murmured: 'But you won't do nowt rash, will y', Ned – Ah mean, Sal. Oh, Ah don't want him t' . . .'

'Ne'er heed what *you* want.'

They had been conversing on the doorstep of No. 17; the street lamps had just been lit; children were playing around the lamp-posts; groups of the neighbourhood's young men stood talking at the street corners. Frequently middle-aged and old men and women passed to and fro carrying jugs filled, or to be filled, with supper beer. A blaze of light flooded the pavement immediately outside the open doors of the Duke of Gloucester: from where Kate and Sally stood they could hear, above the conversation, laughter and the rattle of glasses, the hoarse voice of the bar-tender calling: 'Time, gen'l'men. Time there, please.'

'Come on,' said Sally, with determination, as the patrons of the public-house noisily vacated the place.

Ned was one of the last to leave. The doors slammed behind him and the bolts were shot as he stepped heavily into the street where he stood awhile thumbs in belt, staring about him with an air of indecision.

Sally tapped him on the arm. He turned. She interrupted his unspoken greeting, eyes blazing, breathing quick and sharp. She said: 'Ah want t' talk to you.' She turned about, walked a half-dozen paces or so from the groups in front the public-house. With a blank expression of mystification he followed, not seeing Kate standing by the dark house walls staring at him with fascinated fixity.

'What's up?' he asked, perplexed, halting in front of Sally and staring down at her.

She curled her lip: 'You ought to know what's up. You and Kate Malloy,' glaring at him: 'Well, what about it?'

'Worrabout wot? Worrabout wot?' he asked, his mouth slightly agape, brows raised.

'Kate's in family way and you're father.'

'Me? Me?' he blustered: 'Aw, come off'n it! Blimey, Ah ain't th' only one as's bin wi' her.'

'Ooo! You dirty dog. You're a specimen, you are,' she exclaimed, supremely contemptuous. She turned to Kate who was holding a hand to her mouth and whimpering: 'Come here, Kate,' she said. Kate obeyed, avoiding Narkey's frowning expression: 'Y' heard what he said. D' y' still want t' have owt t' do w' such a rotten lot?'

''Ere, 'ere. Shut y' trap, or Ah'll shut it for y',' Narkey cried, savagely.

'Yes, and the likes o' you *would*, too,' she snapped back, defiantly: 'You. . . . You . . .' eyeing him from head to foot: 'Yaa! You ain't a man. Ten a penny, that's what your kind are. Ten a penny. Allus y' fit for's t' tek best out of a girl like Kate what'll let y' do what y' like, then blame it on somebody else.'

'What about that bloody swine as y' let muck about wi' you? How many times has 'e had wot 'e wants?' he demanded, thickly: 'Up another street wi' him, eh?'

'Leave him out of it,' she replied. Tossing her head, proudly: 'He's doin' more for me than you'll do for her. He *will* marry me.'

'An' so would Ah ha' done. Ah asked y' . . .'

'An' y' asked Kate, too. . . Till y' got what y' wanted out of her . . .'

'Augh! Her!' He turned on Kate, angrily: 'Y' gawmless-lookin' bitch, y'. Why didn't y' do as Ah told y'? Ma Haddock would ha' shifted it for y'. Jesus,' desperately: ' 'n how do Ah know it's mine.'

'Oh, Ned, Ned,' Kate whimpered: 'Y' know there ain't nobody but you.'

'More fool you, Kate. You shouldn't ha . . .'

'You shut it,' snapped Narkey. He raised his fist and sent Sally reeling against the wall with a blow to her bosom: 'Think on, y' bloody interferin' bitch, y'. Ah'll get even with that bastard y' sweet on. S'elp me. Ah ain't done wi' him. Don't you forget it.'

White, holding her hand to the injured spot, she faced him and forced a provocative smile. She tossed her head.

'Ah'll . . .' he began. Then a sudden thought arrested further speech. He paused. If he declined to marry Kate there would be an affiliation order which wouldn't take into consideration the uncertainty of his work. But, if he married Kate he could send her to work after her confinement! She was complaisant, was passionately infatuated with him; the kind who would obey him absolutely, who never would have the nerve to question his comings or goings or the manner he wished to spend his time and with whom he wished to spend it. She would be perfectly subservient. He turned to Sally: 'Ah'll show y' what kind of a bloke Ah am. Ah'll marry her,' to Kate: 'D'y' hear?' with rising impulsiveness: 'Ah'll marry y' this week-end,' to Sally: 'D'y' hear, y' interferin' bitch?'

'So y' ought. Y' doin' her no favour.'

He snarled an oath, turned on his heel and stamped off to his lodgings, nursing bitter grudges against Sally, Larry and Kate. Already he was repenting his impulsiveness. Kate followed in his shadow, a timid smile transfiguring her face.

Sally sighed, stood there awhile staring into nothingness, responding expansively, to the inevitable comparison between Larry and Ned.

Within a fortnight she and Larry would be married! At last she had overcome his caution. Yes, and in the face of their inability to save enough money to buy their furnishings cash down. What few pounds had been saved had been given as deposit against the hire purchase of the furniture now in store. He hadn't anything left, now. Neither had she. And they were in debt to the tune of the balance of the furniture money. Well, she would prove to him that happiness did not depend on money. She would show him how quickly her wages would pay off the debt. She would prove him to be wrong. A soaring of the spirits; an intoxicating picture of themselves in a home of their own.

A door opened opposite; an oblong beam of gaslight stabbed her eyes and attracted her attention. A shabby young man came out and closed the door. He thrust his hands into his pockets, hunched his shoulders and trudged to No. 17 with a slouching gait.

She frowned petulantly; pouted, asking herself, plaintively, whether she could help it if her father and Harry were un-employed. Anyway, Harry should have taken the job in an office when he left school; he wouldn't be advised. Oh, she couldn't take all the world's troubles on her shoulders. Hadn't she enough of her own? Peeved, she followed Harry into the house.

CHAPTER 6

## A MAN OF LEISURE

It got you slowly, with the slippered stealth of an unsuspected, malignant disease.

You fell into the habit of slouching, of putting your hands into your pockets and keeping them there; of glancing at people, furtively, ashamed of your secret, until you fancied that everybody eyed you with suspicion. You knew that your shabbiness betrayed you; it was apparent for all to see. You prayed for the winter evenings and the kindly darkness. Darkness, poverty's cloak. Breeches backside patched and re-patched; patches on knees, on elbows. Jesus! All bloody patches. Gor' blimey!

'Remember t' day when me ma bought me new pair over-alls!' he murmured, to himself.

He halted, unconsciously, by a street corner, stood staring at nothing, seeing himself, on that occasion, stalking the streets a beaming smile on his lips: rejuvenated, full of confidence and daring. Unashamed; hopeful.

Daring! Round Trafford Park and to all the other engineering shops: 'Any chance of a job, mister?'

'No.'

'Any vacancies, mate?'

Snappily: 'Get off, out of it. Open y' eyes,' a thumb jerked towards a board: NO HANDS WANTED.

Trudging home, dispirited, tired. Pausing on Trafford Bridge to stare at the ships in the Ship Canal.

Ships! Cliffs; afterglow on calm seas; gulls; blue skies, heather and gorse; tiny, whitewashed cottage 'To Let', half a crown a week. Walking home with Helen in the bright moonlight.

Helen! He saw her face in the murky water below; felt tight in the throat, turned away to slink homewards. Home! His spirits retched with nausea. How much longer? Daren't go to see Helen. Couldn't bear to look at that question eternally in her eyes: 'Have you got a job, yet?'

No money. She'd be like you, fed up. 'Ah'm goin' barmy. Ah'll jump in cut one o' these days.'

There was a dull vacuity in his eyes nowadays; he became listless, hard of hearing, saying, 'Eh?' when anybody asked him a question.

Nothing to do with time; nothing to spend; nothing to do tomorrow nor the day after; nothing to wear; can't get married. A living corpse; a unit of the spectral army of three million lost men.

Hands in pockets, shoulders hunched, he would slink round the by-streets to the billiard hall, glad to be somewhere out of the way of the public gaze, any place where there were no girls to see him in his threadbare jacket and patched overalls. Stealing into the place like a shadow to seat himself in a corner of one of the wall seats to watch the prosperous young men who had jobs and who could afford billiards, cigarettes and good clothes.

Watch that bloke there, Harry. . . . He'll be chucking his tab-end away in a minute. There it goes! Stoop, surreptitiously, pretend you are fastening your bootlace. Grab the cigarette end now . . . there's no one looking. Aaaah! A long puff; tastes good. But it wasn't always so easy as that. Sometimes his vigilant eyes would see the butt end disappear into the spittoon, or its careless owner might crush it beneath his heel.

At other times his heart would vomit at the thought of the billiard hall. He would saunter about the streets, aimlessly; kick at a tin can lying in the gutter, shoo an alley cat: 'Pshhhh! Gerrout of it!' hum or whistle some daft jazz tune, stand transfixed at street corners, brain a blank. Then, waking to a deep hungering for a smoke, would drift inevitably, to the billiard hall. Or he might forget where he was going; have his attention diverted by the play-bills of the picture theatres; half-naked tarts being mauled by dark haired men in evening clothes. Daft. Sometimes there were interesting police notices in the chip shop window: 'Lost, a Toy Dog. £5 Reward.' Jesus! A fiver for a blasted mongrel. Go'n look for it, Harry. A fiver, though! 'Wanted for Murder'. A fellow who's murdered a bank clerk for money: 'All y've got t' do, Harry, is t' sneak into a bank, land the clerk a good 'un over the head then help y' self.'

'Oh, it's daft. Ah'm barmy,' he said, aloud. A passing woman looked at him and wondered. He read the movie play-bills again, groaned, inwardly, that he lacked the necessary three-pence – no, sixpence, threepence each for Helen and he.

They'd have a night at the Flecky Parlour and he'd buy her a tanner's worth of chocolate, a box of twenty cigarettes; a new suit for himself and a rig-out for her; afterwards they'd catch the train, off for their honeymoon. Barmy. What am Ah talking about? Dreaming daft day-dreams until you were dizzy. Oh, Oh, how much longer? Fall, pitchy night, he now was a creature of the dark. This sunlight was reproachful; it sang of the cliffs and the bracken. The very houses pained the inward eye; spoke of homes, of happy marriages. He eyed them, hungrily, saw himself coming home from work, Helen, bright and clean, meeting him at the door. Blind ole Riley! Imagine it! Having a home of your own where you could love Helen and be sure that nobody could trespass upon your love-making! No more dodging it on Dawney's Hill or in a dark back entry. Blimey! Allus Ah want is a job an' we could do it! A job; money!

Money.

'Ah may as well be in bloody prison.' He suddenly wakened to the fact that he was a prisoner. The walls of the shops, houses and places of amusement were his prison walls; lacking money to buy his way into them the doors were all closed against him. That was the function of doors and walls; they were there to keep out those who hadn't any money. He was a prisoner at large. Instantly, the confines of the world shrank. He felt a contraction within him; tremors plucked his heart; stare-eyed fears tiptoed through his brain. Walls and doors everywhere closing in on him; towering, taking upon themselves ominous qualities. No matter where he went there would be walls and doors and he would have to remain on their outsides. Walls and doors guarding from him the things he wanted. Where can a man go who hasn't any money? Wide, wide world; boundless firmament. He stood, wide-eyed, staring, palpitant, afraid.

There were other ways of killing time than brooding. The boiler-house at Marlowe's cotton mill. The firehole gave on to the street. And Bob Russell, whose backyard door faced the Hardcastle's, worked here as stoker. Fascinating to stand there watching him stripped to the waist, his body bathed in the fierce yellow glare of the firehole; glorious the sight of the sweep of Bob's strong arms as he chucked shovel after shovel of fuel into the heart of the fire. Harry could feel energy creeping up his arms, tingling under his skin: 'Hey, Bob, lad . . . let's have a try, will y'?' ingratiatingly: 'Go on. Just one or two shovels.'

Bob grinned, flicked a sweat rag out of his belt and wiped the back of his neck: 'Aw reet. He'y'are,' he said. Harry, grinning, slid down the heaped fuel eagerly, threw aside his coat and picked up the shovel whilst Bob watched him, smiling. After two or three minutes Harry paused, breathless, exhausted, unable to continue. Bob laughed: 'Y're out o' fettle, Harry, lad. Here, gie us y' shovel. Tha'll ha' fire goin' out.' Guiltily, Harry put on his coat and drifted away.

This vicious fear of deterioration drove him to seek the companionship of the others, Jack Lindsay and the rest. Being all in the same boat, as it were, was something of a consolation.

Swinbury Park, about a couple of miles in a westerly direction from Hanky Park, a place of meadows, trees, with a wealthy person's mansion here and there, was their favourite haunt. The attraction was the new Liverpool–Manchester road, the spectacle of its making was interesting. A brand new thirty-odd-mile road, magnet for unemployed men of all trades who lined the cutting, lounging in the grass. Not in the expectation of work; it was merely an interesting way of killing time. Men of all trades, joiners, painters, bricklayers, engineers, dockers, miners and navvies; all watching a handful of men working. Watching.

This section of the new road ran through undulating parkland skirting a golf course. Progress had razed to the ground some of the mansions of the wealthy Manchester merchant princes, had driven a line through the park's centre, devouring, crushing all in its path.

Modern progress; a handful of men working; crowds of unemployed watching. The road grew, perceptibly. A light, narrow gauge railway, a line of jubilee wagons and a steam-navvy demolished inclines and tipped the superflux into declivities making the crooked straight and the rough places plain.

It became tedious to hear the old men repeating, time and time again: 'Luk at yonder,' indicative of the steam-navvy: 'Begob, there used t' be a gang o' hundred men every fifty yards. But luk at that bloody thing. Eats the bloody work. Blimey, we'll ne'er get work while them things're bein' used.' Those who listened grunted and watched the scoop of the steam-navvy biting away tons of earth and tearing up ancient tree boles as though they were weeds.

Sometimes a band of unemployed mill girls would saunter by, exchange banter with the four young men and depart shrieking with laughter as Tom Hare made a suggestive gesture at them with his fingers after they had declined his invitation to join them on the grass.

He spat on to the grass when the girls had gone: 'Yaaa,' he said: 'They're all the same. When y've got nowt they don't want y'. That whore of a Maggie Elves, her as'd go wi' anybody for a tanner, tole me as she wasn't a blackleg when Ah asked her for a bit for nowt. Blimey, they must be in a bloody union, all on 'em.'

'Christ,' muttered Sam Hardie, the long armed, stocky, muscular young fellow, 'Christ,' he said, gazing after the party of girls: 'Ah wisht Ah'd yon fat 'un i' bed for hafe an hour.'

Tom Hare showed his decayed teeth in a grimace: 'Wait 'ntil Ah get a job,' he muttered, narrowing his eyes: 'Fust week's

pay Ah get Ah'll be after fust old tail (prostitute) Ah see,' fervently: 'Gor, Ah wish they'd ha' tuk me in th'army. Ned
Narkey ses it's the life. Nowt t' worry about an' a fresh tart
when e'er y' feel like it. It's all right for them fellers as is
married on dole. They can tek their wives t' bed in th' afternoon. Blimey, n'wonder some on 'em don't want work.'

Jack Lindsay grinned: 'Then why don't y' get wed?'

Tom grunted and told him not to be daft.

Jack grinned anew: 'They're all doing it. Tarts go out t' work
nowadays while th' owld man stops at home,' he glanced at
Tom, eyes twinkling: 'Just suit thee, Tom. Bed, baccy and a
woman all t' y'self,' to Harry: 'What about you, Harry. Your
kid and Larry Meath's goin' off. When're you?'

Harry smiled: 'When Nelson gets his eye back, Ah suppose,'
he answered, with forced facetiousness: he added, quietly:
'We'd ha' done it long ago if Ah'd found a job. An' Larry Meath
an' our kid ain't so sure. He told me things is gone worse at
Marlowe's. Aw, Ah'm sick o' havin' nowt i' me pocket.'

'You ain't th' ony one,' said Sam Hardie, 'An' what about this
here Means Test as Larry Meath was spoutin' about. Ses they're
gonna knock us all off dole. Ah've filled my bloody form in,
anyway. By Christ, if it's true wot he ses we'll be bloody well fed
up then. Ah can see me father keepin' me when Ah'm bringin'
nowt home. Ah don't think. Bad enough as it is. Blast him.'

'Yaah, it's all rot wot Larry Meath ses,' said Tom: 'They
daren't do it. There'd be a revolution.'

Bill Simmons glanced at them furtively, then said: 'Fed up
wi' havin' nowt, eh? Huh! So was I ... until. ...' He put his
hand into his pocket and withdrew a large box of cigarettes.
He grinned, winked secretively and offered the box to his companions: 'Tek one,' he said, 'Plenty more where them come
from.' They accepted, regarding him interrogatively: 'Where
d'y' get 'em?' Tom Hare asked.

'Wouldn't y' like t' know, eh?' replied Bill, evasively.

A pause; they lit their cigarettes. An embarrassing silence
fell. Bill shifted, uneasily, glanced at them and laughed,
forcedly: 'Oh,' he said, with an attempt at bravado: 'Ah'll let
y' in on it'; with a trace of petulance and plaintiveness: 'Sick

Ah am o' pickin' tab ends up,' warmly: 'Damn well sick o' havin' nowt i' me pocket. Blast everybody. Ah don't care . . .'

'But where d'y' get 'em from,' Tom Hare interrupted, greedily: 'Blimey, tell us, will y'?' already he was visualizing a week-end spree on the proceeds of a sale of the stolen goods.

'You come wi' me tomorrow night an' Ah'll show y',' pause: 'Ah y' game?'

'Norrarf,' Tom answered, warmly: to Jack Lindsay: 'A' you?' Jack made a wry face: 'Naa. Ah don't want t' g' t' jail.'

To Harry's relief Sam Hardie also declined. He, Harry, had no palate for such an adventure and was glad to be able to ally himself to Jack and Sam in their refusals.

'Aw,' said Tom, with a grimace: 'Y' make me sick,' then to Bill, eagerly: 'Can't we go now, Bill. . . . Carm on; ne'er heed them.'

'Don't be a bloody fool,' Bill answered, testily, glaring at the others defiantly: 'Y've got t' wait till the place closes. T'morrow night, Ah said. Wait y' sweat.'

The incident engendered an atmosphere of unease. They rose and made towards home, five down at heel young men trudging along in silence.

Harry was viewing the evening's prospect. It would be the same old thing. A meagre tea, a swill under the tap then a mouch round the streets in Helen's company. Revolting. Where was the magic of her presence? the joy of yesterday? She was changed; her company was depressing. Or was it his fault; was he the cause of her indifference? The idea that his lack of money might be partly responsible for her change of heart made him hate her and filled his heart with an overflowing self-pity. Next, he supposed, she'd be telling him that she had found somebody else. That was maddening. 'Ah'll jump in t' cut if she does.'

Gloomily he recalled past happiness; compared it with his present experiences. The contrast was glaring. Suspicion whispered: 'Y'd got money then, Harry.' Days gone by when her eyes searched his with great anxiety; when her lips were constantly asking for his avowals of affection. Poignant! Nothing so exquisite nowadays.

They had nothing to discuss save their own misery. And experience had taught him that to discuss this was to play with fire, to invite a quarrel.

'Ne'er heed, Helen. We'll be all right when Ah get a job.'

Bitterly: 'Aye. . . . *When.*'

Blimey, what could a fellow say to that? Oh, for a fist full of money and a regular job. Oh, for a hole to crawl into so that he might relieve himself in bitter tears.

What the hell use was there in discussing homes, marriage? It was nauseating in its mockery. Reality, imperturbable, sickening, forbidding, rose to his mind's eye and jeered at him, making him feel an incompetent fool.

They were drifting lower and lower. One could feel it.

What a travesty of romantic love this their present courtship. If his present circumstances were to be a subject of a movie play this would be the opportunity for him to rescue, from some sort of danger, the only child of a wealthy man who rewarded his heroism with money and a good job. Oh, what was he thinking about?

He shuddered, inwardly, as his mind switched back to the contemplation of what would happen this evening, when, clad in his eternal shabbiness he would meet her, clad in *her* eternal shabbiness. There would be that question in her eyes: 'Have you found a job yet?'

'Aw. Have Ah bloody hell as like,' he cried, aloud, in desperation.

Jack Lindsay, walking by his side, himself in a brown study, looked at him and said: 'Eh?'

'Nowt,' Harry answered, without looking at him: 'Ah was talkin' t' meself.'

That question: 'Have you found a job yet?' It raised its presence between them like a barrier.

He found himself half in agreement with Tom Hare: 'When y've got nowt they don't want y'.' That seemed to sum up the situation. Money, the thing that stood between them. With it, they could marry; lacking it. . . . Oh, there were no demonstrations of affection, no embraces, no loving, now. Blimey, a fellow couldn't help feeling that way. Was it likely that a fellow would permit all the miserable plaguings of sexual impulse if it could be helped? And discussion of the subject was taboo: 'Oh, all you men think about is *that*!'

Interminable walks round and round the streets in silence, both brooding. Sometimes he would warm to remembrances of when, under such circumstances as now, they would gravitate towards Dawney's Hill to love. That had been quite recently, too. Strange that it should have ceased. He recalled the last occasion when they had sat there; recalled the incident which had, as it were, severed the present from the past, which had inaugurated the present tension. They had been sitting on the hill when one of those fearful sensations of desperate loneliness assailed him, when all his woes had risen up personified into a single, monstrous pessimism. He had turned to her as for protection; had put his arm about her.

The touch of his hand interrupted her brooding thoughts. She, meditating resentfully on her own impotence against the frustration of all her dreams, was caught on the crest of a wave of discontentment. She had frowned as one irked, had made the shadow of a movement away from him: 'Don't,' she said, pettishly, translating out of the gesture of affection something of suspicious significance.

He stiffened, affronted, transfixed. It had been so unexpected. Could it be that – ? He hadn't meant – . Rudely awakened he had been too shocked to speak. Mechanically he had withdrawn his arm and had stared over the lamplit townscape overwhelmed with mortification.

Until then there had been rare compensating moments when they had cast aside all their troubles and had lost themselves in love. How precious they seemed now that they were gone. But now – . It seemed as though they were entering a new and altogether antagonistic phase of life. Suspicion whispered to him; filled him with frantic fears with its dreadful insinuations. Suppose her change towards him was as a consequence of her having met some other fellow! He remembered millions of small instances of her coolness to him in confirmation of the doubt. Terrifying.

Oh, he didn't want to see her; it was obnoxious, sickening,

to imagine one of those sulky walks round the streets each holding their tongues, brooding, lest words should invite the ever imminent quarrel. And now that this suspicion was in his heart extreme caution would be necessary. He felt he would die if he had to hear his dismissal from her lips.

Blimey, if on'y Ah could get a job. His heart warmed to the thought of how different everything would be. His spirits writhed; he asked himself, in desperation, whether it was possible for things to be worse. For a while he toyed with the idea of what would happen, say, were he to be denied the dole altogether under this 'Means Test' which Larry Meath had been warning everybody about before the election. Larry had said that if something called the 'National Government' went back they would remove many people from the dole altogether. Well, this here National Government had gone back and the bloody swines had already cut the dole from seventeen bob to fifteen. Aw, what the hell does it all matter, anyway. His dull brain refused, listlessly, to care what happened next. 'Let 'um tek me dole away altogether. What's fifteen bob. Ah see none of it. As soon as Ah draw it Ah've t' tip it up.'

Money! For a brief instant he was appalled by its significance and potency. Its influence on his life was immense. Why, it was everything! He was *as* he was simply because he had no money. He could reason no further than an uneasy dissatisfaction of the mind which told him that something was wickedly wrong in such a state of affairs.

Mill and factory sirens roused him. Five-thirty. He looked about him; he was alone. His companions, after their usual wont, had drifted their several ways without a word; or they may have said: 'S'long,' and he had not heard them. He turned into Hanky Park, tried to make himself unnoticeable to the eyes of the passing girls by pulling the neb of his cap down and by walking close to the wall. Better hurry or he would meet Helen. And it was daylight; bad enough having to meet her in the dark; even *that* couldn't altogether hide one's shabbiness.

He saw her standing at the corner of North Street. She was alone. Her gaze was fixed in his direction. He pushed his cap upward, blushed as his heart rose, apprehensively. What was the matter now? She had never waited there before.

Ah, yes, he knew it. It was the worst. Her coolness towards him had been proof. She had transferred her affections to some other fellow and now was waiting to tell him, Harry, that she did not wish to have anything more to do with him. It, obviously, must be this. What had he to offer her? They were both growing older and he had no signs of a livelihood. He marvelled that she should have tolerated him so long.

He felt dazed, limp, disembodied, horribly isolated; he could not think; wanted to run away to hide in a hole; wanted to be spared that awful humiliation of hearing the words fall from her lips. Never before had he known how deep was his love of her; never before had she appeared so shining and desirable; never before had he known the utter littleness of himself. And only a moment gone he had been wondering whether it was possible for his circumstances to be worsened; had been telling himself that nothing mattered, anyway!

He approached her and stood in front of her, eyes staring, fascinated.

Extreme nervousness dominated her, a kind of suppressed hysteria; her cheeks were flushed and her eyes red-rimmed; she had been weeping. Neither spoke for a while, then, with an effort, Harry, raising his brows, whispered 'What's up, Helen?'

On a sudden she clutched his arm, replying, fixing him with a terrified stare: 'Ah knew it'd happen. ... Ah knew it'd happen.'

He eyed her, blankly: 'Eh?' he said.

'We should ne'er ha' done it. ... Ah've bin feard for a fortnight. ... Ah went t' t' doctor at dinner time. ... He told me. ... Ah'm, – y'know.'

His mouth opened; he swallowed hard, and blinked.

Fearfully she gripped his arm tighter and said, in low, scared, tones: 'What shall we do, Harry ...?'

He felt choked, stared back at her, a freezing sensation creeping up his body. He could find no words.

# DIRTY WORK AT THE CROSSROADS

OUTSIDE Marlowe's engineering works, squatting by the high enclosing wall, standing in groups, hundreds of the employees, smoking, chatting, arguing, whiled away the remaining minutes separating them from one o'clock and a recommencement of work.

Two young men were contending, hotly, on politics. They were surrounded by an audience interested enough to be attentive, of whom, Ted Munter, the would-be bookmaker, was one.

Impatiently, from one, a powerfully built young man: 'You're a bloody fool, that's what you are. Here we are, workin' like hell until we're twenty-one. Then wot happens, eh? They give us the bloody sack an' don't care a damn wot becomes of us, the bastards,' fiercely: 'Jesus! An' these here society dames, muck 'em, spendin' more on pet dogs 'n we earn in a year. Aye, an' then they go on the Riv-bloody-eera when weather changes. By – Christ! Ah'd give 'em Riveera if Ah'd me way.'

Ted Munter lifted his lip and stared at the speaker through his thick pebble spectacles: 'Don't talk so daft,' he said: 'Y'd do t' same if y' was in their place.'

The young man turned on him savagely: 'What's up wi' you, y' big fat sod?' Ted stared, surprised: 'You keep y' trap shut,' the young man continued thickly: 'Ah'm about fed up wi' such as you. Ready to crawl in front of anybody as y' think can do y' a bit o' good. Y' bloody snake. Go on, out of it. An' go'n report *me* t' t' foreman.' Ted's jaw dropped. He held his tongue, though.

The other young man, to whom the powerfully built speaker had addressed his remarks originally, said: 'Aye, but you ain't answered me. Ah still say as y' can't do without capikle. Ah'm all out for them wi' the dough as can find us work. Yaah, that talk about socialism's all rot,' warmly: 'You answer me.

*Can* y' do without capikle, eh? Answer that, owld clever devil.'

The powerfully built young man spluttered, impotently, then, on a sudden, broke through the group, stared fiercely up and down the lines of men leaning against the wall. He turned to the other and said: 'You wait there a minute,' and strode away.

He confronted Larry Meath standing by the gates smoking a cigarette. Larry grinned at the young man before he opened his mouth: 'You've no need to tell me, Jim,' he said: 'I know what you're going to say,' throwing the cigarette end away: 'Well, what mess has that temper of yours got you into this time?'

'Aw, come on,' said Jim: 'It's them bloody fools again. They're daft.' Larry walked with him back to the group, saying: 'When will you take notice of me, Jim? You . . .'

'Oh, Ah know. But them damn fools'd mek anybody get their hair off.'

'I've told you before, Jim,' replied Larry, quietly: 'If you'd learn your subject properly, nothing would make you get your hair off.'

They halted by the group: 'He,' said Jim, jerking his thumb towards his opponent: 'He ses y' can't do without capikle.' He glared.

'Yes, Ah do,' retorted the other, staring defiantly at Larry.

'But nobody wants to do without it,' said Larry, with a disarming smile. 'All that we say is that it's wrong if you use it as a means for making profit.'

'But that's all rot,' said the young man: 'They've got t' mek profit else place'd close down.'

'Yes. And Marlowe's are making so little profit nowadays that it's possible that we'll all be out of work in a month's time. But that doesn't prove that Marlowe's – or this engineering works – couldn't carry on simply because shareholders aren't getting any dividends. The machinery's still there ready to be used, and all of us are willing to use it, and there's plenty of raw material in the world, and people want things making. So what's stopping us all from working full time?'

'Aye, that's all right. But who's goin' t' invest their money if they ain't goin' t' get nowt back agen?'

'Do you know what money is?' Larry asked, patiently

'Ha! Course Ah do.'

'Then what is it?'

'It's. .... It's. .... Well, it *is* a daft question. Anybody knows what money is.'

'He doesn't know, the gawmless sod,' said Jim.

'Be quiet, Jim,' said Larry. He reached into his overall pocket, extracted a piece of chalk and turned to the wall on which he scrawled the symbol of a sovereign '£'.

'You know what that means,' he said: 'Pounds, shillings and pence. The things they give you as wages. Pounds. Those are what millionaires are supposed to possess. Now, when you get your wages you don't set them on a plate to eat them, do you?'

'D'y' hell. Y' spend 'em.'

'What d' you spend them on?'

'Well,' hesitantly: 'You ought t' know. Y' spend 'em on things y' want.'

'Then the things you want are the things you go out to work for?'

'Ah suppose so. .... Aye.'

'In that case you don't really work for money at all, do you? You work for the things you want.'

'Aye, if y' like t' put it that way.'

'So money's no use in itself, is it? You can't eat it or wear it. If there weren't any things to buy with your money, it wouldn't be any use.'

'If there wusn't. .... But there *is*!'

'That's true. But remember, there wouldn't be if such as you and me – working people – didn't make them. Would there?'

'You can't do without capikle,' the other persisted, stubbornly.

'Ach, y' silly, daft, crackpot,' cried Jim, furiously: 'Where's y' blasted brains?'

'Hush, Jim, hush,' Larry protested. To the dogged one: 'Listen, I've never once suggested that we *could* do without capital. I'm only trying to show you what it is. You said it was money. You admitted that money was the things everybody wants, didn't you?'

A non-committal grunt.

'Well, let's call the things you want "commodities",' he turned to the wall to make an addition to the pound sign: ' ≡ commodities'. 'Remember,' he said, 'that the word means anything, everything, that people need. Food, clothing, houses, motor-cars, trips in ships and on railways. Do you understand that?'

Another grunt.

'Very good,' Larry continued: 'Now, you know that there's only one class of people who provide all these commodities, don't you? And those people are us. We, you and I and the rest of the working folk. We are the ones who plough the soil and grow food; we make the clothes and the houses and the motor-cars and the ships and trains; and we man the ships and drive the trains. In short, it's our labour power that makes all and every one of the commodities. You never see a rich man doing any of these things, do you?'

'Course y' don't. They've got the capikle, as Ah've told him,' jerking his thumb towards Jim: 'An' if you'd got it you wouldn't g' t' work, either.'

'I wouldn't have any need to,' replied Larry, smiling: 'Because money means commodities and if I'd enough of it I'd have enough commodities. Suppose' – a smile – 'Suppose I was a millionaire. My million pounds would only mean that I could buy a million pounds' worth of commodities. And remember, *I* wouldn't have made them, *you* would have done that, you and all the other working folk. You see, then, money means commodities, and commodities are made out of two things.' He turned to the wall to write: 'Raw materials plus labour power = commodities. That's what a rich man's millions represent: the accumulation of the labour of such as you and I.

'Raw materials and working people's labour; combine the two and there you have commodities. Let me make it clearer. Imagine a tree growing in a field. Call the tree "raw material" instead of a "tree". Now, if somebody – say a millionaire – wanted the tree making into a table, he could pile his million sovereigns in front of it and say: "Change yourself into a table". But he wouldn't get his table despite his million pounds. What he would have to do would be to hire working people; a wood-man to chop the tree down, a carter to haul it away, a sawyer to saw it up and a joiner to fashion the planks into a table. Then the tree wouldn't be raw material any more; it would be a commodity because it had had labour power expended on it. Money means commodities and commodities mean raw materials and labour power. So money, really, means the fruit of labour. And if you did without *that* – labour – everybody would starve. And whenever you use the word "capital", again, remember that it only means raw material and the labour of working people combined, saved, stored up: then you'll also remember that millionaires are men who possess millions of pounds' worth of working people's labour. That is all that money is; your labour, our fathers' and our fathers' fathers' labour. You must ask yourself whether we can do without that. Do you think we can?'

'Y' can't do without capik . . .'

The remainder was lost in the howl of the hooter.

Ted Munter stared at Larry and the powerfully built Jim as they and the rest chatting and arguing made for the gates. He kept a couple of paces to their rear: 'Ah'm a big fat sod, am Ah?' he said to himself: 'Ah'm a bloody snake, am Ah? Awright. Ah'll just show you bloody Bolshies what Ah *can* do for that.'

His thoughts wandered; he forgot his grudge against Jim in the pleasing, newly-conceived anticipation of the possible out-come of, say, Larry's displacement. Blimey, wouldn't Sam Grundy be tickled. Sam who had sworn like the devil when he, Ted, told him of Sally Hardcastle's forthcoming marriage to Larry Meath. How he, Ted, gloated, silently, in Sam's discomfi-ture. Of course, he hadn't sufficient influence to procure Larry's discharge, damn it. Blimey, if only such a matter were left to his arbitration! By gad, Ah'd mek Sam Grundy pay. Aye, an' pay he would if there wus a chance for him t' get hold o' that bloody tart. Alas, the most he could do would be to report sub-versive political activity – the evidence was chalked on the wall – and to hope that this would be remembered when next the staff was depleted, a not distant probability if the news-papers were to be relied on.

Everybody was acquainted with the rumours; only yesterday they had been confirmed by the newspapers. Indeed, Ted had the clipping in his pocket. He already had frightened his wife by reading it aloud to her, and in such inflexions and with such significant glances as though to suggest that the paragraph referred to nobody but himself. One could tempt fate when one's job, as timekeeper, was more or less secure. He had fetched the clipping to work with the intention of reading it, in condescending tones of sympathy and commiseration, to those whose jobs were not so secure as his own.

And it was very agreeable to visualize an interview this evening with Sam Grundy, when Ted, first telling how he had reported Larry to the proper quarter, winked, slyly, and, without another word, passed the clipping for Sam's perusal:

Interview today, the manager of Messrs Marlowe's Ltd explained to our representative the possible consequences of the difficulties placed in the way of trade with Russia by the Government. 'We have much work for Russia in hand,' the manager stated, 'which is being gradually brought to a standstill by the Government's attitude. Their failure to cooperate with us in this direction will mean that we shall have to discharge a good many of our workpeople. It may even mean the closing down of our machine shops altogether as our order books are practically empty but for our contracts with Russia.'

Ted passed his hand across his mouth and narrowed his eyes. That, surely would be sufficient to induce Sam Grundy to stand him a couple of double Scotch whiskies . . .

That evening, passing the wall on his way home, Larry smiled to see a bill pasted over his chalkings:

> Anyone found chalking on,
> or otherwise defacing these walls,
> will be dealt with severely.
> By Order

'Look, Jim,' he said, to the powerfully built young man accompanying him.

'Ach,' Jim responded, with a scowl: 'Y'know who did that. . . . The bloody big fat toad.'

## CHAPTER 8

## IT IS DRIVING HIM BARMY

LARRY MEATH shrugged his shoulders and stared, moodily, at the sandy floor of the foundry. The foreman, standing by, eyed him with curiosity: 'Well,' said the foreman, 'Well, p'raps this'll learn y' t' keep y' trap shut for future. Yaach! Y've bin a silly devil, Larry,' spitting: 'This lousy lot o' devils here, d'y' think *they* give a cuss what y' say?' a pause: he added, in changed tones: 'Ah must say as y're tekkin' it different from most o' t'others. Say what y' like, things is bad when reg'lars like us get sack. Blimey, wot the 'ell's comin' o'er t'world? It's fust time this's happened i' my recollection,' another pause: 'Y' should have heard Ned Narkey an' t'others when Ah told 'em. Ay, 'n Ned on'y just married. 'Tain't s'bad for you, Larry, a single bloke. It's us married 'uns wot feels it.'

'I should have been married next week,' Larry replied, dully, adding, musingly: 'I dunno what I'm going to do,' with sudden impatience: 'Ach! anybody with a pair of eyes could have seen this coming weeks ago.'

The foreman raised his brows then shook his head: 'Eh, Ah'm sorry, lad,' he said, sympathetically: with feeling: 'But be glad y' still single,' indignantly: 'What a' we gonna do? Wharram *Ah* gonna do? By the Christ, it was tekkin' us all our time t' manage on me wages. But when Ah think o' the seven of 'um at home, an' her ma livin' wi' us, all on what they'll gimme at dole. . . . Yaaa! an' the bloody liars at election said everythin'd be apple pie if National Gover'ment went back. Well, where are we?'

Larry clenched his fists and flushed: 'Where we deserve to be,' he answered, eyes shining: 'And let me tell you, Bob, it's going to be a sight worse yet,' contemptuously: 'National Government. Ach! Ha, well, they told us what they'd do if they went back; wage cuts and all the rest. But everybody was too busy with their daft Irish Sweepstakes and all the rest of it. It makes y' want to chuck up the whole sponge. . . .' He perspired in hopeless impotence of the utter futility of it all. 'I tell you, Bob, it's driving me barmy to have to live amongst such idiotic folk. There's no limit to their daftness: won't think for themselves, won't do anything to help themselves and. . . . Augh! Watch them waken up when they get it in the neck with this Means Test. You'll hear some squawking then.' He flung aside the piece of cotton waste on which he had been wiping his hands: 'But you 'n me's got to suffer wi' the rest. . . .' He remembered Sally. What was he to do? How could he tell her this? With a final gesture of desperation he turned and made for the time office, leaving the astonished foreman gaping after him.

2

'. . . turning *me* down. *Me*, an' all Ah could gie y'! Turning me down for *him*. Yaa! y' barmy.' Sam Grundy the fat bookmaker, eyed Sally with an expression of forced amusement as he stood, thumbs in waistcoat armholes, billycock at the back of his head, barring her path at the corner of North Street immediately outside the doors of the Duke of Gloucester. She flashed him a glance of scorn: 'Gerr out o' me way, *you*,' she snarled: 'Ah don't want t' even talk t' the likes o' you. You 'n Narkey mek me sick. Luk better o' y' both if y'd spend more time wi' y' wives 'stead o' pestering girls as wouldn't wipe their feet on y',' threateningly: 'Y'd better luk out if y' won't let me be . . .'

'Oh, now, Sal, now. That ain't way t' talk to a friend wot wants t'help y',' solicitously: 'Has that Narkey bin pesterin' y' agen?'

At that moment Ned Narkey stepped out of the public-house wiping his mouth on the back of his hand. He glowered as he heard Sam's interrogation. He hitched his belt, set his jaw and took the step separating him from Sam and Sally: 'Eh?' he said, glaring at Sam: 'Eh? Wot's that? Wot was y' saying about me?'

'Augh!' cried Sally, with a toss of her head: 'Augh, let me pass.' She pushed by Sam Grundy and strode down the street tingling with indignation.

The empty condition of Ned's pocket reflected itself in his temper. The landlord of the Duke of Gloucester, regretfully, but firmly, had just informed him that no more credit could be given him: 'You'll have to ease up now on the slate, Ned,' adding, hurriedly, as he noticed the scowl appear on Ned's face: 'Though it'll be all right agen, y'know, when y' get back t' work.'

Ned snarled an oath, raised his glass and drained it: 'Y're all same, all the lot o' y'. . . . A feller's on'y welcome wi' a full pocket. . . . But Ah'll remember.'

'Aw, now Ned, now Ned. Ah'm on'y thinkin' about y' o' week-end when y've t' sekkle up. Y' ain't a single feller no more, y' know.'

Ned swore, swung around and stamped out of the public-house in time to hear Sam Grundy saying to Sal Hardcastle: '. . . Narkey bin pesterin' y' agen?'

'Eh? Wot's that?' he snapped, glaring at Sam: 'Wot was y' sayin' about me?' He eyed Grundy balefully; did not hear what Sally said nor took any notice of her.

Instantly he appreciated Grundy's prosperity, its easy source, the smug complacency of the man, his affluence, influence and ability to indulge his every whim. Comparing it with his own barren indigence made his poverty doubly maddening. Blind hate and envy dominated him; his impulse was to snatch at Grundy's throat, fling him to the floor and kick his brains out as he had done those German boys, who, scared stiff, he had captured in a pill-box, a feat of heroism which had earned him the medal and the commander's commendatory remarks. He could feel a torrent of energy rushing down his arms and tingling his fingertips.

Grundy's tongue peeped furtively between his suddenly parched lips. Narkey's ugly mood was genuine. He flashed a quick glance up and down the street to see whether there was a policeman about. There were none.

Policemen!

An idea struck him. He gazed at Narkey and smiled with forced expansiveness: 'Luk here, Ned, lad,' he said, paternally, good-naturedly, raising a hand to Narkey's shoulder. Ned knocked it away, savagely: 'Don't you come the soft soap on me,' he snapped: 'Wot was y' sayin' to her about me, eh?' He thrust his face forward.

Sam sighed in simulated despair: 'Suppose Ah told y' it was for y'r own good, eh? Suppose Ah told y' Ah knew y' was out o' work an' that Ah could fix a good job for y' – if on'y y'd do as y' bid,' warming to the subject as he perceived the impression he was making on Ned: 'Suppose Ah told y' that y' wouldn't stand a cat in hell's chance o' gettin' it the way y' carry on about every bit o' skirt as teks y' fancy,' mildly reproachful: 'Eh, Ned lad, Ned lad, an' you a married man.'

'Wot about y' self?' countered Ned, petulantly, puzzled as to Grundy's intentions. He still was suspicious.

'Ne'er mind me. Ah'm in no need of a job,' warmly: 'But you. . . . Ha! Y'd be a fool, all right, t' let a bit o' skirt ruin y' chance o' becomin' a copper,' winking and slapping Ned on the chest with the back of his hand: 'Three ten a week, lodgin' allowance, uniform and boots an' all y' bloody holidays paid for. . . . On'y for walking about streets eight hours a day.'

Ned blinked; his fists unclenched; his tensed muscles relaxed: 'Me – ? Y' can get me on as a copper . . .?' he murmured, staring at Grundy, blankly.

Sam thrust his thumbs into his waistcoat armholes, smiled and winked: 'Ah've a *bit* o' influence,' he remarked, casually.

Ned stared at him, dubiously. He muttered, suspiciously: 'But what's y' game, Grundy? How is it y've on'y just found Ah'm alive?'

'On'y just, eh? Ha! Ah like that,' he put his hand to the side of his mouth and strained up to Ned's ear: 'Ah've bin asked by a certain party t' recommend a likely lad or two. You're an owld sweat an' y've Military Medal. Ah can see to it that y' name guz in first . . . but y've got t' lay off the skirt. If y' don't it'll put paid t' y' chances. They won't have anybody, y' know,' resuming his original position and glancing shrewdly at Ned: 'But, think on, now, *how* y' got job ain't nobody's business. Mum's the word. An' see as y' don't let me down.' He reached into his pocket for a cigar.

Ned licked his lips. Seventy shillings a week regularly; holidays paid for and clothes free. Better than being in the army for, here, after the eight hours duty, one was a civilian for the remainder of the day: 'An' when do Ah start, Sam?' he murmured, with suppressed eagerness.

Sam tapped him on the shoulder, jerked his thumb towards the open doors of the Duke of Gloucester: 'Come'n have a couple wi' me an' Ah'll explain,' he said.

Ned went in first, Sam followed, the smoke from his cigar curling gracefully over his shoulder like the flung ends of a conspirator's cloak.

CHAPTER 9

NOW IT'S DRIVING HER BARMY

'COME in,' said Larry, from the back kitchen, as a knock sounded on the open front door of his lodgings. He was alone in the house as generally was the case since his landlady's and her husband's occupations – they were stewards and caretakers of the Labour Club rooms – kept them from home for the greater part of the day. He paused in his shaving to listen.

Sally entered smiling and announced herself. He asked her to be seated until he had finished shaving.

She complied, sighed contentedly, and relapsed into silence as her gaze idly roved this, his room. Exactly the same kind of front room as at No. 17, yet how different. It and its furnishings breathed his name. Books arranged on shelves either side the fireplace. A comforting sight; so extraordinary a furnishing of a North Street front room. Their presence enhanced, lent an intangible part of themselves to the meagre rickety furniture provided by the landlady.

She sighed anew; felt the blood coursing quicker about her body as she visualized herself, within a week's time, dusting those volumes with loving care and in a home of their own. Tonight they were to inquire concerning the tenancy of a house in the next street. Then –. Fly time!

In the room at the back Larry stood staring at the slopstone as he dried his shaving tackle mechanically. His fagged brain cast about listlessly, wearily, for a way out of this present predicament. There was only one solution: his thoughts returned to it with the inevitability of a magnetic needle to the pole: 'I'll have to tell Sal that we'll have to postpone the wedding.' To marry on the money they would give him at the dole would be the height of folly. Seventeen shillings a week was an impossible pittance. No, not seventeen shillings, even: in the interests of national economy this had now been reduced to fifteen shillings.

Was it all a dream? Could life be really so inexorable and harsh? He stood staring at the slopstone drying his shaving tackle mechanically.

You're sacked, and there's a girl in the other room whom you've promised to marry. His dizzied brain revolved. Then a sensation of suffocation insinuated itself; he felt cramped, stifled, exhausted. His breath caught in his throat and, next moment he was seized with a paroxysm of violent coughing.

Instantly, Sally, full of anxiety appeared in the doorway. Her heart rose apprehensively as she stared, fascinated, mute, frightened. Suppose she had been premature in condemning as unjustifiable Mrs Bull's comment on Larry's health: 'Yon lad'll have t' be tuk care of, lass. That there cough ain't no ordinary cough an' calls for doctor if Ah know owt about it. You see as he guz, lass. Men allus neglec' 'emselves. Allus.' Sally had deprecated the idea. Who hadn't a cough at this time of the year in Hanky Park? She had only just rid herself of one.

Yet – apprehensive tremors fluttered her heart as Larry straightened himself. His eyes were brimming, his cheeks burned, he panted and steadied himself by leaning on the table: 'A'y' all right, Larry?' she murmured, stealing to his side.

He nodded, raised the towel he was holding to his eyes and to his perspiring brow: 'It was a touch of a cough, Sal,' he said: 'I'm all right, now.'

She regarded him with an interrogative stare, puzzled, indecisive. Suddenly, she cried, accusingly: 'Y' should ha' bin t' the doctor before now,' she continued, warmly: 'It ain't fair to you and it ain't fair to me . . . us going to be married.'

The last phrase of her utterance froze him. His pulse quickened; he felt afraid. He laid aside the shaving tackle, regarded her and murmured, in a voice that sounded unreal: 'We'll have to postpone it, Sally . . . I'm come out of work.' He blushed; his dry lips parted slightly. Like a boy waiting on tenterhooks for a firework to explode he held his breath listening for her answer.

She raised her brows; her eyes widened, her mouth opened slightly and her hands fell to her side limply: 'Postponed . . .? But . . .'

'As soon as I find work we'll be married,' he said.

She remembered her brother. Helen Hawkins had confessed that Harry had promised her similarly: *their* marriage was further off than ever. If Harry did succeed in finding work it would take six months of his wages to replenish his clothing. He was walking about in shameful condition. She flushed. Was Helen Hawkins's experience to be hers too? Her breathing quickened: 'Why can't we be married as we arranged?' she demanded, impatiently. She brushed aside his attempt at interruption and continued: 'There's nowt t' stop us. You'd get your dole, and I'm working.'

A humiliating picture of himself living under such an arrangement flashed through his mind. It stank: it smacked of Hanky Park at its worst. He felt weak, powerless, capable of no resistance. Then he fancied he could feel the district's tentacles feeling to get a grip on him, feeling for a hold with which to pull him down: 'No . . .' he said, sharply, suddenly animated: 'No, no, Sal. No, I can't do it.'

'Y' don't *want* to do it,' she flashed back, here eyes staring. An expression of bitterness contorted her face.

'I . . .' he replied, warmly, then he checked himself. Some panic-stricken part of him forbade him speech; forbade him hazard her irreplaceable companionship in tempestuous words. He dared not, could not risk losing her. Should he, after all, capitulate? What else remained Sally but her present attitude in the face of so keen a disappointment? He composed himself with an effort: 'Listen Sal,' he said: 'It's as hard on me as it is on you. . . . *Don't* you think that I'm as disappointed as you are? I'll soon find another job . . .' pause; he compressed his lips to stop their nervous trembling; then, in an unguarded moment, and as he noticed that her expression of bitterness was unrelaxed: 'Aw, I should never have encouraged you in the first place.'

Hotly: 'Then why did y'?'

Wearily: 'Why, oh, why? I *did* encourage you, didn't I? I still love you.'

She curled her lip: 'Fine way this is o' showing it.'

He looked at her appealingly: 'Can't you understand, Sal?' He felt bothered, harassed by this need of continual explanation; felt his patience and composure crumbling. Was this himself saying: 'I'm tired of it all. Sick and tired of everything. How the devil d'y' think I'm going to manage on fifteen bob a week ...?' He stopped short. Inconsequently a vivid appreciation of the present situation spouted in his mind. This present was love's young dream. This, which should be the peak of lovers' happiness, harshly shattered by lack of money. What recourse was there? 'Please, sir, are there any vacancies?' 'Please, sir, *please* let me live.' 'Please, sir, in God's name let me work.' He saw himself, these past few nights, chalking pavements and walls with the legend: 'Thursday next, 10.30 a.m. Unemployed Rally. Mass Protest Demonstration and March to Two Cities' Town Hall.'

What was he thinking about now? Was he going off his head altogether? He gathered his wits and said, staring at her: 'It's no use arguing, Sally. It'd be daft to do it. Yaa! Fifteen bob a week! D'y' think I'm going to sponge on you. What the devil d'y' take me for?'

'Don't you talk like that ...' she cried, shrilly: 'Don't you talk like that!' her voice rose; hysteria contorted her face: 'Ah'm sick o' hearin' y'. ... Y're drivin' me barmy. Why don't them Labour Councillors as're allus makin' a mug out o' y' find a job for y'? They're all right, they are; don't care a damn for us. They've all landed good jobs for 'emselves. And – Oh, I – I – Ah *hate* y'.' She turned and ran sobbing to the front door, burying her face in an old coat of his hanging there.

He stood staring at the floor; felt himself diminishing in stature; felt a helpless fool, utterly negligible.

After a minute or so the riot in her brain subsided; she began to hate herself. What must he think of her? Obstinately she told herself that she didn't care what he thought. Reproach stung her. It was as though she had taken advantage of him. She half turned, sniffed, paused, took a hesitant step and paused again. Head bent she retraced her steps to the room at the back.

What a fool she made of herself in her tantrums; making things uncomfortable for him whom she was supposed to love; making things unbearable at a time when he needed her kindnesses most of all. Look at Helen Hawkins's example. She, Sal Hardcastle, wasn't the only woman in the world who'd been disappointed.

In a sudden access of remorse and affection she rushed to him and flung her arms about him: 'Ah'm sorry, Larry. Ah'm sorry,' she buried her face in his bosom.

He put his arms about her, closed his eyes and rested his cheek on her soft hair. Oh, the utter, complete, ineffable solace! He felt a tightening in the throat, did not speak, hugged her tightly, jealously.

### CHAPTER 10

## HISTORICAL NARRATIVE

HARRY HARDCASTLE was staggered: 'Y' what ...? What did y' say?' he asked, staring, incredulously, at the unemployment exchange clerk on the other side of the counter.

'A' y' deaf?' retorted the clerk, pettishly: he added, snappily: 'There nowt for y'. They've knocked y' off dole. Sign on of a Tuesday for future if y' want y' health insurance stamp. Who's next?'

The man behind Harry shouldered him away. Dream-like, he turned and paused, holding the dog-eared, yellow unemployment card in his hand. This was catastrophic: the clerk was joking, surely; a mistake must have been made. He hadn't asked the clerk the reason why they had stopped paying him his unemployment benefit: 'Gor blimey,' he muttered: 'Hell, what am Ah gonna do?' He remembered Helen, instantly. The people here didn't realize, didn't know that he'd *got* to marry her. Nobody but themselves and Sally were aware that she was an expectant mother. He licked his lips, and, dazed, turned to the counter once again in time to hear his unspoken question answered indirectly. The man who had succeeded him was angrily demanding an explanation of the clerk; those in the queue behind and those on either side listened attentively. That which passed concerned them all.

Hearing the man's indignant expostulations, a policeman, on duty at the door, came nearer, silently. The man, grey-haired, middle-aged, a stocky fellow in corduroys, clay-muddied blucher boots and with 'yorks' strapped about his knees, exclaimed: 'What d'y' mean? Nowt for me. Ah'm out o' collar ain't Ah?'

The clerk put aside his pen and sighed, wearily: 'Doan argue wi' me,' he appealed: 'Tain't my fault. If y' want t' know why, go'n see manager. Blimey, you blokes're bloody well drivin' me barmy this mornin'.'

'Manager, eh?' the man snapped: 'You bet Ah'll see the manager. Wheer is 'e?' The clerk jerked his thumb towards the far end of the counter. 'Ask at "Enquiries",' he said: 'Who's next?'

Harry followed the man.

The manager ordered a clerk to look up the man's particulars; the clerk handed over some documents after a search in a filing cabinet. His superior, after perusing some notes written upon the forms, looked at the applicant and said: 'You've a couple of sons living with you who are working, haven't you?'

'Aye,' the man answered: 'One's earnin' twenty-five bob an' t'other a couple o' quid, when they work a full week. An' th'eldest . . .'

'In view of this fact,' the manager interrupted: 'The Public Assistance Committee have ruled your household's aggregate income sufficient for your needs; therefore, your claim for transitional benefit is disallowed.' He turned from the man to glance interrogatively at Harry.

The man flushed: 'The swine,' he shouted: 'Th' eldest lad's

gettin' wed ... 'as 'e t' keep me an' th' old woman?' raising his
fist: 'Ah'll. ...' But the attendant policeman collared him and
propelled him outside, roughly, ignoring his loud protestations.

Harry learnt that, in the opinion of the Public Assistance
Committee his father's dole and Sally's wages were sufficient
to keep him. No more dole would be forthcoming. And when
he asked whether he could re-state his case the manager informed him that there was no appeal. He didn't argue; went
outside, dazed.

A quite different atmosphere from the usual enlivened the
adjacent streets. Police were conspicuous. Knots of men barred
pavements and roadways listening and interjecting as various
spokesmen voiced heated criticisms of this, the latest economy
move on the part of the National Government. Occasionally, the
spokesmen's words would be lost in rowdy, jumbled torrents of
cursings and abusive oaths. From the labour exchange there
came a continuous trickle of men wearing appropriate expressions as became their individual dispositions. Men of Harry's
kind dazed, mystified, staring at the ground; more spirited indi-
viduals, flushed with anger, lips trembling, eyes burning with
resentment. They joined the groups, finding a sorry sort of
relief in the knowledge that all here assembled were similarly
affected. Most of those more fortunate ones whose benefits had
remained untouched cleared off home jealously hugging their
good fortune and telling themselves that what was passing was
no concern of theirs.

Harry's thoughts, in general, represented those of his companions. This sudden cessation of their pittances was as an unexpected douche of cold water. Unexpected. Of course, all had
known that something was in the air: all had received the
official forms which had inquired, thoroughly, into their means.
But nobody had believed that they themselves would fall victim. To them all it had concerned others than themselves; each
had found adequate excuse and reason why *his* benefit should be
continued, though each had selected somebody else who, in his
opinion, would suffer no hardship in having his unemployment
pay stopped. 'Ha! Means Test, eh? They can't knock *me* off.
Blimey, it's tekkin' us all our time t' manage as it is. ... Now him

as lives next door; Ah could understand 'um knockin' *him* off. He's got more coming in than me. Yaach, they won't touch the likes of us. They daren't. There'd be a bloody revolution.'

Like an unexpected douche of cold water. And dismay was made all the more complete by the knowledge of their own impotence. What could they do about it? What?

Crowds of ill-dressed men, growing crowds on whom the heavens had just fallen.

Suddenly, the several crowds integrated into one large assembly as a youngish man, wearing an open-neck shirt was lifted shoulder high: 'Comrades,' he shouted, spiritedly, and proceeded to an inflammatory speech which communicated restless animation to his audience. In conclusion he invited them to follow him to the place where hundreds of unemployed already were assembled preparatory to marching to the city hall in protest against the Means Test. They followed in a body, some arguing volubly, some wearing grim expressions, some grinning or laughing and treating the affair as a joke; over all, the confused tramping of many feet.

A stone's-throw distant was the assigned meeting place. A patch of waste land upon which the biting north-east wind descended ruthlessly. To the right rose huge gasometers, to the left slumdom squatted. The place was black with men and youths continually augmented by batches of new arrivals. Shabby fellows, scrawny youths mostly wearing caps, scarves and overalls, coughing, spitting, those on the fringe of the crowd stamping their feet and beating their arms against their sides. Blowsy women, limp hair blowing about their faces, stood in large groups at the street corners opposite, their arms and hands enwrapped in their aprons as shelter from the perishing wind. Bitter expressions contorted their lips as they loudly criticized the Means Test and the presence of the strong force of uniformed and plain-clothes police, the latter mingling with the great crowd of men across the way, some surreptitiously making shorthand notes of speeches, the former lining the pavements, one every yard or so, most of them wearing expressions similar to Ned Narkey's, who, too, was on duty, regarding the proceedings with amused tolerance.

By the wall of the gas works rested a number of crudely hand-painted placards fixed to flimsy sticks, and a large black, double-poled banner bearing a slogan surmounted by a skull and crossbones. By its side was a big drum over which a diminutive, pugnacious individual mounted guard.

The great pale sea of faces were turned to an improvised rostrum where a stocky, wire-haired fellow speaking in a strong Scots accent, passionately inveighed against the government and urged all to resist, by force if necessary, the threat to their standard of life. His words were greeted by a roar of approval, and, this much encouraged, he jabbed the air in the direction of the plain-clothes police, their size rendering them conspicuous, standing in the crowd. He condemned them as 'traitors to their class', as 'enemies of the workers', 'servants of the boss class'. He concluded on a threatening note, glaring at the police. Then he stepped down and was lost in the crowd who applauded mightily.

Ned Narkey, his magnificent physique set off to perfection in his new uniform, winked at his nearest companion in blue and muttered, out of the side of his mouth: 'Ah hope t' Christ the bastards start summat. Ah'll. . . .' He stopped and stared. A few beats on the big drum commanded silence for the next speaker.

Larry Meath appeared on the rostrum, cleared his throat and surveyed the crowd as he wiped his moist brow with his handkerchief. He wished all this over so that he might return home to go to bed. This present indisposition, this severe cold, was a nuisance; it left him enervated. He had been foolish to come.

Ned's eyes narrowed; he strained his ears to catch what Larry said, inwardly cursing the noisy traffic and the bell-ringing errand boy cyclists who paused awhile to investigate what all this to-do was about.

Larry began with a repudiation of the previous speaker; urged his audience to appreciate the preparations, in the way of attendant police, which had been made in anticipation of any disorderliness; reminded the crowd that the cause of their protest was of their own making; recalled the scares and the people's response at the general election. A spasm of coughing interrupted him; he recovered and continued, urging the need of working-class organization. Again he was incapacitated. This time he stepped down, went over to the wall and rested a hand against it in support of himself as the cough racked him bathing him in perspiration.

A finely featured young man with long hair took his place on the rostrum instantly winning the acclamation of the crowd by heaping invective upon all with whom he disassociated himself in the social scale.

Harry, on the appearance of Larry, had pushed his way to the front and now stood by him with an expression of excitement on his face. Like most of the crowd his bewilderment and resentment had disappeared for the nonce in face of the imagined possibilities engendered by the speech-making. Each had taken courage in the presence of his neighbour; the protest, surely, in face of their numbers, must be effective. The very atmosphere tingled with expectancy.

A man came up to Larry: Harry heard him say: 'You're in the deputation, aren't you? There's six of us. We'd better lead the march then we can go into the city hall without having to hunt for one another when we get there.'

Larry nodded: 'I wish we'd done. I feel as weak as a kitten. . . . This cold, I suppose.'

The man looked at him, concerned: 'Why don't y' clear off home? Ah'll tell 'm, y' feel bad.'

'No, I'll be all right. What time's the mayor expecting us?'

'In about half an hour,' the other answered, looking at his watch.

'Hadn't we better be forming the procession? It's going to take us all our time to be there punctually. Which way do we go?'

'Round by labour exchange, then round by Crosstree Lane 'n' Consort Road.'

'We'll not do it in half an hour,' said Larry: 'Still, form the ranks. . . . Who's in charge?'

The man nodded in the direction of the finely featured young man addressing the crowd.

Larry frowned: 'Hadn't you better inform him of the time?'

'Ah've told him once.' He went to interrupt the speaker

again who ignored him and continued speaking for another ten minutes. When he stepped down, hair in disarray, eyes burning with passion, Larry went up to him and said, with a touch of impatience: 'D'y' know what the time is? We'll have to take a tram if we're to keep the appointment.'

The organizer stared at Larry with a mixture of surprise and indignation: 'Eh?' he said, then added, warmly: 'They'll wait *our* pleasure. We're not kowtowing to them,' with dilated nostrils and staring eyes. 'We lead the procession. And if the arrangements don't suit y' can drop out.'

'All right, all right,' returned Larry, angrily: 'You're in charge. It won't be my fault if they refuse to meet the delegation. They'll not delay their business indefinitely.'

'No business is more important than the starving proletariat,' replied the organizer, as angry as Larry.

'Oh, don't talk so damn daft, man. Get something done, for God's sake.' He about faced, disgusted, recognized Harry, grabbed a placard and pushed it into his hand: 'Here, Harry,' he said, 'Hold that up. Stand where you are,' to the pugnacious drummer: 'Some music, please.' The man responded, setting himself in front of Harry and beating loudly upon the drum. Larry asked a number of his immediate neighbours to form themselves four deep behind Harry: they complied, obediently. The large, black double-poled banner was unfurled and set in front of the drummer preceded by a man carrying a red flag. The nucleus formed, the remainder followed automatically. Men detached themselves from the main body to form up behind those already in line.

It happened so speedily that the organizer, momentarily, was at a loss; then, piqued, he found his voice and strode to Larry's side, indignant at his assumption of control: 'Here . . .' he protested. Larry picked up a megaphone from the side of the rostrum, handed it to him and said: 'You'll want this to ask the crowd to assemble, won't you? What do you want me to do next? Shall I distribute the remainder of the placards down the line?' His request for orders pacified the organizer, who, with a grunt, nodded curtly, stepped on to the rostrum and bawled at the crowd through the megaphone.

Buzz of voices, jostlings, pushings. Larry found himself overcome by a peculiar faintness. He went over to the wall, leaned against it, brain spinning, a sensation of utter uselessness in every member of his body. He closed his eyes: a cold sweat broke out all over him. By Jove, he'd never felt like this before in all his life. This was a severe cold, to be sure. Still, he soon would be free to return home to go to bed. Bed! To be there now. A couple of days in bed, with Sally to sit with him of an evening, he pretending to be an invalid so that she might indulge him with all due pampering.

The pretty prospect revived him. He opened his eyes, mopped the perspiration from his face and shivered. He unbuttoned his coat and took in his belt a couple of holes. He felt warmer now.

He gazed down the long, serpentine column of men. Most of them were betraying excessive self-consciousness; unmistakable signs, voluble speech, furtive, shamefaced glances toward the growing crowd of sightseers lining the pavements: bluff, noisy invitations to all to join in; attitudes consorting ill with the arbitrary imperiousness of their placarded demands: 'Not a penny off the dole.' 'Hands off the people's food.' An inspector passed amongst the police giving instructions: press photographers appeared. Boys, come from nowhere, called the midday racing edition in shrill voices, darting in and out the crowd, pausing by the blowsy women who rummaged in their plackets for their purses.

The procession moved off preceded by a police inspector and four stalwart policemen. The remainder of the constables flanked the procession, a couple – one either side – every six yards or so. Grinning spectators, youths mostly, marched along the pavements whilst those in the ranks jeered at them for not falling behind. The jeers were taken up; many who walked the pavements were shamed into swelling the numbers in the roadway.

Occasionally, the monotonous beat of the big drum was varied by the insistent clamour of a handbell; sometimes they were banged and rung in concert, their din attracting the attention of all within earshot.

Quite unexpectedly the demonstrators received a shock and an ominous intimation.

Their proposed route would have led them past the labour

exchange, but, as the leader of the procession wheeled to the right towards a side street, the policemen in front about faced and formed a cordon.

The column halted: drum and bell were silenced.

The organizer stepped forward desirous of an explanation, receiving scant courtesy of the inspector, who, pointing his stick down the road and staring elsewhere than at the man to whom his remarks were addressed, said: 'Keep straight on.'

The organizer protested, indignantly.

Larry touched him on the arm: 'We'd better do as we're told,' he said: 'It's useless arguing with these men.'

The finely featured young man ignored him. With blazing eyes he asked instructions of the demonstrators. Which were they to do, obey the police or follow out their original intention of marching past the labour exchange? A new spirit stung the marchers; it was as though they were set on their mettle; faces could be seen assuming expressions of defiant pugnacity. A confused murmuring grew; the front portion of the procession broke ranks and pressed forward in a body, eyeing the cordon threateningly. The police farther down the line behaved strategically, breaking up the column into several small portions, preventing further augmentation of the crowd blocking the roadway higher up.

Pale, lips pursed, the organizer took the initiative in stepping forward and motioning to the crowd to break through the cordon. A handful of men made a rush; some broke through into the desert patch of street beyond where they stood staring foolishly at the policemen's backs and at the rest of their companions who were being pushed back roughly.

Larry, heart fluttering with apprehension, trembling with incredulity, faced a part of the crowd, held up his arms and enjoined them to re-form the ranks. Surly, muttering, casting baleful looks at the police, some obeyed. Hesitantly others followed. The procession was re-formed. The police inspector ordered his men to the procession's head. Ned Narkey spat on to the ground and grinned exultantly at Larry as he passed.

The new spirit immediately manifested itself when the march continued. Down the long column and on the pavements the incident was passed on, explained and discussed excitedly. Those who had been concerned in the clash demeaned themselves with conscious pride; hostile glances were thrown policewards, and, in general, an air of animated expectancy pervaded the demonstrators. Somebody produced a mouth organ and commenced to play the 'Red Flag'. Those unacquainted with the words la-la'd the tune.

The crowds grew denser and denser the nearer the long column came to its destination, and, by the time the main thoroughfare leading to the city hall was reached, pavements and roads were a moving river of humanity, impassable, on the Manchester approach, to traffic. At each street corner a tributary of new arrivals immersed itself in the main river, most of them in the nature of curious spectators.

Women pushing bassinettes or carrying their children; young unemployed men and women hurriedly pulling on their coats or setting caps and neckcloths straight, doubtless, having just rushed out of their homes; old men and women, doddering, roused out of their hovels in adjacent slumdom by the clamour. Shop windows, rows of them, used as grandstands by the shop assistants. Winged rumour had flown on in front, enlarging and exaggerating the story of the recent clash. Already, expectant crowds were blocking the pavements by the city hall, craning their necks and waiting as they would have had royalty been expected to pass.

With the foretaste of constabulary intolerance in mind, Larry feared for the outcome of this demonstration. The crowd was become enormous.

Two dozen yards or so away, drawn across the entrance to the city hall square, he saw a strong cordon of police. He turned to the organizer, puzzled: 'I say,' he said, 'I understood that we were to be permitted to enter the square.' The square, a not very large enclosure, facing the city hall and flanked either side by municipal show rooms, a bank and solicitors' offices, was the meeting place of all interested in election results at the appropriate time; a rallying point and had been from time immemorial.

The finely featured young man did not answer; he seemed to be as puzzled as Larry, who now was coughing violently as he walked. When the procession halted outside the square he was catching his breath with exhaustion. With the other five dele- gates he approached the cordon. He'd be glad to get inside the city hall to sit down. Perhaps he'd better excuse himself when the mayor had received them; better take a tramcar home and get to bed.

A uniformed police official, resplendent in gold braid, met the six delegates: 'Here,' he cried, impatiently, 'Get this crowd shifted and be bloody quick about it.'

'But – Here – I say . . .' protested the organizer.

The police official turned, signed to the four constables and the inspector who had headed the procession, turned his back on the delegation and faced his men in the square. Orders passed. Moun- ted police appeared at the trot, and, on a sudden, a swarm of plain-clothes men descended from nowhere and began to snatch the placards from the hands of the demonstrators, flinging the posters to the ground and trampling them underfoot. A- mazed, incredulous, all who had witnessed the incident were shocked to inaction.

A murmur rose, grew in volume to a roar of protest: men turned to expostulate with the plain-clothes men; the object of the march was forgotten instantly: arms gesticulated, eyes flashed angrily. The police advanced and began to push the crowd back; tempers, already short, snapped. The pugnacious individual in charge of the drum, provoked beyond endurance by the repeated pushings and digs of a policeman, and after almost losing his balance by an excessively vigorous push, threatened the policeman with one of his drumsticks. Instantly he was arrested, the drum removed, flopped on the ground to be res- cued by somebody and taken away quickly.

Traffic accumulated behind the surging crowd: lines of tram- cars, motor-cars and lorries going to and coming from Man- chester. Clanging of tram bells; hooting of motor horns; faces pressed against the glazing of the upper decks of the trams; Press men leaning out with cameras in their hands.

With a rush, and as though in obedience to a command, a new force of police, truncheons drawn, charged the crowd.

Harry, jostled this way and that, dodging blows, caught a

glimpse of the finely featured young man set upon by a couple of constables, knocked down savagely, and frog-marched away by three hefty policemen.

Narkey's great bulk was conspicuous as he laid about him, right and left, recklessly indiscriminate. A woman, whom he struck across the bosom with his truncheon, screamed; her companions, shouting protest, cursed and spat at him; one of them, with an expression of intense savagery, reached forward and clawed Ned's cheek, drawing blood. Harry cheered, excitedly, and, next moment, Harry saw Ned hustled away by a sudden rush of angry men who broke through to engage the police in a futile struggle.

Fascinated, scared, Harry gaped at the spectacle of helmets rolling on the setts, truncheons descending on heads with sickening thuds; men going down and being dragged off, unceremoniously, to the cells.

Then he gasped, flushed, and, on a sudden, raised his cupped hands to his mouth and bawled: 'Larry! Larry! Luk out!'

He saw Larry standing in the midst of the tussle, an expression of shocked bewilderment on his face. He saw a policeman's hand fall on his collar, a truncheon strike thrice, twice on Larry's back and once on his head. He went down on his knees, head drooping forward. A couple of constables took him under the armpits and pulled him towards thé cells, his legs dragging behind him.

Speechless, Harry stared for a moment. He gulped, made a dive for Larry's hat, then, dazed, hysterical, brain a riot of confusion, he, hugging Larry's crumpled hat, pushed his way into the crowd on the pavement and was lost in the surging masses.

CHAPTER II

UPSET IN NORTH STREET

GASPING for breath, a wild light in his staring eyes, Harry ran into North Street.

It was turned noon; the mills had loosed the operatives; he had expected to find the street quiet, had pictured himself dropping the bombshell of what he had witnessed and causing great commotion in the neighbourhood. To his surprise he found a crowd of neighbours congregated outside the home of Bill Simmons. A policeman was walking away.

Harry fell into a walk as he passed the policeman whom he eyed furtively, his heart rising apprehensively to remember his guilt in having been one of the demonstrators.

Helen and Sally detached themselves from the group of neighbours and came forward to meet him. Both wore expressions of anxiety. He licked his lips: 'Have y' heard, then?' he asked.

'Aye,' said Sally: 'Were you one of 'em?'

Harry nodded; then, blushing: 'But they'd no right t' do what they did!'

Sally puckered her brows and regarded him interrogatively. Helen clutched his arm: 'But you never stole any, did y', Harry?'

He stared at her, blankly: 'Stole any? What y' talkin' about?'

'Why, the cigarettes. Y'know, don't y'? Bill Simmons and Tom Hare? They've been caught stealin' out of a shop ...'

Harry ran a finger round his neckcloth; he could not withdraw his gaze from Helen's; he began to beat Larry's hat against his leg. Bill and Tom 'pinched'! And they'd invited him join them in their felony.

He felt a tug at his hand: startled, he heard Sally's voice: 'Whose hat's this? Where've y' got it from?' She looked from it to him: 'Where did y' get it?'

The group of neighbours, noticing Harry, and thinking that he might have been in some way connected with Bill's and Tom's misdemeanour, clattered to him, curious. Harry saw the unspoken question in his mother's eyes; he reassured her, then, turning to Sally, took a deep breath and related the occurrence of the clash with the police, deeply conscious of the impression his narrative was making on his audience.

'... and they told us at dole as we'd all bin knocked off so we marched t' t' city hall and they charged out wi' their truncheons. An' a copper collared hold o' Larry an' laid him out ... an' two slops (policemen) dragged him off t' prison. Aye, unconscious, too. Ah saw 'um, Ah tell y'. Knockin' fellers out all over t' show. ... He was unconscious, Ah tell y', an' he was doin' nowt, neither. None of us were. An' women coppin' (catching) it too. .... Thousands and thousands o' people there. .... Aye, 'n coppers walked wi' us all way t' city hall. They could ha' stopped us at fust if they didn't want us t' go . . .'

Towards the end of his story his auditors began to exchange glances of wild surmise; then, as with one accord, they inundated him with questions.

'Was our Dick there, Harry?'

'Oh, my God. Ah knew summat had happened. My bloke weren't ne'er so late home from dole in his life before. Ah've bin on pins this last hour. .... An' me thinkin' he's broke teetotal.'

'Did y' see our Jack, Harry?'

'Eee, Ah'll murder ar Albert if he was among 'um . . .'

The babel of voices receded to an incomprehensible jumble in Sally's ears. For a brief space she stood there dazed, holding Larry's hat, limply. Then her bosom heaved; her breathing quickened, sharply as she pictured Harry's story of Larry's assault. She gazed about her, wildly; her flashing glance fell upon Kate, Ned's wife, and, in a burst of rage she exclaimed: 'Ah'll *murder* that pig-swine of a husband o' yours if he's had owt t' do wi' it. Ah will, s'help me. .... The rats. .... The dirty, bloody dogs Ah'll, ... O. .... *Get* out o' my way.' Sobbing, without returning home for her shawl, she pushed her way through the group and ran off. Kate, shrinking, clasping and unclasping her hands nervously, watched her go.

Mrs Bull grunted: 'Well, did y' e'er hear owt like *this*?' to Mrs Hardcastle, who was standing there, whimpering indecisively, not knowing what to do. She was plagued with the thought of Sally's dinner growing cold and as to whether or no Sally would return in time to be punctual at the mill. Mrs Bull frowned upon her: 'Well,' she snapped, 'What y' standing there squawkin' for. Why don't y' tek y' rent book an' follow that lass o' thine. Y'll want it t' bail Larry out wi' . . .'

Her advice sent most of the group, whose husbands and sons might, for all they knew, be under arrest at this moment – sent them clattering home for rent books.

One woman stopped half-way across the street and shouted:

'Do it matter, Mrs Bull, if y' rent book's in arrares? Ah ain't paid ma rent f' three week . . .'

'Tike it'n see,' suggested Mrs Jike, adding, with a chuckle: 'I iyn't pide mine this last two months, sow it iyn't no use tikin' mine.'

'An Ah'll go down f' seven days afore he gets another penny from me,' said Mrs Bull: 'Ah've reckoned it up . . . leastways, Larry Meath reckoned it for me. Forty years Ah've lived there an' paid him five bob a week an' more, an' it comes to more'n five 'undred pounds. Sod 'im. If Ah'd knowd then what Ah knows now he'd ha' bin singin' for his money afore t' day. Ha, who cares o' goin' in chokey? It'll teach owld Jack Bull what it means t' have somebody t' wait on him hand an' foot like as though he was Lord Mayor's Fool. P'raps he'll understand what an easy time men have of it when they've got t' luk after themselves.'

When they had gone, Harry, sighing, turned to Helen. Instantly his spirits withered when he noticed her expression, such a one which told him that he had offended her in some way. She was pouting, staring away from him.

She found herself resenting his spending time on such affairs as this morning's. What was it to him that he should be mixed up in it? To her way of thinking their own difficulties of the present were serious enough to engage his whole attention. And to get as excited as he had been a few minutes ago, wholly absorbed in the narration of an incident that should never have concerned him, argued that there *were* some things in which he could forget all about her completely. And this when he knew her condition. She stood there pouting in sulky silence.

'What's up, Helen?' he asked, resentful of her mood: 'What's up wi' y'! What have Ah done now?' She turned on her heel and sauntered homewards, slowly, he following looking at her, brows raised. 'Nothin',' she said. Gloomily he thrust his hands into his pockets and stared at the pavement, wondering whether it had occurred to her that he might require a little sympathy. Might he not have been a victim to the police assault? Oughtn't she to be glad that he had escaped unhurt. Blimey, and here he'd been priding himself on his bravery. Oh, girls! they were always different from what you expected: 'Ah'm goin' 'ome,' he mumbled, when they paused by her home. She did not answer, went into the house: he trudged across the roadway, miserable.

'Well,' said Mrs Bull, gazing at Mrs Nattle, Mrs Jike and Mrs Dorbell, all that remained of the group: 'Well, that's *that*. What next, Ah wonder?'

Mrs Dorbell raised a yellow, clawlike hand to her hair and scratched: 'Thank God,' she said, crossing herself: 'Thank God as Ah'm a widder an'll me fambly's growd up an' out o' my sight. Dammum. Not one of 'um ever come t' see me. Yaah! Ah wouldn't have the worrit of 'em agen not for a king's ransom. When they've gone y' can have a nip when y' like wi'out askin' anybody's leave . . .'

'If y've got thrippence, y' mean,' said Mrs Jike.

Mrs Dorbell felt in her placket and withdrew her purse, opened it and glanced within. There were many pawntickets there, and there were five halfpennies and a penny.

Threepence for a nip left only a halfpenny. And the egg she required for her dinner would cost a penny. Unless, of course, she could find a cracked one amongst Mr Hulkington's stock which could be procured half price: 'Ah don't see why Ah shouldn't,' she said to herself, aloud, picturing herself surreptitiously cracking one of Mr Hulkington's choicest eggs with the shiny doorkey in her pocket. She looked at Mrs Nattle significantly and said: 'Ah'll follow y' down. Ah've a bit o' shoppin' t' do.' The party broke up, Mrs Bull and Mrs Jike following Mrs Nattle to her home, Mrs Dorbell shuffling towards Mr Hulkington's shop, talking to herself on the way.

CHAPTER 12

THE COVERED WAGON

THE main corridor of the Esperance Infirmary gave you some idea of the size of the place.

Bare and draughty, as monotonous as a vigil, old folk who come to visit relations are wearied by the walk if necessity obliges them to traverse it from end to end.

Its uncovered concrete floor emphasizes every footfall,
throwing up the loud sounds to the dark ceiling where they echo
hollowly.

Sometimes a uniformed nurse will appear out of one of the
tunnel-like arches set at regular intervals along the corridor,
proceed, with a starchy rustling of apron and skirts, to disappear into another tunnel mouth farther removed. Such a transit
is a series of contrasts in white and grey: passing the windows
she would be a nurse clothed in flashing white, but, in the gloom
between, she, but for her echoing footfalls, would be a wraith,
mantled eerily.

The tunnel-like arches gave on to flights of worn stone steps
leading to higher floors: by their sides, the open doors of the
ground floor wards revealed rows and rows of iron beds, some
concealed by red screens where a patient was either dead or
dying. If he or she were dead they would remain screened until
the witching hour, when a couple of porters, pushing a long
truck hooded like an American pioneer's covered wagon, would
remove the body to the mortuary.

Next day the occupants of the bed either side that of the one
from which the corpse had been removed, would have to accus-
tom themselves to a new arrival, who, oftener than not, had to
put up with a running reminiscence, from both sides, of the vir-
tues and manner of death of their predecessor.

At one of the tunnel mouths half-way down the corridor
stood a woman dressed in clogs and shawl. Now and then she
would peep down the tunnel and into the ward. But she could
see no sign of Sally. She fretted and fumed, experiencing
pinches of petulance that Sally should have caused her this inconvenience. Why couldn't she come home? For a day and a
night she'd sat by Larry's bedside. As though her presence here
would assist his recovery. Surely she was alive to circumstances
at home; should know the havoc the lack of her wages would
create in the household exchequer this week-end. Of course, it
was natural that she should be distressed on Larry's account;
and even though it *was* a pity the way the police had treated
him, yet this excessive devotion on Sally's part was unnecessary.
There was a trained staff here to minister to him; there was no

reason why Sally shouldn't come to spend her evenings here after work. But her present behaviour was indefensible; it was detrimental to her health; human nature couldn't stand it. Mrs Hardcastle sighed that hers was so self-willed a daughter.

She would gaze, urgently appealing, at each nurse who passed; would find herself on the point of speaking to them, then her courage would ebb and the nurses were gone in a flash.

Finally, her wearied impatience grew stronger than her timidity. She intercepted a rheumy-eyed old man dressed in a suit of hospital blue a couple of sizes too large. He scratched the back of his ear, wrinkled his brow and stared at the floor: 'Oh,' he said, looking up: 'Y' mean yon lass sittin' wi' yon lad wi' the pumonia?' He put out his lips and shook his head, slowly: 'Ay, aye, oo! Well, lass, if she's thy dowter she won't ha' much longer t' sit. For yon lad's dyin'. Ah know. Ah've sin 'em tuk out o' this ward b' the score. Bin here eight months Ah have, e'er sin she died, bless her soul. None o' me childer'd ha' me so Ah'd t' come t' t' grubber, 'cause they said Ah'd rheumatics bad. That's what me childer said, mind y': though they ne'er thought o' that afore they got wed an' when Ah wus fetchin' me wages home t' keep 'em all on. . . . Ne'er forgive 'um. . . . Not one of 'em e'er comes t' see me t' ask me have Ah got a pipe o' baccy. Three days Ah've bin wi'out a puff. They tek y' pension off y' when y' come in here, an' grub's pison.'

Mrs Hardcastle felt sorry for him but she wished he would inform Sally of her presence in this cold corridor. Perhaps, if. . . . She produced her purse in which she knew were a few coppers. She gave a couple to the old man saying: 'That's all Ah've got. Perhaps y'll be able t' get a pipe o' baccy wi' it,' adding, as she drew her shawl tightly about her person once again: '*Would* y' tell me daughter Ah'm here, please, mister?'

He took the coins, and, with an expression of sudden enlightenment, said: 'Oh, aye, that lass o' thine. Y'd better come along wi' me an' Ah'll tek y' to her.' He shuffled to the door of an ante-room to obtain the sister's permission. In a moment, Mrs Hardcastle, her shawl shrouding her face, tiptoed after the old man, quaking with nervousness and shame on account of the noise her clogs were making on the ward's bare boards. She was frightened, too, by the unearthly groans of a man dying unattended in some remote part of the ward; and by the jabberings of another patient recovering from a recently administered anaesthetic. Nobody else seemed to take notice of the noises. In fact, four men were playing cards on the bed next the screen where the old man now stood paused. From the other side of the screen came a low, monotonous mumbling.

The old fellow opened one of the screen's leaves, then, perceiving Mrs Hardcastle's hesitation said, with an inclination of the head: 'Go on. Go in, lass.' She obeyed.

She stared, shocked, when she saw Larry. The smile she had put on for his benefit faded the instant her gaze fell on him. The red flannel pneumonia jacket he was wearing exaggerated the intense pallor of his face which seemed to have shrunk to nothing: his mouth, lips dry and slightly parted, moved as he murmured, incoherently, deliriously: his laboured breathing, quick and harsh was painful to hear: his eyes, wide open seemed twice their accustomed size, they burned with a wild, haunting light. The pink coverlet outlined his motionless form like something wet and clinging. Sally, sitting on a chair by the bedside holding one of his hands, did not look up when her mother entered; she was dozing, chin sunk on chest.

For a while Mrs Hardcastle could not remove her fascinated gaze from Larry. At once she appreciated the futility of her mission. Sally never would be induced to leave. Not that she, Mrs Hardcastle, would wish her to do so now that she had learnt how seriously ill Larry was. They would have to manage, somehow, without Sally's wages. How they *were* going to manage now that Harry had been refused the dole didn't bear thinking on. She forgot about it as she stood staring at Larry, an overwhelming sympathy towards him swelling in her heart, a fear treading on sympathy's heels as to the consequences of this to Sally. Mrs Hardcastle licked her lips.

She became conscious of a dull aching in her legs. There'd be no harm in sitting on the edge of the bed. Carefully she seated herself, thrilled with fear as her movement disturbed Sally, who, catching her breath in a weary sigh, looked up. Mrs Hardcastle fixed her gaze on Larry; she did not wish to meet Sally's eyes.

Money jingled as the four card players on the next bed threw their halfpenny bets into the kitty: the man recovering from the anaesthetic chuckled, groans came from the dying man in the remote part of the ward.

Sally gently stroked her disengaged hand across Larry's brow. It was as though he had not seen her hand; his staring eyes did not flicker. He did not murmur now: a crackle crept into his breathing. The two women watched and waited.

CHAPTER 13

# WANTED, A FIVER

'Aʜ think,' said Mrs Bull, warmly: 'Ah think it's a sin an' a shame Ah do.' She turned to her cronies standing in a group about the open door of the house where Larry had lodged. A horse and cart was pulled up by the kerb on and around which hosts of the children of the neighbourhood were playing noisily. Two men were inside the house shifting Larry's possessions. Sally was standing by the doorstep, a dull stare in her eyes.

'Ah think it's a sin an' a shame Ah do,' Mrs Bull said, warmly: 'Huh!' her immense breasts wobbled like Brobdingnagian blanc-manges as she ejaculated: 'Huh! Five quid, mind y'. On'y five quid for all t' lad's belongin's. Bareface-daylight robbery, that's what it is.'

'Sellin',' said Mrs Dorbell, wryly: 'Sellin' ain't buyin'. Ah remember that 'armonium wot belonged t' that there lodger o' mine afore he died. He gev eight poun' ten for it. Ay, an' it were a nice piece o' furniture. Though he couldn't play it an' allus kep' it locked so's nobody else could try. Ne'er played on it wasn't from comin' in t' goin' out. As good day it went as day it came. Kep' it dusted 'issel', he did an' wouldn't let a soul g' near it. Fifteen an' a tanner they gev me for it when he wus dead. Fifteen an' a tanner, mind y' an' it ne'er bin played on. Ay, enough t' mek him turn o'er in his grave, saints preserve 'im,' she crossed herself: 'He were best lodger Ah ever had,' she sniffed; her dewdrop disappeared from the tip of her beak-like nose and slowly grew again.

Mrs Bull grunted, then glanced at Mrs Nattle: 'Y'll be goin' round t'all t' neighbours collectin' for a wreath for t' lad, won't y', Sair Ann?'

'Aye, Ah suppose so,' Mrs Nattle answered, adding, with a shake of the head: 'Though Ah ain't confidential o' gettin ' much. Things're too bad. It's comin' t' summat, Ah must say, when even pop-shop guz bankrupt. Did y' hear tell o' that one i' William Street? Everybody pawnin' an' nobody gettin' 'em out. An' Ah seed bum-bailiffs in yesterday tekkin' all the bungles away on a cart. "Thank God," Ah sez to meself Ah ses: "Thank God as all my customerses bungles is at Price and Jones's." That's what comes o' not goin' to a 'igh-class pop-shop.'

Before Mrs Nattle had finished speaking, Mrs Bull, who had not been listening to her, turned to Sally and said: 'Where are y' buryin' the lad, Sal?'

'He ain't bein' buried,' replied Sally, tonelessly.

'Eh?' said Mrs Bull, incredulously: 'Eh? Not buryin' him . . .?' All stared at Sally, amazed.

Without looking at any of them Sally answered, in the same toneless voice: 'I'm going to have him cremated. He allus said it was proper way.'

'Cremated!' said Mrs Bull: 'Well, did you ever,' to the others: 'That's fust time *that's* happened in Hanky Park,' incredulously: 'Well, now, what d' y' think o' that?'

'Gie me a grave, proper an' Christian like,' said Mrs Dorbell: 'Ah wus brought up t' read Bible, Ah wus.'

Tiny Mrs Jike shivered: a thought plagued her as to how Larry would fare on the day of resurrection; particularly was she troubled in regard to his 'spiret': the consequences seemed so complex that she could find no words with which to express her intense puzzlement. She licked her lips and stared at Sally apprehensively.

'Naa,' said Mrs Nattle, putting out her lips and shaking her head: 'Ah ain't bin allus Ah should ha' bin i' me time, but if that's what them there socialis' fellers believe in, then *Ah'm* ne'er gonna vote for 'um. Huh! Nobody's gonna burn *me*, not if *Ah* know it.'

A thoughtful silence.

Mrs Bull contracted her brows and gazed at Sally: 'It's gonna cost y' a tidy penny, ain't it, Sal?'

Mrs Dorbell pricked her ears: she said, eagerly: 'How much did y' have 'im in for?' She referred to the amount, if any, of Larry's insurance.

Sally answered Mrs Dorbell: 'He wasn't in for nowt. He didn't believe in it.'

Mrs Dorbell's eyes opened wide: 'Didn't believe in insurance . . .?'

Mrs Nattle's mouth opened; she said, in such tones as plainly said that it was inconceivable that anybody could *not* believe in insurance: 'Then how – what – who did 'e expect 'd *pay* for his funeral,' she was as indignant as she would have been had the bill for the funeral expenses been addressed to herself.

'Aaach,' snapped Sally, with sudden animation: 'What was good o' him talkin' to a lot o' owld geysers like you?' with a rising voice: 'He didn't care what become o' him, no more do I.' fiercely 'He's gone, now d'y' hear? He's gone!' Her eyes blazed; she stared piercingly at Mrs Nattle.

'Huh!' said Mrs Nattle, folding her arms and tossing her head: 'Huh! If y' gonna act like that wi' them as is tryin' t' sympathize wi' y', y'd best be left t' y'sel' '; to Mrs Dorbell: 'Come on, Nancy,' adding, to Mrs Dorbell as the pair stalked away: 'Ungrateful madam.' Mrs Jike mumbled some excuse and hurried after her two friends.

'Sally,' said Mrs Bull, when they had gone: 'Tek no heed on 'em, lass. Ah'd many a crack wi' that lad o' thine about one thing an' another, an' he spoke a lot o' sense, he did. Ah've seen too much i' my time t' be tuk in by all parson'd like y' t' swallow. Ah've had no eddication but Ah do know that there ne'er was parson breathed wot preached sermon about resurrection on empty belly, an' mine's bin empty many a time. S'easy for them as live house an' light free an' a regular wage comin' in. . . . Let 'em try clemmin' (going hungry) like us have t' do every day o' our lives. Pay 'em wot they pay them on t' dole an' y'd see plenty o' parsons jobs goin' beggin'. Yaach. What's good o' botherin' about us when we've snuffed it? Luk better o' some folks if they'd do us a bit o' good while we're alive,' pause: 'As for that lad o' thine, Sal, lass, don't you wish him back. All me life Ah've lived, lass, Ah've bin waitin' for summat that's never come. Ah don't wish a day of it back agen. There's nowt for the likes of us t' live for, Sal. Nowt. Religion, eh? Pah. Ah've no patience wi' it.'

'No, nor me neither,' muttered Sally, adding, bitterly: 'Ah've patience wi' nowt nor nobody, now.'

A pause. Then Mrs Bull gazed at Sally perplexed: 'But tell me, lass. How *are* y' gonna manage t' pay for funeral if all y've got's this here five quid they're giving y' for his things?'

Sally sighed wearily, and stared at the roadway: 'God knows,' she said: 'Owld Fogley said it'll cost me twice more than what Ah've got. Ah've offered t' pay him so much a week but he won't take it that way. An' people we bought furniture off won't give us deposit money back. They say that it's in papers that Larry signed that we lose what we paid if we don't have the furniture . . .' half to herself: 'Ooo, Ah wish Ah knew somebody as'd lend it t' me . . .'

'Five quid's a lot o' money, Sal,' Mrs Bull murmured, thoughtfully, slowly lifting the hem of her apron upon which she blew her nose: 'Five quid. . . . Ah wonder, now. . . .' She glanced at Sally sharply: 'Wot about Sam Grundy, eh, Sal? He ain't a bad feller at heart, y' know. He'd do it for y'.'

Sally shrugged: 'Ah know he would. Do it for what he'd like t' get out o' me.'

Mrs Bull grunted: 'That's fault wi' all o' the men. But they don't allus get what they want. Still, Sal, Ah'd think it o'er if Ah was you,' glancing up the street: 'Ah, well, Ah must be off, Sal. Ah've a rare pile o' ironin' t' do t' neet. Poor soul wi' a tribe o' kids as lives in next street's bin confined agen. They'd ha' charged her ten bob for t' washin' if she'd ha' sent it t' t' laundry. Couldn't even afford t' pay me for tendin' her i' childbed, an' him workin', too! Blimey, wot a life, Sal, wot a life.' She shook her head and made as though to go, then she paused and added: 'Ah'll come wi' y' t' t' funeral if y' don't mind, Sal. Ah've allus wanted t' see how they do it.' She waddled away to borrow a flat iron from Mrs Cranford, her next door neighbour.

One of the furniture broker's men, a tall, gaunt individual

with skin-tight clothes, a luxurious moustache and prominent eyes, came to the door of the house carrying a pile of Larry's books slung about with a length of cord. He pushed past Sally then dropped the books on to the pavement as he stared, astounded, at the scene in front of his eyes.

Children everywhere. Swarming and dancing upon the cart bottom; swinging on the choke rail, lying on the axle bars, a couple of boys astride the listless horse, ineffectually urging it to move; another demonstrating his daring by lifting one of the animal's forefeet; one unhooking the traces, another unfastening every buckle he could find; a crowd in front of the horse's head feeding it on stolen handfuls of corn taken from the nosebag swinging on a hook by the shafts; lastly, two small boys who, having first lighted the cart's lamps, now competed with each other in creating the largest flame by turning the wicks higher and higher until thick wisps of smoke began to ascend.

The man, knocking his rusty billycock to the back of his head, stared for a second, aghast. Then, with his intense hatred of all the juvenile world reflecting itself in his suddenly flushed face, he bawled, in a voice amplified by his indignation: 'Hoi!'

Instant silence from the cart alow and aloft. All regarded him impudently: none made the least suggestion of stirring. It was maddening. The man made a sudden rush: 'Gerrout of it, y' little devils y', gerrout,' he roared: 'Blind owld Riley, Ah'll break y' bloody backs if . . .' spotting the smoke: 'Blimey, they've set the cart afire!' He dived beneath to extinguish the lamps: 'An'. . . . Gor. . . . Blimey! They'd ha' pinched the horse if Ah hadn't come out. Hoi, George!' His mate appeared, a short, snub-nosed, pot-bellied man wearing a check waistcoat, a cap and an interrogative expression: 'Wot's up, Bill?' he asked.

'Wot's up, eh? Wot *ain't* up. Bloody kids . . . they're like bloody monkeys,' raising his brows extraordinarily high: 'Even had the 'orse unharnessed. 'S a wonder owld Sam didn't gallop off'n 'urt somebody.'

George guffawed: 'He ain't done no gallopin' sin' he were in t' Fire Brigade,' assuming a stern expression which was extremely incongruous to the humorous cast of his features; turning to the horde of children standing off at a safe distance and in the form of a semi-circle: 'Go on, now. Be off wi' y' or y'll have a bobby round y' tails.' He stopped, picked up the pile of books which George had dropped and flung them on to the cart bottom where they fell with a dull thud.

Sally turned away: it was poignant. She could scarcely lend credence to these happenings; her disbelief sicklied them over with the quality of a dream; to try to convince herself otherwise induced only a dazed torpor of the brain. It was absurd, this imperturbable knowledge that she never would see Larry again. Never? It stunned her. She sighed, wearily, fretfully, felt pinioned; a wild bleakness, a yearning, a striving filled her heart. There was no place she wanted to go; nothing she wanted to see or do. The streets suffocated her, the encompassing walls oppressed her; she felt reckless, desperate, rebellious. She stared about her, wildly – then the sensation subsided; she felt weary again, remembered dully, that she had five pounds to find from somewhere.

She found herself paused by the open doors of the Duke of Gloucester. Sam Grundy's motor-car stood pulled up by the kerb; she heard his raucous laugh within the public-house.

'Five pounds,' the words repeated themselves monotonously. After all, why shouldn't she ask the favour of him? Why? What a question. What alternative was there? Who in Hanky Park possessed such a sum of money: and who, possessing it, would lend it to her knowing her circumstances. Oh, money, money, money. A listlessness overwhelmed her; made her feel as powerless as a straw buffeted on turbulent waters. Then, sudden anger took hold of her, rousing her from her dazed state of brain weariness. She needed money; Sam Grundy had it. With kindling eyes and flushed cheeks she asked herself why she should refrain.

She turned and went into the public-house.

As she entered by the outdoor department the landlord stared at her over the beer engine. Her appearance was arresting; dark hair blown about her face, lustrous eyes burning brighter, as staring over the landlord's shoulder, she caught sight of Ned Narkey, in civilian clothes sitting with a number of other men, among whom was Sam Grundy, in the taproom. Their eyes met. Ned leered, shifted in his seat and spat on to the saw-dusted floor. Her nostrils dilated; she passed a hand across her hair and looked at him with a wide-eyed, intense stare. His gaze wavered and fell; he passed a hand across his mouth and turned to speak to his nearest companion.

'Tell Sam Grundy Ah want t' see him,' she murmured, to the landlord, without removing her gaze from Ned. Then she turned and walked out to stand on the pavement, brooding. She did not see Sam's approach; was not aware that her sudden request had so perturbed him as to cause him to lay aside his freshly lit cigar and to leave his double Scotch untouched, both of which later, were dispatched, mysteriously, by whom none knew. Though Ted Munter left earlier than was usual for him.

Sam's agitation was apparent; he moistened his lips, fur-tively, coughed nervously; there was a stare in his beady eyes: he was at a loss, completely, for reasons to account for this totally unexpected summons: 'What's up, Sal?' he asked, anxiously: 'What's up, Sal? What d'y' want?'

She looked at him awhile, lip curling: 'Ah was going to ask y' t' lend me five pounds,' she said. She paused, interrupted him as, an expression of deep relief causing his features to relax, he took a deep breath and was about to reply with broad gestures of generous compliance – she interrupted him: 'But I'm not so sure I want y' help, now.'

He raised his brows and said, in hurt tones: 'Why, Sal, what d'y' mean?'

'Aaach, Ah'm not so fond of the company y' keep.'

'Company Ah keep? Who d'y' mean?'

Her breathing quickened; she inclined her head, sharply, towards the Duke of Gloucester: 'You know who Ah mean,' with flashing eyes: 'Him. Ned Narkey, that pal o' yours . . .'

Sam's mouth contorted, wryly: '*Him*. Yah! He ain't no pal o' mine, nor none of his kidney, neither.'

She eyed him, suspiciously: 'Y' seemed t' be enjoyin' his company.'

'Aw,' he replied, with a note of querulous appeal in his voice: 'Y've got to be civil to 'em. He's a copper. An' they can turn nasty. On'y last week they booked a couple o' my men an' it cost me ten quid in fines. Yah! He's no pal o' mine. How he got on force Ah don't know,' a pause, then, with suppressed ardour and with a nervous glance towards the door of the public-house: 'Come on, Sal. Come a drive round in me car. Y' don't want t' talk business where everybody can hear.'

She frowned, and, with a sharp gesture of the hand, replied: 'Ah want t' borrow five pounds. Ah want no drives in no cars. An' Ah'm feard o' nobody hearin',' gazing at him, frankly: 'Will y' lend it? Ah'll pay back when mill starts on full time agen . . .'

Instantly he was fumbling abjectly in his pocket. He withdrew a bundle of one pound treasury notes and passed her a number: 'Here, Sal,' he said, with intense eagerness: 'Here, Sal, will that be enough?' adding, as she took them: 'Y've no need to pay me back.' His eyes shone as he looked at the notes in her hand; his overripe complexion took on a deeper shade; he felt unaccountably nervous, pleased with himself.

Mrs Dorbell who was shuffling by, gulped and stared as she saw Sally count five of the notes and pass the remainder back to Sam with a rebuking glance: 'Ah wouldn't ha' come to you if Ah could ha' borrowed it from somebody else,' she said, candidly: 'An' Ah'll pay y' back.' Mrs Dorbell sniffed, passed on her way, lips tightly compressed.

'Aw, Sal, what's up wi' y'? What have y' got agen me?' deprecatingly: 'Ah don't want y' t' pay me back. Ah'm on'y glad Ah can do y' a good turn. Tek it. . . . Tek it all, an' more if y' want it.' She did not answer, pressed the excess back to him: 'Aw, go on, Sal. Tek it an' don't be daft.' She pushed the notes into his breast pocket: he flushed at the contact of her hand, blinked. A sudden appreciation of her unspoilt youth stabbed his age and excess with keen reproach. She was maddening: 'Gord, Sal,' he muttered ardently: 'Y've got me all wrong. Ah'm not tryin' any tricks on wi' y' . . .' with shamefaced hesitation: 'Ah'd. . . . Ah'm. . . . Aw, Ah'd like y' for a pal, that's all,' persuasively: 'Y' must be sick o' havin' nowt t' wear, an' pinchin' an' scrapin' week after week. . . . Blimey. An' what y' could have if y' wanted. Anythin', Sal. Anythin' f'th' askin'.'

She turned on her heel and walked away, Sam's fixed gaze

devouring her until she went into her home. Still he stared, a slow smile breaking on his lips, a sensation of expectancy, of imminent good fortune inflating his heart. Then he experienced an urgent desire to celebrate in anticipation, and, on an impulse, he got into his car and drove away.

The broker's cart followed him out of the street.

CHAPTER 14

## 'VOICE THAT BREATHED O'ER EDEN'

HARDCASTLE regarded his blushing son with growing severity as Harry, hesitatntly, concluded: '. . . so, y' see, Dad, Ah'll have t' marry 'Elen. An' Ah thought, like, that we could come'n live here an' get a bed in back room wi' Sal . . . until Ah get a job, like . . .' he licked his lips and stared at his father.

His mother's fingers played with the hem of her apron as though she was threading it with a bodkin; she stared at the floor.

Hardcastle's shoulders shrugged convulsively; he regarded Harry scornfully: 'Huh!' he said: 'A pretty pickle y've got y'self in, y' bloody fool,' a pause; he added: '*You*, gettin' married. Huh! Who the devil d'y' think's gonna keep y', eh?'

'Ah thought, like . . .' Harry mumbled, averting his gaze.

'Y' *thought*! Yah, y' damn fool, don't y' think there's enough trouble here wi'out you bringin' more?' emphatically: 'Well, no slut like that's gonna come t' live here, d'y' hear . . .'

Harry glared at his father: 'Hey,' he said, warmly: 'Ah'm not havin' you callin' her a slut, d'y' hear? You leave her name out o' it.' He clenched his fists.

Hardcastle half rose: 'Are y' threatenin' *me*?' he demanded.

'Aye, Ah am, if y' call her names. . . . Ah'm askin' *you* for nowt. Ah'm not th' on'y one out o' work i' this house, remember. Yah, y' treat me like as though Ah was a kid, just-a-cause Ah've got nowt an' Ah'm out o' work. . . . Y' didn't talk like this when Ah was sharin' me winnin's wi' y', did y'? Chee! Once let me get hold o' some money agen an' Ah'll ne'er part

wi' a brown (penny). Ah'm supposed to be a man, Ah am. ....
Well, luk at me!' he held out his hands, tears shone in his
eyes.

'Y' bringin' no wife here, d'y' understand?' cried his father:
'Y've made y'r own bed wi' y' fornicatin'; y' mun lie on it. Go'n
stay wi' *her* folk, the low-live lot that they are . . .'

'Stop it!' cried Harry, his voice rising, shrilly: 'Stop it!' then,
with passion: 'Ah don't *want* t' live here. D'y' hear. Ah wouldn't
live wi' *you* if Ah got chance. Y' can g' t' 'ell. Ah'm leavin'
here. . . .' He turned about and was gone, not hearing his mother
who called his name plaintively.

He stepped into the street and slammed the door after him
with such force as rattled the windows. Hands in pockets, burning gaze fixed on the pavement, breathing short and sharp, he
stamped up the street to join Helen, waiting for him at the
corner. She came forward to meet him, an apprehensive stare
in her eyes: 'What did he say, Harry? Will he . . .?'

'No,' answered Harry, savagely: 'An' Ah've left home,' averting his gaze. 'Ach, allus he could say was that we was damn
fools an' we'd made our beds. . . . Oh, y'know th'old tale,' staring at her and raising his brows: 'Said *he* couldn't keep us. *Him*,
mind y'! Him wot's livin' on our Sal,' with a gesture of desperation: 'Aw, carm on, who wants t' live there, anyway? It'll be
a long while afore he sees *me* agen.'

She fell into step by his side, her troubled eyes searching his
profile. 'But who'll tek us in, Harry?' she asked, in a frightened
whisper: 'We've got nowt on'y what Ah'm earnin'. . . . An'
Ah'll be confined soon. You're knocked off dole, an' there's no
room at our house,' pause: fear grew on her face: she repeated,
in tones, which, to his guilty ears, seemed to grow from a
whisper to disturbing loudness: 'What'll become of us? Oh, if
only Ah'd known this was gonna happen. . . .' He glanced about
him, red in the face. He turned to her: 'Aw, Helen, quiet down,
will y'? Y'll have everybody lukkin' at us . . .' persuasively: 'You
leave it to me. Everythin'll be all right. Ah'll find a place for us,
somewhere. Ah'll . . .' passionately: 'Ah'll join th' army, afore
Ah'll be beat. Gor blimey, if Ah won't.'

Either she did not hear him or her mild hysteria refused to be pacified. She kept mumbling to herself in whimpering tones while Harry continued, warming to the optimistic side of the picture: '... Besides, when we're married they'll be bound t' give us money at workhouse. .... An' Ah'll stand a better chance o' gettin' a job wi' bein' married. They're givin' married 'uns a chance before t'others wherever y' go. ... Single blokes don't get a smell in,' eagerly: 'Don't y' see, Helen? Why, Ah bet Ah'm workin' in next t' no time. ... You see. An' by time y' finish work t'day Ah'll have found a place for us. Ah will, really. Ah'll come an' meet y' tonight at mill,' he placed his arm about her shoulder and said, in soothing tones: 'You don't fret y'self, Helen. Ah'm glad as it's happened way it has. We'll be together, anyway, an' that's what Ah've allus wanted,' ardently, vehemently: 'Oh, once let me get a job an' Ah'll show y'. You'll go short o' nowt, s'elp me!'

Gradually, her perturbation subsided: she mumbled: 'If only y' could get a job, Harry. Ah wouldn't care nowt for nobody.'

'Oh, it'll come, you see if it won't,' warmly: 'Y' ne'er know what's in store for us. ... Why, just imagine it, Helen, Ah've on'y t' get a job an' ...' awed: 'Blimey! A job!' The immense consequences that hinged on the possibility amazed him, made him forget everything but itself; for a moment he was staggered by its full significance. She, too, was similarly affected.

They walked along, a shabby, insignificant couple, contributing the negligible quantities of their presence to the hurly-burly of the main thoroughfare; two young people, too preoccupied, too full of their own immediate woes and hopes of relief to suspect like emotions in the hearts of the other passers-by.

They paused outside the workhouse and stared at each other with expressions of shame-faced self-consciousness. Helen withdrew a ten shilling note from her pocket, limp with the perspiration of the hand that had been clutching it. She offered it to Harry: 'Here it is, Harry,' she said: 'Ah borrowed it from a girl at mill. She says we can pay her back when y' get work.'

He took it, slipped it into his waistcoat pocket, then, coughing nervously, licking his lips and running a finger round his loose neckcloth, blinked at her and said: 'Come on, 'Elen. Let's get it over with.' He led the way, she following as he, blushing hotly, walked up the steps of the entrance to a door marked:

REGISTRAR'S OFFICE
EAST DISTRICT

2

Mrs Dorbell, her threadbare shawl wrapped about her head and skeletonic shoulders, shuffled into North Street muttering aloud to herself. Her concealed hands held, in the one, her purse and doorkey; the other, under her chin, clutched a handful of the shawl's folds pulling the covering as tight as a bandage about her face. Now and again the nostrils of her hook nose gave an upward jump as she sniffed, lusciously. Coming to a standstill outside the open door of Mrs Nattle's home, she muttered, concluding her remarks with: 'They wanted enough for their money, an' me wot's a pore widder 'ooman wi' nobody at back of her. But Ah'm all there, Ah am. Nobody's gunna get best o' me.' She stared at the door-knob for a moment and added: 'Ah don't see why Ah shouldn't.' She bowed, as it were, slightly, to the open door, and, keeping her heavy-lidded gaze fixed upon the chipped black door-knob, asked . . .

Mrs Nattle within, pricked her ears as she heard the shuffling footsteps cease outside the door. She quickly drained the glass which lay on the breakfast-littered table, then concealed both glass and bottle beneath her trailing skirts. Afterwards she composed her hands across her stomach, assumed an innocent expression, and waited, a seemingly unconscionable time for the familiar voice which asked: 'A' y' in, missis?'

In response to the invitation, Mrs Dorbell entered: 'Ah've just bin,' she began: 'Ah've just bin t' draw me owld age. Ah'll sit me down for a minnit if y' don't mind.' She did, and it was with a long-drawn groan which employed every vowel in the language: 'Aeiou! Ah'm none so well this mornin'.'

Mrs Nattle sympathized with a glance and with many shakes of the head: 'P'raps,' she suggested: 'P'raps a likkle nip'd do y' good.'

Mrs Dorbell produced her purse, laid the new ten shilling

note, her old age pension, upon the table, and said: 'Three pen-n'orth, Sair Ann.'

The bottle and glass appeared; the drink was carefully dispensed. Mrs Nattle passed the glass to her friend, picked up the ten shilling note, and, nursing the bottle as she would have a baby, took it with her so that Mrs Dorbell might not be led into temptation, saying, as she passed through the doorway to the room at the back: 'Ah'll have t' get y' change, Nancy.'

An intense silence fell on the house. Mrs Dorbell strained her hearing in the hope of learning the approximate hiding place where Mrs Nattle lodged 'it'. Mrs Nattle, Mrs Dorbell knew, distrusted banks, and, in view of her multifarious business affairs, it was obvious that she must have a considerable sum in store somewhere in the house. The obsessing, oft-recurring vision in which Mrs Dorbell saw herself, one day, finding Mrs Nattle a lonely corpse in the house would have done justice to a rightful legatee. It intoxicated her to imagine coming across 'it' under such circumstances.

Mrs Nattle had her suspicions though. And this accounted for the fact of her precaution, every old age pension day, of having handy, on top of the chest of drawers in the room at the back, an amount of silver and copper in anticipation of the demand for change. Thus, she, entering the back room, could stuff the treasury note in a jug, noiselessly pick up nine shillings and ninepence change, then stand there awhile, bottle in arm, listening to Mrs Dorbell's listening, and congratulating herself on the confusion and disappointment she knew her silence was causing Nancy.

Sounds of the 'clop-clop' of clogs, the blending of voices in the street induced a succession of coughs in Mrs Nattle. She shuffled her feet as though returning from some farther re-moved corner then returned to the front room: 'Nine and nine-pence change, Nancy,' she said, handing the money over. In reference to the approaching footsteps: 'Sounds like Mrs Bull and Mrs Jike.' Nevertheless, although she guessed the identity of her prospective visitors, she hid the bottle beneath her skirts, composed her hands in the customary place, excusing her caution with: 'Pays t' be careful, Nance, when y' ain't got a spirit licence. Put y' glass away, lass, y' ne'er know who's sneakin' round. Dammum!'

'Ah'm comin' in,' said the voice of Mrs Bull from the door. She entered, stared at Mrs Nattle and Mrs Dorbell grunting a greeting. Mrs Jike, smiling and wearing her husband's cap, followed: 'Hallo, Mrs Nakkle,' she said, brightly, then turned to Mrs Dorbell: 'Ah, *you're* there, too, Mrs Dorbell. How's y' pore old cough, love?' She fumbled in her placket and withdrew her snuff-box, first proffering it to her companions, then putting a pinch on the back of her hand and sniffing it, deeply. She seated herself next Mrs Dorbell on the sofa: 'How's y' cough, love?' she asked Mrs Dorbell once again.

'As oosual,' replied Mrs Dorbell with a melancholy glance: 'It don't do me no good, thank y'.'

Mrs Bull was about to say something when Mrs Dorbell interrupted her, saying, to the company in general: 'Me spare room's tuk, thank God,' adding, after a slight pause: 'Furnished,' she sniffed and gazed at Queen Victoria's picture on the wall.

Mrs Jike drew back open-mouthed, folded her arms, tightly, and, staring at Mrs Dorbell's Punch-like profile, said, in tones of great surprise: 'Y' down't siy! Well, did y' ever, now!'

Mrs Bull chuckled: 'Furnished,' she scoffed: 'Furnished! Wermin an' all.'

Mrs Nattle, scenting the likelihood of a new 'naybore' who might find cause to wish to be 'obligded', regarded Mrs Dorbell with intense interest: 'Oo is it?' she asked: 'Hanybody we know?'

'It's,' answered Mrs Dorbell: 'It's 'im as got that lass o' Hawkinses into trouble. Hardcastle's lad. His pa wouldn't have him fetch a wife home him bein' out o' work. They bin married at registry office and she's expectin' soon ...' to Mrs Jike, as though in warning: 'That's wot comes o' sittin' on Dawney's Hill wi' lads, an' going' away holidayin' together. Ah'd like t' see feller as'd get *me* sittin' up there wi' him.' She pushed her shawl back and scratched her dirty hair.

'Well,' responded Mrs Jike, breathlessly: 'Y' down't siy!' To Mrs Bull who was chuckling and placing three pennies on the table: 'That'll be a job for you, dearie, when the gel's confined,' sighing: 'Ah, well, eccidents *will* heppen. An' it's one wiy o' gettin' y' blowke.'

Mrs Bull, still chuckling, received the glass of Mrs Nattle. She sipped, then, ceasing chuckling, regarded Mrs Dorbell suspiciously: 'Didn't y' say young Harry'd bin knocked off dole?'

Mrs Dorbell nodded and looked very sad: 'They've told me all their perticlers. *She*'s earnin' eighteen bob at mill when she gets a full week in.'

'Wot about when she's confined?' Mrs Jike asked: 'She wown't be able to work then. How'll they piy y' the rent?'

'Ah suppose,' said Mrs Nattle, curling her lip and putting her head back: 'Ah suppose they'll g' t' their Sally an' ask her t' ask Sam Grundy for a bit o' help,' opening her eyes very wide: '*Ah* heard o' a party wot 'appened t' be passin' Duke o' Gloucester not *very* long ago. An' *they* saw a likkle bit o' business bein' done a-tween her an' him. Gev' her a bungle o' notes, he did. *Wery* nice, Ah *must* say. An' in broad daylight, too!' narrowing her eyes and nodding her head, knowingly ' "Ah'll pay y' back," ses she t' him when she saw this certain party passin'. Huh! As though *we* don't know how she'll pay him back. Nice carryin's on amongst y'r own naybores, Ah must say. Wery nice, indeed. An' him what she was supposed t' marry not buried a month!'

'Yaaa,' snapped Mrs Bull: 'Leave lass a-be (alone). If y' want t' know it was me wot put her up t' ask Sam Grundy. An' if y' can't mind y'r own business then y'd better know wot she wanted money for – It was t' pay funeral expenses o' Larry Meath. *Now* a' y' satisfied?'

'All same,' mumbled Mrs Nattle, who, obviously, was not satisfied: 'All same, Sam Grundy'n her are gettin' pretty thick. Ah see his moteycar everlastin' hangin' about street corner nowadays,' warmly: '*He'll* be gettin' his way wi' her ...'

'More power t' t' lass if he does,' Mrs Bull responded: 'For the more Ah see o' men an' wedlock wi' the likes of us, the more Ah – Aw, what is it, anyway, scratchin' an' scrapin' week arter week; killin' y' sel' mekkin' ends meet an' havin' kids wot y' can't afford t' keep. ... Yaa, an' there ain't no goin' on strike for us women. Neglec' y' childer an' y're hauled afore t' beak. ...

Gor blimey, they think we're magicians, an' Ah ain't sure that we ain't. .... Anyway, if a lass like Sal Hardcastle gets chance t' see summat different an' get a few quid in her pocket, then more power to her. ... Even though it don't last for ever she *will* ha' seen summat different. That's more'n Ah can say for meself.' She glanced at Mrs Dorbell and caused that lady's brows to elevate by saying: 'An' ne'er heed owld Ma Dorbell. *She* ain't one t' go nowt short. Trust her. By time *she's* finished wi' young Harry he'll know all tricks o' the trade.'

Nancy looked hurt and indignant: 'They've got t' give 'em their rent at workhouse,' she protested, 'no matter wot comes or guz,' adding, warmly: 'An' Ah don't see wot or why a pore, lone, widder 'ooman should go bout her due for sake o' a young feller's pride,' with emphasis: 'You betcha! Ah'll show him the ropes. Nancy Dorbell's lived too long t' go owt short. Huh!'

Mrs Jike, who, for the past few moments had been listening to what she thought was the approaching voices of newspaper boys, cried suddenly: 'Hark! Ain't that the one o'clock?' She rose and hurried to the door as one of the boys tore down the street: 'Hiy! Here, sonny,' she shouted, and, as she gave the penny in exchange for the sheet, asked, eagerly: 'What are they backin'? What d' y' know?'

'Dusty Carpet in t' two-thirty,' said the boy, adding, with a snigger: 'It'll want some beatin'.' And he was off in a jiffy, calling his newspapers as he ran fetching many people to their front doors with pennies in their hands.

Mrs Jike muttered something and returned to her companions where to consult the inspired prophecy of the tipster journalists.

CHAPTER 15

'LEANOVER'

For a while Harry was perplexed by his new circumstances. Waking in a strange ramshackle bed in a strange bare room and finding Helen by his side chilled and frightened him. He would lie there, staring at the dirty ceiling or at the colour-washed walls mapped with patches of damp; stare at them feeling as a stranger in a strange town. Then, to escape the fears that plagued him, he would put an arm round Helen, move closer to her to find what comfort and solace he could in her companionable presence, trying to evade the disturbing remembrances which, one after another, jostled him with heart-raising jolts.

He was severed from the old way of life at home, now. Mother, father and sister were as strangers. He lived separated from them! He soon would be a father himself! The thought made him feel scared, guiltily scared. He marvelled at Helen's seeming composure. She did not seem at all disturbed now that they were married. He, a father though! He, a silly, incompetent boy dressed in the ill-fitting clothes of manhood. 'A father! *Me*, a father!' Sometimes he couldn't make sense out of it. Surely everybody must suspect his secret opinion of his own immaturity. He felt afraid to be seen abroad for fear of pointing fingers and muttering mouths.

Then he would be filled with a timid curiosity, a titillating expectation, a shy impatience to know and to see the baby. It was not altogether unpleasant. After all, why need he be ashamed? Ashamed? nay, he was proud. Yet it seemed absurd, really. In his eyes other fathers filled the part. Was he miscast or was he merely scared of himself? He could not decide; could only waver between apprehensive misgiving and secret anticipation. He was grateful that Helen appeared to be insensible to his state of mental unease. Though he dared not delve too deeply into the assumption of her being free from a like tyranny; he liked to think that she transcended it; that she had strength to balance his weakness.

Use, though, accustomed him to the changed conditions; memories of the old way of life receded, became the past. After all, if ever he wished to see the old home it was only a few doors away. Strangely enough, when he did pluck up courage to call on his parents, he found that he had no desire to return. The place, in some mysterious way, was not as it used to be though everything was there. Why, his new circumstances were infinitely to be preferred in one sense. They were trying, betimes, certainly, but there were compensations. There was Helen's home-coming of an evening, a growing source of pleasure. And the preparations for her return was pleasantly disturbing – though this was his own secret; he never told Helen how much he looked forward to seeing her after work. Making the place presentable; putting fresh newspaper on the table: making up the fire with coal that he had picked out of the huge dirt-heap of the Agecroft pit where his father had worked and which now was closed down for ever; setting the kettle in the blaze and cutting the bread and margarine. Altogether new experiences, though, sometimes, the pleasure would be vitiated by remembrances of Jack Lindsay's voice, speaking during those times they sat in Swinbury Park discussing marriage: 'Why don't t' get wed. They're all doin' it. Tarts go out t' work, nowadays, while th' owld man stops at home. . . .' It made him feel mean, parasitical, irresponsible, an urgent, desperate yearning for work made him squirm. 'Ah ne'er thought Ah'd be one o' them fellers whose wives went out t' work,' he mumbled, to the table. Nevertheless, such moments were transitory and would fade with Helen's home-coming. Helen's home-coming! There was a whiff of the holiday spirit about it which gave a flavour to the meagre meal. For brief magic moments when Mrs Dorbell was out on her mysterious errands and they alone in the house, they spent happy moments in each other's arms, furnishing the place after their fancies and finding in their visions momentary relief from harsh reality. The delight of the moments spurred him to renewed efforts in the search for work. But it was the old story. Footsore, weary and dispirited he would return, a prey to gnawing pessimism.

The world was changed. The boys of yesterday – Where were they? Bill Simmons, Jack Lindsay, Sam Hardie and Tom Hare. Two in jail. Sam Hardie – He hadn't seen him this past week or so. Jack Lindsay, the erstwhile merry soul. There was little merriment in his make-up nowadays. Instead, Harry saw a dismal, depressing young fellow shuffling about with a slouching gait in broken boots and shabby suit, a lost expression of worried preoccupation on his face.

'Aye, aye, Jack . . .'

'Aye, aye, 'Arry. Any signs yet (of work)?'

No answer; at least, no answer was the answer. They stood in silence leaning against Mr Hulkington's, the grocer's shop window.

Slowly, there unfolded in Harry's brain, a panorama of this very spot years agone; the meeting place of the boy and girlhood of the district. Halcyon days! Money in pocket and the Flecky Parlour of a Saturday night. And a job to go to on Monday. All gone. Two lads in jail; and Sam Hardie ...

'Hey, Jack,' he said, suddenly: 'What's become o' Sam these days?'

Jack looked up: 'Ain't y' heard? He's joined th' army cause he had to.'

'Had to?' repeated Harry.

'Aye, bloody well had to. His pa kicked him out o' th' 'ouse when he was knocked off dole. Told him t' clear out 'n join th' army cause he wasn't gonna keep him. He wus livin' i' one o' them doss houses i' Garden Place. Poor devil couldn't afford price of a bed. Tuk him all his time t' find for a tupp'ny leanover.'

Harry gazed at Jack, puzzled: 'Tupp'ny leanover. Wha' d'y' mean?'

Jack shrugged: 'Y' should go 'n have a luk at it. It's for t' real down and outs as can't afford price of a bed. They charge y' tuppence t' lean o'er a rope all night. Hell, y' should see 'em. About forty blokes sittin' on forms in a line an' leanin' o'er a rope ... elbow t' elbow all swayin' fast asleep, except the old bastards who're dyin' and can't sleep for spittin' an' coughin' their guts away.... Aye, 'n Sam wouldn't ha' bin able t' afford that if he hadna gone buskin'. ... Jesus! That's work for y' if y' like. ... Trapesin' streets singin' in t' perishin' cold, an' sometimes nobody'd give him a stiver. Anyway, he's joined th' army,' pause, then, savagely: 'Jesus, that's where honesty gets y'. Yaa, luk at me, sellin' *these* lousy bloody things,' he produced a few packets of cheap contraceptives and a bundle of obscene postcards: 'An' luk at Bill Simmons an' Tom Hare.'

'Why ...?' said Harry, with interest: 'What's up wi' ...'

'Here's Bill now,' Jack interrupted: 'Ask him.' He relapsed into silence, stowed the postcards and contraceptives into his pocket again and stared moodily at the toes of his broken boots.

Harry turned his head to smile a welcome to Bill Simmons who approached at a brisk walk. This was the first intimation he had had that Bill had been released, and he could not but feel rather astonished to notice Bill's air of self-confidence and his prosperous appearance. He was puzzled. One would have thought that Bill would be filled with shame, embarrassment and remorse. Quite the contrary.

'Aye, aye, Harry. What ho, Jack,' he cried, breezily, stopping in front of them, grinning and rubbing his hands together: 'How's things?'

'They luk all right wi' you, anyway, Bill,' replied Harry, eyeing Bill attentively.

'Wi' me? Ha! You bet. Ah'm workin', y' know.' His grin broadened; he felt in his pocket and withdrew a shilling packet of cigarettes: 'Have a tab?' Harry's eyes opened wider. Such affluence! He accepted a cigarette without a word, Jack likewise. Harry looked at Bill questioningly, almost suspiciously. Bill laughed: 'Oh, it's all right, Harry,' he said: 'Ah didn't pinch these. Bought 'em, Ah did, out o' me own money.'

'Where y' workin'?' Harry asked, enviously.

Bill winked: 'Th' East City Buses,' he lit a cigarette and inhaled deeply, and with a self-satisfied smirk: 'Fifty bob a week without overtime an' all clothes found. Y' can't whack (improve on) it, lad. Y' can't – whack – it.'

'Ay, Ah shouldn't think so,' replied Harry, in a monotone, adding, with a puzzled expression: 'But how did y' get it?'

'Ah,' Bill grinned, with mock secrecy, then, facetiously: 'Allus y've got to do is t' get y'self pinched and sent to quod, do y' time, an' when y' come out Probation Officer or Court Missionary does rest. It's th' on'y way t' get a job nowadays,' a pause: Bill added, with raised brows: 'Ain't either of y' bin down t' t' bus offices t' try t' get tuk on?'

Jack made a wry face: 'Bin down. Yach! Ah'm sick o' goin' down an' fillin' forms in. What's the use when they've a bloody big board stuck up: "No Vacancies"?' vehemently: 'Christ, it meks y' sick, it does. Y've a cat in hell's chance o' gettin' tuk on if y' ain't got nobody t' speak for y'. If y' ain't got a councillor or somebody else wi' 'fluence behind y', y' may as well

. . . Aw,' disgustedly: 'Ah'm sick o' the whole blindin' show . . .' precipitately, he turned and slunk away, hands in pockets, shoulders hunched, a bulge in his coat pocket where were the obscene postcards and the packets of cheap contraceptives.

Bill put out his lips and raised his brows. Then he shrugged and touched his hat to Harry in a mock salute: 'Well, Harry, Ah'm off for a game o' pills (billiards). Ah'll be seein' y'. S' long.'

'S' long,' murmured Harry, stabbed to the heart with envy.

He stood there, leaning against the window lost in meditation and cursing his prudence and fear that had prevented him from being one of Bill's accomplices when he was apprehended.

Then the newer and younger end of the neighbourhood's unemployed drifted to where he was standing. Blimey, was he to them as Billy Higgs had been to him? He glanced at them, dully, and betook himself out of their way.

## CHAPTER 16

### 'UNTO US . . .'

LATE afternoon.

They, Mrs Dorbell and Harry, had just returned from, to him, a new and unusual expedition. They entered the house together, Harry carrying a brown-paper parcel which he laid upon the table.

He was brimming with gratitude towards the old woman. But for her he never would have found the nerve to do what he had done. Besides, never in his life until now had he heard of the 'Mission to the Respectable and Deserving Poor', from which organization, and after much questioning, he had received a layette and an order for a half-crown's worth of grocery, printed on the back of which was a list of goods, classed as luxuries, which the shopkeeper was instructed not to supply. As for the workhouse. Until Mrs Dorbell had initiated him he had no idea of the procedure necessary when applying for relief. He considered himself rather mean for having been ashamed to have been seen walking in the company of such a dirty old woman after she had taken so much trouble in his and Helen's behalf.

'It was good o' y' to have shown me what t' do, Mrs Dorbell,' he said, as he laid the parcel on the table: 'Ah'd ha' ne'er had nerve t' go on me own.'

'Yaa, y' softy,' she replied: 'Y'll live an' learn. There ain't nowt got i' this world wivout a bit o' cheek (impudence). Besides, it's y' right an' proper due,' a sigh: 'Eh, it's weary Ah am wi' all that walkin',' she flopped into a chair, adding: 'Ah'll rest me pore owld feet for a minnit.' Her mournful gaze rested upon the brown paper parcel: she said: 'Ah'll tek it t' t' pop-shop for y', if y' like.'

'Tek what?' replied Harry, turning to her, puzzled.

'Why, that there that yon besom at Mission gev y'. She's a bitch, if e'er God let one breathe. Dammer! Questions she asks! Pooo!'

Harry raised his brows: 'But Ah don't want it pawned. It ain't mine. . . . It's for Helen an' the baby.'

'Yaaa, softy. Wot does a child want wi' things like that? Ik'll on'y spew all o'er 'em then they'll be all spiled. Yaa, nobody about here e'er uses 'em. Allus they get 'em for 's pop-shop,' warningly: 'Y'll want as much money as y' can get when *she's* confined, lad.'

Harry shook his head: he did not wish to offend Mrs Dorbell, nor did he wish to rob himself of this opportunity of giving Helen a surprise. He shook his head: 'No, Ah'm not sendin' it t' pawn. It ain't mine t' send.'

She eyed him, pityingly: 'Eh, lad, y've a lot t' learn,' she said, adding reproachfully: 'An' after all trouble Ah've tuk, well, Ah *did* think there'd be price of a nip for *me* out of it . . .'

Harry licked his lips, embarrassed: 'Ah'm sorry, ma,' he said: 'But Ah ain't got no money till Friday when they gie me some at workhouse.'

'Wot about that there ticket for a half-crown's worth o' grocery? Mrs Nakkle gi'es one an' thrippence for 'em. You gie it t' me. Ah'll ha' thrippence for a nip an' bring y' t' shillin' back.'

He fingered the order indecisively; could not for shame disappoint her. He held it out without speaking. She took it without a word, rearranged her shawl tightly about her person and went directly to Mrs Nattle's, muttering to herself, aloud: 'If 'e thinks 'e's gunna get any change out o' this arter all trouble Ah've tuk . . . well, he's sadly mistaken, saaadly mistaken. An' Ah'm sure o' me rent from him now as he's goin' t' t' workhouse,' contemptuously, and in reference to Harry's refusal to allow the layette to be pawned: 'It – ain't – mine. It's for her an' babby. Yaaa. Don't know what young 'uns 're comin' to . . .'

Inside the house, Harry was staring at the brown paper parcel, torn between a desire to open it yet hesitating, thinking that such should be Helen's privilege.

He looked up as a peculiar knocking sounded upon the door. Wondering, he walked to the door and opened it.

It was Helen, her face pale and strained: she gripped the door frame for support: 'What's up. . . . What's . . .' he stammered. Then he took her by the waist and assisted her into the house, brain dazed with perplexity and fear.

'Go for Mrs Bull,' said Helen, weakly: 'An' go t' t' mill at five o'clock for me wages. Me number's 215.

'But . . .' he stammered.

'Leave me be. . . . You go for Ma Bull. Ah'll get upstairs meself,' she disengaged herself from him with weak petulance, and walked with laboured gait to the threshold of the doorway dividing the two rooms. He heard her climbing the stairs one at a time.

Panic gripped him: with staring eyes he bolted into the street and dashed into Mrs Bull's house. 'Mrs Bull, Mrs Bull,' he gasped, gesticulating wildly: 'Come quick, will y'. It's Helen. She's tuk bad. Oh, hurry, will y'. . . . Hurry.'

'Aye, lad, Ah'll hurry,' Mrs Bull answered. She was sitting down to the table ironing some clothes. She set aside the flat iron and gripped the table edge for support as she pulled herself to her feet. She was aggravatingly leisurely. She glanced at him: 'Did y' put kekkle on?'

'No, should Ah ha' done?'

'Should y' ha' done. Yaa, get along wi' y'. Put it on an' see've y' can 'urry y'sel'.'

He dashed outside, tears starting, paused in the middle of

the street and returned: 'We ain't got no fire,' he blubbered.
'Ah'll come an' mek it for y', dafty,' she said, impatiently:
'Mine's too low. ... Go'n ask somebody wot 'as, stoopid.' He
ran out again, dashed to Mrs Cranford's house, next door,
pulled up sharp and stepped inside, nervous, agitated.

Two small children sat upon the bare boards pulling and
stretching and trimming with scissors fragments of chamois
leather with which the table and the sewing machine, the
room's only furnishings, were littered. A heap of the stuff lay
by the children's side, one pulled and stretched, the other
trimmed and placed the finished pieces to one side for Mrs
Cranford's attention who, later, would stitch thirty or so more
pieces together into the form of a window leather. Another
little girl, standing on the threshold of the doorway dividing
the two rooms, and staring at her mother in the back room
who was setting the table, pointed her tiny hand towards the
sewing machine under the window where a large rat was chew-
ing a fragment of the chamois leather: 'Mammy,' the child
said, 'Mammy, the big pussy agen.'

Harry gazed in the direction indicated by the child; his heart
leapt; he hated the things. He glanced about, wildly, for a mis-
sile, saw a pair of Jack Cranford's clogs under the table, dived
for one, and, with a great 'Shooo, y' sod, y'!' scared the rat to
the floor and hurled the clog at it as it escaped round his legs
and through the front door. He followed to see it meet a sudden
bloody end in an encounter with a famine-hungry cat which,
swearing like a trooper, dragged the corpse away.

The incident sobered Harry. For a moment he had forgotten
about Helen. He returned to the Cranford home, urgently. Mrs
Cranford, a wearied woman, eyes red rimmed with excessive
stitchery, figure ruined with excessive child-bearing, came,
heavily, to the front room to find the cause of the row.

Harry, stammering, made his request, then, as she said she
could oblige him, told her of the rat: 'Aw, sick Ah am of the
things,' she said: 'Can't leave a bite o' food untended for a
minute. Here, Harry, lad. Tek what y' want out o' t' kettle. Use
the bowl on t' slopstone. Ah'll come across in a minute t' see
if Ah can help any . . .'

A neighbour, standing on her doorstep, seeing Harry's agitated running hither and thither, also seeing Mrs Bull waddling to Mrs Dorbell's home, at once assumed the truth. And when, presently, Harry came out of Mrs Cranford's house carrying an enamel bowl filled with steaming water, the assumption was confirmed. In a moment most of the street was acquainted with the news, and in another moment a group of women had assembled in and about the front door chatting concerning the peculiarities of their confinements.

Mrs Dorbell, sitting on Mrs Nattle's sofa with a glass in her hand and a shilling change in the other, looked up as Mrs Nattle, pricking her ears, asked: 'Wot's all row in street about, Nancy?' She folded the order for a half-crown's worth of grocery which she had just discounted for Mrs Dorbell and placed it carefully into her purse.

Mrs Dorbell trudged to the door to see what the matter was. She returned, pop-eyed, mouth agape, drained her glass and exclaimed: 'They're all i' front o' *my* door . . . !' She gathered up her skirts, went outside and made a ludicrous attempt at running. Mrs Nattle corked the bottle, said to the cat when it yowled as she trod heavily on its paw in her hurry to put the bottle away: 'Shift out o' t' way, then,' took up her key, went out, slammed the door and hurried after Mrs Dorbell to the scene of the commotion.

' 'Ere, 'ere, wot's all this 'ere?' demanded Mrs Dorbell, warmly, of her neighbours: 'This 'ere ain't Liberty 'All!'

'That gel is confined,' said Mrs Jike: 'Pore child, pore child.'

Mrs Dorbell did not stay to hear more. She entered her abode, sniffing and frowning. Mrs Nattle, when she appeared, was intercepted by two neighbours who, until her arrival, had been arguing. Said one, to Mrs Nattle: 'Do it cover death i' childbed when y're insured wi' newspaper, Mrs Nattle?' Her question was couched in such petulant tones as almost appealed for a negative answer.

'Ah neither know nor care,' snapped Mrs Nattle: 'An' shift out o' me way.'

'Besom, slut, bitch,' the woman flung after her. To her disputant in the recent discussion: 'Eh, she's an owld slut if y'

237

like. She'd mek money out o' God Almighty 'issel' if she got chance.' The other lady nodded agreement, adding: 'Though Ah'm sure, *positive*, that newspapers pay when y' die i' child-bed.' The dispute was renewed.

Mrs Jike, in conversation with three other women, suddenly interrupted herself and said: 'I know what I'll do. I'll mike the gel a bowl o' broth ... I'll not be a minute, gels. ...' She trotted off towards Mr Hulkington's shop to obtain a penny beef-essence cube on her credit account.

Within the house, Mrs Bull, sleeves rolled high up her arms, was receiving the bowl of water from Harry. Mrs Nattle was standing by the rickety table in the front room, her lips set in a sneer as she, having opened the brown paper parcel containing the layette, was inspecting each item critically. ''e wouldn't 'ear o' pawnin' it, Sair Ann,' Mrs Dorbell was saying.

Mrs Bull said to Harry: 'Now, lad, sling y'r hook. Y'aint wanted here for hafe an hour an' y'll on'y be in way. Go on, now. Tek a walk.'

Apprehensive, flustered, he obeyed, taking up his cap and walking into the street in time to hear, at its height, the dispute as to whether newspaper insurance covered death in childbirth.

Helen die! The terrifying thought transfixed his brain. Until now such a possibility had never occurred to him. Cold shivers ran up his spine and crept under his scalp: he licked his lips afraid; dazed, shocked, he was too stunned to think. He moved with aimless gait, could not comprehend such an eventuality as Helen's dying. Then, with a vivid flash of understanding, he appreciated how Sally's bereavement must have affected her. A whiff of her bleak loneliness suffused his shrinking spirits: he marvelled, was awed by her fortitude. Suppose such a fate were to overtake him. 'Gosh!' he muttered: 'Ah ne'er thought o' this. Gosh! Suppose 'Elen ...'

Remembering Sally reminded him of Helen's instructions to call at the mill for her wages. He grasped the opportunity grate-fully as a means wherewith to occupy his mind with some-thing other than that awful possibility. He would meet Sally, too; she would be anxious to hear the news.

He hurried forward, eagerly.

## CHAPTER 17

# THE VILLAIN STILL PURSUES HER

IN his preoccupation he passed Sam Grundy's car drawn up at the end of the street where the mill was situated, passed it without a glance in recognition. Nor did the car's fat proprietor, lolling gracelessly in the depths of the upholstery, notice the shabby young man's passing.

The mill and factory hooters were shrieking and moaning the end of the working day before Harry came to the lodge gates of the mill. He found the yard full of queues of loud-voiced operatives; fresh streams of workers from the farther removed weaving sheds streamed across the great yard's cobblestones with a noisy confused clattering of clogs and shoes. Impossible to pick Sally out of such a crush; even so, he doubted whether he would have had the nerve to expose himself to the cynosure of such a multitude of feminine eyes. He moved off to a secluded corner to wait and to keep a sharp watch for a glimpse of Sally amid the constant efflux of women and girls, shawls disarranged as they came sauntering into the street, preoccupied in the counting of their shillings and pence. He did not see her.

Later, when the numbers lessened, he went into the yard and waited an opportunity to approach the lodge window when the wages clerk was disengaged.

He felt an awful fool after he had stated that he had come for 'Helen's wages' The clerk wanted to know who 'Helen' was. 'She's me wife,' Harry murmured, very red in the face: 'Two fifteen's her number. She was tuk bad this afternoon and come home and told me to come for her wages.' The clerk asked for proof of his identity. Harry fished out of his pocket his much-soiled unemployment receipt card, now a historic memento of better days: 'Me sister Sally works here. Sally 'Ardcastle,' he said, staring fixedly at the clerk.

The man nodded, lifted a small tin cylinder marked '215' from a tray and tipped the contents, Helen's wages, into Harry's palm. 'Y'd better count it,' the man said: '... should be twelve and tenpence, that's wi' her insurance an two'n ninepence fines stopped out. She knows about it.' Harry counted the money and found it as the man had said. He thought the amount of the fines rather excessive, but did not say anything to the man about it. He pocketed the money and made way for the fresh queue of operatives who had formed up behind him, then, hot-foot, he hurried homewards.

Approaching the street corner he peered at a girl standing by a stationary motor-car. Was it. . . . It was Sally. She was standing staring at the pavement, an expression, eloquent of indecision, on her face. Sam Grundy's head and a shoulder were out of the car window: he was leaning towards Sally, speaking to her in low persuasive tones. Harry increased his pace, and, coming closer, heard Sam saying: 'Blimey, Sal, wot are y' feared of?' mildly indignant: 'Ah'm not askin' y' t' tek a dose o' poison! Blimey!' For Harry there was nothing significant in the utterance; he hardly listened, was bursting with his news: 'Oh, Sal . . .!' he exclaimed, breathlessly. Sam frowned and glared as he relaxed into the car, a sulky expression super-seding the one of undivided concentration.

'Oh, Sal! Helen's bin tuk bad. Ma Bull's wi' her now . . .'

Sally was confused, momentarily. A tinge of colour appeared in her cheeks. 'She's . . .?'

'Aye,' Harry nodded, eagerly.

She pursed her lips, decisively: 'Come on,' she said, forgetting Sam.

'Hey, Sal,' cried Sam, from the car: 'Hey. Gerrin car. Ah'll run y' 'ome in a jiffy, you an' t' lad.'

Already he was out of the car and holding open the door: 'Come on, Sal,' he urged. She shrugged and stepped inside, Harry following, babbling the inconsequent news of his success-ful application for Poor Relief, and he had scarcely finished when the car pulled up outside Mrs Dorbell's home. Those few neighbours remaining, pursed their lips, exchanged significant glances, winked and nodded knowingly as Sally stepped out, followed by Harry. They smiled, forcedly, as Sam explained his presence and the car as a result of a fortuitous meeting: 'How's the lassie?' he concluded: 'Is it o'er?'

'It's a gel,' replied one of the women, and she was prevented from further speech by her uncollared, unwashed, dishevelled-headed husband standing in the doorway of their home and demanding, loudly and angrily: 'Hey, you, wha'r'about me tea? Come inside wi' y' ... standin' gassin' there ...' glaring at her as she passed him on the threshold: 'Ah suppose it'll be chips'n' fish agen, eh? Y'll have had no time t' do any cookin', eh? Ah'. ...' He slammed the door; a moment later, a child, carrying a basin, appeared and made a bee line for the fried fish shop.

In the Dorbell kitchen, Harry, in the company of Mrs Dorbell, Mrs Nattle, Mrs Bull and his mother, was grinning and blushing, endeavouring to assume an air of composure. His embarrassment was acute; as keen as his desire to be upstairs with Helen that he might smile upon her and glimpse his daughter for the first time. His daughter! He felt choked; his brain refused to lend credence to the unique event; its significance eluded him. The women were speaking to him but he did not hear what they said; smiled and nodded mechanically and fingered, nervously, the greasy gas flex hanging from the gas fitting and fixed to the gas ring on one corner of the food and crockery-littered table. Oh, why couldn't the women clear off so that he might go to Helen ...

In the room above Sally sat on the edge of the bed nursing the baby to her bosom. Helen, smiling, watched her through half-closed eyes, complacent, proud, flattered by the implied jealousy of Sally's present meditative attitude.

As she nursed the baby, vain, agonizing thoughts paced slowly through her dulled brain filling her with a deep brooding. But for a malignant fate this present consummation of Helen's might have been hers, too. Might have been! The phrase, steeped in the venom of bitter impotence, stabbed her. Might have been! Yaa! Her being rose in high revolt; she felt sickened, disgusted, at a harsh discord with life.

Life? Now that Larry was gone what had it to offer to her? *He* had been her prospect; whilst he had lived everything was, and anything would have been, bearable. For *he* was there, *here*, at the end of the day.

*Love on the Dole*

What remained now? Bleakness; daily slaving at the mill: 'clack-clack-clack-clack', the hideous noise of the shuttle's traverse seared her brain with its intolerable dinning. Nineteen shillings a week if work was to be had and if they didn't foist inferior warp and weft on to you. Day in and day out, an eternal grind; coming home at night to sit there, brooding with reproachful thoughts of what might have been as companions. Brother a pauper: 'They're gonna gie me money at workhouse, Sal.' Parents dependent on her; scratching and scraping until the distraught brain shrank and retarded and the mouth sagged and the eyes lost their lustre. And nevermore to see Larry. God, if only he was alive, *half* alive; anything if only he breathed, could look at and smile at her.

Was that his warm breath she felt upon her lips? Her breathing quickened. Fancy spread its wings, and, for a brief moment that was an age she soared in the upper regions of exquisite joy, living with him anew in a synthesis of all their happiness.

It was gone; her spirits tumbled to earth, stunned and gathered themselves together with slow bewilderment, ever increasing despair. Reality was encompassing, crushing her in, suffocatingly; she felt exhausted; no spirit even to protest.

In the swirling chaos of her brain a solitary thought insinuated itself, growing to dominating proportions; Sam Grundy.

Sam Grundy. How long had he importuned her? She had him grovelling at her feet through no effort on her part. He had everything to offer; she had nothing to offer. He had money. Money, change of life. Money, the fast conveyance in the search of forgetfulness; money that would give the quietus to gnawing memory, that would heal this open wound. What was there to hamper her? Compunction pinched her as she imagined what Larry might say to this characterless capitulation to impulse.

Larry? Ha! Dead, and so was Sally Hardcastle. Aaach! Who cared what happened now. It was idle to live in the past. Let things take their course. The worst was over; life could hurt her never more.

She did not hear Harry enter the room with trepidation; did not see the shy fond smile on his lips nor the soft light in his

242

eyes as he peered at Helen over the rusty bed head. She did not see or hear anything, sat there motionless, prey to an irresistible surge of reckless abandonment that blinded all save itself.

Sam Grundy was waiting below.

Suddenly, with burning eyes and flushed cheeks, she replaced the baby by Helen's side and astonished both Helen and Harry by departing, impulsively, without a word.

Harry, amazed, came to the bedside and stared at Helen who returned his wide-eyed questioning: 'Well ...' said Harry. The baby stirred. Helen put her arm about it. Harry smiled, dropped on to his knees and instantly forgot Sally in the all-absorbing contemplation of his daughter.


CHAPTER 18

# NO VACANCIES

'Yᴀᴀᴀ,' said Mrs Bull, impatiently: 'Fuss y' mek of it. Ah reckon she might ha' gone farther an' fared worse.' She was sitting in the Hardcastle kitchen, she, Mrs Hardcastle and Mrs Cranford.

'It's him,' Mrs Hardcastle whimpered: 'He'll murder her if ever he finds out. *Ah* know her father. . . . An' it's such a disgrace. Everybody'll be talkin'. . . . Ah'm feared.' She began to tap with her toes; her hand resting on the table drummed its top with nervous agitation.

Mrs Bull shrugged and grunted: 'Talk's cheap enough,' she said, then listened as the latch of the front door clicked: 'She's here now,' said Mrs Bull.

Sally entered the room with an air of studied unconcern; she greeted the company airily. Her mother eyed her anxiously. Rising, Mrs Bull said: 'Eh, well, Ah guess Ah'd best be goin'.' Mrs Cranford also rose, heavily, to her feet: 'Ah'll see y' agen, Mrs Hardcastle,' she said: 'It's a shillin' a dozen the Jew pays for window leather makin'. Y've t' find y'r own thread. But there won't be no more work for a week or two, he ses. Ah'm havin' t' tek in washin' meself. But when he comes agen Ah'll send him across.'

'Eh, thank y', Mrs Cranford,' muttered Mrs Hardcastle, gratefully.

'Y've no need t' go,' said Sally, gazing at the two women, steadfastly– 'Ah suppose th' whole street knows all my business by this time,' with animation, defiance: 'Well, Ah ain't ashamed.'

'Y'd be a damn fool if y' was,' murmured Mrs Bull. She sat down again; Mrs Cranford followed suit. Here was something of interest to be had without payment. Mrs Bull continued, on a sigh: 'Ay, lass, when y' get as owld as me y'll have learned that there ain't nowt worth worritin' y' head about save where next meal's comin' from. Be God, y' will.'

Sally dropped into the rocker chair, carelessly, linked a leg over the chair arm, leaned against the table edge and stared, thoughtfully, arms folded, into the tiny fire: 'Aye,' she murmured: 'It seems t' me that things allus turn out different to what y' expect. ... Ah thought Ah'd bin married by now. Huh!'

Mrs Cranford lifted her lip: 'Married,' she said, bitterly: 'You ain't missed nowt wi' missin' that. Oh, God, if Ah'd me time t' go o'er agen Ah'd ne'er get wed. Naow, not t' t' best feller breathin' wot hadn't enough t' keep me on proper. An' Ah know o' no married woman i' Hanky Park wot wouldn't do same. Marriage, eh? Yaaa. Y' get wed for love an' find y've let y'sel' in for a seven day a week job where y' get no pay. An' y' don't find it out till it's too late. Luk at me, Sal. Luk at me. Worritin' me guts out tryin' t' mek ends meet, an' a tribe o' kids t' bring up on what he and me can earn.'

'Ha! Then they say we ain't eddicated,' said Mrs Bull. With a grin: 'Ne'er heed, Mrs Cranford, wait till the tribe's all growd up an' bringin' y' wages home.'

'Aye, an' then they'll all get married, like Ah did, damn fool that Ah was. ... Stichin' till Ah'm blind. Then when there ain't no work i' that line Ah'm washin' from Monday till Thursday an' kids t' be tuk t' t' clinic. Aw, Gord! Ah wish Ah wus dead an' out o' t' way ...'

'Naterally dismal, Mrs Cranford,' said Mrs Bull: 'That's allus up wi' you. Y' jest naterally dismal. Y've a lot t' learn, lass, a lot t' learn. Ne'er in all my life have Ah seen anybody as tuk things

244

so serious. Allus y' want's a nip o' Scotch now an' agen. Mek y' forget y' troubles.'

'Aye, 'n wot'd happen t' t' kids if Ah started that . . .?'

'They'd tek no harm,' said Mrs Bull: 'Wot'll happen to 'em anyway? Same as happened t' you, don't worry.'

'Well, that ain't for me,' said Sally. She sighed: 'Ah can't have what Ah wanted so Ah've tuk next best thing. Sick an' tired Ah am o' slugging an' seein' nowt for it. Ne'er had holiday i' me life, Ah ain't. But Ah knows what money means, now. An' he's got it an' by God Ah'll mek him pay. Ah'm gonna tek things easy while Ah've got chance.'

'More fool you if y' didn't, lass,' murmured Mrs Bull: 'Though Ah'd get Sam Grundy t' mek a sekklement on y'. There's nowt like havin' the brass in y'r own name. Y' may as well be wed if y' ain't done that. An' now's y' chance afore he cools.'

Sally shrugged and opened her handbag: 'Ah've seen to that. He's stinkin' wi' brass. He's as daft as the rest of his kind. Ach! What fools they do look slobberin' around y';' a hard light appeared in her eyes: 'But there was nothin' doin' until Ah got my way. He can chuck me over as soon as he's a mind now.' She reached three one-pound notes out of her handbag and offered them to her mother. Mrs Cranford licked her lips and stared at the money fixedly; Mrs Bull rubbed her nose. 'Here, Ma,' said Sally: 'They won't be the last, either.'

Mrs Hardcastle shrank a little as Sally held out the money: 'N' – n' – no, lass, Ah daren't. What'd y' father say?' wringing her hands: 'Oooo, Ah don't know what's come o'er ye. Y' ain't same girl.'

'Oh, don't *you* start,' snapped Sally, impatiently; 'Ah'll have enough from him when he comes in, Ah suppose. . . .' The latch clicked again. Sal snatched at her mother's purse lying on the table top and stuffed the money inside.

An expectant silence fell on the room. Sal's air of unconcern was superseded by one of stubborn determination. Mrs Bull coughed, Mrs Cranford looked at the floor, Mrs Hardcastle, scared stiff, held her breath as she heard her husband pause to hang his hat and coat behind the front door, then his heavy footfalls thumped across the floor of the outer room.

He paused on the threshold; had eyes for none but Sally. Lips set, fists clenched, he demanded, tersely, instantly: 'What's these tales Ah'm hearin' about thee an' Sam Grundy?'

She was on her feet in a flash, facing him with bold defiance: 'Well,' she retorted: 'What about it?' Her bosom heaved, agitatedly; her staring eyes assumed an added lustre.

'Why, y' brazen slut!' he exclaimed, incredulously: 'Have you got cheek t' stand theer an' tell me it's *true*?'

'Yes, I have,' she replied, hotly: 'An' Ah'll tell y' summat else. It's sick Ah am o' codgin' owld clothes t' mek 'em luk summat like. An' sick Ah am o' workin' week after week an' seein' nowt for it. Ah'm sick o' never havin' nowt but what's bin in pawnshop. . . . Oh, Ah'm sick o' the sight o' Hanky Park an' everybody in it . . .'

Hardcastle narrowed his eyes: 'So y'd go whorin' an' mek respectable folk like me an' y' ma the talk o' the neighbourhood, eh? Damn y'! Y'ain't fit t' be me dowter.'

'Yaaa, who cares what folk say? There's none Ah know as wouldn't swap places wi' me if they'd chance. Y'd have me wed, wouldn't y'? Then tell me where's feller around here as can afford it? Them as is workin' ain't able t' keep themselves, ne'er heed a wife. Luk at y'self.... An luk at our Harry. On workhouse relief an' ain't even got a bed as he can call his own. Ah suppose Ah'd be fit t' call y' daughter if Ah was like that, an' a tribe o' kids like Mrs Cranford's at me skirts. . . . Well, can y' get our Harry a job? *I* can an' Ah'm not respectable . . .'

Hardcastle pointed to the front door: 'Get out . . .!' he snarled.

'Oh, Harry,' his wife whimpered: 'Oh, Harry,' she gripped handfuls of the folds of her apron.

'Right,' replied Sally, defiantly: 'Ah can do that, too. Ah can get a place o' me own any time. Y' kicked our Harry out because he got married an' y' kickin' me out 'cause Ah ain't. . . .' Unwisely, in her agitation and in efforts to justify herself, she persisted in the same provocative strain: '*You*'d have me like all rest o' the women, workin' 'emselves t' death an' gettin' nowt for it. Luk at me ma. . . . Luk at Mrs Cranford. . . . Well, there ain't no man breathin', now that Larry's gone, as'd get me like . . .' she stabbed the air in the direction of her terrified mother: '. . . . Get me like *that* for him!' Her voice rose high and shrill.

'Aaaach! Y' brazen bitch,' snarled Hardcastle, thickly. He rushed at her: 'Tek that . . .' he lashed out; his fist caught her on the mouth.

She stumbled sideways, saved herself from falling by clutching the head of the couch. Her mother screamed and rushed to her side. The other two women rose to their feet in protest. 'Hey, don't be a damn fool, Harry,' said Mrs Bull: 'Luk what y've done t' t' lass.'

Hardcastle, white, fists clenched, breathing heavily, ignored them: 'Now,' he said to Sally, harshly: 'Now gerrout o' here: an' Ah don't want t' see y' agen,' to his wife: 'Come away from her. . . . D'y' hear? Come away.'

Sally rose to her feet, hair tumbled about her face, mouth bleeding. Mrs Bull took her arm: 'Come on, lass,' she said, quietly: 'Come an' stay wi' me while y' want'; to Hardcastle: 'Y' bad tempered devil, y'.'

For a moment Sally gazed at her father, then she burst into sobbing. Mrs Bull led her away, Mrs Cranford following.

Mrs Hardcastle flopped on the couch and buried her face in her hands, weeping bitterly.

Her husband stood there, motionless, his anger subsiding like a retreating wave the instant Mrs Bull slammed the front door. Beached on the bleak shore of remorse and self pity he felt he would have given anything to have been able to undo what had been done. Echoes lingered in his mind of Sally's barbed, burning accusations '. . . ne'er havin' nowt but what's bin in pawnshop. . . . Luk at y'self. . . . Luk at our Harry . . . workhouse relief . . . ain't even a bed t' call his own. . . . Ah'd be fit t' call y' daughter if Ah was like that, an' a tribe o' kids like Mrs Cranford's at me skirts . . Y'd have me like all rest o' the women. . . . Luk at me ma. . . . No man breathin' 'll get me like that. . . . Kicked our Harry out because he got married an' y're kickin' me out 'cause Ah ain't. . . .' Her biting phrases lacerated him; such exquisite pain to which the dull senses could not respond, filled the brain with a cowed submission. He sought the support of the rocker chair; seated himself, heavily. Stark truth wouldn't let him alone; it embraced and crushed.

What had he done for his children? Out of his despair rose a counter question which he clutched as a drowning man might a straw: What had he been *able* to do other than what had been done? The responsibility wasn't his. He'd worked all his life; he had given all he had to give . . .

He felt his confidence slipping again. Sally, too, had given her all; so had Harry. They had been living on each other. These last few months since he had been knocked off the dole he had been living on Sally's earnings. Living on a woman, his daughter, whom he had just dismissed for living on a man! She was gone now; had taken her income with her. What was he to do to meet the home's obligations? The workhouse for pauper relief? He shrank from the prospect. Then there only remained Sally. And, to him, the source of her present income was corrupt. Oh, why the devil couldn't they give him work? The canker of impotence gnawed his vitals. He felt weak; as powerless as a blind kitten in a bucket of water.

His wife, frightened by his silence, looked at him through her tears to see him sitting there, head bent, sparse grey hair catching the fire's glimmer, an arm resting on the table, the other on his knee, his hand dangling limply.

2

Mrs Hardcastle, one hand at her throat, the other gripping a fold of the ragged lace curtain, gazed fearfully through the window at her husband standing indecisively outside the closed door of Mrs Bull's home on the other side of North Street.

She hardly breathed fearing lest Hardcastle should change his mind and walk away without fulfilling his promise of a moment agone. It had needed all her powers of supplication and persuasion to overcome his resistance, though she sensed a powerful ally in his ill-concealed shame and remorse. All yesterday, on every possible occasion, she had begged him to go to repair the breach between himself and Sally: 'Oh, Harry, Ah don't know how y' can do it. There's no wrong in lass: she's on'y young and self-willed. . . . She's y' daughter and she's alone. What'll become of her, lad?'

'Ach, leave me be. Ah'm sick o' hearin' y'. She can go no lower than she is now.' He looked away, uncomfortably.

'For shame, Harry Hardcastle. . . . For shame.'

'She made her own bed; she mun lie on it.'

'Aye, y' said that about our Harry.'

'Aw, leave me be, woman, can't y'. Leave me be.'

He had gone to bed out of way of her tongue. But he could not escape his own thoughts. She, lying by his side, sleepless, silent, translated his restless tossing and turning as the manifestations of his inward strife. Then she had dozed off. Sleep evaded him. He stared into the darkness, weary. 'She's made her own bed. . . .' 'Aye, y' said that about our Harry.'

It occurred to him that his arbitrary utterance had the quality of a boomerang; the propensity to return to that point from whence it had been thrown. A voice reminded him that, in turning out first Harry, and now Sally, he, too, had 'made his bed' and must be prepared to 'lie in it'. He found his bed-making most uncomfortable; found himself, economically, up against a blank wall. This week-end would see no money whatsoever coming into the house, unless Mrs Hardcastle succeeded in procuring such work as Mrs Cranford found herself obliged to do. The thought was paralysing: a murderous hate of his own impotence made him squirm. What an utter, complete fool he had made of himself in denying the staring, glaring truth of Sally's accusations. *Did* he really wish her to live such a life as her mother had lived; such a life as was in store for young Harry and his wife? No! he answered himself, emphatically, No! One long succession of dreary, monotonous years, toiling, moiling, with a pauper or near-pauper funeral and the end of it. Then why had he struck her? why had he been indignant that she should choose – what to him had been – a disgraceful way out? What disgrace was there in it? Who made it a disgrace? People's tongues. What business could it be of theirs? None. In what way could Sally's affairs affect them? No way. She was as free to arrange an illicit contract as they were a licit. Furthermore, she had chosen the former already. Again, she was no longer a child; she was a woman. He had not the slightest authority now to interfere with her. She was independent. Nay, financially, he and his wife were her dependents. It had been *her* earnings that had kept the home going.

Once begun he found a million excuses for her and a million condemnations of himself. He found ease; oil was poured on his perturbed spirits. He sighed, relieved, promising that he would permit his wife to persuade him into a reconciliation with Sally in the morning. Try as he would he could not overcome his stubbornness in taking the initiative unaided.

And now he found himself outside Mrs Bull's front door, quaking inwardly with indecision and fear lest Sally should rebuff him. He licked his dry lips, raised his hand and knocked, softly.

Mrs Bull answered the door: ' 'Allo,' she said: 'Ah wondered when y'd be comin'.'

'Is Sal in?'

'Aye, come thee in, lad,' he followed her: 'Sit y' down,' she said, indicating the couch, below whose seat rail could be seen an elliptical curve of hessian where the springs had collapsed. As she waddled to the room at the back, Mrs Bull announced, loudly: 'Hey, Sal, lass. Here's thi' dad.'

He heard the creaking of a chair in the other room. Sally appeared. He dropped his gaze, shamefaced after a glance at her swollen lip. Staring at the floor he mumbled, in a hesitant monotone: 'Ah've come t' say Ah'm sorry, lass. Ah must ha' lost me temper . . .'

His abjectness touched her. She felt the effort this apology must have cost him. Her heart expanded; she felt near to tears. But she smiled: 'That's all right, Dad. Ah guess y' weren't the only one t' lose y' temper,' pause; she added, still smiling: 'Ah've a surprise for y'. . . . Ah think Ah've got y' a job . . .'

He looked up quickly: 'Eh?' he said, incredulously.

'Yes,' she answered, then she interrupted herself, as, out of the tail of her eye and through the open door, she saw Harry passing on the other side of the street. She called his name. He paused, arrested, peered across the street and approached, slowly, wondering. 'Come in, Harry,' she said. He stared to see his father sitting there; had heard of the quarrel, plus a few enlargements, of Mrs Dorbell. The present situation electrified him; he felt as one who finds that he has strayed into the middle of no-man's-land. He smiled forcedly at Sally; avoided looking at his father.

He blinked as he heard his father repeat: 'A *job*, did y' say, Sal?'

He gaped when Sally, opening her handbag, fetched out a couple of letters, passed one to his father and one to him, saying: 'Y've t' tek these t' th' East City Bus offices, and give 'em t' Mr Moreland. There'll be a job each for y'. . . . But remember, say nowt t' nobody how y' got it. An' give the letters to nobody else than Mr Moreland.'

They took the letters, awed; they exchanged glances of perplexed surmise. Harry found his tongue: 'Bus offices, Sal? They don't want nobody there, though. There's a big notice stuck up there, warnin' y' off. . . . "No vacancies", it ses.' He stared at her blankly and licked his lips.

'Aye?' she answered: 'Well, tek those letters as Ah've told y', then see. Here,' she passed her father some small change: 'This'll get y' a few smokes each.'

Harry remembered Sam Grundy. He remembered Helen. What would she say to this? A smile grew on his lips and broadened: 'Oh, ta, Sal, ta . . .' to his father, whom he had sworn never to acknowledge again: 'Say, Dad, can y' imagine wot Helen'll say? Gosh!' knocking his cap upwards: 'Ah dunno. . . . Oh,' eagerly: Oh, come on, Dad, let's go . . .'

Hardcastle, still holding his letter in his hand, followed his son outside. There was a far-away, childlike stare in his eyes; his brain retarded, bewildered.

Sally watched them go, torn between conflicting emotions, a fugitive response to their pleasure, then a blank, forlorn sense of utter loneliness which made her feel as one apart, a trespasser, unable to share in that happiness of which she had been the cause. She roused herself, shook off the creeping hand of introspection and went into the room at the back to escape from herself in talking to Mrs Bull.

3

Friday afternoon, the same week.

A knot of neighbours standing outside the home of Mrs Nattle, regarded, pensively, the front door of Mrs Hardcastle's home from which a taxi had just driven away.

'High-ho,' sighed Mrs Jike: 'I wouldn't turn me nowse up at a fortnight's holidiy where she's gorn. Strike me pink, I wouldn't!'

'She's a hinterferin' young 'ussy, that's what she is,' snapped Mrs Dorbell, angrily: 'It's her doin's as's got me lodgers t' tek th' empty house at top o' street. Aye, an' him just startin' work when he'd ha' done me a bit o' good. *Me*,' indignantly: '*Me*, mind y', as got him pay from workhouse an' a parcel o' clouts from t' Mission. Yah! That's thanks y' get.'

'Hold y' noise, hold y' noise,' snapped Mrs Bull; 'the lass has done best thing she could. "Get away," ses me to her: "Get away from these here owld bitches, 'cause no matter what y' do, they'll find summat t' say agen y',"' loudly: 'Luk at her across street; that pal o' thine, Mrs Jike. Too religious t' live – her an' her spirits,' she nodded towards Mrs Alfred Scodger, the spiritualist mission's lady performer upon the trombone, who stood upon her doorstep, her back as straight as a poker, her arms as tightly folded as her lips were compressed, her clean, starched apron rustling in the bitter March wind.

Mrs Scodger closed her eyes and retorted: 'The carryings on o' some folks wot could be named ain't fit for the ears o' res*pect*-able folk,' opening her eyes: 'An Ah'm sur*prised* at you, Mrs Jike. Ah'm sur*prised*!'

'It don't tek much t' surprise some folk,' Mrs Bull retorted. She turned, waddled down the street and into the Hardcastle home.

She found Mrs Hardcastle in tears. Helen, nursing her baby, was sitting in the rocker chair watching her, sympathetically. ''Allo, more tears,' said Mrs Bull, flopping down. She gazed at Mrs Hardcastle with disapproval, then said, impatiently: 'Aw, ne'er in all me life did Ah see such a one as thee for shrikeing. Lord, what ails thee now?'

'What'll become of her. Oh, what'll become of her?' Mrs Hardcastle wailed.

'Yah, ain't that just way o' the world, eh? Her dowter gets a sekklement made on her then her ma wonders what gonna become of her. Yah, y' don't deserve nowt, y' don't. Why don't y' ask what's gunna become o' all of us wot's left i' Hanky Park?' sighing: 'Ah dunno; some folks don't know when they are well off,' pause: 'She'll tek no hurt. She ain't the kind. She'd ha' bin a sight worse off hangin' about here doin' nowt but thinkin'. If y' *want* t' know, it was *me* as 'inted t' Sam Grundy that she'd tek no hurt if she went away for a while. Three or four months at that there place o' his in Wales, wi' all nice weather i' front of her – Why, woman, she'll be new-made-o'er-agen. Allus she wants is summat t' mek her forget. Everlastin' thinkin' about that Larry Meath, an' livin' here right opposite place where he used t' live. ... It's more'n flesh an' blood can stand. Use y' head, woman, use y' head.' She enlarged upon the theme relating her own experiences regarding her bereavement of her first husband. 'Ah'd ha' gone barmy if Ah hadn't tuk a job i' service up i' the country. Bein' away tuk me right out o' meself an' got me out o' me sorrer twice as quick.'

Mrs Hardcastle sniffed: 'There's t'other thing,' she whimpered: 'Her an' Mr Grundy. Ah don't like it. ... It's – It's. ... We've allus bin respectable. An' now neighbours 're all talking.'

'Lerrem talk. While they're talkin' about you, they're leavin' other folks be.' She gazed at Mrs Hardcastle, critically: 'Y'know,' she said: 'Ah do believe y' thinkin' more about y'self than about yon lass. Yah, *do* y' understand y'r own daughter? A bellyful o' trouble she's had, aye, a proper bellyful. Her pa comes out o' work; then the bloke she's set on marryin' dies. She's workin' at mill an' all her money's goin' t' keep your house goin'. Yaa. Y've bin tekkin' too much for granted, like a few more Ah know. Y' want t' forget y'self for a bit an' try t' understand how t' young 'uns must feel about all these here goin's on i' t' world t'day. Every cent they earn bein' tuk in keepin' their owld folks an' any o' t' family as is out o' work. World ain't wot it used t' be when we wus young, an' don't forget it, neither. Let me tell y' this: if she'd 'ad much more

of it Ah'm certain that she'd ha' done wot yon poor soul i' next
street did yesterday ... cut his throat an' jumped out o' bedroom window when he got letter from Guardians sayin' he'd
got t' give five bob a week to his wife's people wot come under
Means Test. Five bob a week, poor soul, an' he couldn't keep his
own, proper. Yes, Ah could see it i' your Sal's face all right;
moonin' about like a lost soul; sittin', night after night on this
here couch gawpin' at nowt. ... It all come out night as y'
'usbant landed her one, now didn't it, now? Wot she said was
only wot she'd bin thinkin' e'er sin' Larry kicked bucket,' a
deep breath: 'Aye, *she's* had a bellyful all right. An' she'd ha'
gone melancholy mad if it'd ha' lasted much longer. An' it's
glad y' ought t' be, all o' y', that chance come for her t' get
away from it all. Bless the lass, she's seen none o' you go short.'

Helen sighed: 'If it hadn't bin for her, Mrs Bull, Ah don't
know what me'n Harry would ha' done. ...' With restrained
excitement: 'We've got th' 'ouse at top o' the street. An' we're
goin', t'night, t' see about gettin' the furniture on the weekly
(the instalment plan). Y'see, Ah'm startin' work agen soon so
we'll be able t' pay money off quicker. An' Ah'll want somebody t' luk after baby. ... Y've bin so good. ... Ah wondered,
like. ... Ah'd pay y' if y'd see to her durin' day for me. ...
Would ...?'

'Aye, lass, she'll be all right wi' me.' She gazed at Helen,
steadfastly, 'An' if y' tek my advice, lass, y'll mek this one y'
last. One's too many sometimes where workin' folk're concerned. 'Tain't fair t' you an' 'tain't fair t' t' child. Luk at Mrs
Cranford. One reg'lar every year, an' half of 'em dead. An'
Kate Narkey shapin' same way. Yah, them two fellers ought t'
be casterated.'

Helen shifted uncomfortably, glanced at the clock then said,
in genuine alarm: 'Ooo, luk at time. ... Harry's tea'll ne'er be
ready when he comes,' smiling at her mother-in-law and Mrs
Bull: 'Ah'll have t' be goin'. He'll be home in a minute,' rising
and arranging the baby's shawl: 'Ay, Ah bet he's excited –
drawin' his first week's wages t'day. G'night, Mrs Hardcastle.
G'night, Mrs Bull. ...' She went out, hurrying to Mrs Dorbell's,
a set smile on her lips.

A young man strode down Hankinson Street, beaming, full of self-confidence. His right hand, thrust deep into the pocket of his trousers, clutched a small envelope containing a week's pay. The seal of the envelope was unbroken. To open it was Helen's privilege. Oh, to see her face when he placed it into her hands! 'Blimey, an' think of it, though! T'night Ah'll ha' some money o' me own t' do what Ah like wi'! Blimey, though! Blimey!'

Harry, in his exuberance, lengthened his stride. Then, suddenly, his pace slackened as he caught sight of a solitary figure standing on the corner of North Street. The smile died on his lips.

Jack Lindsay.

He was standing there as motionless as a statue, cap neb pulled over his eyes, gaze fixed on pavement, hands in pockets, shoulders hunched, the bitter wind blowing his thin trousers tightly against his legs. Waste paper and dust blew about him in spirals, the papers making harsh sounds as they slid on the pavement.

No influential person to pull strings on his behalf; no wages for him tonight; no planning for the morrow. He was an anonymous unit of an army of three millions for whom there was no tomorrow.

Harry faltered, licked his lips then stole away, guiltily, down a back entry unable to summon the nerve to face his friend.

5.30 A.M.

A drizzle was falling.

Ned Narkey, on his beat, paused under the street lamp at the corner of North Street. Its staring beams lit the million globules of fine rain powdering his cape. A cat, sitting on the doorstep of Mr Hulkington's, the grocer's shop, blinked at Ned, rose, tail in air, and pushed its body against Ned's legs.

'Gaaa-cher bloody thing,' he muttered, and lifted it a couple of yards with his boot. Then he glanced up and down Hankinson Street, afterwards footing it quietly to his house to rouse his wife. The idea of her lying abed whilst he was exposed to the raw elements annoyed him. Anyway, he would be finished work in a half hour; she should be up and preparing against his return. ... Aye, and that blasted Sal Hardcastle and Sam Grundy. Damn 'em both! Sam had worked his cards prettily. Yaaa! What y' can do when y've got money! ...

A man wearing clogs and carrying a long pole tipped with a bunch of wires came clattering into North Street. His back was bent, beard untrimmed, rusty black bowler hat tipped over his eyes. He stopped at No. 17, raised his pole and laid the wires against the window, rattling them loudly against the panes. A voice responded. Joe moved on to Mrs Dorbell's, where he repeated the performance. 'Come thee on, lass,' he said, when Helen's voice acknowledged the summons: 'Come thee on, lass. Hafe past five, Monday mornin' an' pourin' o' rain.' He shouldered his pole and clattered out of the street. Those who were unemployed slumbered on.

Silence.

Lights began to appear in some of the lower windows of the houses.

The grocer's shop at the street corner blazed forth electrically. Occasionally, women, wearing shawls so disposed as to conceal from the elements whatever it was they carried in their arms, passed, ghostlike, the street corner. In the gloom they looked like fat cassocked monks with cowls drawn.

In Mrs Dorbell's house, Helen came downstairs, 'Ah-ah-ing' sleepily. She groped on the tiny kitchen's mantelpiece for the matches, struck one and lit the gas. The glare hurt her eyes; she blinked, stifled a yawn, scratched her head with one hand whilst she stretched with the other. She shivered and shrugged. It was cold. She stooped, raked out the grate and stuffed it with paper, picked up the shovel and trudged to the backyard, pausing by the stairs to shout: 'Come on, Harry, lad. Five an' twenty t' six, Monday mornin' an' pourin' o' rain.'

She unbolted the door and went to the corner where the coal was stored. Other people in neighbouring backyards were shovelling coal, the gratings of the shovels rasped harshly in the still air of early morning.

The melancholy hoot of a ship's siren sounded from the Salford Docks ...